BILLION DOLLAR
Temptation

DANI COLLINS   **CLARE CONNELLY**   **TARA PAMMI**

MILLS & BOON

CONTENTS

Canadian **Dani Collins** knew in high school that she wanted to write romance for a living. Twenty-five years later, after marrying her high school sweetheart, having two kids with him, working at several generic office jobs and submitting countless manuscripts, she got The Call. Her first Harlequin novel won the Reviewers' Choice Award for Best First in Series from *RT Book Reviews*. She now works in her own office, writing romance.

Books by Dani Collins

Harlequin Modern

Cinderella's Royal Seduction
A Hidden Heir to Redeem Him
Confessions of an Italian Marriage
Innocent in the Sheikh's Palace
What the Greek's Wife Needs

Once Upon a Temptation

Beauty and Her One-Night Baby

One Night With Consequences

Innocent's Nine-Month Scandal
Bound by Their Nine-Month Scandal

Secret Heirs of Billionaires

The Maid's Spanish Secret

Visit the Author Profile page
at millsandboon.com.au for more titles.

Ways To Ruin A Royal Reputation

Dani Collins

To my fellow authors in this trilogy, Clare Connelly and Tara Pammi.

Writing is a strange beast and can be lonely at times, but when a fun project like this one comes along, it reminds me I have watercooler colleagues who know exactly how my workday is going.

I can't wait until we can get together to celebrate these books in person!

CHAPTER ONE

"RUIN ME."

Amy Miller blinked, certain she'd misheard Luca Albizzi, the king of Vallia.

She'd been reeling since she'd walked into this VIP suite in London's toniest hotel and discovered who her potential client would be.

Her arrival here had been conducted under a cloak of mystery. A call had had her assistant frowning with perplexity as she relayed the request that Amy turn up for an immediate consultation, now or never.

Given the address, Amy had been confident it was worth pandering to the vague yet imperious invitation. It wasn't unheard-of for managers of celebrities to conceal a client's identity while they brought Amy and her team into a crisis situation.

Amy had snatched up her bag and hurried across the city, expecting to meet an outed MP's son or an heiress being blackmailed with revenge porn.

The hotel manager had brought her to the Royal Suite, a title Amy had not taken seriously despite the pair of men guarding the door, both wearing dark suits and inscrutable expressions. One had searched through her satchel while the other inspected the jacket she had nervously removed in the lift.

When they opened the door for her, Amy had warily entered an empty lounge.

As she set her bag and jacket on a bar stool, the sound of the main door closing had brought a pensive man from one of the bedrooms.

He wore a bone-colored business shirt over dark gray trousers, no tie, and had such an air of authority, he nearly knocked her over with it. He was thirtyish, swarthy, his hair light brown, his blue eyes piercing enough to score lines into her.

Before she had fully recognized him, a hot, bright pull twisted within her. A sensual vine that wound through her limbs slithered to encase her, and yanked.

It was inexplicable and disconcerting—even more so when her brain caught up to realize exactly who was provoking this reaction.

The headlines had been screaming for weeks that the Golden Prince, recently crowned the king of Vallia, would be coming to London on a state visit. King Luca had always been notorious for the fact he was powerful, privileged and sinfully good-looking. Everything else about him was above reproach. According to reports, he'd dined at Buckingham Palace last night where the only misstep had been a smoky look of admiration from a married duchess that he had ignored.

"Call me Luca," he said by way of introduction, and invited her to sit.

Gratefully, Amy had sunk onto the sofa, suffering the worst case of starstruck bedazzlement she'd ever experienced. She spoke to wealthy and elite people all the time and never lost her tongue. Or her hearing. Or her senses. She refused to let this man be anything different, but he was. He just was.

She saw his mouth move again. The words he'd just spoken were floating in her consciousness, but his gorgeously deep voice with that Italian accent evoked hot humid nights in narrow cobblestone alleys while romantic strains of a violin drifted from open windows. She could practically smell the fragrance of exotic blossoms weighting the air. He would draw her into a shadowed alcove and that full-lipped, hot mouth would smother—

"Will you?" he prodded.

Amy yanked herself back from the kind of fantasy that could, indeed, ruin him. *And* her. He was a potential client, for heaven's sake!

A cold tightness arrived behind her breastbone as she made the connection that she was, once again, lusting for someone off-limits. Oh, God. She wouldn't say the king of Vallia reminded her of *him*. That would be a hideous insult. Few men were as reprehensible as *him*, but a clammy blanket of apprehension settled on her as she realized she was suffering a particularly strong case of the butterflies for someone who potentially had power over her.

She forcibly cocooned those butterflies and reminded herself she was not without power of her own. She could turn down this man or this job. In fact, based on this off-the-rails attraction she was suffering, she should do both.

She would, once she politely heard him out. At the very least, she could recommend one of her colleagues.

Why did *that* thought make this weird ache in her diaphragm pang even harder?

She shook it off.

"I'm sorry," she said, managing to dredge the words from her dry throat. "Did you say someone is trying to ruin you? London Connection can definitely help you defuse that." There. She almost sounded like the savvy, confident, cofounder of a public relations firm that her business card said she was.

"I said I want *you* to ruin me."

You. Her heart swerved. *Did he know?* Her ears grew so hot, she feared they'd set her hair on fire. He couldn't know what had happened, she assured herself even as snakes of guilt and shame writhed in her stomach. Her parents and the school's headmistress had scrubbed out that little mess with all the alacrity of a government cleanup team in a blockbuster movie. That's how Amy had learned mistakes could be mitigated so well they disappeared from the collective consciousness, even if the stain remained on your conscience forever.

Nevertheless, her hands clenched in her lap as though she had to physically hang on to all she'd managed to gain after losing everything except the two best friends who remained her staunchest supporters to this day.

"Our firm is in the business of *building* reputations." Muscle memory came to her rescue, allowing her voice to steady and strengthen. She said this sort of thing a million times a week. "Using various tools like media channels and online networking, we protect and enhance our clients' profiles. When a brand or image has been impacted, we take control of the narrative. Build a story." Blah, blah, blah.

She smiled while she spoke, hands now stacked palm up in her lap, ankles crossed. Her blood still sizzled because, seriously, he was positively magnetic even when he scowled with impatience. This was what a chiseled jaw looked like—as though a block of marble named "naked gold" or "autumn tan" had been chipped and worked and shaped to become this physical manifestation of strength and tenacity. Command.

"I know what you do. That's why I called you." Luca rose abruptly from the armchair he'd taken when she'd sat.

He paced across the spacious lounge. His restless movement ruffled the sheer drapes that were partially drawn over the wall of windows overlooking the Thames.

She'd barely taken in the decor of grays and silver-blue, the fine art pieces and the arrangements of fresh flowers. It all became a monochrome backdrop to a man who radiated a dynamic aura. He moved like an athlete with his smooth, deliberate motions. His beautifully tailored clothes only emphasized how well made he was.

He paused where the spring sun was streaming through the

break in the curtains and shoved his hands into his pockets. The action strained his trousers across his firm behind.

Amy was not an ogler. Men of all shapes, sizes and levels of wealth paraded through her world every day. They were employees and clients and couriers. Nothing more. She hadn't completely sworn off emotional entanglements, but she was exceptionally careful. Occasionally she dated, but even the very nice men who paid for dinner and asked politely before trying to kiss her had failed to move her.

Truthfully, she didn't allow anyone to move her. She preferred to keep her focus on her career. She'd been taught by an actual, bona-fide teacher that following her heart, or her libido, or that needy thing inside her that yearned for someone to make her feel special, would only leave her open to being used and thrown away like last week's rubbish.

But here she was acting like a sixth-former biting her fist because a particularly nice backside was in her line of sight. Luca wasn't even coming on to her. He was just oozing sex appeal from his swarthy pores in a passive and oblivious way.

That was ninja-level seduction and it had to stop.

"I'm asking you to reverse the build," Luca said. "Give me a scandal instead of making one go away."

She dragged her attention up to find him looking over his shoulder at her.

He cocked his brow to let her know he had totally and completely caught her drooling over his butt.

She briefly considered claiming he had sat in chewing gum and gave her hair a flick, aware she was as red as an Amsterdam sex district light. She cleared her throat and suggested gamely, "You're in the wrong part of London for cheap disgrace. Possibly hire a woman with a different profession?"

He didn't crack a smile.

She bit the inside of her lip.

"A *controlled* scandal." He turned to face her, hands still in his pockets. He braced his feet apart like a sailor on a yacht, and his all-seeing gaze flickered across her blushing features. "I've done my research. I came to *you* because you're ideal for the job."

Whatever color had risen to her cheeks must have drained out of her because she went absolutely ice cold.

"Why do you say that?" she asked tautly.

His brows tugged in faint puzzlement. "The way you countered the defamation of that woman who was suing the sports league. It was a difficult situation, given how they'd rallied their fans to attack her."

Amy released a subtle breath. He wasn't talking about *her* past.

"It was very challenging," she agreed with a muted nod.

She and her colleagues-slash-best friends, Bea and Clare, had taken on the case for a single pound sterling. They'd all been horrified by the injustice of a woman being vilified because she'd called out some players who had accosted her in a club.

"I'm compelled to point out though—" she lifted a blithe expression to hide the riot going on inside her "—if you wish to be ruined, the firm we were up against in that case specializes in pillorying people."

"Yet they failed with your client because of *your* efforts. How could I even trust them?" He swept a dismissive hand through the air. "They happily billed an obscene amount of money to injure a woman who'd already been harmed. Meanwhile, despite winning, your company lost money with her. Didn't you?"

His piercing look felt like a barbed hook that dug deep into her middle.

Amy licked her lips and crossed her legs. It was another muscle memory move, one she trotted out with men in an almost reflexive way when she felt put on the spot and needed a brief moment of deflection.

It was a power move and it would have worked, buying her precious seconds to choose her words, if she hadn't watched his gaze take note of the way the unbuttoned bottom of her skirt fell open to reveal her shin. His gaze slid down to her ankle and leisurely climbed its way back up, hovering briefly on the open collar of her maxi shirtdress, then arrived at her mouth with the sting of a bee.

As his gaze hit hers, his mouth pulled slightly to one side in a silent, *Thank you for that, but let's stay on task.*

It was completely unnerving and made her stomach wobble. She swallowed, mentally screaming at herself to get her head in the game.

"I would never discuss another client's financial situation." She would, however, send a note to Bea advising her they had some confidentiality holes to plug. "Can you tell me how you came by that impression, though?"

"Your client was quoted in an interview saying that winning in the court of public opinion doesn't pay the way a win in a real court would have done, but thanks to *Amy* at London Connection, she remains hopeful she'll be awarded a settlement that will allow her to pay you what you deserve."

Every nerve ending in Amy's body sparked as he approached. He still seemed edgy beneath his air of restraint. He dropped a slip of paper onto the coffee table in front of her.

"I want to cover her costs as well as my own. Will that amount do?"

The number on the slip nearly had her doing a spit take with the air in her lungs. Whether it was in pounds sterling, euros, or Russian rubles didn't matter. A sum with that many zeroes would have Bea and Clare sending her for a cranial MRI if she turned it down.

"It's...very generous. But what you're asking us to do is the complete opposite of London Connection's mission statement. I'll have to discuss this with my colleagues before accepting." Why did Clare have to be overseas right now? Starting London Connection had been her idea. She'd brought Amy on board to get it off the ground, and they usually made big decisions together. Their latest had been to pry Bea from slow suffocation at a law firm to work for them. Bea might have specific legal concerns about a campaign of this nature.

"I don't want your colleagues," Luca said. "The fewer people who know what I'm asking, the better. I want *you*."

His words and the intensity of his blue eyes were charging into her like a shock of electricity, leaving her trying to catch her breath without revealing he'd knocked it out of her.

"I don't understand." It was common knowledge that the new king of Vallia was nothing like the previous one. Luca's father had been... Well, he'd been dubbed "the Kinky King" by the tabloids, so that said it all.

Amy's distant assumption when she had recognized Luca was that she would be tasked with finessing some remnant of Luca's father's libidinous reputation. Or perhaps shore up the cracks in the new king's image since there were rumors he was struggling under the weight of his new position.

Even so... "To the best of my knowledge, your image is spotless. Why would you *want* a scandal?"

"Have I hired you?" Luca demanded, pointing at the slip of paper. "Am I fully protected under client confidentiality agreements?"

She opened her mouth, struggling to articulate a response as her mind leaped to her five-year plan. If she accepted this assignment, she could reject the trust fund that was supposed to come to her when she turned thirty in eighteen months. Childish, perhaps, but her parents had very ruthlessly withheld it twice in the past. Having learned so harshly that she must rely only on herself, Amy would love to tell them she had no use for the remnants of the family fortune they constantly held out like a carrot on a stick.

Bea and Clare would love a similar guarantee of security. They all wanted London Connection to thrive so they could help people. They most definitely didn't want to tear people down the way some of their competitors did. Amy had no doubt Bea and Clare would have the same reservations she did with

Luca's request, but something told her this wasn't a playboy's silly whim. He looked far too grim and resolute.

Coiled through all of this contemplation was an infernal curiosity. Luca intrigued her. If he became a client... Well, if he became a client, he was absolutely forbidden! There was a strange comfort in that. Rules were rules, and Amy would hide behind them if she had to.

"I'll have to tell my partners something," she warned, her gaze landing again on the exorbitant sum he was offering.

"Say you're raising the profile of my charity foundation. It's a legitimate organization that funds mental health programs. We have a gala in a week. I've already used it as an excuse when I asked my staff to arrange this meeting."

"Goodness, if you're that adept at lying, why do you need me?"

Still no glint of amusement.

"It's not a lie. The woman who has been running it since my mother's time fell and broke her hip. The entire organization needs new blood and a boost into this century. You'll meet with the team, double-check the final arrangements and suggest new fundraising programs. The full scope of work I'm asking of you will remain confidential, between the two of us."

His offer was an obscene amount for a few press releases, but Amy could come up with a better explanation for her friends later. Right now, the decision was hers alone as to whether to take the job, and there was no way she could turn down this kind of money.

She licked her dry lips and nodded.

"Very well. If you wish to hire me to promote your charity and fabricate a scandal, I would be happy to be of assistance." She stood to offer her hand for a shake.

His warm, strong hand closed over hers in a firm clasp and gave it a strong pump. The satisfaction that flared in his expression made all sorts of things in her shiver. He was so gorgeous and perfect and unscathed. Regal.

"Now tell me why on *earth* you would ask me to ruin you," she asked, trying to keep her voice even.

"It's the only way I can give the crown to my sister."

CHAPTER TWO

LUCA RELEASED HER hand with a disturbing sense of reluctance. He quickly dismissed the sexual awareness dancing in his periphery. Amy Miller had a scent of biscotti about her, almonds and anise. It was going to be incredibly distracting to sit with her on the plane, but she was now an employee and he finally had a foot on a path that would allow his sister to take the throne. His entire body twitched to finish the task.

"Eccellente," he said in his country's Italian dialect. "Let's go."

"Go?" Amy fell back a half step and blinked her sea green eyes. "Where?"

"I'm needed in Vallia. We'll continue this conversation on our way."

He glimpsed a flash of panic in her expression, but she quickly smoothed it to show only professional calm.

"I have to take your details first. Prepare and sign the contract. Research—"

Impatience prickled his nape. "I want a secure location before we discuss this further."

"My office is secure. We don't have to go to Vallia." She made it sound like his home was on another planet.

"It's only three hours. My jet is waiting."

Amy's pretty, glossed mouth opened, but nothing came out.

Luca had had his doubts when she had first come onto his radar. He didn't trust anyone who seemed to enjoy being the life of the party, and her job involved nonstop networking with spoiled, infamous attention-seekers. Her online presence was filled with celebrity selfies, club events and influencer-styled posts. It all skated too close for comfort to the superficial amusements his father had pursued with such fervor.

Along with awards and praise from her colleagues, however, she came highly recommended when he'd made a few discreet inquiries. In person, she seemed levelheaded and knowledgeable—if aware of her ability to dazzle with a flick of her more-blond-than-strawberry locks and not the least bit afraid to use such tactics. She was mesmerizing with her peaches and cream skin. Her nose was cutely uptilted to add playfulness to her otherwise aristocratic features, and there was something intangible, a certain sparkle, that surrounded her.

But the very fact she entranced him kept him on his guard. He was long practiced at appreciating the fact a woman was attractive without succumbing to whatever lust she might provoke in him. He was *not* and never would be his father.

Even if he had to convince certain people he was *enough* like him to be undeserving of his crown.

"But—" She waved an exasperated hand. "I have other clients. I can't just drop them all for you."

"Isn't that what I just paid you to do? If you needed more, you should have said."

"You really don't know what my work is, do you?" She frowned with consternation before adding in a disgruntled voice, "I'll have to shift things around. I wish you'd made it clear when you called that you expected me to travel. I would have brought a quick-run bag." She moved to the leather satchel she'd left on a stool at the bar.

"Are you a PR rep or a secret agent?" Luca asked dryly.

"Feels like one and the same most of the time. At least my passport is always in here."

He eyed her slightly-above-average height and perfectly proportioned curves. Amy wore nothing so pedestrian as a skirt suit. No, her rainbow-striped dress was styled like an ankle-length shirt in lightweight silk. She'd rolled back her sleeves to reveal her bangled wrists and left a few buttons open at her throat and below her knees. It was a bohemian yet stylish look that was finished with a black corset-looking device that made him want to take his time unbuckling those five silver tongue and eye closures in the middle of her back. Her black shoes had silver stiletto heels that glinted wickedly, and the shift of filmy silk against her heart-shaped ass was positively erotic.

Not her, Luca reminded himself as a bolt of want streaked from the pit of his gut to the root of his sex. He was woke enough to know that objectifying women was wrong, that women who worked for him were always off-limits, and that grabbing anyone's backside without express permission was unacceptable—even if she'd gawked at his own like she'd wanted to help herself to a handful.

When he'd caught Amy checking him out a few minutes ago, he'd considered scrapping this whole idea in favor of suggesting he refile his flight plan so they could tour the king-size bed in the other room.

Luca didn't place nascent physical attraction over real world obligations, though. Whether it looked like it or not, allowing his sister to take his place was the greatest service he could do for his country. He wouldn't be swayed from it.

If that left room in his future to make a few less than wise decisions with a woman who attracted him, that was icing. For now, he had to keep his mind out of the gutter.

Or rather, only go there in a very shallow and deliberate manner.

Look at the bar Papa set, his twin had sniffed a few weeks ago when he'd been relaying his frustration with the Privy Council's refusal to allow him to abdicate. *You have a long way to sink before they would even think of ousting you in favor of me.*

Luca didn't want to put the country into constitutional crisis or start firing dedicated public servants. He only wanted to make things right, but there were too many people invested in the status quo. He'd tried cultivating a certain incompetence as he'd adopted the duties of king, pushing more and more responsibilities onto Sofia to show she was the more deserving ruler, but the council dismissed his missteps as "adapting to the stress of his new role." They hovered more closely than ever and were driving him mad.

Sofia's casual remark had been effortlessly on the nose, providing Luca with the solution he'd been searching for. He needed to sink to that unforgivable depth in one shot, touch bottom very briefly, then shoot back to the surface before too much damage was done.

Amy Miller was uniquely positioned to help him make that happen, having bailed countless celebrities out of scandals of their own making.

She was helping herself to items from the hospitality basket, dropping an apple and a protein snack into her bag before adding a water bottle and a bar of chocolate.

"I'll deduct this from your bill," she said absently as she examined a lip balm before uncapping it and sweeping it across her naked mouth. She rolled her lips and dropped the tube into her bag. "I'll buy a change of clothes from the boutique in the lobby on our way out."

"We don't have time for a shopping spree. I'll make arrangements for things to be waiting for you when we arrive."

"I'm hideously efficient," she insisted. "Shall I meet you at the front doors in fifteen minutes?" She plucked the black motorcycle jacket off the back of the stool and shrugged it over her dress.

Something in that combination of tough leather over delicate silk, studded black over bright colors, fine blond hair flicked free of the heavy collar and the haughty expression on her face made him want to catch her jacket's lapels in his fists and drag her close for the hottest, deepest kiss of their lives. His heart rate picked up and his chest heated.

Their eyes met, and they were close enough that he saw her pupils explode in reaction to whatever she was reading in his face.

Look at the bar Papa set.

"Car park. Ten minutes." He pushed a gruff coolness into his tone that made it clear he was not invested in her on any level. "Or the whole thing is off."

She flinched slightly, then gave him what he suspected was a stock keep-the-client-happy smile, saying a very unconcerned, "I'll risk it."

It was cheeky enough to grate, mostly because it lit an urgency in him, one that warned him against letting her get away. He started to tell her that when he said something, he meant it, but she was already gone.

Amy fled the suite. She had reached the limit of her ability to pretend she was cool with all of this and desperately needed to bring her pulse under control, especially after what had just happened.

What *had* just happened?

She had found an excuse to escape his overwhelming presence, dragged on her jacket, glanced at Luca, and a crackling surge of energy between them had nearly sucked her toward him like a tractor beam pulling her into an imploding sun. For one second, she'd thought he was going to leap on her and swallow her whole.

Much to her chagrin, she was a teensy bit disappointed he hadn't. In fact, she was stinging with rejection at the way he'd so quickly frozen her out, as if he hadn't handpicked her to make his worst nightmare come true.

As if she'd been obvious in her attraction toward him and he'd needed to rebuff her.

As if she had consciously been issuing an invitation—which she hadn't!

She was reacting on a purely physical level and was mortified that it was so potent. So *obvious*. She didn't understand why it was happening. Even before all her PR management courses, she'd had a knack for being dropped into a situation that demanded swift, decisive action and turning it around. Now it was her day job to create space for clients to freak out and sob and come to terms with whatever drama might have befallen them. She was adept at processing her own reactions on the fly, but today she was shaking and wishing for a paper bag to breathe into.

Luca was the diametric opposite of everything she'd ever encountered. He wasn't a boy from the council flats who'd stumbled into stardom and didn't know how to handle it. He'd been raised to be king. He was a man of impeccable reputation who wanted her to engineer his fall from grace. Instead of his looks and wealth and privilege getting him into trouble, he needed her to make that happen for him. *I want* you, he'd said.

He'd made it sound as if he saw her as exceptional at what she did, but there was that niggling fear deep in her belly that she'd been chosen for other, bleaker reasons.

Even as she was texting Clare and Bea from the lift, informing them she was leaving town with an important new client who'd offered a "substantial budget," she was stamping her feet to release the emotions that were accosting her.

There was no tricking herself into believing Luca Albizzi was a client like any other. He wasn't. Not just because he was a king. Or because he radiated more sex appeal than a whole calendar of shirtless firefighters. He was…magnificent.

He was causing her to react like a— She pinched the bridge of her nose, hating to admit it to herself, but it was true. She was behaving like damned *schoolgirl*.

That would not do. She was older and wiser than she'd been back then. Infatuation Avenue was firmly closed off. Men were no longer allowed to use her very natural need for affection and companionship as a route to taking advantage of her. Besides, he was a client. Their involvement had to remain strictly professional. It *would*, she vowed.

As the lift doors opened, Clare texted back that she would run things remotely. Bea promised to email their boilerplate for the contract. Neither protested her disappearing, darn them for always being so supportive.

Amy hurried to the boutique. Thankfully, she was blessed with a body that loved off-the-rack clothing. It took longer for the woman to ring up her items than it did for Amy to yank them from the rod. She didn't need to buy a toothbrush. She always kept the grooming basics in her shoulder bag since she often had to freshen up between meetings.

She was catching her breath after racing down the stairs to the car park when the lift bell rang. Luca's bodyguards stepped out. One checked as he saw her hovering, nodding slightly when he recognized her. An SUV slid to a halt, and Luca glanced at her as he appeared and walked across to the door that was opened for him.

"I didn't believe you could find what you wanted in less than an hour." His gaze dropped to the bag she swung as she hurried toward him. "Your ability to follow through on a promise is reassuring."

"Reassurance is the cornerstone of our work. I'm not being facetious. I mean that." She let his bodyguard take her purchases and climbed into the vehicle beside Luca, firmly ignoring the cloud of the king's personal fragrance, which may or may not have been a combination of aftershave, espresso and undiluted testosterone.

Whatever it was, it made her ovaries ache.

As the door shut and the SUV moved up the ramp into the

daylight, Amy withdrew her tablet from her satchel, determined to do her job, nothing more, nothing less.

"I was going to look up some background information unless you'd rather brief me yourself?"

He pressed the button on the privacy window, waiting until it was fully shut to ask, "How much do you know about my family?"

"Only the—" She pursed her lips against saying *sketchiest*. "The most rudimentary details. I know your father passed away recently. Six months ago? I'm very sorry."

He dismissed her condolence with an abbreviated jerk of his head.

"And your mother has been gone quite a bit longer?" she murmured gently.

"Twenty years. We were eleven." The flex of agony in his expression made Amy's attempts to remain impervious to him rather useless.

"That must have been a very hard loss for you and your sister. I'm so sorry."

"Thank you," he said gruffly, and something in his demeanor told her that even though his mother's death was two decades old, he still mourned her while his grief over his father was more of a worn-out fatalism.

"And Princess Sofia is…" Amy looked to her tablet, wishing she could confirm the impressions that leaped to mind. "I believe she's done some diplomatic work?" Amy had the sense it was far more substantial than a celebrity lending their name to a project.

"Sofia is extremely accomplished." His pride in his sister had him sitting straighter. "She began advocating for girls when she was one. We both studied political science and economics, but when I branched into emerging technologies, she pursued a doctorate in humanities. More recently, she played an integral part in the trade agreements in the Balkan region. She's done excellent work with refugees, maternal health and global emergency response efforts."

"I had no idea," Amy said faintly. Her parents had disinherited her and she'd come a long way from a hard start, but women like his sister made her feel like a hellacious underachiever.

"She's remarkable. Truly. And has way more patience for politics that I do. I don't suffer fools, but she's willing to take the time to bring people around to her way of thinking. We both know where Vallia needs to go, but my instinct is to drag us there through force of will. She has the temperament to build consensus and effect change at a cultural level. She's better suited to the role, is arguably more qualified and, most importantly, she's an hour older than I am. The crown should be hers by birthright."

"Wow." If her voice held a touch of growing hero worship for both of them, she couldn't help it. "It's rare to hear a powerful man sound so supportive and willing to step aside for anyone, let alone a woman. That's so nice."

"I'm not 'nice,' Amy. Shake that idea from your head right now," he said tersely. "I am intelligent enough to see what's obvious and loyal enough to my country and my sister to make the choice that is right for everyone concerned. This has nothing to do with being *nice*."

He was using that voice again, the one that seemed intent on warning her that any designs she might have on him were futile.

Message received, but that didn't stop her from lifting her chin in challenge. "What's wrong with being nice? With being kind and empathetic?"

"I'm not advocating cruelty," he said with a curl of his lips. "But those are emotions, and emotions are hungry beasts. Soon you're doing things just so you *feel* kind. So you have the outside validation of people believing you're empathetic. Ruling a country, doing it *well*—" he seemed to pause disdainfully on the word, perhaps criticizing his father's reign? "—demands that you remove your personal investment from your decisions.

Otherwise, you'll do what appeases your need to feel good and lose sight of what's ethically sound."

She considered that. "It seems ironic that you believe giving up the crown is the right thing to do when your willingness to do what's right makes you ideal for wearing it."

"That's why my sister won't challenge me for it. She refuses to throw Vallia into turmoil by fighting for the right to rule, not when I'm healthy, capable and wildly popular. From an optics standpoint, she can't call me out as unsuited and install herself. She has to clearly be a better choice, recruited to save the country from another debacle."

"Why was she passed over in the first place? Primogeniture laws?"

"Sexism. Our father simply thought it would make him look weak to have a woman as his heir. He was too selfish and egotistical, too driven by base desires to see or do what was best for Vallia. When it was revealed my mother was carrying twins and that we were a boy and a girl, he declared the boy would be the next king. Even though Sofia was born first, making her the rightful successor, the council at the time was firmly in my father's pocket. No one pushed back on his decree."

"Does that council still have influence? Can't you simply abdicate?"

"I've tried." Impatience roughened his tone. "Once I was old enough to understand the reality of my position, I began to question why the crown was coming to me." He pensively tapped the armrest with a brief drum of his fingers. "Our mother knew Sofia was being cheated, but she worried that pressing for Sofia's right to inherit would cost her what little influence she had. She used her mandate of raising a future king to install a horde of conservative advisers around us. They genuinely wished to mold me into a better king than my father was, and they are extremely devoted to their cause. That isn't a bad thing, given the sort of people who surrounded my father." He side-eyed her.

Amy briefly rolled her lips inward. "I won't pretend I haven't read the headlines." Countless mistresses, for instance, sometimes more than one at a time. "I don't put a lot of stock into gossip, especially online. Paparazzi will post anything to gain clicks."

Even if Luca's father had been into polyamory, it was merely a questionable look for someone in his position, not something that negated his ability to rule.

"Whatever you've read about my father is not only true," Luca said in a dark voice, "it is the whitewashed version." His voice rang as though he was hollow inside. "When he died, I brought up crowning my sister despite the fact I've always been the recognized successor. It was impressed upon me that Vallia was in too fragile a state for such a scandal. That we desperately needed to repair our reputation on the world stage and I was the man to do it."

"It's only been six months. Is Vallia strong enough to weather you renouncing your crown?" she asked skeptically.

"It's the perfect time to demonstrate that behaviors tolerated in the previous king will not be forgiven in this one. A small, well-targeted scandal that proves my sister is willing to make the hard decision of removing me for the betterment of our country will rally the population behind her. I need something unsavory enough to cause reservations about my suitability, but not so filthy I can't go on to hold positions of authority once it's over. I don't intend to leave her in the lurch, only restore what should be rightfully hers."

"What will you do after she ascends?" she asked curiously.

"Vallia's economy has suffered from years of neglect. Recent world events have not helped. Before the duties of a monarch tied up all my time, I was focused on developing our tech sector. We have a small but exceptional team working in solar advancements and another looking at recovering plastics from the waste stream to manufacture them into useable goods."

"Be careful," she teased, noting the way his expression had

altered. "You almost sound enthusiastic. I believe that's known as having an emotion."

His gaze clashed into hers. Whatever keenness might have briefly brimmed within him was firmly quashed, replaced by something icy and dangerous.

"Don't mistake my frankness for a desire to be friends, Amy," he warned softly. "I'm giving you the information you need to do your job. You don't know me. You can't. Not just because we'll never have a shared frame of reference, but because I won't allow it. I've lived in the shadow of a man who made everything about himself. Who allowed himself to be ruled by fleeting whims and hedonistic cravings. If I thought my desire to go back to reshaping our economy offered anything more than basic satisfaction in pursuing a goal, I wouldn't do it. It's too dangerous. I won't be like him."

They were coming into a private airfield and aiming for a sleek jet that had the Vallian flag painted on the tail. A red carpet led to the steps.

Amy squirmed internally. He might not have emotions, but she did. And she was normally well-liked. It bothered her to realize he not only didn't like her, but he didn't want to. That stung. She didn't want to feel his rebuff this keenly.

"Developing a rapport with a client is a way of building trust," she said stiffly. "Given the personal nature of this work, and how I live in my client's pockets through the course of a campaign, they like to know they can trust me."

"I've paid top price for unquestionable loyalty. I don't need the frills of bond-forming banter to prove it."

Keep your mouth shut, she warned herself.

"Lucky you. It's included with every purchase," she blurted cheerfully.

The SUV came to a halt, making it feel as though his hard stare had caused the world to stop spinning and her heart to stop beating.

"Dial it back," he advised.

She desperately wanted to tell him he could use a laugh. *Lighten up*, she wanted to say, but the door opened beside her. He was the customer and the customer might not always be right, but they had to believe she thought they were.

She buttoned her lip and climbed aboard his private jet.

Did he feel regret at taking her down a notch? If Luca allowed himself emotions, perhaps he would have, but he didn't. So he sipped his drink, a Vallian liquor made from his nation's bitter oranges, and watched her through hooded eyes.

He told himself he wasn't looking for signs she'd been injured by his cut. If she was, she hid it well, smiling cheerfully at the flight attendant and quickly making a work space for herself. She made a call to her assistant to reassign various files and eschewed alcohol for coffee when offered, tapping away on her tablet the whole time.

She seemed very comfortable in his jet, which was built for comfort, but she was relaxed in the way of someone who was not particularly impressed by the luxury. As though she was familiar with such lavishness. Took it for granted.

She catered to celebrities so she had likely seen her share of private jets. Why did the idea of her experiencing some rock star's sonic boom niggle at him, though? Who cared if she'd sat aboard a hundred yachts, allowing tycoons to eyeball her legs until she curled them beneath her like a cat while tracing a stylus around her lips as she studied her tablet? It was none of Luca's business if she traded witty barbs with stage actors or played house with playwrights.

He was absolutely not invested in how many lovers she'd had, rich, poor or otherwise. No, he was in a prickly mood for entirely different reasons that he couldn't name.

He flicked the button to bring down the temperature a few degrees and loosened his tie.

"I'm sending you the contract to forward to your legal department." Amy's gaze came up, inquiring. Professional, with a hint of vulnerability in the tension around her eyes.

Perhaps not so unaffected after all.

A tautness invaded his abdomen. He nodded and glanced at his phone, sending the document as quickly as it arrived. Seconds later, he realized he was typing her name into the search bar, planning to look into more than her professional history. He clicked off his phone and set it aside.

"How did you get into this type of work? The company is only two years old, isn't it? But it won an award recently?"

"For a multicountry launch, yes. Specifically, 'Imaginative Use of Traditional and Social Media in a Coordinated International Product Launch Campaign.'" She rolled her eyes. "These types of awards are so niche and specific they're really a public relations campaign for public relations." She shrugged. "But it's nice to have something to brag about and hopefully put us at the top of search engines for a few days."

"That's how your firm came to my attention, so it served its purpose."

"I'll let Clare know." She flashed a smile.

"Your partner." He vaguely remembered the name and photo on the website. The dark-haired woman hadn't projected the same vivacity that had reached out from Amy's headshot, compelling him to click into her bio and fall down an online wormhole of testimonials.

"Clare is one of my best friends from boarding school. London Connection was her idea. She came into some money when her father passed and wanted to open a business. I worked the social media side of things, organizing high-profile events and managing celebrity appearances. Once we were able to expand the services beyond straight promoting into problem-solving and crisis management, we exploded. We're so busy, we dragged our friend Bea from her law firm to join our team." Her face softened with affection. "We're all together again. It's the best career I could have imagined for myself."

"Boarding school," he repeated. That explained how Amy took to private jets like a duck to water. She'd probably been raised on one of these. "I thought I detected a hint of American beneath your accent. Is that where you're from?"

"Originally." Her radiance dimmed. "We moved to the UK when I was five. I went to boarding school when my parents divorced. I was just looking up your foundation. Do I have the name right? Fondo Della Regina Vallia?"

"That's it, yes."

"I have some ideas around merchandise that would double as an awareness campaign. Let me pull a few more details together." She dipped her attention back to her tablet, corn-silk hair falling forward to curtain her face.

And that's how it was done. Replace the thing you don't want to talk about with something that seems relevant, but actually isn't.

Amy Miller was very slick and not nearly as artless and open as she wanted to appear.

Rapport goes both ways, he wanted to mock, but he didn't really want to mock her. He wanted to know her.

Who was he kidding? He wanted to know what she *liked*. She was twenty-eight, and at least a few of the men photographed with her must have been lovers. Maybe some of the women, too. What did he know? The fact was, she was one of those rare creatures—a woman in his sphere who attracted him.

His sphere was depressingly empty of viable lovers and historically well guarded against them. His mother had surrounded her children with hypervigilant tutors, mentors and bodyguards. It had been the sort of blister pack wrapping within a window box frame that allowed others to look in without touching. He and Sofia had been safely admired, but never allowed out to play.

Mostly their mother had been trying to protect her children from learning the extent of their father's profligacy, but she'd also been doing what she could for the future of Vallia. There'd been a small civil war within the palace when she died. Luca and Sofia's advisers had collided with their father's cabal—men who had had more power, but also more to hide.

In those dark days, while he and Sofia remained oblivious, deals had been struck that had kept everyone in their cold war positions. Their father's death had finally allowed Luca and his top advisers to carve the rot from the palace once and for all. Luca had installed his own people, and they all wanted to stay in the positions to which *they* had ascended—which was how he'd wound up in this predicament.

And the reason he was still living a monk's existence. He had no time and was monitored too closely to burn off sexual calories. At university, potential partners had always been vetted to the point that they'd walked away in exhausted indifference rather than run the gamut required to arrive in his bed.

As an adult moving through the hallowed halls of world politics and visiting allied territories, he occasionally came across a woman who had as much to lose by engaging in a loose-lipped affair as he did. They would enjoy a few private, torrid nights and part ways just as quickly and quietly. The few who had progressed into a longer relationship had been suffocated by his life, by the inability to make the smallest misstep with a hemline or a break with protocol without suffering cautionary lectures from his council and intense scrutiny by the press.

Luca didn't blame women for walking out of his life the minute they saw how little room there was to move within it.

Amy would die in such a confined space. She was too bright and vivacious. It would be like putting a burning light inside a cupboard. Glints might show through the cracks, but all her heat and power would be hidden and wasted.

Why was he dreaming of crawling in there with her? Imagining it to be like closing himself within the cradle of a suntan bed, surrounded in the sweet scent of coconut oil and a warmth that penetrated to his bones.

He dragged his gaze from where the barest hint of breast swell was peeking from the open buttons of her dress and set his unfinished drink aside. Best to slow down if he was starting to fantasize about a woman he'd hired—to *ruin* him.

He bet she could ruin him. He just bet.

His assistant came to him with a tablet and a handful of inquiries, and Luca forced his mind back to who he was and the obligations he still had—for now.

Perhaps when this was over, he promised himself, he would be able to pursue the iridescent Amy. Until then, he had to remain the honorable and faultless king of Vallia.

CHAPTER THREE

AMY'S FATHER USED to joke that he had oil in his veins and a rig where his heart ought to be. His great-grandfather had hit a gusher on a dirt farm in Texas, and the family had been filling barrels with black gold ever since. Her father was currently the president of Resource Pillage International or whatever name his shell company was using these days. He had moved back to Texas shortly after the divorce, remarried, and was too busy with his new children to call his eldest more than once or twice a year.

Amy's mother came from a family of bootleggers, not that she would admit it. *Her* great-grandfather had been born when Prohibition ended. The family had quickly laundered their moonshine money into legal breweries throughout the Midwest. Two generations later, they had polished away their unsavory start with a chain of automobile showrooms, fashion boutiques, and most importantly, a Madison Avenue advertising firm.

Amy's mother had taken the quest for a better image a step further. After pressing her husband to move them to London, she had traded in her New York accent for an upper-crust British one. Since her first divorce, she had continued to scale the social ladder by marrying and divorcing men with names like Nigel who held titles like lord chancellor.

Amy had to give credit where it was due. Her mother had

taught her that if reality wasn't palatable, you only had to finesse the details to create a better one. *Of course I want you to live with me, but boarding school will expose you to people I can't.* And, *Delaying access to your trust fund isn't a punishment. It's a lesson in independence.*

People often remarked how good Amy was at her job, but she wasn't so much a natural at repackaging the truth as a lifelong victim of it. Case in point, her mother's first words when Amy answered her call were, "You wish to cancel our lunch Wednesday?"

As if Amy had been asking for permission.

Amy reiterated what she'd said in her text. "I had to run out of town. I can't make it."

"Where are you?"

In a car with the king of Vallia, winding up a series of switchbacks toward the remains of a castle that overlooked the Tyrrhenian Sea.

"I'm with a client."

"Who?"

"You know I can't tell you."

"Amy, if he won't let you talk about your relationship, it's not going anywhere." Perhaps if her mother had worked at the family firm instead of choosing "heiress" as her career, she would know that Amy's job was not a front for pursuing men with fat money clips.

"Can I call you later, Mom? We're almost at our destination."

"Don't bother. I can't make lunch, either. Neville— You remember him? He's the chargé d'affaires to Belgium. He's taking me to Australia for a few weeks."

"Ah. Lovely. Enjoy the beach."

"Mmm." Her mother sniffed disdainfully. She was more vampire than woman, eschewing sunshine in favor of large-brimmed hats and absorbing her vitamin D through high-priced supplements. "Behave yourself while I'm gone. Neville is ready to propose. I wouldn't want to put him off."

Seriously, Mom? It's been ten years. But her mother never missed an opportunity to remind her.

Amy's stomach roiled with suppressed outrage, but she only said through her teeth, "You know me, all work and no play. Can't get into trouble doing that."

"You wear short skirts to nightclubs, Amy. That sort of work is— Well, I'm sure I can persuade Neville to introduce you to someone if you manage not to mess this up for me."

Could Luca hear what her mother was saying? He'd finished his own call and pocketed his phone. This town car was the sort that made the drive feel like a lazy canal ride inside a noise-canceling bubble.

"I have to go, Mom. Travel safe." Amy cut off the call, which would result in a stinging text, but she wasn't sorry. She was hurt and angry. Bea and Clare always told her she didn't have to talk to her mother if it only upset her, but Amy lived in eternal hope that something would change.

"Everything all right?" Luca was watching her with a look that gave away nothing.

She realized she had huffed out a beleaguered sigh.

"Fine," she lied sunnily. "Mom's off to Australia."

"You didn't mention any siblings earlier. Are you an only child?"

"The proverbial spoiled kind. I had one of everything except a brother or sister, which is why my friends are so special to me. Will I meet your sister?"

There was a brief pause that made her think he knew she was deliberately turning the question around to avoid delving into her own past.

"She's traveling, due home later this week," he replied evenly.

They were driving past the shell of the castle. As they came even with a courtyard bracketed by two levels of arches in various states of disintegration, she glimpsed a young woman in a uniform leading what looked like a group of tourists. They all turned to point their phones at the car's tinted windows as it passed.

Seconds later, when they halted to wait for golden gates to crawl open, Amy glanced back, curious.

"The castle is a heritage site," Luca explained. "Open for booked tours. The island of Vallia was a favorite summer destination for Roman aristocracy. The palace is built on the remains of an emperor's villa. You'll see what's left in one of the gardens." He nodded as the palace came into view.

"Wow."

At first glance, the imposing monument to baroque architecture, ripe with columns and domes and naves, was almost too much. Amy could hardly take in everything from the serpentine balcony to the elaborate cornices to the multitude of decorative details like seashells and ribbons. Stone angels held aloft what she presumed to be Vallia's motto, carved into the facade.

"This is amazing."

"You can accomplish a lot when you don't pay for labor," Luca said, mouth twisting with resigned disgust. "Vallia was a slave trading post through the Byzantine era. Then the Normans used them to build the fortress while they were taking over southern Italy." He nodded back to the castle. "They sent the slaves into the fields to grow food, and the first king of Vallia used them again to build this palace in the late 1600s, when the Holy Roman Emperor established the kingdom of Vallia."

Despite its dark history, she was in awe. The white stone of the palace was immaculately tended and blindingly beautiful. The gardens were lush, the windows reflecting the blue skies and colorful blooms.

"It's not showing its age at all."

"My father had it fully restored and modernized."

"The workers were paid this time, I hope?" It was out before she thought better of it.

Luca's expression hardened. "A livable wage for honest employment, thanks to efforts by my sister and I, because he couldn't be dissuaded from doing it. Hardly the best use of Vallia's taxes, though."

Amy managed to bite back her observation that he didn't sound as though he had been super close with his dad.

They stepped from the car, and the comforting warmth of sunbaked stones radiated into her while a soft, salt-scented breeze rolled over her skin. The palace was set into terraced grounds facing the sea, but the view stretched east and west on either side. Flowers were bursting forth in splashes of red and yellow, his country's colors, in the gardens and in terra-cotta pots that sat on the wide steps. New leaves on the trees ruffled a subtle applause as they climbed toward the entrance.

A young man hurried to open a door for him.

Entering the palace was a step into a sumptuous garden of white marble streaked with pinks and blues, oranges and browns. Ornate plasterwork and gold filigree climbed the walls like vines, sweeping in curves and curls up to the sparkling crystal chandeliers. The fresco painted on the dome above had her catching at Luca's arm, it made her so dizzy. Amid the cerulean skies and puffy clouds and beams of sunlight, the angels seemed rather...sexual.

They weren't angels, she realized with a lurch of her heart. That satyr definitely had his hand between the legs of a nymph.

A man cleared his throat.

Amy jerked her gaze down to see a palace sage of some type, middle-aged, in a dark suit. His gaze was on her hand, which still clutched Luca's sleeve.

She let it fall to her side.

"Amy, this is Guillermo Bianchi, my private secretary. Guillermo, Amy Miller. She's with London Connection, a public relations firm. She'll assist with the foundation's gala."

"I received the email, *signor.*" Guillermo nodded as both greeting and acknowledgment of her role. "Welcome. Rooms have been prepared and appointments arranged with the team."

"Thank you. Er...*grazie*, I mean."

"Amy will join me for dinner in my dining room while she's here."

Guillermo gave an obsequious bow of his head that still managed to convey disapproval. He asked Amy to accompany him up a wide staircase beneath a massive window that allowed sunlight to pour in and shoot rainbows through the dangling chandelier.

She looked back, but Luca was already disappearing in another direction toward a handful of people waiting with tablets, folders and anxious expressions.

Amy went back to gawking at the opulence of the palace. She'd grown up with enough wealth to recognize hand-woven silk rugs and antiques that were actually priceless historical artifacts. She lifted her feet into a slight tiptoe when they reached a parquet floor, fearful of damaging the intricate artistry of the polished wood mosaic with her sharp heels. She could have stood upon it for hours, admiring the geometric designs.

This whole place was a monument to ancient wealth and abundance that stood on the line of gaudy without quite crossing it.

After a long walk through a gallery and down a flight of stairs, she was guided into a lounge that was a perfect mix of modern and period pieces. It had a wide gas fireplace, tall windows looking onto a garden with a pond, and Victorian furniture that she suspected were loving restorations. Everything in the room was the height of class—except the pornographic scene above the sofa. Amy blinked.

"The previous king commissioned a number of reproductions from Pompeii," Guillermo informed her in bland, barely accented English. "I've ordered tea and sandwiches. They'll be here shortly. Please let the maid know if you require anything else."

Amy almost asked whether the sofa was a pullout, but he was already gone.

She poked around and discovered this was a self-contained

flat with a full kitchen, a comfortable office with a view to the garden, and two bedrooms, each with more examples of Pompeii's salacious artwork.

Her meager luggage was waiting to be unpacked in the bigger room alongside a handful of clothes that were unfamiliar, but were in her size. There was a luxurious bath with a tempting, freestanding tub, but she only washed her hands.

A three-tiered plate arrived full of sandwiches, savory pastries and chocolate truffles, and was accompanied by coffee, tea and a cordial that turned out to be a tangy sweet liquor meant to be served with the soda water that accompanied it.

She did her best not to reveal she was completely bowled over, but she was only *around* wealth these days. London Connection was doing well, but they were reinvesting profits and using them to hire more staff. Amy had conditioned herself to live on a shoestring after being expelled from school. She'd been unable to take her A-levels and had had to sell what possessions she'd had at the time—mostly designer clothes and a few electronics—to set herself up in a low-end flat. She'd come a long way since then, but the maid probably had a higher net worth than she did.

Amy asked her to set the meal on the table outside her lounge. The patio overlooked a man-made pond full of water lilies where a weathered Neptune rose from the middle, trident aloft. Columns that were buckling with age surrounded the water. This must be the ruins of the Roman villa that Luca had mentioned, she thought.

Between the columns stood statues that looked new, though. Huh. The gladiator had a bare backside that rivaled Luca's, and the mermaid seemed very chesty.

After the maid left, Amy gave in to curiosity. She set aside her tea to walk out for a closer look.

"My father's taste was questionable," Luca said behind her. "To say the least."

She swung around, but had to look up to find him. He stood

on a terrace off to the right that she surmised was the best vantage point to admire the pond. He wore the clothes he'd had on earlier, but his jacket was off again and his sleeves were rolled back. His expression was shuttered, but once again she heard the denigration of his father's waste of taxpayers' money.

"I thought I wouldn't see you until dinner." She had been looking forward to reflecting, putting today's events into some sort of order in her mind. Now she was back to a state of heightened awareness, watching his long strides make for a set of stairs off to the left. He loped down them and came toward her in an unhurried stride that ate up the ground easily.

"I don't want any delay on your work."

"Oh, um." Her throat had gone dry, and she looked longingly back at her tea. "I was about to sit down and brainstorm ideas, but I'm having trouble understanding why you'd willingly give up all of this." She waved at her small flat. His private quarters were likely ten times more luxurious and grand. Looking up, she suspected his was that second-level terrace that looked out to the sea unobstructed.

"Allow me to enlighten you." He jerked his head at the pebbled path that wove through the columns around the pond, indicating they should walk it.

She started along and immediately came upon a soldier performing a lewd act with a nymph, one that made her cheeks sting with embarrassment. It grew worse when she darted a glance at Luca and discovered him watching her reaction.

Her heart lurched, but he didn't seem to be enjoying her discomfiture. If anything, his grim expression darkened.

"Oh, those Romans," she joked weakly.

"My father commissioned them. He could have used the funds in a thousand better ways. My first act once I was crowned was tax relief, but I couldn't offer as much as was needed. Our economy is a mess."

Their footsteps crunched as they wound between the columns and wisteria vines that formed a bower, filling the air with their potent fragrance.

The statues grew increasingly graphic. Luca seemed immune, but Amy was as titillated as she was mortified. She was mortified *because* she was titillated.

Even more embarrassing was a stray curiosity about whether Luca would have the strength to have freestanding sex like that, arms straining as his fingertips pressed into her bottom cheeks. His shoulders would feel like marble beneath her arms where she clasped them tightly around his neck, breasts mashed to his flexing chest as her legs gripped around his waist. They would hold each other so tightly, they would barely be able to move, but—

"Do you know why Vallia needs a queen, Amy?"

"No," she squeaked, yanking her mind from fornication.

"Because the king of Vallia is this." He nodded toward the statuary. "A sex addict who never sought help. In fact, he used his position to take advantage of those over whom he had power."

The butterflies in her stomach turned to slithering snakes that crept up to constrict her lungs and tighten her throat.

Amy knew all about men who took advantage of their position of power. It was adding a razor edge of caution to every step as they walked among these erotic statues.

Luca was a client, which made her feel as though she had to defer to him, but he wasn't forcing her into an awkward situation for his own amusement. She might be blushing so hard the soles of her feet hurt, but he was radiating furious disgust. He was trying to explain why he was so committed to her doing this odd job for him.

Not that kind of job, Amy! She dragged her gaze off the woman whose hands were braced on a naked gladiator's sandals as he sat proudly feeding his erection to her.

"You're not like him," she managed to say. "Your father, I mean."

"No, I'm not," he agreed, jaw clenched. "But I have to make

at least a few people believe I could be. Briefly." He glanced from the narrow shadow of the trident on a stepping-stone to his watch.

She followed his gaze and said with delight, "It's a sundial! Half-past oral sex and a quarter till—" She slapped her hand over her mouth, cheeks flaring so hotly, she thought she'd burn her palm. "I'm sorry." She was. "I use humor to defuse tension, but I shouldn't have said that. This is a professional relationship. I'll do better, I promise."

She was still stinging with a flush of embarrassment that boiled up from too many sources to count—the situation, the blatant thing she'd just said, the lack of propriety on her part and, deep down, a pang of anguish that she was giving him such a terrible impression of herself when she wished he would like her a little.

His mouth twisted. "You'll have to say a lot worse than that to shock me. The Romans themselves couldn't hold a candle to some of the obscene things my father did."

He veered down a path to a small lookout that was mostly overgrown. A wooden bench faced a low, stone wall, but they had to stand at the wall to see the blue-green water beyond.

Compassion squeezed Amy's insides as she sensed the frustration rolling off him.

"I've worked with a lot of people trying to keep scandals under wraps. It's very stressful. I can only imagine the pressure you've been under since you took the throne."

Luca made a noise that was the most blatantly cynical sound Amy had ever heard.

"For my whole life," he corrected her grimly. "As long as I can remember I've been trying to hide it, fix it, compensate for it. I've had to be completely different from him despite looking exactly like him while training for his job. A position he made seem so vile, there is absolutely no desire in me to hold it."

At his own words, he swore under his breath and ran a hand down his face.

"That sounds treasonous. Forget I said it," he muttered.

"This is a safe space. It has to be." Amy had long ago trained herself not to judge what people revealed when they were in crisis. "Are you still under pressure to hide his behavior? If there are things you're worried could come out, I might be able to help manage that, too." She looked to where the array of erotic statues was shielded by shrubbery. "I could put out confidential feelers for a private collector to buy those, for a start."

"That's well-known." He dismissed the statues with a flick of his hand. "There's no point trying to hide them now."

His jaw worked as though he was debating something. When he looked at her, a cold hand seemed to leap out of his bleak gaze and close over her heart.

"The way he died may yet come out," he admitted in a voice that held a scraped hollow ring, one that held so much pain, she suspected he was completely divorcing himself from reality to cope with it.

"Do you want to tell me about it? You don't have to," she assured him while her heart stuttered in an uneven rhythm. "But you can if you want to."

His father's death had been reported as a cardiac arrest, but there'd been countless rumors about the circumstances.

"My sister doesn't even know the full truth."

It was all on him and the secret weighed heavily. Amy could tell.

She wanted to touch him, comfort him in some way. She also sensed he needed to be self-contained right now. It was the only way he was holding on to his control.

"If you're worried there are people who might reveal something, we could approach them with a settlement and a binding nondisclosure," she suggested gently.

"That's already been done. And the handful of people who knew where he was that night were happy to take a stack of cash and get away without a charge of contributing to manslaughter, but they're not the most reliable sort." He searched her gaze with his intense one. "Frankly, I wish he'd hired pros-titutes. They would have acted like professionals. This was a party gone wrong. There were drugs at the scene. Nasty ones."

"Here? In the palace?" That was bad, but she'd cleaned up similar messes.

"In the dungeon."

She didn't school her expression fast enough.

"Yes. *That* kind of dungeon." His lips were snarled tight against his teeth. His nostrils flared. "I wouldn't normally judge how people spend their spare time, but if you rule a country, perhaps don't allow yourself to be tied up and flogged by a pair of women who get so stoned they don't know how to free you when your heart stops. Or who to call."

Amy caught her gasp in her hand. Talk about making a trau-matic situation even more distressing for all involved!

"Luca, I'm so sorry." Her hand went to his arm before she realized she was doing it.

He didn't react beyond stiffening under her touch.

She'd seen clients shut down like this, doing whatever they had to in order to carry on with their daily lives. It told her ex-actly how badly his father's behavior had affected him.

"Look, I have to ask before we go any further. Are you sure you're not just reacting to what you've experienced? I'd want to wash my hands of this role if I were in your shoes. That's un-derstandable, but what you've asked me to do is not a decision you should make in haste."

"It's not one incident, Amy. It's everything he stood for. All of the things I've learned he was capable of, now that I'm privy to it. It's appalling. There was a thorough cleaning of house once I took the throne, but how can I claim to be righting his wrongs if I ignore the very basic one where he installed me as monarch instead of my sister?"

The flash of a tortured conscience behind his searing blue eyes tempted her to shift her fingers in a soothing caress. She moved her hand to the soft moss that had grown on the stone wall and scanned the view through the trees.

"And no one will listen to this extremely rational argument? Let you turn things over without drastic measures?"

"My supporters see Sofia as an excellent spare, but they are extremely attached to keeping me exactly where I am. Our constitution doesn't allow an abdication without proper cause. Even if I was incapacitated, I would keep the crown and Sofia would rule as a regent until I died. I've exhausted all other avenues. This is what's left. I have to prove myself a detriment to the country. An embarrassment that can't be tolerated because I'm too much like my father after all."

"Okay. Well…" She considered all she'd learned, formally and informally. "Most scandals fall into three categories—sex, drugs and corruption. It sounds like your father had his toe in all of those?"

"He did."

"It's hard to come back from embezzlement or political payoffs. I wouldn't want to tar you as a crook, especially if you're planning to take an active part in improving Vallia's economy afterward."

"Agreed."

"Drug scandals usually require a stay in a rehab facility and ongoing counseling. Addiction is an illness, so there's a risk you'd be expected to continue to rule. It's also very complicated to manage image-wise. There has to be sincere, visible effort, and it becomes a lifelong process of proving sobriety. There's always a certain mistrust that lingers in the public eye. The world expects a recovering addict to trip and is always watching for it. I would prefer not to use a drug scandal."

"So that leaves us with sex." His mouth curled with dismay.

"Yes. People love to act outraged over sexual exploits, but they all have their own peccadillos to hide so they tend to move on fairly quickly."

"It can't be anything harassment related or exploitative," he said firmly.

"No," she quickly agreed. "I couldn't defend that, even a manufactured charge. London Connection is always on the victim's side in those cases. It will have to be something compromising, like cheating or adultery." She tapped her chin in thought.

"That would mean courting my way into a relationship with someone in order to betray her. I don't want to use or hurt an unsuspecting woman."

"Something that suggests you have a streak of your father's tastes, then?"

"I'm won't be tied up and spanked. That's not my thing."

"Like anyone would believe you're a bottom. I'm sorry!" She hid her wince behind her hand. "These are habits of a lifetime, trying to be funny to keep a mood light."

After a silence that landed like a thump, he drawled, "I'm definitely a top." The firmness in his tone underscored his preference for dominating in bed.

Which caused the most inexplicable swoop in her stomach. Runnels of tingling intrigue radiated into her loins, much to her everlasting chagrin.

When she risked a glance up at him, she saw humor glinting in his eyes along with something speculative that noted the blush on her cheekbones.

Her heart swerved, and she shot her attention to the sea while her shoulders longed for the weight of his hands. Something wanton in her imagination pictured him drawing her arms behind her back by the elbows while he kissed the side of her neck and told her not to move.

While he held her. *Claimed* her.

Her scalp tingled in anticipation and she refused to look down, deeply aware her nipples were straining against the soft silk of her dress, swollen and tight and throbbing with lust.

"Perhaps...um..." Her voice rasped and her brain was wandering around drunk in the dark. "Something with role-play?" she suggested tautly.

"Leak a photo of me wearing pointy ears or dressed like one of those gladiators?" He thumbed back toward the path. "No, thanks."

He would so *rock* a leather sword belt. She licked her lips. "Voyeurism?"

"Hidden cameras? Gross."

"What if you, um, did something questionable in public?"

"Caught with my pants down? Like a flasher?"

"*With* someone."

"Mmm." He grimaced as he considered it. "It has potential, but it means compromising someone else, and naked photos are forever. Keep going."

"You're really hard to please."

"You'll get there," he chided.

A fluttery excitement teased through her.

"Group sex?" she suggested, then realized that might be *too* reminiscent of his father.

Luca's gaze held her own in a way that made her stumbling heart climb into her throat.

"I prefer to give one woman one hundred percent of my attention," he stated. "And I refuse to compete for hers."

So dominant.

Bam, bam, bam went her heart, hammering the base of her throat while the rest of her was slithery honey and prickly nerve endings.

"The only thing left is tickle fights and foot fetishes." She turned her gaze to the water, nose questing for any hint of breeze to cool her blood. She was boiling inside her own skin.

"I like a pretty shoe," he allowed in a voice that angled down to where her silk dress fluttered against her ankles. His voice climbed as his attention came up. "Quality lingerie is always worth appreciating."

He could see the sea-foam green of her lacy bra cup peeking

from the open buttons at her chest; she was sure of it. Could he also see she was fighting not to pant in reaction? Why, oh, why was she responding to him so strongly?

"But it's hardly a crime to admire a beautiful woman, is it?"

Was that what he was doing? Because she was pretty sure she was being seduced.

"I want to do something *bad*, Amy."

She choked on a semihysterical laugh, fighting to stay professional and on task while imagining him— *Don't*, she scolded herself. *Don't imagine him doing anything, especially not making babies with y—*

"Oh! Baby daddy!" She leaped on it, pointing so hard toward him, she almost poked him in the chest. "A woman claims to be pregnant with your baby."

His brow went up toward his hairline. "That sort of extortion died when DNA tests came along, didn't it?"

"That's why it would be taken seriously." She spoke fast as she warmed to it. "Women don't make the claim unless they've actually slept with the potential father. Here's what I like about this idea." She excitedly ticked off on her fingers. "It's a very human mistake that still makes you seem virile, and you'll take the honorable steps to accept responsibility. But, because she's not suitable as a queen, it opens the door for your sister to question your judgment and take over."

"It won't work." He dismissed it flatly. "If I conceive a baby while I'm on the throne, my honor would demand that I marry her. That child would become the future ruler of Vallia and my sister would be sidelined forever."

"There is no baby." Amy opened her hands like it was a magic act. "We'll keep the timeline very short. We leak that a woman approached you and *thinks* she's pregnant. You take the possibility seriously, but even while the scandal is blowing up, she learns it was a false alarm. She wasn't actually pregnant. That way the trauma of a pregnancy loss can be avoided. The scandal will be about you taking reckless chances with your country's future. Your sister can call you irresponsible and take the throne."

His brow was still furrowed. "There's no actual woman? I'm the only name in the press? I like that."

"I think you need a living, breathing woman." She wrinkled her nose. "Otherwise the public will search forever for this mystery woman. You'd have people coming forward for generations, claiming to be your long-lost descendant. No, you need someone you conceivably—ha-ha—could have met and slept with. Perhaps a reality star or a pop singer. Let me go through my contact list. I'm sure I can find a few women who would be willing to do something like this as a publicity stunt."

He cringed.

"You hate it?" She had been so proud, convinced this was a workable plan.

"I don't love that I have to use someone, but if she's in the know from the beginning and getting something out of it, I can live with it. This sounds effective without being too unsavory." He nodded. "Run with it."

CHAPTER FOUR

A DISTANT NOISE INTRUDED, but Luca ignored it and continued indulging his lascivious fantasy of Amy's dress unbuttoned to her waist, held closed only by the wide black corset-style belt. Her lacy green bra and underwear would hold the heat of her body and have a delicious silky abrasive texture against his lips and questing touch. She—

"Signor?" His private secretary and lifelong adviser cleared his throat very pointedly, forcing Luca to abandon his musing and focus on the fact that Guillermo was standing in his office, awaiting acknowledgment.

"Yes?" Luca prompted.

"About Ms. Miller's work with the charity..." Guillermo closed the door.

"Is she shaking things up? Because that's what I hired her to do." If she appeared to be an impulsive, misguided decision on his part, all the better.

Guillermo's mouth tightened before he forced a flat smile. "The palace PR team is perfectly capable of handling this last-minute promotion of the gala. In fact, the foundation's board could carry the event over the finish line without any help at all so I'm not sure why Ms. Miller is necessary."

This was the sort of micromanaging Luca had suffered all

his life and would have burned to the ground if he'd been planning to remain king. Given their lifelong relationship, Luca could also tell Guillermo smelled an ulterior motive and was digging to find it.

"The board of directors are my mother's contemporaries," Luca said. "They're committed and passionate, but at some point, adhering to tradition only demonstrates a lack of imagination. We're there."

"Have you seen Ms. Miller's contemporaries? Her online presence is very colorful." It wasn't a compliment.

"She's well-connected and understands how to leverage that community."

"But to *whom* is she connected, *signor*? That is my concern. She's photographed with a lot of men, often in relation to a drug charge or the like."

"It's her job to mitigate scandals."

"Are we certain she's not actually the source of them?" Guillermo wasn't being an alarmist. Their previous head of PR had been an enabler to the former king's vices. "Even if she's aboveboard, she wishes to pitch the directors on having the foundation's logo embroidered onto pajamas to be sold as a fundraiser. She thinks celebrities could be encouraged to post photos of themselves wearing them. Might I remind you, *signor*, of your standing instruction that all those associated with royal interests project a more dignified profile than we've seen in the past? Have I missed an announcement that your attitude has changed?"

"You know it hasn't," Luca said flatly. "I'll have Amy tell me about the pajama idea over dinner and judge for myself."

Guillermo didn't take the hint that he was dismissed. "Is dining with her a good idea? She's very familiar. She makes frequent jokes."

Dio aiutami, his patience was hanging by a thread. "Off with her head, then."

"I'm merely pointing out that if she were a true British subject, she might understand the role of a sovereign, but she was born in America—"

"She has the gall to be an American? What *will* we do?"

"*Signor*, I wouldn't want her levity or imprudence to cast any shadows upon you."

"A moment ago, she was too colorful. Would she not cast rainbows?"

"She is already rubbing off on you if you're not taking my counsel seriously. Ms. Miller is a poor fit for any palace endeavor," Guillermo insisted.

"On the contrary, Amy understands influence and image better than you or I ever will. That's why I hired her." Luca was genuinely annoyed by his secretary's snobbish dismissal of a woman who was a font of problem-solving ideas. She had quickly grasped the pros and cons of his unusual request and shaped a workable plan in the shortest possible time. She was the type of person he loved to hire. Instead, he was surrounded by stodgy relics who started their day by shooting protocol directly into their veins.

"I'm sure her *image* is what influenced you," Guillermo sniffed.

"What are you implying?" Luca narrowed his eyes.

"Only that she's very beautiful. The sort of woman who might charm and distract a man from his duties. Impact his judgment."

"I hadn't noticed," Luca lied flagrantly, adding with significant bite, "But if you're having trouble seeing past the fact she's attractive, I'll work with her personally. Safer for all."

"*Signor*, I am perfectly capable of working with her."

"But I'm not?" Luca was down to his last nerve. "I am thirty-one and the king. It's time you trust me to know what I'm doing." *As I nuke my own life...but needs must.*

Do you? Guillermo didn't say it, but the words echoed around the room all the same.

"You're dismissed."

Guillermo closed the door on his way out with a firm click.

Luca hissed out a disgusted breath. Guillermo wasn't stupid. Or wrong. If he'd been a true detriment to the family, the palace, or Vallia, he wouldn't hold the position he did.

Luca was resolved, however, in giving up the crown. The part where he was all too aware of Amy's attributes wasn't part of the plan. He was crossing certain lines if only within his own mind, imagining how snugly silk and lace would sit against Amy's skin. It reinforced temptations that were already difficult to resist.

And much as he was willing to appear fallible, he didn't want to do anything that would sit on his conscience—like make an unwanted pass at an employee. Dignity and responsibility had been his watchwords all his life. He had never had room for even those small human mistakes that Amy found so forgivable.

Her accepting nature was as disarming as her sense of humor and sparkling beauty. He'd signed the contract she'd sent him so he knew she was legally bound to keep his secrets, but he was still unnerved at how easily he'd told her about his father. The night of his father's death had been horrific and something he'd expected to take to his grave—even though it sat inside him like a boil.

Lancing that poison had been a profound relief. Maybe she was onto something about building rapport with her clients.

He choked on a fresh laugh as he recalled her blurted joke. *Half-past oral sex and quarter till—*

What had she been about to say? Doggy-style?

So inappropriate, considering their professional relationship, but damned if he wouldn't recall that remark every time he looked at the sundial in future. And laugh instead of wanting to bash it apart with a sledgehammer.

He'd fought noticing how the graphic statues were affecting her as they walked through them. She'd been curious, as anyone would be. They were meant to be sexually provocative. He'd seen her blushes and lingering looks and the way her nipples had poked against the cups of her bra beneath the layer of her silk dress.

He'd had his own stiffness to disguise. In another life they might have had an entirely different sort of conversation among those athletic examples of libidinous acts, one that might have ended in an attempt to emulate—

Stop. He couldn't let himself do this. He had *hired* her.

To ruin him.

And their conversation on how best to go about that had been some of the most amusing banter he'd enjoyed in ages.

Guillermo was right. Amy could be very dangerous to him on a personal level.

Even so, he glanced at his watch and decided he was hungry for an early dinner.

Amy eyed the slim-fit chive-green pants and the madras patterned jacket in pink and green and gold that she'd bought from the hotel boutique. They would work for tomorrow's meeting with Luca's gala committee, but it wasn't a formal enough outfit for dining with a king.

She debated between the two tea dresses in the closet. One was a pale rose, the other a midnight blue. Both were exceedingly good quality, elegant and pretty, but so demure as to bore her into a coma while looking at them. That pastel pink with the long sleeves would make her skin look sallow, and its sweetheart neckline would have her begging for an insulin shot.

She tried on the blue. It had a round collar, cap sleeves and a sheer overlay on the A-line skirt. She was tempted to put her own leather corset belt over it, but tried the belt off the pink dress. It was a narrow plait with a spangled clasp that added some pop against the blue.

She ignored the closed-toe black patent leather pumps and put on her own silver-heeled stilettos. Then she pushed all her bangles so they sat above her elbow. She couldn't hide the tattoo on her upper arm and shoulder, so she underscored it.

Her hair was in a topknot with wisps pulled out at her temples. Simple eye makeup made her new crimson lipstick all the more dramatic. She was ready to face Luca.

She hoped.

The young man who escorted her—was he a footman?—glanced at her in the various reflective surfaces they passed. She wasn't falsely modest. She knew she attracted the male gaze. Even before her curves had developed, her mother had coached her to play up her femininity and keep the men around her happy and comfortable.

Manipulate them, was what her mother had meant. Trouble was, she'd taught Amy to hunt without teaching her to kill. Thus, Amy's first experience had been to successfully stalk a predator and become his prey without even realizing what was happening.

But she wouldn't think about that right now. The footman was letting her into an office that held a small lounge area and a scrumptious king.

"Amy," Luca greeted.

The impact of his presence, of a voice that sounded pleased to see her, was a blast of sensual energy that made all the hair on her body stand up.

He was freshly shaved and wore dark pants with a pale blue shirt. Both were tailored to sit flawlessly against his muscled frame. Funny how she almost wished he wore a jacket and tie so this would feel more formal. She wasn't sure why she wanted him to put up armor against her, but it would have made her feel safer.

Not that she felt *un*safe as the door closed, leaving them alone. She just wanted him to put up barriers because she couldn't find any of her own. She suddenly felt very raw and skinless as she faced him.

So she turned her attention to the old-world decor, the fine rugs and carved wooden columns. No overtly sexual images in here. It was decorated in a combination of modern abstracts, contemporary furniture and a few period pieces. His desk had to be three hundred years old. It was all very beautiful and... impersonal.

He hadn't moved in. Not properly. He might have erased his father's presence, but he'd made no effort to stamp the space with his own. He'd been planning his abdication from the day he was crowned.

When she looked at him, she caught him staring at her tattoo.

"You really don't care for convention, do you?" he said.

Her toes tried to curl, reacting to the conflicting mix of approval in his tone with the suggestion of disapproval in his words.

"Does that bother you?" she asked, voice strained by the pressure in her chest.

"Some." He poured two glasses of white wine and brought them across the room to offer one. "This is our private reserve. If you don't care for it, I have a red that's not as dry."

"I'm sure it will be fine." She accepted it, and they touched the rims of their glasses before she tried the wine. It was icy and very dry, but complex with a fruit forward start, a round mouth feel and a brief tang before its soft finish. "This is lovely. I'll take payment in cases."

His mouth twitched. He nodded at her shoulder. "Do you mind? I saw online that you had one, but I didn't see what it was."

She angled slightly so he could examine the inked image of a bird flying free of a cage suspended from a branch of blossoms.

"Colorful," he murmured. Something in his amused tone was drier than the wine. It made her feel as though he was making a joke she didn't understand, but his thumb grazed her skin, blanking her mind while filling her body with heat. "It must have taken a lot of time."

"Four hours. It hurt so much," she said with a laugh that was shredded more by her longing for another caress than any memory of pain. "It's too on-the-nose and was a foolish expense since I was broke at the time, but my mother had always threatened to disinherit me if I got a tattoo. Since she'd gone ahead and done that, I saw no reason to wait."

"The same mother you spoke with in the car today? The one who spoiled you because you were an only child?"

"Yes. But then she stopped." She wrinkled her nose. "I'd rather not talk about my parents. It's a complicated relationship."

"That's fine," he said mildly. "But you *can* talk about them if you decide you'd like to. This is a safe space," he added in a sardonic tone that threw her own words back at her.

She choked back saying it didn't feel like it and said, "Good to know." She gulped wine to wet her dry throat. "Do you have any?"

"Tattoos?" He snorted. "No." He sipped his own wine, then walked his glass to an end table and set it down. "I was also forbidden to get one, but that didn't bother me. I've never had much appetite for rebellion. My father thought being king gave him license to do whatever the hell he wanted despite the responsibilities that come with the title. I was taught differently."

"By your mother and her team."

"Yes. And his behavior impacted her. She had mental health struggles. That's why the foundation exists. She started it because she understood the hurdles people face when seeking treatment. She passed away from an unrelated condition, but I often think her depression affected her…" Agony tightened his expression. "Her will to fight. She loved us, but she was very disillusioned. Humiliated by my father's conduct. Or lack thereof," he said with a twist of his lips. "He was completely indifferent to the effect he had on her. Not oblivious. He simply didn't care. If anything, he was spiteful about it. He didn't *want* to be a good husband or father or ruler. He set out to prove he didn't have to conform or put anyone's needs above his own. As a result, I find rebellion a selfish and unattractive behavior."

"Ouch," she said blithely as she set aside her own wine, fighting not to let him see how deeply that knife had plunged.

"I didn't mean to suggest you're selfish. I was speaking of the characteristic in general."

"Oh, but I was," she assured him. "I was a self-involved brat until such time as that luxury was denied me." She'd been hurt and feeling abandoned by her parents after they'd divorced and shuffled her off to boarding school. She'd made demands for things she didn't even want in a clichéd cry for the love and attention she really craved.

Her behavior had spiraled from there and yes, Amy carried some of the blame for what had happened with the field hockey coach. She had known what she was doing was wrong, but so had he. And he'd been a man of twenty-nine while she'd been an eighteen-year-old student in his class.

"I didn't always direct my independent streak in the best way," she admitted. "But it annoys me that pushing back on how girls and women are 'supposed to' behave is considered rebellion. That's what I was really fighting. My mother was always saying, 'Don't speak up. You have to fit in.' She buys into this silent agreement with society that women aren't supposed to draw attention to ourselves because it pulls the spotlight from the really important people. Men," she stated with a scathing eye roll.

"Ouch," he said ironically.

She bit her lip, quelling her smile.

He was shaking his head, but taking her remark with good-natured amusement.

She liked him, damn it.

Best to focus on why she was here. "Can I show you the women I've identified who might be willing to ruin you?"

"I thought I was already looking at her," he drawled.

Amy faltered in retrieving her phone.

He sobered. "That was a joke."

"I know. I didn't realize you knew how to make one." She shakily breezed past her tiny betrayal of a guilty conscience and brought her phone to him. "These are celebrities I know well enough to approach. I am neither confirming nor denying they are clients."

"Noted."

They stood so closely, she could feel the heat off his body and detected the mellow scent of his aftershave. He picked up his wine and she heard him swallow as she began to thumb through images, providing a brief biography for each.

"German car heiress trying to start her own fashion line. Country music star, American, won an award for a song about her messy divorce. This is a cousin of a British ambassador. She has a popular online cooking series."

Luca rejected them all just as quickly. "Too young. No one will believe I listen to American country music. Where would I have met an online chef?"

Six more went by and Amy clicked off her phone. "You're being too picky. *No one* will be perfect. That's the point."

"If I don't believe I'm attracted to her, no one else will." He set aside his glass again.

"What kind of woman do you want, then?" she asked with exasperation.

His gaze raked down her face and snagged on her mouth, then swept back to her eyes. The heat in the depths of his blue irises nearly set her on fire before he looked to a corner.

Amy caught her breath, swaying on the skinny heels of her shoes. She had really hoped this attraction was only on her side. It would have made this a silly infatuation where she was reaching out of her league and had no chance.

It was a lot harder to ignore when she knew he felt the same. The space between them seemed to shrink, drawing them in. Her gaze fixated on the tension around his mouth.

"I…" She had no words. She should have moved away. "I thought you were…" She thought back to that dismissive rebuff he'd given her in London. "Indifferent to me."

His lips parted as he exhaled roughly. "You do speak your

mind, don't you? I *want* to be indifferent." The air crackled between them. "But I'm not."

What was she supposed to do with that? She could only soften with helplessness. He had to be the strong one.

As they both fell silent, she felt the pull of an invisible force. He moved in such small increments, she thought she imagined that he was drawing closer; but he was suddenly so close that a prickle of anticipation stung her lips. She dampened them with her tongue.

"Amy." It was a scold that rang with defeat. His hand found her hip as though to ground them both as his head dipped and he covered her mouth with his own.

Sensation burst to life in her. His lips were firm and smooth and confident. Smothering in the most delicious way as he angled and fit and claimed her. Devastated her.

How long had it been since she'd kissed a man? Really kissed one with hunger and passion and a hand that went to the back of his head, urging him to ravish her?

His arm banded across her lower back, dragging her in so her body was plastered to the hardness of his. They rocked their mouths together, pressing tighter, opening wider, exploring deeper.

A moan left her throat and she wound her arms around his neck, clinging weakly as she lost herself to the delirium. No one had ever made her feel like this. Never, ever.

Suddenly he took her by the shoulders and set her back a step. The regressive light in his eyes stopped her heart before he ruthlessly leashed whatever animal was alive inside him.

His hands dropped away as he turned to stand directly in front of her.

"*Sì,*" he barked and the door opened.

Oh, God. Someone had knocked and she hadn't even heard it. She dropped her face into her hands.

She recognized Guillermo's voice, but stayed exactly where

she was, hidden by the wall of Luca's back as she tried to gather her composure.

The men exchanged words in crisp Italian and the door closed again.

"There's a call I must take." Luca's arm reached past her to snag his wine. She heard him finish it in one gulp. "I'll be tied up for hours. Your meal will be delivered to your room."

She nodded jerkily and made herself lift her head and turn to face him. She cringed as she saw him, saying remorsefully, "My lipstick is all over your mouth."

He swore and swiped the back of his hand across his lips, noted the streak of red and swore again, this time with resignation.

"I shouldn't have done that. I'm sorry." A muscle in his cheek ticked.

Her stomach clenched around the pang his regret caused her.

"I know better, too." Her voice rasped and the backs of her eyes were hot. "I'll go."

"Amy."

She turned back.

Compunction was still etched across his face, but he held out a handkerchief. He touched her chin, urging her to lift her mouth. In a few gentle swipes, he cleaned the edges of her lips.

He then used the same soft linen to wipe his own mouth. He dropped his hand and let her examine his work. All trace of their kiss was gone as though it had never happened.

She nodded, too empty to feel anything but despondency. She swallowed a dry lump from the back of her throat, turned and left.

CHAPTER FIVE

LUCA TOOK THE CALL regarding a handful of Vallia's elite military serving overseas on a humanitarian mission. No one had been injured, but there'd been an incident that required he draft a statement and follow up with calls to overseas contacts.

By the time the whole thing was put to bed, it was long past time he should have been asleep himself.

"Take the morning off," he told Guillermo as he rose from his desk.

"Signor." Guillermo had an uncanny ability to inject a host of meaning into that single word. This one held appreciation for the sentiment, protest that the extra sleep wasn't necessary, caution and concern and a waft of smugness that he'd been right to warn Luca against Ms. Miller.

"I'll speak to the Privy Council in the morning," Luca said, meeting Guillermo's gaze with an implacable one. "You needn't make any reports to them on this evening. At all."

Guillermo's mouth tightened. "As you wish. Sleep well."

Luca didn't. He got slightly drunk while roundly berating himself even as he stood on the terrace off his bedroom, overlooking the Roman pond surrounded by sexual gymnastics.

If Amy had been wandering around there like a lost ghost,

he would have had a reason to go out to see her, but she hadn't given him one.

Kissing her had been such a stupid thing to do. A mistake. Mistakes were something else he'd never had the appetite for. He'd been so scrutinized all his life, so quickly corrected for the tiniest errors, he had little tolerance for imperfection, especially within himself. He was the Golden Prince, after all.

And Amy was...

The image of her tattoo came into his mind, oddly pretty and feminine despite the jailbreak it depicted. He had wanted to clasp his hand around her warm arm and set his mouth against the ink. Taste her skin and kiss that small, pretty bird that he instinctively knew had been as chirpy inside that cage as she was outside it.

What kind of woman do you like, then?

Not anyone like her—with her cheeky remarks and hair that looked like it had already been mussed by raunchy sex. Not someone who didn't so much get under his skin as draw him out of his own. One who made him want to shake off his restraints, self-imposed and otherwise.

One with whom he'd already broken a cardinal rule of keeping his hands to himself.

He managed to sleep a few hours, then got an early start on his day. He met with his Privy Council, spoke briefly with his sister who was distracted as she wrapped up a diplomacy conference in North Africa, then made his way to the meeting of the gala committee.

Amy was holding court and faltered when he entered. She was like a tropical bird in pinks and greens and gold. Beautiful, if projecting an air of delicacy that he hadn't expected. There were hints of shadows beneath her makeup and a wary fragility in her smile.

"Your Highness," she greeted.

"Continue," he said, waving everyone to stay seated while

he remained on his feet at the back of the room. "I want to hear your pitch on the pajamas."

"I'm almost there." She glanced at her slide presentation and finished talking about the recruitment of influencers. She switched to photographs of elegant satin pajamas.

"Sometimes we want to call in sick to life." Her apprehensive gaze flicked to him and her laser pointer wasn't quite steady as she circled the pajama shirt. "Sometimes we need to feel safe and cozy as we navigate personal challenges. Asking celebrities to model the foundation's merchandise isn't about making mental health struggles seem glamorous. Yes, it's a fundraiser and some people will be motivated to buy the pajamas because of who wore it best, but we're also promoting self-care. We're saying it's okay to have a pajama day."

Amy paused for reaction, seeming to hold her breath.

Heads turned to gauge his reaction. One voice said pithily, "There's no way to have them printed before the gala."

"No," Amy agreed. "The campaign would be announced at the gala with an opportunity for those attending to place preorders. People love to be on the ground floor of something new. When they received their pajamas, it would bring the foundation back to their minds. In a few months, you could offer a new color and send out reorder forms. Later in the year, you could host a low-key pajama party."

"*That* doesn't sound very dignified," someone murmured.

"I like the central message," Luca stated firmly. "And it offers flexibility moving forward. My vote is to go ahead. Amy, I'd like to meet with you on another matter when you've finished here."

The attitude in the room changed as Luca left. A few old guard on the council were sitting as though perched on a pin, but they were the type who didn't like change. The rest had been hiding their interest for fear of offending them. Now that Luca had granted royal assent, several people had excited questions and seemed eager to carry the campaign forward.

Amy contributed as best she could, but she was having trouble concentrating. She'd nearly fainted when Luca walked in. She had half expected him to announce she was off the case and should catch the first flight back to London. Last night had been a rough one full of self-recriminations—and not just because their kiss had been so improper.

Was it, though?

Or was she searching for a way to rationalize her own poor judgment?

She wasn't an impressionable student any longer. She was an adult and their kiss had been completely consensual, but Luca did have power over her, most of it financial. He also had enough influence politically and socially to destroy London Connection if he wanted to call her out as offering sex to entice his business or some other twist of the truth.

Was it naive of her to believe he would never do such a thing? She barely knew him, but she didn't believe that he had it in him to act so dishonorably.

No, the real power Luca wielded was his ability to make her cast aside common sense.

As she'd ruminated alone last night, over a meal she'd barely touched, part of her had been tempted to tear up their contract, pack up and disappear in the dead of night.

It would cost her a nonperformance fee and impact her own reputation as dedicated and reliable, but Amy had suffered through hard times before. She wasn't as vulnerable and cushioned from reality as she'd been when she'd first been expelled, either. She didn't *want* to start over, but she knew how to do it. And she had modest savings set aside for exactly the sort of emergency that would arise if she turned her back on Luca as a client.

Amy wasn't a quitter, though. And she didn't want to believe she was so weak she could fall under a man's spell and ruin her own life in the process. Not again.

Eventually, to quiet her mind, she had gone back to working on the gala presentation and the other, private assignment. If Luca decided to fire her for lacking professionalism, so be it. She, at least, would carry on as if she still had the job.

Which, it turned out, wasn't any easier than being fired. It meant facing him again. In front of a crowd. She had tried to sound knowledgeable and unaffected by the memory of their kiss while her ideas were picked apart and his laser-like gaze watched her every move.

Now the meeting had broken up and a footman was leading her back to the private wing of the palace. He showed her into a different room from last night, this one a parlor in colors of olive and straw and pale, earthy reds.

"The king will be with you shortly," he said before he evaporated.

Amy took a cleansing breath and allowed the open doors to draw her out to a small, shaded courtyard. It was full of blooming roses exuding fragrances of lemon and raspberry, green tea, honey and cloves. She felt like a bee, incapable of deciding which to sniff first.

A small round table was set with snow-white linens and a splendiferous table setting fit for—well. Duh.

She studied the gold pattern on the china plates and the scrolls of what had to be real gold applied to the glasses. A yellow orchid blossom sat on the gold napkin ring. The flatware was gold, too. Intricately patterned and heavy and engraved with the Italian word for—

"Caught you," Luca said, startling her into clattering the gold knife back into its spot.

She sent him an admonishing look while his mouth curled into an amused smirk.

He was so effortlessly perfect. Lean and athletic, confident in his own skin, moving as an intrinsic part of the beauty and luxury that surrounded him.

"I was trying to make out what it said," she grumbled. "My Italian needs work."

"The setting was commissioned for my grandparents' wedding by my great-grandmother." He touched different pieces of cutlery as he translated the various words etched upon each. "Respect, honesty, trust, loyalty. The foundation of a strong marriage."

Don't read anything into it, Amy ordered herself, but couldn't help the way her pulse quickened and her cheeks grew warm with self-consciousness.

"My grandmother always used it when she had private luncheons with her women friends." He touched a fork to minutely adjust its position. "So did my mother."

"What a lovely tradition." Her heart twisted as she realized she was being very firmly friend zoned. "It puts a literal spin on women coming together to dish the dirt, doesn't it? I'm honored you would share it with me."

"I'm sure it made the women feel privileged to hear palace gossip from the queen herself, but if we're being honest?" He gave the knife with *Lealtà* scrolled upon it a sardonic nod. "I think it was also a reminder that the secrets she revealed were meant to be kept."

"The qualities of any good relationship, then." Amy spoke with casual interest, but her veins stung with indignation. She wasn't going to tell anyone that they'd kissed, if that's what he was worried about. "I've signed a nondisclosure contract," she reminded him, chin coming up a notch. "You don't have to drive it home with a golden spike."

"I thought you'd think they were pretty," he said in a blithe tone that disconcerted her because why would he care what she thought about anything? "The dishes and the courtyard."

"They are," she allowed, feeling awkward now. Privileged and entrusted.

He nodded past her and staff approached to seat them. Wine was poured, and as they took their first sips, her gaze clashed with his over their glasses. His expression was inscrutable, but the impact of looking him in the eye caused her to rattle the rim of her glass against her teeth. Her throat contracted on the wine, so she choked a bit, which she tried to suppress. The burn of alcohol seared a path behind her sternum.

An antipasto course was served. The staff didn't leave so they spoke of general things. Luca asked about the rest of her presentation, and Amy managed to say something lucid.

"What drew you to public relations as a career?" he inquired.

"Dumb luck. I was serving drinks at a pub. They had a band coming in, and I put it on my social media feeds. My circle was quite posh from school, daughters of celebs and such. One was a girl from a movie that was a cult favorite. She came out, and it turned the pub into that summer's hot spot. Another pub asked me to put them on the map, and word got out on the music circuit. Instead of serving drinks, I started planning and promoting events. The more people I knew, the more I got to know."

"I presumed you'd taken a degree, not learned on the job."

"I've since taken a vocational qualification." She didn't have to elaborate on why she hadn't gone to uni. Rice and fish were served, delicately spiced with saffron and scallions.

While they enjoyed it, he told her some more history about the palace and his country.

By the time they'd finished with a custard tart topped with whipped cream and fresh berries, they had discovered they both enjoyed mind-teaser puzzles, horseback riding—though they found little time to pursue it—and shared a fascination with remote places on Earth.

Amy had forgotten who he was and why she was here. This had become the most effortless, enjoyable date she'd been on in ages.

Then Luca told the server, "We'll take coffee in my drawing room," and Amy crashed back to reality. This wasn't a date.

She found a smile and said, "Coffee sounds good."

A few minutes later, they walked down the hall to the room where they'd kissed last night. The drapes were open, allowing sunshine to pour into the expansive space, but it still felt intimate once the espresso had been served and they were alone.

She understood the expression "walking on eggshells" as she approached the sofa. Each step crushed something fragile underfoot. Should she acknowledge last night? Express regret and move on? Ignore it completely and see if he brought it up?

"I saw your press release this morning," she said, deciding on an oblique reference to the phone call that had pulled them apart last night. "I'm glad things weren't more serious."

After a brief pause, he drawled, "You ought to defuse bombs for a living."

"I do," she replied mildly, obeying his wave and sinking onto the cushion. "Proverbial ones." She felt as though a sizzling string was running toward a bundle of dynamite sitting beneath her.

She added a few grains of raw, golden sugar to her coffee. He took his black.

"It's fine if we're not going to talk about it," she said in the most unconcerned tone she could find, sitting back and bringing her cup and saucer with her. "I respect boundaries. Yesterday's evidence to the contrary," she added with a wince of self-recrimination. "I don't make a habit of behaving so unprofessionally."

"My behavior was wildly inappropriate, given my title and the fact I've hired you. I want to be clear that I expect nothing from you beyond the work I've commissioned from London Connection. If our contract is something you'd prefer to dissolve now, I would understand."

Weren't they the most civilized people on the planet? And why did it make her feel as though she was swallowing acid?

"We bear equal responsibility."

"Do we?" He sounded so lethal, it struck her as an accusation. Her heart lurched.

"I'm not a victim." Conviction rang in her tone. She refused to be one ever again. "I don't think you are, either. Are you?" It took everything in her to hold his gaze and not shake so hard she'd spill hot coffee on her knee.

"No. On the contrary, I can have nearly anything I want." He smiled flatly. "It's up to me to exercise control and not take it."

"You didn't take anything I wasn't giving. I'm not afraid to tell you no, Luca. I've done it before, I can do it again." *If I want to.* The problem was, she didn't really want to.

His expression shifted into something close to a smile, but his exhalation gave away his annoyance.

"What?" she asked caustically.

"It makes you even more attractive," he said bluntly. "That toughness inside that angelic persona you project. I find it infinitely fascinating. Which I shouldn't tell you, but we're past pretending we're not attracted to each other. Better to name the beast."

Was it? Because something ballooned in her chest, cutting off her airways. She really was going to freak out and spill hot coffee all over herself.

"It's not like we can do anything about it," she reminded him. "You're about to publicly tie yourself to another woman."

His expression shuttered, and he didn't sound pleased as he said, "True."

"I think I've found a good fit." Amy forced herself to plow forward.

"Oh?" Luca sat back, projecting skepticism. Reluctance, perhaps?

"She's an actor." She leaned forward to set her coffee on the table. "She plays a spy on that cold war series that's streaming right now. Even if you haven't seen it, people would believe you might have. It's very popular, and they film all over Europe so it's feasible you would have been in the same city at some point. We could say you were introduced by a mutual acquaintance who remains nameless. She's very pretty." Amy flicked through her phone for the woman's image.

Luca took the phone long enough to glance at it before handing it back. "Why didn't you suggest her yesterday?"

Amy almost said, *Because she's very pretty.*

"I don't know her that well. We met at a club a few weeks ago." Amy had provided a shoulder while the woman poured her heart out over a man she was having trouble quitting. "I reached out last night with a very superficial mention of a potential 'unique opportunity.' She said she'd take a meeting. I'm waiting to hear where and when."

"How much do you think she would want?"

"That's why I think she would be a good fit. Obviously, she should be compensated, but I don't think she'll care about money or publicity. She generates plenty of both on her own. But when we met, she said something that leads me to think she would find it useful to be seen as being committed to a man of your caliber."

His brows went up in a silent demand for more info.

"Romantic troubles. I don't want to gossip out of turn. I'm sure she would be more forthcoming if you formed a liaison."

He hitched his trousers as he crossed one leg over the other, looking toward the windows with a flinty expression.

Amy bit her lip, well practiced in giving a client time to process her suggestions. In this case exercising patience was especially hard. She was eager to please, but was so aware of their kiss—their mutual attraction—that it twisted her insides to suggest he even pretend to see another woman.

After a long minute, he said, "I hate this."

Her heart lurched.

Did he hate that he was sabotaging his own reputation? Or that he'd behaved badly with her and the repercussions were still coloring their discussion?

Or was he harboring a secret regret, the way she was, that

they had to relegate their kiss and any potential relationship firmly offstage?

"I have to do this," he said, bringing his gaze back to hers in an ice-blue swing of a scythe. "You understand that? I don't have a choice to put it off or..." His hand scrolled the air and it sent an invisible lasso looping around her, strangling her. "I can't chase what I want at the expense of what is right. I couldn't even offer you— It would be *once*, Amy. Nothing more. And the window for that is already closing."

Amy supposed his words were a compliment, but they slapped like a rejection. Through the fiery agony, she reminded herself that she was respecting boundaries and nodded acceptance. "Don't worry about me. My job comes first."

"Same." His mouth twisted in dismay. "She sounds like a good option. Meet with her. Keep my name out of it until we're further along."

"Of course." She ignored how heavy it made her feel. "I'll have her sign confidentiality agreements before I pitch it, and I'll gauge better whether she's a good fit before you're mentioned at all."

"When will you see her?"

"I've asked for tomorrow afternoon." Her heart was pounding so hard, her ears hurt. "Do you want a slower rollout? If she turns it down, we'll have to find someone else."

"I want my sister installed as quickly as possible," he said decisively, rising.

"I think we're on the right track." She rose too, getting the message that this meeting was over. "I'll finish up my gala work while I wait to hear."

He nodded and she started to leave.

"Amy," he growled, sounding so deadly, her breath caught. She swung around.

He wore a look of supreme frustration. His hands were in his pockets, but were fisted into rocks.

"It would only be once," he repeated grittily.

Such a bright light exploded within her, she was ignited by the heat of a thousand suns.

"Once is better than never." She ran into his arms.

CHAPTER SIX

HE CAUGHT HER, barely rocking on his feet. His arms wrapped tightly around her, holding her steady even as he hesitated. His lips peeled back against his teeth in a moment of strained conscience.

"It's just once," Amy blurted in a bleak urgency that awakened old ghosts inside her. The wraiths slipped and swirled in cool trails of guilt, hissing, *You shouldn't. You know you shouldn't. Nothing good will come of this.*

"Just once," he echoed in groaning agreement as he claimed her mouth with his own.

She'd been in a state of deprivation since last night. Relief poured through her as he dragged her back to where they'd left off. White heat radiated from his body into hers, burning away her cobwebs of misgivings. This was nothing like that tainted, ancient memory from years ago. It was sweet and good and right.

Amy felt safe and cherished in these arms that could crush, but didn't. His mouth rocked across hers, seducing and ravaging, giving as much as he took. He stole soft bites of her tingling lips, and the heat in his eyes sent shimmering want through her limbs.

"Will anyone come in?" She wasn't ashamed of what they were doing, but she dreaded another discovery.

"No," he murmured, adding, "But let's make sure."

He moved as if they were dancing, smoothly pivoting her before he caught her hand and swirled her toward an unassuming door. It led to an anteroom and from there they entered a massive bedroom.

This was the king's chamber, a mix of the palace's opulence and Luca's spare, disciplined personality. Huge glass doors led to a terrace that overlooked the sundial and the sea. The glass was covered in sheer drapes that turned the light pale gold. The marble floor was softened with a thick rug in shades of gold and green, the ceiling painted a soothing blue between the white plaster and gold filigree. There was a fireplace and a comfortable sitting area, and a button that he touched caused all the doors to click.

"We have complete privacy now. Even the phone won't ring."

He turned to her and she stepped into his arms with a sigh of gladness, wanting to be swept away again into that place where second thoughts were impossible.

He cupped her face. His spiky lashes flickered as he scanned her features.

"What's wrong?" she asked, uncertainty creeping in.

"Absolutely nothing, but if we only have today, I'm damned well going to take my time and remember every second."

"Oh," she breathed. His words dismantled her at a very basic level. She wasn't that special. Didn't he realize that? She was actually tarnished and broken. What she was doing right now with him was akin to stealing.

But as the pad of his thumb slid across her bottom lip, she whispered, "I want to savor you, too." She lifted a hand to touch his hair, startled to find the strands so soft and fine when it looked so thick.

He adjusted their stance so their bodies aligned perfectly. His feet bracketed hers, and his thighs were hard against her own.

He was aroused, the stiffness of him undeniable against the part of her that was growing soft and damp and ripe.

She slid her arms around his strong neck. His touch slipped under her jacket so his hands splayed across her back while they crashed their mouths together.

Something wanton in her wanted—needed—to know he was as helpless against her as she was against him. She arched, inciting him with a grind of her hips against that alluring ridge of hardness, seeking the pressure of him *there*.

Lust exploded between them. His whole body jolted, and his arms tightened before he backed her toward the high bed.

Her thighs and bottom came up against the edge of the mattress. He held her there, pinned against the soft resistance while his legs went between hers. Now he was the one who gave muted thrusts, his gaze holding hers, watching as she released a soft mew of helpless, divine pleasure. She felt herself dissolving.

"Good?"

He had to know it was. She couldn't even speak, only nod and brace her hands on the mattress behind her, arching to encourage his rhythm, sharp heels liable to snag his expensive carpet and who the hell cared because this was the most incredible experience of her life. Every breath was filled with his scent. All of her muscles were shaking with sexual excitement.

His hands swept forward and opened her jacket so he could roam his hot palms over the lime-green camisole she wore. A tickling touch danced across her chest and shoulders as he spread the jacket to expose all of her torso. The hot caress of his hands enclosed her breasts.

She groaned and he caught that with his mouth. His thumbs worked over her nipples through the layers of silk and lace. His tongue brushed against hers, and she groaned again as the coiling pleasure in her center became a molten heat. An unstoppable, screaming force.

She had wanted to push him past his own control and here

she was losing hers, fists clenched in his bedspread, hips buck-ing with greed.

When he lifted his head, she dragged her eyes open, dread-ing how smug he must be at doing this to her, but she saw only a glow of barely leashed lust in his sharp gaze. He was with her, deep in the eye of the hurricane.

"What do you need?" His voice was a rasp that made her skin tighten. "This?" His head dipped and his mouth was on her breast, fingers pulling aside her camisole and the cup of her bra. His touch snaked across her nipple before he exposed it and enveloped her in the intense heat of his mouth.

A lightning bolt of pleasure went straight to where they were fused at the hips and she groaned, moving helplessly against that lethal shape lodged in the notch of her thighs. Acute sen-sations were taking over, heat and pleasure and a need so great she couldn't resist succumbing to it.

As he pulled on her nipple, a muted climax rose and broke and cascaded shimmering sensations through her.

Ragged noises left her lips as his hand replaced his mouth, tucking inside the cup of her bra to hold her breast as his mouth came back to hers, tender yet rough, soothing, but determined to catch all of her moans.

The pleasure continued to twist inside her, sweet and deli-cious and teasingly unsatisfying. She was more aroused than ever. Ready to do *anything*, which caused a twinge of anxiety as she weakly sank onto her back on the mattress, legs still dan-gling off the side, essentially offering herself to him.

He stayed hovering over her. He could persuade her to do anything right now, she acknowledged. He stood with his thighs between her splayed ones, his thick erection pressed indelibly to the swollen, aching flesh between her legs.

He could have lorded her abandonment over her, especially because she was lifting her hips in a muted plea.

He looked wild, though. Barbaric in the most controlled way possible. If he was an animal, he was the kind that might chase his mate to ground, but he would kill *for* her before he'd allow her to be harmed in any way.

Amy might have reached past that veil of savagery if she'd wanted to, but as he raked his hand down the front of his shirt, tearing the buttons loose and baring his chest, she was lost. He was pushed to the limits of his restraint, and she was bizarrely reassured since she had no ability to resist him, either.

His shirt landed on the floor, and he popped the button on the fly of her new green trousers. His hand swept up, urging her to lift her arms. He lifted her jacket up and threw it off the far side of the mattress. She left her arms up so he could sweep the camisole up and away, as well.

His nostrils flared at the sight of her bare belly and pale breast overflowing the dislodged cup of her green bra, she arched to tease him with the sight, inviting him to skim his hand behind her back to find the hook.

He whisked away the bra, then traced each shadow and curve of her torso, claiming her with tickling touches and firm flicks of his thumbs. He bent to nuzzle her skin with his lips, pooling his hot breath in the hollow of her collarbone before taking a blatant taste of each pouting nipple, leaving them erect and gleaming.

The zipper of her pants gave with a snap as his hands raked them down her hips.

She didn't protest the damage. She was too caught up in the urgency he was projecting. It was mesmerizing to see the intensity in him as he dragged her pants down her legs and gave each cuff a yank to pull them free of her shoes.

"I can take them off."

"I don't want you to," he said, voice distant, fingertips sliding across the sensitive skin on the top of her feet and encircling her ankles. "I want to do this."

He set the shoes on his shoulders as he lowered to his knees beside the bed.

She strangled her groan of helplessness with the back of her wrist, lost before he'd even touched her.

He delicately moved side the damp silk of her panties. His touch traced between her folds, making her groan again and twist in tortured anticipation. In the self-conscious knowledge he was looking and touching and—

She gasped as his mouth grazed the inside of her thigh, then the other one. He slowly, slowly kissed toward her center.

She shifted her feet so she could urge him with a heel in his back—forgetting the sharp shoe until he laughed starkly and said, "*That's* what I wanted."

His hot chuckle was her only warning before his mouth was on her and she nearly came off the bed. No restraint in him now. He claimed her unabashedly, tasting, teasing, learning, then mercilessly pleasuring her until she had her thighs locked to his ears.

"Luca. Luca." She lost all inhibition, fist knotted in his hair and hips lifting to meet the swirling pressure of his tongue.

This time her orgasm shattered her. It was one crescendo after another because he made it so, continuing to pleasure her as each wrenching burst of joy contracted through her. He didn't stop until her weak, quivering thighs fell open.

Then he rose to survey the destruction he'd caused. She was in pieces before him, stomach quivering, limbs weak. She was no longer autonomous. She belonged to him.

Which made the way he paused as he hooked his hand in her knickers somewhat laughable, but she lifted her hips in silent consent. Satisfaction came into his stark features then, along with an undisguised possessiveness. His gaze swept down her nudity as he drew the wisp of green off her ankles.

His gaze came back to hers, glints of untamed desire in his fiery blue eyes.

That primeval heat called to her. Drew her to sit up on the edge of the bed and reach a hand to the back of his neck to drag him into kissing her.

His hands went down her bare back and cupped her bottom as he thrust his tongue between her lips, flagrantly making love to her mouth. She sucked on his tongue and blindly fumbled his fly open, then slid her hand inside the elastic of his boxer briefs to clasp the thickness of his shaft and trace her touch to caress his wet tip.

He tangled his hand in her hair and kissed her so deeply, she could hardly breathe, especially when his hand arrived at her breast, reawakening all her erogenous zones as he delicately pinched her nipple.

She squeezed him in reaction, and that seemed to be his snapping point.

He lurched back and shoved his pants down, taking his underwear at the same time. His shoes were toed off and he was naked in seconds, reaching to the nightstand drawer.

She should have removed her own shoes, but she was too caught up in watching his deft movements. He smoothed a condom into place and moved to stand before her.

Her bones softened and she melted onto her back.

Intense pleasure was stamped into his expression and his hands went over her, claiming hip and waist and breast and belly and the tender heat between her thighs as he spread her legs to make room for himself. His elbow hooked under one of her knees and he pushed her farther onto the bed so he could get his knee onto the mattress between her own.

His gaze snagged on her shoe where her leg was draped over his arm. "Perhaps I do have a fetish after all."

He lined himself up against her entrance and watched her face as he began to press into her.

She bit her lip.

He paused.

"Don't stop," she gasped. "It just so good."

Her eyes were wet with some emotion between joy and intense need, her sheath slick and welcoming his intrusion with shivering arousal. She couldn't touch enough of him—

shoulders, chest, straining neck, the fine strands of his hair on his head.

He made a noise that was a mangled agreement and let his weight ease him deeper, sliding all the way in and coming down onto his elbow so he hovered over her. Her one leg was hooked high on his arm. His free hand tangled in her hair and his mouth covered hers.

She wrapped her arms around his neck and arched her back, signaling how eager she was for the feel of him moving over her. Within her.

He began to thrust.

It was mind-bendingly good. She brought her free leg up to wrap around his waist and felt his knees bracket her backside. He rocked them and pushed his arm under her lower back, lifting her hips so he could thrust more freely. With more power.

The new angle caused his next thrust to send a hot spear of intense pleasure through her, one that had her tearing her mouth from his to cry out with tormented joy.

His mouth went to her ear and he sucked on her lobe while their heat and energy built. Their lovemaking turned raw and primal, then. The room filled with their anguished grunts of growing tension and clawing need.

"I need you deeper. Harder," she begged, pulling at his hair.

He caught her other leg and released his full strength, holding back nothing as he drove her higher and higher up the scales of what she could bear.

"Don't stop," she demanded. Pleaded. "Luca! Luca!"

"Let go. You're killing me," he growled, holding both of them trapped on a precipice with his rhythmic, powerful thrusts. "I won't come until you do and I *need* to."

His jagged voice pulled at her while his hard body shifted over her, his mouth taking hers. He surrounded her so fully, there was barely any place he didn't touch. Didn't claim. She was all his. At the mercy of his unconstrained sexual heat.

He slammed into her and rocked against her swollen, delirious flesh. The universe opened into an expansive void. For an infinite moment, they were suspended like stars in the universe, caught in the peak of supreme perfection for all eternity.

Then his tongue touched hers and reality folded in on itself. Orgasm struck like a hammer, and she was moaning against his own noises of supreme gratification while waves of culmination rolled over them, again and again.

Luca woke to the sound of the door locks releasing.

He kept his head buried in his pillow, willing himself to let her go.

"Just once" had turned into twice. Twice was not a slip of control. Twice was unabashed self-indulgence. He had deafened himself to his internal voices of caution and abandoned himself to sheer lust. It had been incredible.

And disturbing to realize he was so capable of immersing himself in base desire. He was not so far above his father as he liked to believe. He was just as capable of pursuing immediate gratification.

When sexual exhaustion had crept over them, he'd thrown himself into a hard nap so he wouldn't have to face this reckoning—which was another facet of abandoned responsibility. On the few occasions when he had made a mistake, Luca always confronted and corrected it. He didn't play denial games.

Sleeping with Amy was definitely a mistake. He'd known it even as her name had left his lips after their lunch. He should have let her walk away.

At least he was doing it now. She was making it easy for him by slipping away while she thought he was sleeping. He would make it easy for her by not trying to stop her, even though his shoulders twitched with the need to come up on his elbows. *Wait*, hovered unspoken on his lips.

What time was it? Beyond his lowered eyelids and the mound of the pillow, he had the sense that daylight was fading. He didn't look. He held still with belated but ruthless control, waiting to hear the door close behind her.

The sound came from the wrong side of the room. The air moved. It tasted cool and carried the scent of the sea. He lifted his head and glanced toward the terrace.

The sight of her knocked his breath out of him.

Amy, bare-legged and shoeless, strawberry blonde hair streaked with gold wafting loosely down the back of his rippling shirt, was backlit by one of Vallia's signature sunsets.

A trick of air and water currents beyond their west coast caused wispy clouds to gather on the horizon at the end of the day, providing a canvas for dying rays. As the air cooled, the sea calmed to reflect sharp, bright oranges that bled toward streaks of pink and purple while indigo crept in from the edges. Couples came from around the world to photograph their wedding against it.

Luca rose and was outside before he'd consciously thought to join her. He was *drawn*. That power she exerted without effort should have scared the hell out of him, but he was too enchanted by the expression on her face when he came alongside her.

She had moved to the northern end of the terrace and was looking back toward the castle ruins where the colors of the sunset were painting the gray stones bronze and red, throwing its cracks and crevices into dark relief.

He joined her and took in her profile with the same wonder she was sending toward the castle. Her mouth was soft, eyes lit with awe. Her creamy skin held the magical glow off the horizon.

"This is so beautiful. I've never seen anything like it."

"Me, either." The compliment was meant to be ironic, but his voice was lodged in his chest where thick walls were fracturing and tumbling apart.

He gave in to the compulsion to draw her into his arms. His hand found the curve of her bare backside beneath the fall of his shirt, and he reveled in the way his caress fractured her breath.

Let her go, the infernal voice inside him whispered. It was more of a distant howl, like wolves warning of the perils that stalked him if he continued to linger with her.

But she was fragrant and soft and shorter without her heels. She sent him a smoky, womanly smile as she realized he was naked and traced patterns at the base of his spine that tightened his buttocks with pleasure.

Her expression grew somber. Vulnerable. "Thank you for this. I haven't been with anyone in a long time. I needed to know I could be intimate with a man and not lose everything."

Tension invaded his limbs. Not jealousy or possessiveness, but a primitive protectiveness that tasted similar. His arms unconsciously tightened, wanting to hold on to her because he understood from her remark that she was afraid of being caged again.

She was reminding him this couldn't be anything more than this one day.

He knew it as well as she did, but he moved his hand into her hair and gently dragged her head back, mostly to see if she'd allow it. They'd grown damned familiar in the last couple of hours, and he wanted that small show of trust from her.

Her lips parted in shock while lust hazed her gaze.

A self-deprecating smile tugged at the corners of his mouth. "I should hate myself for enjoying this as much as I do." Her capitulation. The surge of virility it gave him that she allowed him to dominate her this way. He was an animal, just the same as everyone else. He had never wanted to admit that. "Sex was *his* thing. It's hard for me to give in to desire without thinking there's something wrong with me when I do." He had never told that to anyone. He'd barely articulated it to himself. "It's probably best that today is all we have." Otherwise, they might destroy one another.

With absolute gravity, she said, "There is nothing wrong with the way you make love."

They should be exchanging playful banter, preparing for a

lighthearted parting. Instead, he kissed her, hard. He wanted to imprint himself on her.

The wolves were continuing to howl, but he let himself absorb the fullness of the moment. The way her nails dug into his scalp as she pressed him to kiss her more deeply, the way her tongue greeted his own... This was all they had. This moment. This kiss.

That's all it should have been. But as the fine hair on her mound tantalized his erection and her toes caressed the top of his foot, his heart pounded hard enough to crack his sternum. "Once more?" he asked through his teeth.

She was as powerless to this force as he was and didn't bother trying to hide it. "Once more," she breathed.

With a savage smile, he pressed her toward the doors. "Get back in my bed then."

Amy woke in the early morning, naked and alone in her bed in the guest suite. She stretched and let out a sigh that was both enjoyment of the luxurious thread count and a half moan as her sore muscles twinged. She was glowing with the lingering sensuality of their lovemaking, but beneath it was despondency.

Once had not been enough, even when it turned into an afternoon and evening.

Yesterday was all they would have, though. One golden memory. She worked for Luca. She had an assignment to complete, one she had neglected because they'd been so wrapped up in each other. She'd stolen from his room near midnight like Cinderella, shoes in hand, jacket held in front of her to hide her broken fly. A footman had escorted her, but she trusted he wouldn't say a word.

She was starving and desperate for coffee, so she rose to find the French press in the kitchen. There was cheese, fresh berries and yogurt in the refrigerator, too. Perfect.

She set them out and started the kettle, then went in search of her phone. It was still in her jacket pocket from last night, still set on Do Not Disturb from when she'd joined Luca for lunch. They'd skipped dinner, which was why she was ready to gnaw her own arm.

Still yawning, she touched her thumb to unlock her phone and it flashed to life with notifications. She had several alerts set for her own name since she was often attached to press releases for clients, but this wasn't a press release.

It was about her client. And *her.*

The photos showed her and Luca with the sunset behind them, and each headline slanted them into a different, damning light.

Like Father, Like Son! one headline blared.

The king of Vallia continues a tradition of depravity by seducing his new hire, socialite Amy Miller of London Connection, who caused a stir in the late queen's foundation with her publicity campaign for an upcoming gala...

Victim or Villain? the next asked while the photo's angle revealed her seductive profile and Luca's riveted expression.

The Golden Prince is dragged into the gutter by a gold digger...

Crown Jewels on Display! screamed the most tawdry headline.

They'd blurred the photo, but she knew he'd been naked and fully aroused.

"Oh, Luca," she whispered.

How had something so perfect and unsullied become...this?

As her unblinking eyes grew hot, Amy sank onto the sofa, crushed by the magnitude of this development. Her stomach churned while her brain exploded with the infinite agonies that were about to befall her—the sticks and stones and betrayals and blame.

Her life would disintegrate. Again.

And, just like last time, she had no one to blame but herself.

CHAPTER SEVEN

"Photos were published overnight, *signor*. They are... unfortunate."

"Of *who*?" It was a testament to how thoroughly Amy had numbed his brain that he didn't compute immediately that it was, of course, about the two of them.

Guillermo thrust a tablet under his nose.

Luca's head nearly exploded. The foulest language he'd ever uttered came out of his throat. "Where the *hell* was security?"

"They went up to the castle as soon as they realized they had a stray hiker, but he had already departed."

The guards wouldn't have sensed any urgency. Despite the regulations against visiting the ruins without a guide, the odd tourist still made their way up there, usually photographing the silhouette of the palace against the sunset. Since the lighting was so poor at that time of day, and all the private rooms faced the sea, the chance of compromising a royal family member was low. The paparazzi who'd made the trek had never struck pay dirt because even Luca's father hadn't been stupid enough to stand naked on the *one* visible corner of the terrace.

"We presume it was taken by an amateur," Guillermo continued stiffly. "Given the photo's quality and the fact it was initially posted to a private account. The images have since been reposted by the tabloids with… As you can see."

Unspeakable headlines.

Golden Prince: Feet of Clay, Rod of Steel?

At least they'd blurred his erection, but they'd set his image beside a grainy one of his father in a miniscule swimsuit.

King of Vallia Inherits the Horny Crown

When he saw *Another Molesting Monarch*, he thought he might throw up.

"The PR team is discussing damage control. I've made arrangements for Ms. Miller to return to London."

Luca barely heard him. For his entire life, he had kept to the straight and narrow and the *one time* he had stepped out of line, he was caught and being compared to his father in the most abhorrent way—

Wait. His heart clunked its gears, shifting from reflexive shame and fury to a glimmer of possibility. This was bad. But was it bad *enough*?

This wasn't the scandal he'd wanted. Amy was being derided as badly as he was, but his heart lurched into a gallop as he suddenly spotted the finish line after a marathon that had gone on for two decades.

"She'll be mobbed in London," Luca said, his mind racing. "She doesn't go anywhere until I've spoken to her. PR doesn't take steps without my input."

Guillermo's mouth tightened, but he moved to the door to relay that instruction.

Luca drummed his fingers on his desk. This was far messier and more degrading than he'd wanted it to be, but he would owe London Connection an efficiency bonus if it worked.

It had to work. He would *make* it work.

"Has my sister been informed?"

"A secure line has been established." Guillermo nodded at the landline on Luca's desk. "The Privy Council is divided on how to react." He looked like he'd swallowed a fish hook. "Some are alarmed and suggesting a review of the line of succession. I did try to warn you, *signor*. I *strongly* suggest Ms. Miller be returned to London—"

"I'll speak to my sister." With a jerk of his head, Luca dismissed him.

"I can't believe you did that," Sofia said. There was no ring of outrage or remnants of the secondhand embarrassment they'd both suffered after their father's various exploits. No, there was a far deeper note of stunned comprehension in her tone.

Luca bit back trying to explain it wasn't how he'd meant for this to happen. It was worse and he was genuinely embarrassed, but this was their chance. They had to run with it.

Also, focusing on his goal allowed him to sidestep dealing with the fact he was now the poster boy of depravity.

"You have no choice but to take this to the nanny panel," he said gravely, using their childhood reference to the ring of advisers, now the Privy Council, which kept such a tight leash on both of them. The same ones who had insisted Luca take the throne despite Sofia being entitled to it by birth.

"My travel is already being arranged. I'll meet with them the minute I'm home. I've drafted a statement that I'll release the minute we hang up." She paused, then asked with soft urgency, "Are you *sure*, Luca? Because I'm taking a very assertive stance on this. I don't want to undermine you."

"Sofia. Be the ruler you *are*. It's what is best for Vallia. Don't worry about me."

"Impossible. You're my one and only brother." She took a steadying breath. He thought she might be choking up with emotion, but she was well practiced in keeping a cool head. She cleared her throat. Her voice was level as she continued. "I have questions that can wait, but I plan to make the case for you to stay on as my heir provided you're willing to express your sincere regret and assurance that nothing like this will ever happen again?"

Which part? Being caught naked with a woman? Trysting with an employee? Or making love to Amy in particular?

Some nascent emotion, a grasping sense of opportunity, rose in him, but he firmly quashed it before it could become a clear desire. An *intention*.

Their "just once" might have turned into three times, but their connection was exposed to the entire world, and it was completely inappropriate. *He* didn't want to be labeled the sort of man who took advantage of women in his employ.

"You have my word," he said, feeling a tear inside him as he made the vow.

"*Grazie*. I'll see you soon. *Ti amo*," Sofia said.

"I love you, too." Luca hung up and a cool chill washed over him, like damp air exhaled from a dark cave. It was done.

Amy hadn't stopped shaking, even after a hot shower and too many cups of scalding coffee. The fact that she couldn't seem to leave this room, let alone this palace or this country, didn't help at all.

"I'll pay for the taxi myself," she beseeched the maid, Fabiana.

"It's not my place to call one, *signorina*." Fabiana set out ravioli tossed with gleaming cherry tomatoes and pesto. It looked as scrumptious as the fluffy omelet Amy had ignored midmorning, the focaccia she'd snubbed at lunch and the afternoon tea of crustless sandwiches and pastries she'd disregarded a few hours ago.

There was only room in her stomach for nausea. Her whole world was imploding, and she couldn't even reach out to the best friends who had got her through a similar crisis in the past. Her Wi-Fi connection had been cut off while she'd still been reeling in shock.

Then an ultra-calm middle-aged woman had appeared and identified herself as the senior Human Resources manager for the palace. She was genuinely concerned and had urged Amy to "be honest" if her night with Luca had been coerced in any way.

Amy had insisted it was consensual, but she now wondered if she'd strengthened Luca's position and hindered her own.

She was cold all over, sickened that she'd let this happen and angry with herself because she knew better. She had been fully aware of the potential dangers in sleeping with him, and she had gone ahead and put herself in this awful position anyway.

"My instructions are to ensure you're as comfortable as possible," Fabiana was saying. "Is there anything else I can bring you?"

"Hiking boots," Amy muttered peevishly. She had already asked a million times to speak to Luca. She'd been assured he would see her as soon as he was available.

Fabiana dropped her gaze to the bedroom slippers Amy was wearing with yellow pajama pants and a silk T-shirt. "I wouldn't recommend trying to leave on foot. Paparazzi are stalking the perimeter. Security is very tight at the moment."

Amy hugged the raw silk shawl she'd found in the closet and wrapped around her shoulders. "Restore my Wi-Fi." It wasn't the first time she'd asked for that, either.

"I've passed along your request. I'll mention it again." Fabiana gave her yet another pained smile and hurried out.

Amy was so frustrated, she stomped out the doors of her lounge to the garden patio.

A security guard materialized from the shrubbery. He'd been there all day and once again held up a staying hand. "I'm sorry—"

She whirled back inside.

She needed to get back to London. She needed to know exactly how bad this was. How could she control the damage to London Connection if she was cut off like this?

She ached to talk to Bea and Clare. What must they be thinking of her? She'd told them she was dropping everything for a big fish client with a substantial budget and an "unusual request." Would they question her tactics in getting Luca's business? They had stood by her last time, but they would be fully entitled to skepticism of her motives, especially since her actions were jeopardizing their livelihood along with her own.

Amy's mother was likely having fits, too. Even without a call or text, Amy knew what Deborah Miller was thinking. *Again, Amy? Again?*

She felt so helpless! Crisis management was her bread and butter. She ought to be able to *do* something. As she paced off her tension, she took some comfort in methodically thinking through her response.

In any emergency, there were three potential threats to consider. The first was physical safety. This wasn't a chemical spill. Innocent bystanders weren't being harmed. She forced herself to release a cleansing breath and absorb that tiny blessing.

The second threat was financial loss. She sobered as she accepted that she would take a hard hit from this. There was no way she was taking Luca's money now. That meant all of the expenses for this trip along with the travel home were hers. She had reassigned several of her contracts to other agents at London Connection so she had lost a substantial amount of income. There would be costs to salvaging London Connection's reputation and, since this was her mistake, she would bear that, as well.

How would she pay for it all?

Here was where panic edged in each time she went through this exercise. She was standing hip deep in the third type of threat. Her credibility was in tatters.

She looked like a woman who slept her way into contracts and had no means to spin that impression. In fact, somewhere in this palace, a team of professionals exactly like her was deciding how to rescue Luca from this crisis, and Amy knew exactly the approaches they were taking—deflect the attacks on him. Blame her. Claim she had seduced him. Say she had set him up for that photo to raise the profile of London Connection.

Heck, the headlines she'd glimpsed before losing her connection had already been suggesting she'd had something to gain. They only had to build on what was already there.

What if they found out she had a history of inappropriate relationships?

Her stomach wrenched so violently, she folded her arms across it, moaning and nearly doubling over.

Luca wouldn't hang her out to dry like that. Would he?

Of course, he would. The teacher, Avery Mason, had. The headmistress and her own parents had.

In a fit of near hysteria, she barged out of her suite to the hall.

She surprised the guard so badly, he took on a posture of attack, making her stumble back into her doorway, heart pounding.

She was so light-headed, she had to cling to the doorjamb. She sounded like a harridan when she blurted, "Tell the king I'll set my room on fire if he doesn't speak to me in the next ten minutes. Punch me unconscious or call the fire brigade because I *will* do it."

The guard caught the door before she could slam it in his face. He spoke Italian into his wrist. After the briefest of pauses, he nodded. "Come with me."

Now she'd done it. He was taking her to a padded cell. Or the dungeon.

Yes, that kind of dungeon.

She sniffed back a semihysterical laugh-sob.

He escorted her through halls that were familiar. She was being taken to Luca's office. The scene of their first criminal kiss. And their second.

People filed out as she arrived, but she didn't make eye contact. She stared at the floor until she was told to go in. She went only as far as she had to for the door to close behind her.

"Will you introduce us, Luca?" a woman asked.

Amy snapped her head up to see only Luca and his sister were in the room.

Luca was as crisp and urbane as ever in a smart suit and tie, freshly shaved with only a hint of fatigue around his eyes to suggest he'd had a long day. His gaze sharpened on her, but Amy was distracted by his twin.

Sofia Albizzi was a feminine version of Luca, almost as tall, also athletically lean, but with willowy curves and a softer expression. Where the energy that radiated off Luca was dynamic and energizing, Sofia's was equally commanding but with a settle-down-children quality. She wore a pantsuit in a similar dark blue as Luca's suit. Her hair was in a chignon, and she offered a calm, welcoming smile.

Amy must look like a petitioning peasant, slouched in her shawl and slippers, hair falling out of its clip and no makeup to hide her distress. She felt *awful* coming up against this double barrel of effortless perfection. She wanted to turn and walk back out again, but Luca straightened off the edge of his desk.

"Your Highness, this is Amy Miller. Amy, my sister Sofia, the queen of Vallia."

"Queen?" Amy distantly wondered if she was supposed to curtsy.

Sofia flicked a glance at Luca that could only be described as sibling telepathy.

"My new title is confidential," Sofia said. "Only finalized within the last hour. There will be a press release in the morning. I hope I can trust you to keep this information to yourself until then?"

Amy choked on disbelief. "Who could I tell? You've cut off my online access."

"We did do that," Sofia acknowledged. "The prince said you understand the importance of limiting communication during a crisis, so we can project a clear and unified message."

Prince. He'd been dethroned. *By her.* She was definitely going to faint. Amy blinked rapidly, trying to keep her vision from fading as she looked between the two.

Sofia came toward her, regal and ridiculously attractive while exuding that consoling energy. "I appreciate how distressed you must be, Amy. It's been a trying day for all of us, but I hope you'll allow us to show you the best of our hospitality for a little longer? And not frighten staff with threats of setting the palace on fire?"

Emotion gathered in Amy's eyes, beleaguered humor and frustration and something that closed her throat because she suddenly had the horrid feeling she had disappointed Sofia. Not the way she consistently disappointed her mother. She wasn't being held to impossible, superficial standards. No, Sofia simply projected a confidence that Amy was better than someone who made wild threats. *Let's all do better*, she seemed to say.

Luca was right. She was an ideal ruler.

But there was no comfort in being the instrument that had installed her on the throne, not when it had cost her the life she'd worked so hard to build.

"I want to go h-home." She was at the end of her thin, frayed rope.

"Our people will arrange that soon," Sofia began, but Luca came forward with purpose.

"I'll walk you to your room."

Sofia shot him a look, but Luca avoided her questioning gaze and held the door for Amy.

From the moment the photos had emerged, he had been buried in meetings, phone calls and demands for his attention. He felt as though he'd gone twelve rounds, taking hits from every angle.

It was *not* in his nature to throw a fight. Keeping his mouth shut while his sister called for an HR investigation had been particularly humiliating. To protect the integrity of that report, he hadn't spoken to Amy.

While they'd awaited a determination on whether Amy had been harassed by Luca, other factions had proposed throwing her to the wolves of public opinion to save Luca's reputation. Several voices on the council had tried to cast him as the victim of a scheming woman, eager to make excuses for Luca's lapse in judgment so they could maintain the status quo.

Sofia's supporters had been equally quick to question what kind of queen Amy would make, forcing Luca to declare his intentions toward her.

"We seized a moment, that's all." He hated to reduce her to a one-night stand, but it was what they had agreed and it was better for her to be seen as collateral damage, not a contributor.

"The media storm will rage forever unless we take decisive action," Sofia had pressed. "No matter how we attempt to explain it away, the photos will be reposted every time the king of Vallia is mentioned."

"I've become synonymous with our father," Luca said grimly, hating that it was true, hating that this was the only way, but he threw himself on the proverbial sword. "I won't have his transgressions pinned on me." On that he wouldn't budge. "Vallia's queens have always been bastions of dignity and honor. If I step aside, that's what you'll have again."

That had been the turning point. Discussions had moved from if to how.

Luca had spared a thought to ensure Amy's comfort, but he hadn't allowed memories of last night to creep in. It would have destroyed his concentration.

That fog of desire was making him light-headed now, but he continued to fight it. He had sworn his misstep wouldn't be repeated. His libido might have other desires, but tomorrow his sister would take the crown and Luca would once again become the Golden Prince, honorable to a fault.

Nevertheless, he owed Amy an explanation for how things had played out today.

"It's standard protocol to shut down all the open networks

and allow only secure messaging when incidents occur," he told her as they walked. "And I wanted to shield you from the worst of what's happening online."

"I understand." She nodded jerkily, looking like a ghost.

A pocket of gravel formed in the pit of his gut, a heaviness of conscience he wasn't familiar with because he so rarely made mistakes.

"I assumed you would have an idea what was going on behind the scenes."

"I did." She was nothing but eyes and cheekbones and white lips, her profile shell-shocked.

It hit him that she did know—all too well. He wanted to stop and touch her. Draw her into his arms. Kiss her and swear he wasn't pinning the blame on her.

He settled for following her into her suite.

"I couldn't bring you into the discussions today. I realize, given our contract, that you expected to be consulted, but I had to sideline you. It was best to let the process play out through normal channels."

"You think I'm upset because I feel 'sidelined'? I wish I was a footnote! Why didn't you tell me we were exposed out there? Did you *plan* this?"

"Of course not!" He hadn't given thought to anything but *her* last night. Did she think he would walk outside naked for anyone else? He was still uncomfortable with how immersed he'd been in their mutual desire. "It was a fluke. For God's sake, Amy. How could I plan it?"

"A fluke?" she scoffed. "You just happened to pick *me* to come here and take on the task of *ruining* you. You just happened to kiss me and take me to your room—" She cut herself off, shielding her eyes in what could only be described as shame.

The rocks in his belly began to churn.

"When I heard the door, I thought you were leaving." He started forward, drawn by her distress. "I didn't know you were going outside. I didn't *take* you out there."

As soon as his feet came into her line of sight, she brought up her head and stumbled back, keeping a distance between them.

That retreat, coupled with the trepidation in her face, was like a knee to the groin.

He held very still, holding off a pain that he barely understood. It was new, but so acute he actually tasted bile in the back of his throat.

"I'm not going to touch you if you don't want me to." He opened his hands in a gesture of peace.

"I don't want you to scramble my head again," she muttered, arms crossed and brow flexing with anguish. "This wasn't supposed to happen, Luca. No one was supposed to know about us. You made me think that's what you wanted."

"It was." But affirming it made his mouth burn. "Look, I know this wasn't the way we planned it, but once the photographs were out there, I had to seize the opportunity. This is what I hired you to do."

"You did *not* hire me to sleep with you. I won't take money for it," she said jaggedly.

He was insulted by her implication. "I hired you to ruin me. You have."

She gasped if he'd struck her. Her hurt and distress were so clear, his arms twitched again to reach for her.

"I honestly thought you would understand this was the incident I needed," he said. "I'm not clear why you're so upset."

"I was supposed to find someone who *wanted* the attention. Someone prepared for it." She kept pulling at her shawl until it was so tight around her, the points of her shoulders and elbows looked as though they would poke holes in the raw silk. "I was supposed to control the message to minimize the damage. It wasn't going to be ugly exposure where a woman's reputation is torn to shreds."

When her gaze flashed to his, there was such agony in the green depths, his heart stalled.

"My team won't crucify you," he swore, and started to take

a step forward, but checked himself. "I won't allow it. I'm taking responsibility. This was my slipup—"

"I slept with a client, Luca!" Her arm flung out and the shawl fell off her shoulder. "I compromised him so badly I caused a *king* to be *dethroned*. It really doesn't matter what you or your team say. People will come to their own conclusions."

He briefly glimpsed her tattoo before she shrugged the shawl back into place.

She was shaking so hard, he started to reach for her again and she stumbled back another step.

"I won't touch you." He couldn't help that his voice was clipped with impatience. "But I'm worried about you. Sit down. Have you eaten? I told them to make sure you had food."

"I'm not a dog!" she cried, eyes wild. "You don't get to hire someone to check if I have food and water and call it good. Although, at least I would have got a proper walk today instead of being held like a prisoner."

"That—" He squeezed the back of his neck. "I realize you're angry, but stop saying such ridiculous things."

"Oh! Am I overreacting?" She shot him a look that threatened to tear his head from his shoulders. "You know nothing about what I'm going through. *Nothing.*"

"So explain it to me," he snapped back. "Because I don't see this as the disaster that you do. You said it yourself. People love to clutch their pearls over a sexy escapade. I'm the one who's naked in that photo, not you! Are you upset that *we* happened?" It took everything in him to ask that. It wasn't an accusation, he really needed to know, but he braced himself. "Are you feeling as if I took advantage of you? Like you couldn't say no last night?"

HR had interviewed her. She'd reported that Amy had confirmed their involvement was consensual. Even so, Amy's chin crinkled. Her eyes welled.

His heart lurched and he couldn't breathe.

"I should have said no." Her shoulders sagged. "I knew it

was a mistake and I want to take it back." She buried her face in her hands. "So badly."

That sent a streak of injury through him because the thing that unnerved him most was how little he *didn't* regret sleeping with her.

As the dominoes had fallen today, he'd disliked himself for playing manipulative palace politics the way his father had. He'd met the disillusioned gazes of mentors and advisers and understood he'd fallen miles in their estimation. He loathed feeling fallible.

He had suffered through all of that to correct a thirty-one-year-old wrong and, unpleasant as proceedings had all been, at least he had the extraordinary memory of *her* to offset it.

Even now, as he saw how devastated she was over their exposure, he couldn't make himself say he was sorry. Did she remember how much pleasure they'd given each other?

He pushed his hands into his pockets so he wouldn't try to remind her.

"The announcements will be made tomorrow. I'll step down, and Sofia will be recognized as the rightful ruler. My coronation ceremony was scheduled to happen before our parliament sits in the autumn. It will be revised for her, but she's taking control immediately. Let the dust settle on some of this before you assume you'll take the fall for it."

She snorted, despondent, and turned her back on him. She looked like a tree that had been stripped bare. She was a hollow trunk swaying in the dying winds of a storm.

Was she hiding tears?

His guts fell into his shoes and his heart was upside down in his chest. He wanted to take her in his arms, hold her and warm her and swear this would be okay. *Come to my room.* He kept the words in his throat, but they formed a knot that locked up his lungs so his whole torso ached.

"When can I go back online? Bea and Clare are probably frantic." Her voice was a broken husk.

"My people have provided them with a statement."

That had her whirling around to face him, eyes shooting fires of disbelief that were quickly soaked by her welling tears. "You don't speak for me, Luca. You don't get to tell your side without giving me a chance to tell mine!"

"It's only a standard 'not enough information to comment—'"

No use. She disappeared into the bedroom and slammed the door on him.

CHAPTER EIGHT

AMY TOSSED AND TURNED and finally quit fighting her tears. When she let go, she cried until her eyes were swollen and scratchy, then rose and set a cool, wet cloth over them. Her stomach panged so hard with hunger, she dug up cold leftovers the maid had left in the fridge.

It was almost two in the morning. She didn't know if the guard was still in the garden and didn't check. Her one brief thought about trying to run away was stymied by exhaustion.

She crawled back into bed and didn't wake until midmorning when her phone came alive with alerts and notifications. Her internet access had been restored.

Tempted as she was to post *I'm being held against my will*, she was quickly caught up in reading all the news updates, emails and texts along with listening to her voice mail.

She brought her knees up to her chest, cringing as her mother's message began with an appalled "For God's sake, Amy."

Beyond the bedroom door, she heard the maid enter the suite, but kept listening to her mother harangue her for making international headlines "behaving like a trollop."

It wasn't the maid. Her heart lurched as Luca walked into the bedroom with a tray. He was creaseless and stern, emanating the scent of a fresh shower and shave.

Amy was nestled in the pillows she'd piled against the headboard, blankets gathered around her. She clicked off her phone mid maternal diatribe and dropped the device.

"You really have been demoted, haven't you?"

He stilled as he absorbed the remark, then gave her a nod of appreciation. "Nice to have you back. I was worried. Especially when I was told you didn't eat a single bite yesterday. That changes now." He touched something on the tray and legs came down with a snick.

"Your spies don't know what I do when no one is around." She was dying for coffee, though, so she straightened her legs, allowing him to set the tray across her lap.

"They're spies, Amy. Of course, they do." He sat down next to her knees and poured coffee from the carafe into the two cups on the tray.

"Are you really having me watched?" She scowled toward the ceiling corners in search of hidden cameras.

"No." His mouth twitched. "But I'd be lying if I didn't admit to concern over how you might be handling the restoration of your internet connection. You were very angry last night." He sipped his coffee. "Anything we should know about?"

She followed his gaze to her phone, facedown and turned to silent, but vibrating with incoming messages.

"I've been reading, not responding. My social feeds are on fire. In times like this, you find out very quickly who your real friends are." A handful of clients were ready to die on a hill defending her. Others were asking about terminating their contracts. "Bea and Clare have asked me to call when I can. They won't judge, but I don't know what to tell them. The rest of the office is used to being left in the dark with certain clients or actions we take on their behalf. They're reaching out with thoughts and prayers, but I can tell they're dying of curiosity, wondering if this is a stunt or if I'm really this stupid." Her hand shook as she dolloped cream into her coffee. "Our competitors are reveling in my hypocrisy, of course, crossing professional lines when

I'm usually defending victims of such things. They'll dine on this forever, using it to tarnish London Connection's integrity and my competence."

"London Connection won't be impacted." Luca's expression darkened. "I've set up the transfer. That will keep things afloat until you're able to right the ship."

"I told you not to pay me." She clattered her cup back into the saucer, spilling more coffee than she'd tasted. "I won't accept it. Taking money for this makes me feel cheap and dirty and stupid. Don't make me refuse it again, Luca."

He set his own cup down with a firm clink while he spat out a string of curses and rose to pace restlessly. "You did what I hired you to do," he reminded Amy as he rounded on her. "I want to compensate you."

"I ruined *myself*. I ruined my friends' livelihood."

"Quit being so hard on yourself."

"Quit being so obtuse! Just because I don't run a country doesn't mean my actions don't have consequences." She snatched up her phone and tapped to play her mother's message from the beginning, increasing the volume so Luca got the full benefit of her mother's appalled disgust.

"For God's sake, Amy. You've really done it this time, behaving like the worst sort of trollop. Neville is putting me on a plane back to London. He doesn't want to be associated with me. I've had your father on the phone, too. How can I tell him you're reliable enough to take control of your trust when you do things like this? You really never learn, do you?"

Amy clicked it off so they didn't have to hear the rest.

"I thought you were already disinherited."

"My father has control of a trust fund that was set up for me when I was born. I was supposed to start receiving income from it ten years ago, but I was expelled from school." She didn't tell him why. "They decided I wasn't responsible enough. I was supposed to assume full control at twenty-five, but my career promoting high-society parties online wasn't deemed serious enough. Daddy moved the date to my thirtieth birthday, eighteen months from now. Apparently, that's now off, as well." She threw her phone back into the blankets.

Luca swore again, this time with less heat, more remorse.

"I don't care." It was mostly true. "I've learned to live without their financial support. But when I took your contract, I had a fantasy of finally telling them to shove it. I wanted to prove I'd made my fortune my own way, which was pure pride on my part. Looks like I've got more time to make that dream come true. Problem solved," she said with facetious cheer while bitterness and failure swirled through her chest.

Why was life such a game of chutes and ladders? Why did she always hit the long slide back to zero?

"I had no idea." He came back to sit on the bed.

"Why would you?" She wrapped her cold hands around the hot cup of coffee, ignoring that it was wet down one side. She couldn't help fearing her earlier mistake with Avery Mason would emerge. It had been covered up, and all the key players had more reason to hide it than expose it, but it was still there, lurking like a venomous snake in the grass.

His firm hand gripped her calf through the blankets. "You have to let me help you, Amy."

"Luca." She jerked her leg away. "If you offer me that money one more time, you're going to get a cup of hot coffee in the face. It will turn into a whole thing with your bodyguards, and I'll wind up Tasered and rotting in jail. Not the best path to saving my reputation so leave it alone."

He didn't back off one iota. He found her leg again and gave it a squeeze. "Are you really prone to arson and violence?"

"No," she admitted dourly. "But after my own parents left me fending for myself at eighteen, I've become hideously independent. The worst thing you could have done yesterday was leave me alone like this, helpless to solve my problem."

"Because it's not your problem," he insisted. "That's why I didn't ask you to solve it." He shifted so he was looking at the wall, elbows on his knees, hands linked between them. He sighed. "I didn't see how much damage this would do to you. I want to help you fix it, Amy. Tell me what I can do."

She sank heavily into the pillows. "If I had a clue how to fix it, I would have busted out of here and done it already."

"Let me talk to your parents. I'll take responsibility, patch things up."

"Pass. There's too much water under the bridge there…" Her nose stung with old tears she refused to shed. "And I don't want someone to talk them into forgiving me. I want them to want to help me because they love me." She was embarrassed that they didn't and turned her mind from dwelling on that old anguish since it would never be resolved. "I'm more worried about London Connection. I might have to resign."

"You're not losing your career because you did your job," he said forcefully.

"No one can know that, though, can they? To the outside world, I got involved with a client and caused him to lose *his* job. No one is going to hire the sordid one-night stand who caused a king to be overthrown. If I resign, London Connection can at least say they cleaned house in the same way that Vallia is dumping you."

"That's rubbish." He rose again, all his virile energy crackling around him like a halo. "You're not a martyr and you're not a tramp. You're not something that needs to be swept under a rug or out a door. The answer is obvious."

"A tell-all to the highest bidder?" she suggested with a bat of her lashes.

"Pass," he said with flat irony. "No. Once Sofia is clearly established as Vallia's queen, you and I will take control of our narrative, as you like to say. We'll reframe our affair as a more serious relationship."

"You want to keep sleeping together?" Shock echoed within her strained words.

He wanted that so badly, he had to stand on the far side of

the room so he wouldn't crowd her or otherwise pressure her into it. "Appear to, at least. I understand if you'd prefer to keep things professional."

"Because we're so good at *that*." Her chuckle was semihysterical.

He took perverse comfort from the helplessness in her choked laugh. He wasn't the only one who felt this irresistible pull between them.

"I'm just saying, now that I fully grasp how our affair complicates things for you—"

The noise she made drew his glance.

"Do I *not* understand?" He narrowed his eyes, noting the flush that had come into her cheeks, the glow of disgrace in her eyes. "Is there more?"

She bit the corner of her mouth and dropped her gaze. "There are things in my past I only share on a need-to-know basis. Right now, you don't need to know."

She set aside the tray and flung back the blankets. She wore a silk nightgown that rode up her bare legs as she slid her feet to the floor.

"Don't you have a throne to abdicate?" she asked.

He swallowed and forced his gaze upward to the suppressed turmoil in hers.

She was trying to throw him off with a glimpse of her legs and her air of nonchalance.

He couldn't pretend he wasn't falling for the diversion. Sexual awareness instantly throbbed like a drumbeat between them. His feet ambled him closer before he remembered he was trying to give her space.

"I do have a title to renounce," he confirmed, gaze drawn to the way oyster-colored lace coyly pretended to hide her cleavage. It took everything in him to only caress her pale skin with his eyes. "Then I have a gala to attend. *We* do."

"I'm not convinced our continuing to see one another is the

best way forward." Her head shake was more of an all-over tremble.

He closed his fists so he wouldn't reach for her. "If you go scurrying home in disgrace, you really will be painted as the scarlet woman who toppled a kingdom. If you stick around and attend the gala where the new queen will speak to you, the whole thing will be reduced to a family squabble between my sister and I. You made arrangements to be here for two weeks, didn't you?"

"Yes, but—"

"You don't have to decide this instant. Let me finish my business, then we'll talk more. Away from the palace," he said. "We'll shop for a gown for the gala. Do you prefer Paris or Milan for evening wear?"

"The Glam Shed," she said haughtily, giving her hair a flick. "I quid pro quo promotion campaigns for red carpet rentals."

"I'll pretend that was a joke and make arrangements for Milan. It's closer than Paris and I have a cottage in Northern Italy. We can talk there about how we'll portray our relationship." For the first time in a very long time, he could be with a woman openly with few distractions. He wanted to take her there right now.

Perhaps she read that urgency in him. She flashed him a nervous look, but there was no fright in the depths of her pretty green eyes. Only a vacillating nibble of her lip and another, slower study of his chest and upper arms.

She was going to be the death of him, teasing him so unconsciously and effortlessly.

"Cottage?" she asked skeptically.

He tilted his head. It was an understatement. "A castle on a private island in one of the more remote lakes. The key word is 'private.' We can let this furor die down before our attendance at the gala stirs it up again."

"Are you sure you want to continue associating with me?" she asked anxiously.

She couldn't be that obtuse.

"I want to do a damned sight more than 'associate.'" He snagged her hand with his own and brought her fingertips to his mouth, dying to taste her from brows to ankles, but he had places to be. And he was trying not to take when she was vacillating and vulnerable.

She caught her breath and looked at him with such defenseless yearning, he gave in and swooped his free hand behind her waist to draw her close.

She suddenly balked with a press of her palm to his chest. "I haven't brushed my teeth."

"Then I'll kiss you here." He set his open mouth against her throat, enjoying the gasp she released and the all-over shiver that chased down her body. By the time he'd found the hollow beneath her ear, she was melting into him with another soft cry.

The slippery silk she wore was warm with the heat of her body as he slid his hands to her lower back and drew her closer, inhaling the scent of vanilla and almonds from her hair.

"Luca." She nuzzled his ear and nipped at his earlobe.

His scalp tightened and a sharp pull in his groin threatened to empty his head of everything except the rumpled bed behind this wickedly tempting woman. One quick tumble to hold him. That's all he wanted.

"Give me a few hours," he groaned, lifting his head, but running his touch to her delectable bottom, tracing the curve and crease through the silk as he drew her into the stiffness her response had provoked. "We'll pick this up later."

She searched his gaze, still conflicted.

He kissed her, quickly and thoroughly, tasting coffee as he grazed her tongue with his.

"Eat something," he ordered, then released her and adjusted himself before he left to end his brief reign.

Amy ate. Then she took her time with a long bath and a quiet hour of self-care where she painted her toenails and plucked her brows and moisturized every inch of her skin. She ignored her phone and let the sickening feeling of having her privacy invaded recede while she considered what to tell her best friends.

She was always honest with Bea and Clare, but aside from emailing a promise to call as soon as she could, Amy hadn't found the right way to explain what had happened between her and Luca.

They would know they were being put off, but Amy would touch base with them as soon as she decided whether she would agree to Luca's suggestion.

He had a point that appearing to continue their affair would soften the photo from being a lurid glimpse at a king's downfall to a private moment between a loving couple, but they weren't a loving couple. They were barely a romantic couple, having met only two days ago.

It shocked her to realize that. They'd shared some very personal details with one another. She'd never talked about her expulsion or her parents' rejection of her so candidly. For his part, Luca had entrusted her with the secret of his father's death. On a physical level, they had opened themselves unreservedly.

That meant they had the seeds of a close relationship, didn't it?

Oh, Amy, she chided herself. She had made the mistake of believing physical infatuation meant genuine caring once before.

Her stomach curdled. She hadn't shared *that* part of her story with Luca, had she?

Her affair with Avery Mason wouldn't come out, would it? Aside from Bea and Clare, who would never betray her, the story had never been confirmed. If any of the catty girls from back then had wanted to take Amy down by repeating that morsel of vague gossip, they would have done it by now. They'd had plenty of opportunities while Amy had been posting photos of herself with movie stars and fashion designers. Even if someone did decide to bring it up, they had no proof. It would be a very watery accusation that would quickly evaporate.

Avery could say something, obviously, as could his mother, but Amy didn't believe either would. There was no value in destroying their own reputations, and Amy's parents were equally determined to keep it a private matter. Her mother much preferred to use it as salt in Amy's wounds, dropping it as an aside to blame Amy for her own tribulations like being dumped by her latest paramour.

That would let up once she realized Amy was still seeing Luca, of course.

There was a bonus! Amy paused the hair dryer to drink in a fantasy of her mother groveling for an invitation to meet Amy's beau, once she believed her daughter had a real future with royalty.

Which she didn't. Amy's soaring heart took a nosedive. Even if they slept together again, their relationship was still about optics. Nothing more.

She ignored the streak of loss that cut through her chest and returned to yanking the brush through her hair as she dried it, ruthlessly scraping the bristles across her scalp as an exercise in staying real.

Luca wasn't a sociopathic lothario like Avery, but he was a man. The wires between heart and hard-on weren't directly connected. No matter what she did, she had to protect her own heart so it might be better if she and Luca only pretended to be involved.

She didn't want to pretend, she acknowledged with a twist of remorse wrapped in wicked anticipation. Despite the fact that sleeping with him had pulled the rug out from under her hard enough to topple her entire life, she wanted to make love with him again. She wanted to run her hands across his flexing back, feel his lips against her skin. Play her tongue against his and lose herself to the grind of his hips—

Whew! Had the AC cut out? She fanned her cheeks and opened the door to let the humidity out of the bathroom.

Fabiana was packing the clothing that didn't belong to her

into a suitcase that was also not hers. "The prince will be ready to travel shortly. He asks that you join him at the helipad in one hour? I've set out your lunch."

A few hours later, Amy was in Milan's fashion district, enjoying a crisp white wine with bruschetta. Luca was beside her, speaking Italian into his phone.

"That looks like it would suit you," he said as he ended his call and pocketed his phone. He nodded at the model on the catwalk.

"I like the train, but I prefer the neckline on the blue." She pointed at the model posing toward the back. "The gala isn't black tie. Could I wear something like that fade?"

"Wear whatever you want," Luca assured her, picking up her hand and touching his lips to her knuckles. "I'm indulging the woman who has captured my heart. I want the world to know it."

Her own heart flipped and twittered like a drunken bird even as she reminded herself it wasn't real. Nevertheless, she leaned in and cut him a sly look that he would recognize as her rebellious streak coming to the fore if he knew her well enough.

"Anything? Because I would love something very avant-garde."

Luca's indulgent nod said, *By all means.* "Control the narrative. Tell them what to talk about."

Amy looked to the designer. "What do you have that says, 'space opera'?"

The woman lit up with excitement and rushed into the back with her models.

Soon Amy was being fitted for a dress that hugged her curves while stiff, saucer-like ruffles gave the impression of a stack of dishes about to fall. The glittering sequins reflected prisms in every direction and a matching hat with a polka dot veil completed the dramatic look.

When she was back in her own clothes, she came upon Luca saying something about Vallia to an attendant. Parcels were being taken to the car.

"That's casual wear for the island," he said. "The rest will be sent to Vallia with the gown for our other events."

"What other events?"

"Cocktail parties. Ribbon cuttings. I'm making an award presentation in Tokyo after the gala."

Then what? There was a small cloud of anxiety chasing her. She had a career to get back to, and she had never aspired to be any man's mistress. She'd cleared a block of time to work with Luca so she still had a few days to consider all her options, but no matter if she only pretended or was really his lover, it wouldn't last.

They left the design house, but word had leaked that they were in Milan. They were chased back to the helicopter, soon landing on a blessedly remote and quiet island.

They disembarked into what could only be described as a fairy-tale setting. A wall of craggy, inhospitable mountains plunged down to the jewel-blue lake. A quaint village sat on the far shoreline. A handful of boats dragged skiers in their wake, keeping their distance.

Luca told her the castle had been built as a monastery in the fifth century. It had a tall, square bell tower in the middle of one outer wall, but the rest was only three stories. The ancient stone walls were covered in moss and ivy. A pebbled pathway led them from the helipad, winding beneath boughs that smelled of Christmas pine and fresh earth and summer vacation.

"No vehicles, just a golf cart for the luggage and groceries by boat," Luca said, pointing into a man-made lagoon surrounded by stone walls as they passed. Two fancy looking speedboats were moored there alongside a utilitarian one that was being unloaded.

They entered through what had once been a scullery room. It was now a very smart if casual entryway with hooks for their jackets and a box bench where they left their shoes.

This was why he called it a cottage, she supposed. It was homey and he exchanged a friendly greeting with the chef as they passed the kitchen, nodding approval for whatever menu was suggested.

"The sun is beginning to set. He asked if we wanted to eat something while we watch it from the terrace or view it from the top of the tower?"

"The tower sounds nice."

He relayed her preference, and they climbed to the belfry where no bell hung.

"I have no plans to ring it, so why replace it?" he said as he led her up a heart-stoppingly narrow spiral of stairs that took them to the roof. "This has been inspected. We're safe," he assured her.

"I forgot my phone," she said with a pat of her pockets. "I want photos!"

She went to the corners of the roof, more awed by the view each direction she looked. She paused to watch where the sun was sinking behind one peak, leaving a glow of gold across the surrounding mountaintops. The air was clean and cool, the height dizzying enough to make her laugh.

"You must have loved coming here as a child. How long has it been in your family?"

"I bought it for myself when it came on the market a few years ago."

"Oh. That's interesting." She glanced at him. "Why?"

"Because it's beautiful and private." His tone said, *Obviously.*

"You didn't buy it to hide your women here?"

"Like a dragon with a damsel? Yes, I've lured you here and you can't leave until your hair grows long enough to climb down. No, Amy. What women are you even talking about?"

"I don't know. The ones you have affairs with. Discreetly. On private islands." She turned to the view because this was a conversation they had to have, but she didn't know how.

"Actually, this is where I hide from those legions of women, to rest and regain my virility," he said dryly. "I've allowed my sister to stay here, but you're the only person I've brought as my guest, female or otherwise."

"Ever?" She moved to another corner.

"Why is that so surprising? Exactly how many lovers do you think I've had?"

"Enough to get really good at sex," she said over her shoulder, as if she didn't care. She did care. A lot more than she ought to.

"*You're* really good at sex." He came up behind her to trace his fingertips in a line down her back. "Should I ask how many men you've been with?"

"How do you know it's just men?" She swung around and threw back her head in challenge.

He didn't laugh. Or take her seriously.

"You really do have to work harder to shock me," he admonished. "I honestly don't care what you've done or with whom so long as it was consensual and safe enough that I don't have to worry about my own health."

Her heart faltered. She wondered if she could shock him with the deplorable thing she'd done with her teacher, but he set his hands on the wall on either side of her waist, crowding her into the corner. Now all she could see was his mouth, and her thoughts scattered.

"I'm *very* interested in what sort of history you'd *like* to have. With me. What do you want to do, Amy?"

"Nothing kinky," she warned, reflexively touching his chest. "Just normal things."

"Normal?" His smile was wide, but bemused. "Like tennis and jigsaw puzzles?"

"Yes," she said pertly. "And read books to one another. Austen preferably, but I'll allow some Dickens so long as we have a safe word."

"*Nicholas Nickleby?*" The corners of his mouth deepened. "Tease. Will you sleep in my bed and continue to ruin me for every other woman alive?"

It was flirty nonsense. Banter. But she was incredibly sensitive to words like "ruin."

She swallowed. "I don't want to be your downfall, Luca. I don't want…"

He sobered and brushed a wisp of hair away from her cheek. "What?"

She didn't want to get hurt. Not again.

"I don't want to get confused about what this is." She touched a button on his shirt. "It's just an affair. Right? For a couple of weeks? To, um, take the worst of the poison out of what's going on out there?" She jerked her chin toward the world at large.

He backed off, equally somber. "We barely know each other," he reminded her. "I'm not saying I don't take this seriously, but I can't promise anything permanent. I've never had the luxury of contemplating a future with anyone. Marriage has always been something I would undertake with a woman vetted by a team of palace advisers." His mouth twisted and he dropped his hands to his sides, fully stepping away. "I still have to think that way until Sofia marries and produces our next ruler."

"So you're offering an affair." She hugged herself. "That's fine, but I need to be clear on what to expect since we'll be pretending it's…more."

After a long moment, he gave a jerky nod. "Yes," he agreed. "Just an affair."

And wasn't that romantic.

She looked to where the sun had set and the sky was fading. The glow of excitement inside her had dimmed and dulled, too.

"We should go down while we still have light," she suggested, more to pivot from how bereft she suddenly felt.

He looked as though he wanted to say something, but stifled it and nodded.

He went in front of her, promising to catch her if she missed a foot on the narrow, uneven steps. It was dizzying and nerve-racking, and she clung tightly to the rope that was strung through iron rings mounted to the wall, thinking the whole time, *Don't fall, don't fall*.

But she feared she probably would.

CHAPTER NINE

LUCA WAS RESTLESS and prickly. He blamed the fact he was at a crossroads, having given up the throne, but not yet having found his place in the new order. The work that typically dominated his thoughts now fell to his sister, and the mental vacuum allowed him to dwell on the public's reaction to his fall from grace.

And the woman who had caused it.

They weren't dressing for dinner, but Amy had disappeared to call her business partners, leaving him to nurse a drink and contemplate how completely she seemed to have shut down once he'd pronounced that this was only an affair.

Did she want it to be more? Did he?

He felt as though he'd disappointed her with his answer. Hurt her. That frustrated him. He'd been as honest as possible. Up until that moment, she'd been her bright and funny self. An amusing companion who made him feel alive in ways he had never experienced.

Damn but that was a lot of feelings. He didn't do feelings. They were messy and tended to create the sort of disaster he'd been scrupulously trained to avoid. He'd accomplished what he wanted by giving in to his lust for Amy, but it was time to go back to being his circumspect, disciplined self.

Which meant he shouldn't have a real affair with her, but the mere thought of denying himself when she was willing caused a host of feelings that were more like a swarm of hornets inside him. Which was exactly why he shouldn't indulge—

He swore aloud and set aside his drink as though he could set aside his brooding as easily. Filtering through his texts and emails, he picked up one from an old friend, Emiliano. They had met through their shared interest in emerging tech. Emiliano had since increased his family's fortune by developing tools for facial recognition software.

News bulletin says you're in Milan? I'm at my villa on Lago di Guarda. Join me if you want to escape the fray.

His villa was a comfortable and well-guarded compound. Luca texted back.

Grazie. We're fine, but I'll be in touch about the solar tiles we discussed last year.

Luca moved on, but Emiliano promptly texted back.

Sounds good. The invitation is open anytime. Tell Amy I said hello.

Just like that, Luca's agitation turned to a ferocious swarm of stinging jealousy.

Jealousy was the most childish of all emotions, but he was bothered and even more bothered by the fact he was bothered. He was having feelings about his feelings, and it was annoying as hell.

Amy returned wearing a concerned frown.

"Is everything all right?" he made himself ask, trying to overcome his sudden possessiveness.

"Clare's overseas and Bea has gone off with a client," she said with a perplexed shake of her head. "When we talked her into joining us, it was purely for legal support, but she got roped into working directly with Ares Lykaios. You would have seen his name on our website. He's our biggest client. We owe him for putting us on the map."

"I know who he is." And there was no reason Luca should feel so threatened that he would ask, "Would you rather be in her place right now?" He hated himself for it.

"A little. Bea must be out of her depth. He's tough and assertive, and Bea's shy by nature. It's always been our dynamic that she helps me work through my internal rubbish and I play her wingman in the external world. She might not know how to handle Ares."

"But you do?"

Her air of distraction evaporated and she narrowed her attention onto him. "He's a client whose professional needs dovetail with the services I offer. Why? What are you suggesting?"

"Nothing," he muttered, disgusted with himself.

"You meant something," she accused. "I don't have personal relationships with clients, Luca. That's why you no longer are one."

"Is Emiliano Ricci a client? Is that how you know him?"

Her expression blanked with surprise, then she shrugged. "Not that it's any of your business, but no. He's not. Why? You said you didn't care what I'd done or with whom."

"I don't," Luca insisted, pacing the lounge. "You were lovers, though?"

"I met him on a weekend cruise for app developers. We talked about social media and how to play the algorithms to become an influencer. I think I'd rather return my mother's phone call than continue *this* conversation."

He let her walk out. He told himself to let her go, to hold himself at a necessary distance. His feelings were too strong as it was. But the farther away she got, the more he knew he was totally blowing this.

"Amy," he called from the bottom of the main staircase.

She paused at the top to give him a haughty look from the rail.

"I don't *want* to care—" he bit out what felt like an enormous confession "—but I do."

"Good for you. I don't." She sailed along the gallery.

The hell she didn't! He took the stairs two at a time and opened the door to the guest bedroom that she had just slammed in his face.

She swung around to glare at him.

"I don't like having emotions I can't control," he said through his gritted teeth. "Perhaps I should ask your friend Bea to help me work through them?"

Such outraged hostility flashed in her bright green eyes, he nearly threw his head back and laughed. "See? You don't like it, either."

She folded her arms, chin up. "You chased me all the way up here to see if you could make me as pointlessly jealous as you are?"

"I'm not proud of it." He closed in on her. "But I needed to know whether you were capable of it."

"Jealousy comes from insecurity. I'm not an insecure person." She narrowed her eyes and held her ground. Temper crackled around her. She resisted his attempt to unfold her arms.

"Neither am I." He managed to draw her stiff arms open and kissed the inside of each of her blue-veined wrists. "But we haven't had time to become confident in each other, have we? So we're failing the test."

"You specifically told me not to believe in this!" She freed a hand to fling it out with exasperation. "You're the one who said it was a meaningless affair."

"I never said meaningless."

She tried to pull her arm away, but he held on to her wrist. Her struggle drew her closer. Her nose was even with his chin, her gaze wide and surprisingly defenseless beneath the sparks of anger.

That vulnerability dug into him the way her temper and his

own conflicting emotions hadn't. He drew her in with great care, twining her one arm behind his lower back, then massaged her stiff shoulders.

"I've always known exactly what was expected of me," he said. "And I've always met and exceeded those expectations." His lips were tickled by flyaway strands of her hair. "But from the moment I met you, I have been off-center. I know what I should be thinking and saying and doing, but I can't make myself do it. Every instinct in me wants to *have* you." His arms tightened around her. "But I can't let that animal win. Not when I know how dangerous it is. The war inside me is killing me so you'll have to forgive the snarls." He ran his hand into her lower back.

It took a few circles of his palm before she released a noise that landed somewhere between defeat and petulance.

"This is new for me, too. From the job you hired me for to how I react to you..." She picked one of her red-gold hairs off his sleeve, then rested her hand where it had been. "I'm not being coy. This is hard to navigate."

"I know. I've made it hard. You have a right to be angry with me, which makes me less sure of you." He let one hand settle above her tailbone.

"I'm not angry or blaming you." Her brow pulled with consternation. "I took the job and slept with you. I caused us to be seen. I know how much of this is on me and that's hard, too. I'm worried about how our efforts to turn this around will pan out."

"It's going to be harder if we're fighting, no?"

"Whose fault is that?" she admonished, but grew pliant, leaning her thighs against his.

"Guilty." He let his fingers fan out to graze the upper curve of her backside. "Maybe we should kiss and make up. For the sake of our image."

"Humph." Her lips twitched. "Here in the privacy of this bedroom? Where no one can see us? A strong brand has to be reinforced consistently."

"Ooh. More shop talk, *amata mia*." He nuzzled his mouth into her throat, groaning with mock lust. "It makes me so hot."

She laughed and tried to shrug away from his tickling kiss. "Does it? Because I was going to say that I'm currently with the only man who interests me, but okay. Let me tell you about shareable infographics."

He lifted his head, accosted by the most intense flush of pleasure. The kind that should have had an orgasm as its source. And yes, he hoped to experience one of those very soon, but this was even more deeply affecting because it wasn't a biological reaction. It was an expansive, chaotic and thrilling reaction to a throwaway remark she had buried in nonsensical teasing. It was terrifying how much it meant to him.

"What?" she asked, smile faltering.

"Nothing." He cupped her cheek and set his mouth across hers, the avaricious beast in him howling to consume her, but something soft and equally ravenous urged him to be tender. To savor as he plundered. To pour himself into her even as he felt her start of surprise and tasted her broken sigh of capitulation.

Amy had been confused after their rooftop discussion, coming away wondering if she was allowing herself to be used again. She had wanted desperately to reach out to her friends to start putting all of this into perspective.

Neither had been available and for a few minutes, when she'd come back to the lounge, things between her and Luca had seemed to devolve into chaos. She had stalked up here insulted and filled with misgivings and now...

Now she was more confused than ever.

If he was using her, it was in the most tender way possible. His kiss was fierce and insatiable and shatteringly gentle. He was treating her like she was precious and irresistible. He unraveled her ability to think clear thoughts.

She knew nothing but her body and the feel of him where he touched her. The fingerprints he traced on her cheeks near her ear, the playful scrape of his teeth on her bottom lip, the brush of his thighs against hers and the wonderous way he cradled her breast.

The onslaught wasn't only physical. There was tremendous emotion welling in her as she heard his muted groan ring in his chest. She thrilled to the press of his erection into her middle and sighed with adoration when he touched his lips to her brow.

And she trembled. It was nearly too much, the way he made her feel so beautiful and treasured at once. The way he had shared his struggle. She felt it in the brief bite of his fingertips into her hips before he slowly eased her clothing away. Tasted it like whiskey on his tongue when he made love to her mouth before he kissed the nipples he'd exposed and slowly, erotically, made her writhe with need by sucking on them.

"Luca," she gasped.

His eyes were incandescent as he backed her toward the bed. Then he was over her, both of them with their clothing askew, but neither was willing to break apart to undress completely.

"I need you to take me inside you. I need that like I need air to breathe," he said, making her shiver.

With damp eyes, she nodded, needing it too. Needing the physical closeness to seal the schism that had been wrought by the betraying photo and everything that had come after.

Moments later, he had sheathed himself and, both still half-dressed, disheveled and frantic, they came together with a shudder of grand surrender to the passion they couldn't resist.

He held himself inside her as he brushed her hair from where it was caught on her eyelashes. She turned her mouth into the flexing curve of his biceps, tasting his skin and feeling drunk.

"I don't know if I'll ever be able to live without this." As the words left her, she realized she had spoken them aloud.

She saw the beast then. Caught the flash of feral possessiveness before his mouth was at the corner of hers, soft and tender and sweet again.

"Be with me now," he commanded.

He began to move. She had no choice but to lose herself to the exaltation that was the result of their lovemaking. The pleasure lifted her even as it seemed to strip her of any outer, protective layers, until she was nothing but pure being. Pure reaction.

Undone and completely vulnerable.

But he took care of her. Such care. Drawing her to the peak with those kisses of reverence and blatant hunger. Watching her with such pride and pleasure in her joyous ascent to climax.

"I want you with me," she gasped.

"I'm right here." His voice seemed to speak inside her head, they were so attuned.

And then they were splintering together, writhing and groaning and throbbing in perfectly synchronized culmination.

It was so powerful and magnificent, she couldn't open her eyes after. She stayed in that state of mutual bliss for ages, convinced they were actually one being.

"That was incredible," he whispered when they finally disengaged. He discarded the condom and they shifted to a more comfortable position. His fingers sifted through her hair then settled against her scalp, tangled in the strands. "Green-eyed monster slayed. I was a fool to think any man from your past could have any bearing on what we have."

His words should have been reassuring, but her eyes snapped open as one particular man from her past jumped into her head.

It wouldn't come out, she assured herself, while clammy fingers of apprehension squeezed her lungs. Was she being naive? Forewarned was forearmed. She ought to tell him.

It was so shameful, though. She hated to even recollect it. Trying to explain it, to dredge through the guilt and remorse and betrayal by her parents… His view of her would completely change. She didn't want to ruin this newfound closeness between them. Not right now.

His chest rose and fell beneath her ear as he exhaled into sleep. She snuggled closer and let unpleasant memories drift away.

* * *

"How does it feel to no longer be the most noteworthy person in the room?" Luca's twin asked as she appeared beside him.

Queen Sofia of Vallia was the height of elegance in one of their mother's vintage gowns and a tiara from the crown jewel collection. Her attendance at the foundation's gala was her first public event and their first appearance together since La Inversione, as the press had dubbed her bloodless coup.

Luca noted his sister's gaze was on Amy where she swiveled for the relentlessly flashing bulbs around her. Was Sofia criticizing the attention Amy was garnering? A twist of hostility wrenched through him aimed at the one person he'd always vowed to lay down his life to protect.

He sipped his drink, dampening his desire to remind her that she had been elevated to her current position at Amy's expense. "I never wanted to be. You know that."

"I was teasing." Her gaze narrowed at his tone. "You like her."

Which made him realize he was overreacting, damn it.

"I don't sleep with people I don't like," he muttered.

"Obviously. But you *really* like her. I was under the impression this was all for my benefit," she mused, looking back at Amy with consideration.

He took another gulp of his drink, guilty because this wasn't supposed to benefit him at all. Nothing was. Ever. He hadn't saddled Sofia with running their country so he could enjoy a sexual romp.

"I'll invite her to lunch," Sofia said. "Get to know her better."

"She's due back in London as soon as we return from Tokyo."

Her steady gaze asked, *And then what?*

He rubbed his thumb against the side of his glass, not ready to admit he was thinking of going there with her. There were so many variables and pitfalls. Sofia wasn't married or even looking for a consort. The public might be *for* Queen Sofia, but many were still taking sides *against* Amy Miller for costing them King Luca.

"She handles it well, doesn't she? Being in the sun," Sofia mused.

Amy was winning people over one bright smile at a time, but the attention would never stop. Nor would the judging. It was a sad and relentless fact of his life that he had to remain above reproach. He couldn't sentence her to those same strictures. Not forever.

Not when her smile was already showing signs of strain.

"Yes, but she's not wearing sunscreen." He set his glass on a drinks tray carried by passing waitstaff. "Excuse me while I rescue her."

Amy gratefully went into Luca's arms when he invited her to dance.

"How are you holding up?" he asked as he led her into a smooth waltz. Was there *nothing* this man didn't do perfectly?

"I underestimated what I was asking of my clients in the past, when I've said, 'Just smile while they take your photo.' My fault, I guess, for choosing this dress."

His expression flickered through amusement and ended up as something more contemplative. "There's a commentary there on how much attention we give to what women wear, but I'd rather not think too hard when I've finally got you to myself."

"I'll wear a tuxedo next year," she said, then faltered as she realized it sounded like she assumed she would be with him next year.

"Or pajamas," he suggested.

She relaxed. "I'm glad they've been well received, but I can't take the credit."

"Why not? Sofia and I wouldn't have ordered any if the option hadn't been presented."

Even so, the queen and former king had each preordered a hundred pair, asking that they be donated to long-term care facilities throughout Vallia. With that example set, guests were ordering in factors of ten, rather than the one or two pair Amy had anticipated.

"Do you want to visit the pajama factory while we're in Asia?" Luca asked.

"Oh. Um…" She nearly turned her ankle again. "While you're doing that award thing in Tokyo? I mean, yes. I'd love to connect with the manufacturer and be sure it's a fair wage factory, like they claim. Double-check the quality."

"Get a photo op? We'll go together."

"Look at you, doing my job for me."

"I'm in the midst of a career change. Willing to try new things."

She chuckled, more from happiness than humor, but he made her *so* happy. Glowingly, deliriously lighthearted and hopeful and filled with a sense that she was the luckiest person alive. Especially when his gaze swung down to connect with hers, conveying pride and sexy heat.

This optimism was strange because she had learned the hard way not to look to a man to make her happy. She knew it had to come from within, but even though she would have said she was very content prior to meeting Luca, she felt far more alive and excited now that she was with him. Colors were brighter, music more tear-inducing, her confidence unshakable.

She wondered if this was what being in love felt like—

Oh.

He steadied her, pausing to give her a small frown. "How much have you had to drink?"

"One glass. I was just…distracted for a moment," she lied.

They resumed dancing, but her whole body was fizzing with the realization that her heart had gift wrapped itself and stolen under his tree.

She was in love with him. How it had happened so quickly didn't matter. It had. Because this wasn't a hero-worship crush gone wrong. Or sexual infatuation—although that was definitely a big part of it.

It was deep concern for his well-being. Admiration for his principles and intelligence and laconic wit. It was a compulsion to trust him with all of her secrets and a depthless yearning for him to return her regard.

The words clogged her throat, but it was too soon. Too public. Too new.

But as they continued dancing, she thought it with each step. *I love you. I love you.*

The next days were busy.

Luca was in meetings to redefine his new role and Amy worked remotely, attempting to mitigate the damage her scandal had done to London Connection and her career.

She rarely had Luca to herself, and when she did, it was in bed. There they communicated in ways that were as profound as any conversation she might have wished to have, so she didn't worry that they weren't dissecting their relationship. It was growing stronger by the day.

The unrelenting media pressure only pushed them to rely on one another, rather than rending them apart. If an awkward question was directed at her, his hand would come out of nowhere to interlace with hers. When his bearing grew rife with tension over a late-night pundit's joke at his expense, she would slide her arms around his waist, asking nothing except that he allow her to soothe him. He would sigh and gather her in.

This morning he had commented to someone, "I'm likely to be in London for the next while—"

It had been part of a broader discussion, and she hadn't had an opportunity to ask if that meant he wanted to continue their relationship. They had agreed on two weeks, but she didn't need to do any soul-searching. Of course, she wanted to keep seeing him!

They were both in love. She was sure of it. If that put a dreamy, smitten look on her face, she couldn't help it.

Perhaps that's why she was garnering so many stares right now.

Or maybe it was because this morning, she and Luca had been granted an exclusive visit to Shinjuku Gyoen National Garden to view their cherry blossoms with some Japanese dignitaries. A handful of photographers had followed them, and those shots were likely being published right now.

Either way, her phone, which was facedown on the table and set to silent, was vibrating incessantly.

She ignored it and kept her attention on Luca. He spoke at the podium, switching back and forth between Italian and Japanese so she missed much of what he was saying. She could tell there was praise for collaboration and innovation on some tech solution commissioned for Vallia. He showed a photo of a port in Vallia, then one here in Japan, highlighting some advancement that had made a difference in both countries.

One of Luca's handlers stood behind him. The young man sent her an urgent glare.

Seriously? He could hear the buzz of her phone all the way over there?

She slid the phone off the table without looking at it and dropped it into her bag.

She had the sense of more glances turning her way, but reminded herself that a few rude stares were a small price to pay for the absolute wonder of being Luca's... They didn't need a label, she assured herself. None of the usual ones fit them anyway. "Girlfriend" was too high school. "Lover" was too edgy for a prince, "mistress" too eye-rollingly outdated.

Luca *had* been footing her bills since she'd met him. Even her charge from the hotel boutique in London had been reversed. Apparently, he'd had the clothes she'd bought that day put onto his own account.

That made her uncomfortable, but she pulled her weight in other ways. She was still managing the pajama campaign and offered constructive ideas to his team on how she and Luca were presenting themselves. They were equals.

Luca came to the good part, announcing a pair of names and

the company they represented. Everyone clapped as a husband-wife team rose to collect the statuette Luca held.

The audience took advantage of the applause break to set their heads together and murmur, flicking speculative glances toward her. Luca joined his assistant behind the winners and glanced at the screen his assistant showed him.

He stiffened and his gaze lifted in a flash to hit hers like a punch.

Amy's stomach clenched. *What?*

As the couple at the podium finished speaking and left, they seemed disconcerted by the growing undercurrents in the room.

The cameraman who'd been filming the event turned his lens on her. A reporter shoved a microphone in Amy's face.

"Is it true? Did you cause a teacher to lose his position with Upper Swell School for Girls? Do you have a history of destroying men's lives?"

CHAPTER TEN

LUCA DISAPPEARED OFF the stage behind the curtain, abandoning her to the reckoning of harsh stares and harsher questions.

As Amy was absorbing the profound pain of his desertion, another reporter joined the first. People stared while she desperately tried to gather her handbag and light jacket, which was being pinned by a reporter. On purpose.

Panic began to compress her lungs. She struggled to maintain her composure. She was hot and cold and *scared*. As scared as she'd been the day she was told to leave the school and had no idea where she would go.

Do not cry. Do not, she willed herself while her throat closed over a distressed scream.

And these damned buzzards kept asking their cruel questions.

"Did you lure the prince into that nude photograph? Did someone hire you to do it? His sister?"

One of Luca's bodyguards shoved into the fray and shielded her with his wide body and merciless bulk. He grabbed her things and escorted her out of the nearest exit, but it was still a gauntlet of shouted questions and conjecture.

When he shoved her into an SUV, Luca was already in it. His PA sat facing him; his other bodyguard was in the front.

The bodyguard who had rescued her took the seat facing her and pulled the door shut behind them.

"Is it true?" Luca asked stiffly. She hadn't seen this particular shade of subdued rage under his skin since he'd spoken of his father's death.

"I'm not talking about it here." Her voice was hollow. All of her was. It was the only way she could cope, by stepping outside her body and letting the shell be transported wherever he was taking her. If she let herself see and think and feel, she would buckle into hysterical tears.

"That's not a denial," he growled.

How had this happened? Why?

"Who—" She had to clear the thickness from her throat so her voice was loud enough to catch the PA's attention. "Who released this story?"

He told her the name of an infamous gossip site. "Their source is the wife of Avery Mason. She claims he confided in her early in their marriage."

Amy set her hand across her aching stomach and looked out the window.

"The flight plan has been changed, sir," Luca's PA informed him after tapping his tablet. "The team will meet us when we refuel in Athens."

No photo op at a factory in Jiangsu then. Big surprise. "The team" would be the same group of lawyers, spin doctors and palace advisers who had handled his first damning scandal and were continuing to massage it.

Obviously, *she* was off the job. Amy couldn't be trusted. Luca would control the messaging, and his lawyers would likely press her to sign something. Maybe Luca would sue her for defamation. The contract she'd signed with him hadn't stated explicitly that she was supposed to ruin him. They'd left that part as a handshake deal. Could that come back to bite her? She needed Bea!

The private airfield came into view. They drove up to his private jet, and even that short walk of shame was photographed from some hidden location that turned up on her phone when she checked it as the plane readied for takeoff.

"You're shaking," Luca said crisply. "Do you need something?"

A time machine? Her friends? She dug up one of the sleeping tablets she'd taken on the flight here, requested a glass of water and swallowed the pill.

Luca answered a call and began speaking Italian. His sister perhaps. He was cutting his words off like he was chopping wood. Or beheading chickens.

"Sì. No lo so. Presto. Addio."

She handed back her glass and texted Bea and Clare, already knowing it was futile. They were tied up with other things, and she didn't know how to ask for forgiveness when she was piling yet more scandal onto London Connection.

In a fit of desperation, she sent out a text to a few of her closest contacts, fearful she would be locked down in Vallia again. A commercial flight was out of the question. She'd be torn apart, but a handful of her clients flew privately throughout Europe. There was a small chance one of them might be going through the airfield Luca used in Athens.

As she was texting, her mother's image appeared on her screen as an incoming call.

Don't cry. Do not cry.

Amy hit ignore, then tapped out a text that she was about to take off and had to set her phone to airplane mode. It wasn't true, but she couldn't face the barrage that was liable to hit her. She turned off her phone and set it aside.

Luca tucked away his own phone and studied her.

The plane began to taxi. The flight attendant had seated herself near the galley. The rest of his staff were sequestered in their own area, leaving them alone in this lounge, facing one another like duelists across twelve paces of tainted honor.

"Yes. It's true," she said flatly, appreciating the cocooning effect of her sleeping tablet as it began to release into her system, reducing her agitation and making her limbs feel heavy. It numbed her to the profound humiliation of reliving the most agonizing, isolating experience of her life. "I had an affair with my teacher in my last year of school. That's why I was expelled and why my parents disinherited me."

"How old was he?"

"Twenty-nine. I was eighteen."

He swore. "That's not an affair, Amy. He should have been arrested."

"Oh, he's a disgusting pig. I won't argue that, but I came on to him, even after he said we shouldn't. I told you I was spoiled. I wasn't used to taking no for an answer. I loved how enamored with me he seemed. How helpless he was to resist me."

She saw how deeply that hit Luca, pushing him back into his seat. Making him reconsider his own infatuation with her.

Was she *trying* to hurt him with this chunk of heavy, sharp-edged history? Maybe. Kicking it at him felt like the only way she could handle touching it at all.

"I'd never had to face any consequences before that. If I was caught bringing alcohol into the dorm, my parents would make a donation to the school and smooth things over." That had been her father's solution, to avoid a fight with his ex over which one of them had to bring Amy back into their home. "I was friends with everyone. It was a point of pride that even if someone thought I was full of myself, I would win them over by flattering them and doing them favors." That had been her mother's legacy. If you didn't have a clear pressure point like money or maternal guilt to bring to bear, fawning and subtle bribery were good substitutes. "I refused to let up when he tried to turn me down."

"Grown men are not victims of teenage girls," he said with disgust.

"Not until his mother, the headmistress, discovers them. Then he's apparently a defenseless baby and the harlot who seduced him is served with an overdue notice of expulsion. *That's* when her parents finally decide she should be taught a lesson about the real world."

His flinty gaze tracked across her expression.

It was all she could do to hide how devastated she'd been. Still was. She looked away, out the window to where Tokyo was fading behind wisps of cloud.

A tremendous melancholy settled on her. The sleeping pill, but history, as well.

"It was covered up by his mother and mine. The gossip hadn't really got around anyway. Bea and Clare were the only two people who stood by me. They wanted to quit school in solidarity, but I didn't want them to throw away their futures just because I had. They helped with rent here and there, but I eventually found my feet with the online promotions and I was so...touched. So *proud* when Clare asked me to start London Connection with her. I felt like I was bringing value when I'd been such a mess in those early years. And now... Now I've stuffed it up anyway."

"Why did you take my assignment when you had something like this in your past?"

"I didn't expect to *relive* it. You're the one who decided to use me for your own ends because the opportunity was too good to pass up," she reminded him.

His head jerked back. "I would have made other decisions if I had known."

"Would you?" she scoffed.

"You didn't give me a chance to prove otherwise, did you? I came to you to manufacture a scandal so I wouldn't cause anyone else to be hurt. *I told you that.* But you didn't warn me that something like this was possible. You said this is a circle of trust, but you didn't trust me, did you?"

"Don't lecture me on *honesty*. Not when you—" She leaned forward in accusation, then abruptly had to catch her armrest as she realized the tablet was destroying her sense of balance. "When you were so convinced of your own perfection you had to *hire* someone to make you look bad. You want to talk about respecting a relationship? You hired me so that when you made your *one* mistake—" she showed him her single finger for emphasis "—it wouldn't really be yours. You wanted to be able to tell yourself that whatever happened wouldn't really be your fault. You want to believe this image—" she gestured to encompass his aura "—of being completely flawless, is *real*. Here's news, Luca. We all make mistakes. That's why my job exists! I'm *your* mistake. And now you'll have to live with that. So suck it."

She dropped back into her seat, feeling like a sack of bruised apples. The entire world was upon her, crushing her. She propped her cement-filled head on the weak joint of her wrist, growing too tired to cry, even though sobs were thickening her throat and sinuses.

"My mistake was believing the scarlet harlot of Upper Swell was going to live happily ever after with the Golden Prince."

"I never promised you that." He didn't shout it, but it struck like a sonic boom she felt with her heart.

"No," she agreed with growing drowsiness. "No, you said it was only going to be an affair and I believed you. But you made me fall in love with you." She blinked heavy lids over wet eyes. "That's on you, Luca."

Amy woke in Luca's stateroom several hours later. She wondered if he had carried her here or had one of his bodyguards do it. Whoever it was had removed her shoes and draped a light blanket over her.

She finger-combed her hair and used the toothbrush that had been designated hers when they'd embarked from Vallia, back when she and Luca had been in perfect sync and she'd believed...

She clenched her eyes. Had she really believed they had a chance at a future? *Come on, Amy. You're smarter than that.*

Wrinkled and fuzzy-headed, she crept back to her seat.

Luca was reclined in his seat and fast asleep. Her heart wrenched to see him there when he could have slept beside her in his own bed. If he had wanted to send the message that she would no longer wake to the sight of him sleeping beside her, this was it.

A flight attendant started to approach, and Amy waved her off. She should eat something so she didn't get air sick, but she was too anguished.

She turned on her phone and was tempted to turn it right back off again, but made herself go through some of the messages, looking for...

Her heart lurched as she picked up a reply to her SOS. One of her clients, Baz Rivets, was sober a year now, but had had addiction problems from the time she'd met him at one of his early pub gigs through to the international fame he and his rock band enjoyed today. She'd been beside him every time he'd gone in or come out of a program and regarded him as a friend, but she would never have expected him to go out of his way for her.

I thought I'd have to go back to rehab to see you again. We're detouring to Athens from Berlin. Will wait for you there, ducky.

It was enormously heartening, but also like hearing she could have lifesaving surgery on condition half her heart be removed.

With her throat aching, she replied with a heartfelt, "Thank you," and set aside her phone. Then she stared at the flight tracker, taking way too long to comprehend that they were above Turkey. Only a few hours to go before she would have to say goodbye to Luca.

He woke as they began their descent into Athens.

For one millisecond, as he glanced at her with disorientation, she saw a flash of the complex *hello* he usually wore when he woke next to her. It was discovery and pleasure and something magnetic and welcoming that always warmed her deep in her center.

This time, it was gone before it fully formed. She saw memory strike him so hard, he flinched. His expression blanked into steely, unreadable lines.

Whatever spark of hope still flickered within her died, leaving her more bereft than she'd ever felt. She looked to the window, teeth clenched against making apologies. Was this her fault? Not really. Everyone had a past, and she hadn't aired hers on purpose.

Did that matter when it was impacting him anyway? Her parents hadn't cared who was at fault ten years ago. *This can't get out, Amy. How did you let it happen?*

Her ears popped and, moments later, they were on the ground, taxiing to a stop outside a private terminal for personal and charter jets.

"I have to speak with my sister," Luca said, glancing up from his ringing phone. He unbuckled and rose, bringing the phone to his ear as he moved into the stateroom for privacy.

Amy searched wildly out the window as she began gathering her things. A team of trench coats and briefcases came out of the terminal and headed toward the plane. Fresh air came in as the steps were lowered.

Where was Baz? There! She saw the plane with the psychedelic logo on its tail and rudely shuffled her way past the confused faces of people trying to board.

It was raining and she hadn't bothered to pull on her light jacket, so she felt each stinging drop as she ran the short distance across the tarmac. Stairs appeared as the hatch was lowered on Baz Rivets's plane.

"Welcome to the naughty side, ducky!" Baz wore jeans, a torn T-shirt, a man bun and a scruffy beard. He opened his arms in welcome.

She ran up the steps, starting to cry, she was so overwhelmed. "I didn't know how to get home without being swarmed, but I didn't expect you to make a special trip for me!"

"You flew to Thailand and kept me out of *jail*. Giving you

a lift home is the least I can do." He wrapped his arms around her. "You messy, messy girl."

"I never claimed to be otherwise, Baz. I really didn't."

"Oh. He doesn't look happy."

Amy turned to see Luca had come onto the steps of his own plane. He stared across at her, his dumbfounded rage so tangible she felt a jolt of adrenaline sear her arteries.

Baz kept one arm around her and drew her closer to his wiry frame. He wore the most neighborly of smiles as he waved and spoke with quiet cheerfulness through his clenched teeth, "That'll teach you, ya royal bastard. Amy should be treated like the queen she is."

I'm not. I was never going to be.

For a long moment, she and Luca stared at one another. He didn't call her back or come get her, though. And he turned away first.

It was a knife straight to her heart, one that would have kept her standing there waiting for the rest of her life in hopes he'd reappear to pull it out, but Baz nudged her inside.

"Come tell Uncle Bazzie all about it. Lads, put the kettle on for our sweet Ames."

Luca was clinging to his patience by his fingernails. His brain kept going back to asking *Why didn't she tell me this could happen?*

It didn't matter why. She hadn't. Intellectually, he understood that Amy was the victim of exploitation. That wasn't something she needed to tell anyone unless she wanted to.

But now his sister was in his ear saying, "I appreciate this isn't something she could control, but it's time to distance yourself from her."

"I know." His goal had been accomplished, and Amy's connection to him was making things worse for her.

The woman who had leaked the story wouldn't have been so well rewarded if she'd only been taking down a PR agent who worked with celebrities. No, Amy's romantic link to royalty had been the gold the story was really mining. It was a vein that would continue to be exploited as long as he and Amy were together.

Even so, when Luca saw Amy darting across the tarmac to the waiting plane, he nearly lost his mind.

He'd hung up on his sister and shoved his way outside in time to see her with— Who the hell was that? Some demigod celebrity, Luca realized as he took in the flamboyant logo that spoke of a live fast, die young rock culture. The jackass wore professionally distressed clothing and a smug grin as he claimed Amy.

Luca hated him on sight.

You made me fall in love with you.

If she loved him, she should have trusted him enough to tell him about her past. Enough to *stay*.

That's all he could think as he stared across at her standing in that other man's embrace, the image like radiation that destroyed his insides the longer he stared.

"Sir, there are people in the terminal getting all this on their phones," someone said from inside his plane.

Brilliant. His final humiliation was being recorded for uploading to the buffet of public ignominy that was already so well stocked. Outstanding.

He went inside to take his seat, sick with guilt that he'd wanted to right a wrong and it had resulted in yet more wrong.

Everyone stared at him while he settled into his chair.

"Our first step is to make clear to her the legal and financial consequences she will face if she divulges any of this to the press," one of his lawyers piped up.

"We should make an immediate statement that she was *asked* to leave. Get in front of whatever photos come out from this." Another one tapped the window.

Luca had had the team meet him here in Athens in hopes they could find a way forward that wouldn't destroy both him and Amy. He had expected her to weigh in.

Now he could only stare in disbelief while another backstabbing idiot said, "Given her history, we could reframe the photos and make a case for you to take *back* the throne."

Luca swore and waved his hand. "Get off my plane. All of you."

Neither Bea nor Clare were in London when Amy arrived.

Bea, bless her, said Amy could use her flat. She was deeply grateful and sank into the familiar oasis of Bea's personal space.

But with both of her friends still away, it fell to Amy to keep London Connection running. She popped an email to her assistant to say she would do it remotely to minimize the disruption she was already causing at the office. She didn't mention her plan to resign. She would wait until Clare and Bea were back to tell them personally. For now, she focused on drafting a statement about her past and most recent disgrace.

It started out very remorseful, but the more she looked up statistics on sexual harassment and noted the delight trolls took in being sadistic toward women, and the punishment gap when a woman made a mistake versus a man, the more incensed she became.

She wound up writing:

How is it that a twenty-nine-year-old man was deemed to have more to lose than an eighteen-year-old woman?

Everyone had something to lose when this affair happened, but I—the person with the least life experience and fewest resources—became the scapegoat. I was expelled before I could take my A levels, destroying my university aspirations.

No one cared that my future was derailed. It was far more important to Avery's mother, the headmistress, that she keep her job and avoid a disciplinary hearing over her son's behavior. She convinced my parents to sweep it under the rug. They agreed because they had financial, social, and career pressures to protect.

Instead of urging me to call the police, which I was too humiliated to contemplate on my own, my parents cut me off financially. I was literally left homeless while Avery was immediately transferred to a position at another school.

What began as a PR spin became an essay on feminism and the distance that still needed to be traveled. When she was done, there was morning light outside.

Amy hit send to a senior editor of an old-school but well-respected newspaper in America, then hired bodyguards to escort her to her own flat.

"'The king of Vallia hired me to assist with the Queen's Foundation,'" Sofia read aloud from the same open letter that Luca was reading on his own tablet. "'At the time of my professional engagement, we discussed extending my purview to other assignments, but those discussions were discontinued after we became personally involved.'"

Mio Dio, she knew how to gracefully pirouette with prose, Luca thought.

Perhaps Sofia was thinking it, too. He could feel her staring at him from her position at the opposite end of the table, prodding him for details on those halted discussions.

Luca and his twin had always breakfasted together if they were both in the palace, even after Luca took the throne. It allowed them to connect personally, but also discuss any political developments or other rising concerns. Luca had wanted Sofia to be in the know so she could seamlessly take over when the time came. She was keeping him equally well-informed as a courtesy. She certainly didn't need him weighing in with advice or opinions. Vallia's populace was adapting well to the change-over, seeming energized and eager for the new order.

Luca wished he could say the same. He was miserable.

While I regret the anguish King Luca must have suffered from the photos of us that emerged, I feel no remorse over the fact he was pressured into giving up the crown as a result of our affair. Men should be held to account when they cross a line.

"I like her," Sofia mused.

Me too, Luca thought, heart so heavy in his chest it was compressed and thumping in rough, painful beats that echoed in the pit of his gut.

He reached the end where an editorial note stated that Avery Mason's wife had recently retained an extremely pricey and ruthless divorce lawyer.

"Do you suppose that's why she sold the story?" Sofia asked as she clicked off her tablet. "To pay for her divorce?"

"And bolster her petition for one," Luca surmised. Perhaps she'd seen this as her only avenue for escaping her marriage. He couldn't spare much thought or empathy for her, though. Not when she'd ruthlessly used Amy to achieve her own ends.

The way you did? his conscience derided.

"A rebuttal is being drafted," Guillermo said, ever the helicopter guardian, hovering and batting away threats to his charges.

"Why?" Luca asked. "Do you not think men should suffer the consequences of their actions?"

"Signor." It was one of Guillermo's scolds that backpedaled even as his haughty demeanor reinforced his position. Luca Albizzi was never allowed to be seen as anything but faultless.

You were so convinced of your own perfection you had to hire someone to make you look bad.

"Guillermo, will you leave us please?" Sofia said.

Luca brought his focus back to his sister as Guillermo slipped away.

"I regret nothing," he said, which felt like a lie, but he still waved a dismissing hand at his tablet. "This will pass."

"Luca, I know," Sofia said in a voice that sent a chill of foreboding through him. "About the night Papa died. I made Vincenzo tell me everything." Vincenzo was the head of the palace's legal department.

Luca looked away, instantly thrown back to that grim night. "I was trying to spare you, not hide it from you."

"I know." She rose and came down the length of the table to stand behind him.

He tensed, not wanting comfort. He resisted her touch when her narrow hands settled on his shoulders and she squeezed his set muscles.

"I'm sorry you felt you couldn't tell me. That you've had to carry it alone."

"What was the point in forcing one more ugly memory onto you?"

"I know, but I needed to understand. Something changed in you after that night. At first, I thought it was the pressure of having to ascend. That you were angry the crown hadn't come to me, but it was more than that. I saw it more clearly when you were with Amy. She makes you happy, Luca, but you're fighting that every step of the way. Why?"

"Because look what happens when men in positions of power follow their base instincts!" He waved at the tablet where Amy's words were imprinted for the world to see. "Do you think that would have happened to her if she hadn't been tied to *me*?"

He would have risen to pace, but she didn't let him shrug her off. Her hands pressed him to stay in the chair as if she could impress her views into him with the action.

"You saw how upset she was the day our affair was revealed." He was still haunted by Amy's bleak expression. "She threatened to burn down the palace because she was terrified of exactly *this*."

"You didn't know about it, Luca."

"But I still wouldn't have done anything differently if I had. That's what makes me sick with myself. From the minute I saw her, I wanted her. I was attracted to her and yet I hired her anyway. I brought her here and gave in to what I felt. Pursuing what *I* wanted has destroyed her. So yes, she makes me happy. What the hell can I do about it when I'm a cancer that will only harm her?"

You made me fall in love with you.

He had to breathe through the pain every time he thought about her saying that. In the moment, he'd refused to let it in. His reflex had been to control the damage they faced, but while she'd been sleeping, her words had begun to penetrate and they'd replayed in his head continuously ever since, torturing him. Making him ache with what might have been.

"Do you know why I was away when Papa died?" Sofia asked.

"You were at a UN conference," he recalled dimly.

"The conference was over. I was hiding in a hotel room, worried I was pregnant."

Luca abruptly twisted in his chair to stare up at her.

"It was a false alarm," she hurried to say.

"Who?" he demanded in astonishment.

"Someone who was not anticipating being a father, let alone a queen's consort," she said tartly. "What I'm saying is, you are not the only person who has moments of weakness and fallibility." She cupped his cheek. "You're not the only one who wants to find a life partner and feel loved."

"I will stand behind you no matter what, Sofia. You know that." He took her hand to impress the words into her with a squeeze of her fingers. "You could have told me. If anything like that ever happens again, you can tell me."

"I know. And *I* stand behind *you* no matter what. Despite recent appearances," she said with a quirk of her mouth. Then she waved at his tablet. "Look how strong she is, Luca. Do you really think she's going to let *any* man destroy her? No. She has publicly declared she's keeping the life she has made for herself, and good for her. She is exactly the sort of woman you should be pursuing. She'll keep you honest."

You said it was only going to be an affair and I believed you.

He had tried to believe it himself, but he'd known that every minute with her was more than some flickering memory. It had been a stone in the foundation of something bigger. Something he wanted to make permanent. He'd already been contemplating going to London so they could continue to see one another.

"Do you have any idea how annoying it is that the women in my life are smarter than I am?" He rose.

"At least you're smart enough to realize that."

"Be warned, Sofia. If I'm going after *everything* I want, for me and you and Amy and Vallia, blood may get spilled. I won't always be nice about it."

She smiled. "I've always known you would slay dragons if you were allowed to carry a sword and weren't weighed down by a crown. You've made it possible for me to be who I need to be. I want you to be who *you* were meant to be." She offered her cheek for a kiss. "I love you and trust you."

"*Ti amo, sorella.* Don't wait up. I'll be gone as long as it takes to win her back."

I was going to resign, but you'll have to fire me.

Amy wrote that to Bea and Clare as she prepared to go into work two days later.

Clare was uncharacteristically silent, not answering texts or emails for the last few days, which was worrying, but Bea called her immediately. "I vote you be promoted to Executive Director of Executing Bastards. You're my hero. I love you."

"Where *are* you? When are you coming back?" Amy asked her.

"It's a lot to explain," Bea began.

"Oh, God. Wait," Amy said as her phone pinged with a text.

"My mother is threatening to come see me. I haven't spoken to her since before Tokyo."

"You don't have to see her," Bea reminded her.

"That's what I'm going to tell her." Sort of. "I'll call you back soon." Amy signed off and tapped her mother for a video call.

Her mother looked surprisingly frail, not wearing her usual makeup and designer day dress. Instead, she was in her dressing gown. Her skin looked sallow and aged and, if Amy wasn't mistaken, she was putting out a cigarette off-screen.

"There's a lot of paps outside, Mom. And I'm heading into work so don't come over here. I won't drag them to you, either."

"That's fine, but I *wish* you would have seen all of that old business from my point of view, instead of airing it publicly. In *New York*. Do you have any idea how traumatizing it would have been to put you through a court case over that prat? It was the best thing for you that we made it go away like that. You should be thankful."

"You have a right to your opinion. Is that all?" Amy propped up her phone so she could use two hands to load her bag.

"I've spoken to your father. He's arranging to release your trust fund as soon as possible."

"I don't need it, Mom." She kind of did, but... "I never wanted *money* from you and Dad," she added with a sharp break in her tone that she couldn't help.

"For God's sake, Amy. Have you never realized there was none? It was a recession! Your father borrowed from the trust to keep his company afloat. He stopped paying me support. That's why I married Melvin, so I could sell the house and make your tuition payments. You were adamant that you finished school with your friends. Then you got yourself expelled. I honestly didn't know what to do. We both thought you needed a dose of reality."

"And the reality was, I couldn't count on my parents to be honest with me."

"Do not play the victim here, Amy. You were an absolute pill."

"This is not a productive conversation, Mom. Let's take a break. A long one. I'll call when I'm ready to chat. If you don't hear from me by my birthday, you can call me then."

"In *five months*? No. That stupid Mason fool will not cost me my only child again. I swear, I want to track him down and stab him in the eye."

"Let me know what they set your bail at. I'll see if I can raise it online."

"You think I'm joking."

"You think I am."

"I'll see you at Wednesday's lunch," her mother declared.

Amy rolled her eyes, not caring that it made her mother sigh the way it always had, ever since she'd been a young, rebellious pill.

"I'll text you once I've checked my schedule at work," Amy conceded. "Bea and Clare are away and this is my first day back. It will be hectic."

A short time later, her bodyguards cut through the paparazzi and she entered London Connection. Despite Bea's supportive phone call, however, she wasn't sure of her reception.

"Amy!" someone shouted, and everyone stood up to applaud her.

Which made tears come into her eyes. She was deeply touched and had a queue of hugs to get through before she arrived at her desk and began putting things in order there.

It was a busy day. Some clients had dropped her and the agency, claiming they were "no longer a good fit," but the phones were even busier with potential new ones. Even more heartening were the emails from colleagues in her industry who not only expressed support for her personally, but told her how much they admired her professionally.

"I would rather work for you than the agency I'm at," more than one said. "Please let me know when you have an opening."

As Amy absorbed what an opportunity for growth they faced, she held a quick meeting with the department heads. She tasked them with helping her make a case for expanding London Connection that she could present to Bea and Clare the minute they were back.

It was exciting and consuming and kept her mind occupied so she wouldn't think about how thoroughly her letter had dropped the ax on any chance she might have had of a relationship with Luca. She kept waiting for his rebuttal to hit the airwaves, maybe something that would deride her for daring to be so comfortable with costing a king his crown. The arrogance! The cheek! Did she not know she had destabilized a nation?

There was only a short statement from the palace that they would not comment on the prince's personal life. When she arrived home, however, a pair of stoic-faced men in dark suits were waiting in the lobby of her building.

"Will you come with us, Miss Miller?"

"She will not," one of her own bodyguards said firmly, placing himself in front of her.

"It's fine, I know who he is," she said, nudging her man aside. Her heart began to race and she searched the face of Luca's bodyguard. He gave away nothing.

He probably didn't know what she faced any more than she did.

Would Luca rail at her? Force her to write a retraction? Have her thrown off a bridge?

There was only one way to find out. Despite her trepidation, she dismissed her own guards and went with the men.

They took her to a beautiful Victorian town house in Knightsbridge. The facade was white and ornate. Vines grew up the columns on either side of the black front door. She was shown across a foyer with a lovingly restored parquet floor and into a lounge of predominantly white decor. Three arched windows, tall and narrow and symmetrical, looked onto a garden where a topless maiden poured water from a jug into a fountain.

She looked at the figure and all she could think of was her walk with Luca the first day at his palace, when he'd confided in her about his father's death. He'd been so hurt by the things his father had done, and she'd set him up for more of it.

She rubbed her sternum, hating herself for that.

"It felt like home the minute I saw her," Luca said behind her.

Amy spun to find him leaning in a doorway, regarding her. Her heart leaped a mile high. She had missed him. So much. Then her heart took another bounce because he was so fiercely beautiful. And a third time because there was no anger in his expression. No vilification.

But no smile, either. The one that tugged at her cheeks fell apart before it was fully formed, but she couldn't help staring at him. Drinking him in.

His neat, stubbled beard was perfectly trimmed across his long cheeks. His mouth was not quite smiling, but wasn't tense, either. Solemn. His blue eyes searched more than they offered any insight to his reason for bringing her here.

He had the ability to wear a blue button-down shirt and gray trousers as though it was a bespoke tuxedo. A suit of gleaming armor. Whether he called himself a king, a prince, or a man, he could lean in a doorway and command a room. He projected authority and strength, and despite his intimidating and unreadable expression and the very unsettled way they'd left things, her instinct was to hurry toward him.

She touched the back of a chair to ground herself. To hold herself back.

They'd been apart only four days. Their relationship from "ruin me" to being ruined had been a short ten. How was it possible that her feelings toward him were paralyzing her? She was on a knife's edge between hope and despair. There *was* no hope, she reminded herself.

But still he'd brought her here. Why?

"I—" she began, but had no clue what she wanted to say.

Then his words struck her. "Wait. Did you just buy this?" She pointed at the floor to indicate the house.

"I did. Would you like a tour? It's not a faithful restoration. It was gutted and modernized. I think you'll agree that's a good thing."

He offered his hand.

She hesitated, then moved as though in a trance, desperate for this small contact. This was how miracles worked, wasn't it? Without explanation? She took his hand, and the feel of his warm palm against hers as he interlaced their fingers nearly unhinged her knees.

"I thought you'd be angry with me," she said shakily. "About the letter." Each cell in her body was coming back to life.

"I am. But not with you. I'm angry that you had to write it. The kitchen." He identified the room with a wave as they walked into an airy space of cutting blocks and stainless steel, pots and pans suspended from the ceiling, and French doors that led to a patio herb garden. "The chef has yet to be hired, but you remember Fabiana? I poached her from the palace."

"Yes, of course. Hello," Amy greeted the maid. "It's nice to see you again."

"*Ciao.*" Fabiana gave a small curtsy before she went back to putting away groceries.

"You can access the stairs to the terrace out there. You've seen the garden through the windows. Staff quarters are downstairs. Dining room, office, powder room, you've seen the main lounge," he said as he walked her through the various rooms, all bright and fresh and sumptuously decorated in a soft palette of rose and gray, ice blue and bone white. Shots of yellow and burnt orange, indigo and fern gave it life.

"It's a charming touch to keep this," she said as she paused on the landing to admire the window seat that looked over the road. "I can imagine callers waiting here to see if they would be allowed upstairs by the duke or—" *Prince*.

"There might have been a receiving room up here once, but it's all master suite now."

It was. There was a sumptuous yet intimate lounge with a television and a wet bar, a dining nook for breakfast and other casual meals, a beautiful office with floor-to-ceiling bookshelves and a fitness room that would catch the morning light. The actual bedroom was enormous, and the master bath had a walk-in shower, two sinks, a makeup vanity and…

"That tub!" Amy exclaimed as she imagined stepping into what was more of a sunken pool. It was surrounded by tropical plants and candles, begging for an intimate night in.

"I thought you would like it. Look at the closet." It had an access from the bathroom and was the size of a car garage. There was a bench in the middle and a full-length, three-way mirror at the back. Alongside his suits hung gowns and dresses and a pair of green pants with a mended fly.

It struck her then, why he'd bought this magnificent house. She'd seen the headlines since their breakup.

King's Mistress Dethrones and Departs

Whatever magic had begun to surround her flashed into nothing. She was left with singed nostrils, and a bitter taste in the back of her throat.

She twisted her hand free of his and stalked through to the more neutral living area. Her adrenaline output had increased to such a degree that her limbs were twitching and her stomach ached. She couldn't decide if she wanted to spit at him or run to Baz Rivets again.

"I'm not making any assumptions," he began as he followed her.

"No?" she cried. "I won't live here. I won't be your—your *piece* in London, keeping your bed warm for when you happen to be in town."

"Stop it," he commanded sharply. "Think better of yourself."

His tone snapped her head back. He'd never spoken to her like that.

She folded her arms defensively. "I *am*."

"No, you're jumping to conclusions."

"What other conclusion is there?" She waved toward the closet.

In the most regal, pithy, arrogant way possible, he walked to a painting and gave it a light nudge to release a catch. It swung open, and he touched a sensor on a wall safe. It must have read his thumbprint because it released with a quiet snick.

He retrieved something before closing both the painting and the safe. Then he showed her a red velvet ring box and started to open it. "This was my grandmother's."

Amy was so shocked, so completely overwhelmed, she retreated in a stumble and nearly landed in an ignominious heap against the sofa.

She caught herself and managed to stay on her feet, then could only stare at him.

He gently closed the box. His expression became watchful, but there was tension around his mouth and a pull in his brows that was...hurt?

"As I said, I'm not making assumptions." He set aside the box—which made her feel as though he was setting her heart over there on a side table and abandoning it as he took a few restless steps, then pushed his hands into his pockets.

He snorted in quiet realization.

"Am I making another mistake? I don't like it," he said ironically. "I hurt you, Amy," he admitted gravely. "I know I did. I hate myself for it. Especially because I don't know that I could have prevented it. As long as you were interested in me, I was going to pursue you and we would have wound up where we did. That's been hard for me to accept. I don't like thinking of myself as having such a deep streak of self-interest."

He glanced at Amy for her reaction, but she had no words. He *had* hurt her. "I didn't exactly run away."

Until she had.

She bit her lip.

He nodded. "You hurt me when you left the way you did. That's not a guilt trip. I only want you to know that you can. I stood there telling myself I was doing us both a favor by letting you go, but I was so damned hurt I could hardly stand it."

"Nothing happened with Baz," she muttered.

"I know. He's a client and you don't have relationships with clients." He sounded only a little facetious. More of a chide at himself, she suspected. "It was genuinely shocking to me that anyone could hurt me so deeply just by standing next to another man, though."

She was reminded of their spat about jealousy when they were at his villa on the lake. When he had pointed out they were too new to have confidence in their relationship.

"I want you to come to *me* when you're hurt and scared and don't know what to do." He pointed to the middle of his chest, voice sharpening, then dying to sardonic. "And I want you by my side when *I* don't know what to do. I've hardly slept, I was trying so hard to work out how to spin things so you wouldn't be destroyed by all of this. I wanted to talk it out with you." He laughed at the paradox.

"And then I threw you under the bus," she said contritely, mentioning what was looming like a bright red double-decker between them.

"Don't apologize for what you wrote."

"I wasn't going to." But she clung to her elbows, deeply aware that she couldn't do that to a man and not have him hate her a little.

Which made her gaze go to the velvet box. Maybe it wasn't a ring. Maybe she *was* jumping to conclusions. How mortifying.

She jerked her gaze back to his, but he had seen where her attention had strayed.

"I want to marry you, Amy."

She ducked her face into her hands, all of her so exposed she couldn't bear it, but there was nowhere to hide.

"We don't even know each other, Luca!"

Gentle hands grazed her upper arms, raising goose bumps all over her body before he moved his hands to lightly encircle her wrists.

"I'm telling you what I want, that's all. What I know to be true. You don't have to answer me right now. I'll propose properly when you're more sure."

"What would our marriage even look like?" she asked, letting him draw her hands from her face. "We're not a match that people want to accept. We don't even live in the same country!"

"We can work all that out," he said, as if it was as simple as buying groceries. "My future is up in the air right now. The only thing I know for certain is that I want to be with you. So I bought a house here. We can date or you can move in. You can work or not. I'll get started with my own ventures. Maybe we'll move to Vallia at some point if it feels right. We can have a long engagement, so you have time to be sure. All of that is up for discussion, but I'd love for you to wear this ring when you're ready. I want people to know how likely I am to kill them if they malign the woman I love."

"You love me?" She began to shake.

"Of course, I love you."

"But you said..." She tried to remember what he'd told her about marriage. "You said you'd only marry someone vetted by... I'm not exactly the best choice of bride, Luca."

"If we make each other happy, that's all that matters. No. Wait," he corrected himself, cupping her face. "You are a bright, successful, badass of a woman who makes me a better man. How could anyone say that's a bad choice?"

"I make *you* better?" she choked out. "Hardly. You're perfect." It was annoying as hell.

"Exactly," he said with a shrug of casual arrogance. "I don't make mistakes. How could the woman I choose to spend my life with be anything but a flawless decision?"

"Oh, my God," she scoffed, giving him a little shove, before letting him catch her close. "You are a bit of a god, you know. It's intimidating." She petted his stubbled cheek before letting her hand rest on his shoulder.

"This is you acting intimidated? I can't wait until you're comfortable. You'll be hell on wheels once you trust me, won't you? Pushing back on me at every turn."

A pang of remorse hit her. "I should have trusted you and told you about Avery."

"It's a difficult subject. I understand."

"It wasn't just that," she admitted. "I was afraid of how you'd react. Afraid you would push me away and I would never have a chance to get to know you better. Then I was afraid you'd judge me. That I'd lose you." Her eyes dampened. "And then I did lose you."

"No, you didn't. I'm right here." A smile ghosted across his lips. "We had a fight, and we'll have others because we're both headstrong and used to thinking independently. But we'll always come back to each other. Wear my ring and I'll prove that to you."

"You really think we could make this work?"

"There's only one way to know."

"Okay." Nerves had her hand shooting out between them as though they were finalizing a deal. "I'll live with you here and—"

He yanked her close and swooped a deep kiss onto her lips, one that sent her arms twining around his neck in joy. One of her feet came off the floor.

He used the leverage of taking her weight to pivot her toward the bedroom door, then broke their kiss to walk her backward.

"Wait. I need more of that first." He paused and drew her properly against him, squeezing out all the shadows and filling her with a golden light while his mouth sweetly and lazily got reacquainted with hers.

They both groaned and she whispered, "I missed you."

She might have cringed then because it had only been a few days. They'd been dark ones, though. The beginning of eternity without him.

But here he was murmuring, "Me too," before sweeping his mouth across hers with more heat and passion and craving.

"Luca," she gasped as need sank its talons into her.

"*Sì*. I need you, too," he said in a rough voice and picked her up to carry her through to the bedroom in long strides. When he set her on the bed, he came down with her and framed her face. "I need you, Amy. You. Never leave me again."

"Stay and fight?" she suggested on a shaken laugh.

"*Sì.*" He pressed his smile to hers and they didn't talk again for a long time.

"Amy," Bea murmured. She and Clare widened their eyes with awe as they entered Luca's home several weeks later. Hers too, he kept insisting, but she was taking things slowish.

Not so slow that she didn't introduce Luca by his new title as she drew her friends into the lounge.

"This is Luca. My fiancé." She gave an exaggerated wave of her wrist to show off the ring. It was an oval ruby with a halo of diamonds on a simple gold band, not extravagant, but invaluable for its sentimental and historical significance. He had proposed properly the day she officially moved in with him. She'd been staying with him since he'd come to London so, even though it all happened very quickly, it felt right to make it official. She was beyond honored to be his future wife.

"Oh, my God! Congratulations." Bea and Clare hugged her nearly to death and grew flustered when Luca accepted their congratulations by brushing away an offer to shake hands and embraced each of them.

"I'm delighted to meet you both. And I look forward to getting to know you better, but Amy's been missing you. I'll let you catch up." He touched Amy's arm. "I'll tell my sister she can release the statement on our engagement."

"Thank you." Amy wrinkled her nose. She had asked him to wait on announcing it until she'd had the chance to tell her two best friends in person. "You spoil me."

"Nothing less than you deserve, *mi amore*." He set a kiss on her lips, nodded at the other two women and disappeared up the stairs.

Clare and Bea stood there with their mouths open.

"You've been busy," Clare accused.

"Oh, please. You both have plenty of explaining to do about your own whereabouts these last weeks. Come." Amy led them to where the wine and glasses were waiting. "Dish."

EPILOGUE

"AND THE WINNER for Most Innovative Integrated Media Messaging goes to London Connection, for their Consent to Solar Power campaign on behalf of AR Green Solutions."

Bea and Clare shot to their feet in excitement while Luca said a smug, "I knew it," beside Amy. He rose to help her out of her chair.

Amy needed help. She was eight months pregnant going on eleven. She had been on the fence about attending this ceremony, but it was her last chance for a night out and a rare opportunity to catch up with her best friends.

Of course, when they had planned it, Amy hadn't known she was pregnant again. It had been thrilling news to learn she was expecting their second child, but a surprise, considering it happened a mere twelve weeks after their daughter Zabrina had been born.

Despite how busy she was as a mother, Amy was keeping her hand in with London Connection. She had personally supervised the team who had come up with this promotion for the solar tiles Luca was producing with his partner Emiliano.

They were heading straight to Vallia in the morning, though. Sofia was not even engaged, let alone showing signs of producing the next ruler. This baby would be third in line for the throne after Luca and Zabrina. Everyone wanted this baby to be born there.

For the most part, Amy had been feeling good. Tired, but Luca was a hands-on father, and they had a nanny along with other staff who were always willing to cuddle a princess.

Even so, Amy leaned on Bea and Clare as they all went onto the dais. "Can you believe this is our life?" she asked them.

They were both beaming, all of them at the top of their individual worlds.

But as had always been their dynamic, both women gave Amy a little shove toward the microphone, letting her take the heat of the spotlight for all of them.

"I wouldn't be where I am without these two wonderful women beside me and the brilliant men who conceived these panels, most especially my husband who didn't dismiss me when I said 'What if we show your workers asking Mother Nature for consent?'"

A ripple of laughter went through the room at the unusual campaign.

"I'm the one who said she was out of her mind," Clare interjected, making Amy laugh because that was exactly what her friend had said, before assuring her she trusted her and encouraging her to go for it.

Something happened when Amy laughed, though. A release. She felt the flood of dampness and cringed with an agony of embarrassment.

"Ames?" Bea squeezed her arm. "What happened? Are you okay?"

"This is not a stunt for more publicity, I swear." Amy shaded her eyes and looked for her husband who was already moving quickly toward her, an anxious expression on his face. "But I'm about to make a scene."

"*Amore*, what's wrong?"

"I'm so sorry, Luca. My water broke."

As the whole room erupted, Luca gathered her into his side.

"Of course, it did," he said ruefully. "Never a dull moment. Do you know how much I love you for that?"

Her love for him was touch and go for the next few hours while she labored to bring their son into the world, but at dawn, when she woke to see him cradling their newborn, her feelings toward him defied words.

He barely looked any worse for wear despite the fact he'd been up all night. His love for her and their son glowed from his expression when he noticed she was awake.

"Do you know how much I love *you*?" she asked.

"I think I do," he said, caressing her jaw and kissing her temple. "But tell me anyway."

* * * * *

Clare Connelly was raised in small-town Australia among a family of avid readers. She spent much of her childhood up a tree, Harlequin book in hand. Clare is married to her own real-life hero, and they live in a bungalow near the sea with their two children. She is frequently found staring into space—a surefire sign she is in the world of her characters. She has a penchant for French food and ice-cold champagne, and Harlequin novels continue to be her favorite-ever books. Writing for Harlequin Modern is a long-held dream. Clare can be contacted via clareconnelly.com or on her Facebook page.

Books by Clare Connelly

Harlequin Modern

Redemption of the Untamed Italian
The Secret Kept from the King
Hired by the Impossible Greek
Their Impossible Desert Match

Secret Heirs of Billionaires

Shock Heir for the King

A Billion-Dollar Singapore Christmas

An Heir Claimed by Christmas
No Strings Christmas
(Available from Harlequin DARE)

Crazy Rich Greek Weddings

The Greek's Billion-Dollar Baby
Bride Behind the Billion-Dollar Veil

Visit the Author Profile page
at millsandboon.com.au for more titles.

Cinderella's Night In Venice

Clare Connelly

To the indomitable spirit of the people of Italy,
and for the city of Venice.

CHAPTER ONE

'OH, MY GOD.' Bea stared at the fast-spreading blob of coffee with a look of sheer mortification on her dainty features. 'I'm so sorry. I didn't see you.'

The man—at least, he *looked* part-man, yet he was also part-warrior, all broad shoulders, lean muscle and hard-edged face—stared at her with surprise first, and then displeasure. 'Evidently.'

'Please, let me—' She cast an eye around for something—anything—she could use to mop up the man's shirt, which now bore the marks of her early evening energy boost. 'I just made it. It must be hot. Does it hurt?'

'I'll live.'

She grimaced, looking around the office, but it was past six and almost everyone had left. 'Let me just grab—' She plucked a tissue from a box on a nearby desk, lifting it to his shirt and wiping furiously, all the colour draining from her face when she realised she was only making it worse. Little white caterpillars of tissue detritus were sticking to the coffee stain, damaging the obviously expensive shirt even more.

His fingers curled around her wrist, arresting her progress, and warmth enveloped her out of nowhere, shocking her into looking up into his face properly for the first time. At five foot ten she generally found she was almost at eye level with most men but not this guy. He stood a good few inches above her, at least six foot two, she guessed.

There was something familiar about him, though she was sure they'd never met. She'd definitely have remembered him. His face was angular and strong, like his body, a square jaw covered in dark facial hair—not a look that was cultivated or painstakingly trendy so much as a fast-growing five o'clock shadow. His lips were curved and bracketed on either side by a deep groove, like parentheses in his face, his cheekbones were prominent and his brows were thick and dark, framing his grey eyes in a way that turned the already spectacular specimens into works of art.

Her breath caught in her throat and she pulled at her hand on autopilot, a familiar instinct to deny anything approaching closeness marking her actions, her lips twisting in a silent gesture of rejection and simultaneous apology. 'Naturally the London Connection will cover the dry-cleaning fees,' she offered, her cheeks growing hot under his continued inspection.

He held up a hand in a gesture of silence.

Bea swallowed, taking a step back. 'I didn't see you.' *Quit talking, Captain Obvious*, she derided. It was a tendency she'd worked hard to curb—speaking when nervous was a girlhood habit she'd kicked long ago. Or *thought* she had.

'Where is Clare?'

'Clare?' Bea parroted with a frown, flicking a glance at her wristwatch to be sure she had the time right. Was her friend and founder of the London Connection—a woman who was as well-regarded for her business nous as she was for being notoriously disinterested in romance and relationships—dating this guy? She hadn't mentioned anything, but something *had* been different with Clare recently. Perhaps this explained it?

'Clare Roberts—about this tall, dark brown hair? Given that you work here, I imagine you've heard of her?'

Bea's eyes narrowed at his tone, which was innately condescending. It was on the tip of her tongue to tell the man that not only had she heard of Clare, but they'd gone through almost every major event in their lives, along with Amy Miller, side by side together. The three amigos, from way back.

'We had a meeting and I do not appreciate having my time wasted.'

'Oh.' She grimaced; the oversight was unprofessional and unexpected. 'She's not here.'

'She must be.' His nostrils flared as he exhaled a deep breath. 'Please go and find her.'

'Find her?' Bea felt like a parrot, but her senses were in overdrive.

'You know, walk through the office until you discover where exactly she is?' He spoke slowly, as though Bea was having difficulty comprehending what he was saying, when his English was perfect, albeit tinged with a spicy, exotic accent that was doing funny things to her pulse points.

Old feelings of inadequacy were stealing through her, making her stomach swirl with a very familiar sense of unease. She tried to banish it, forcing a tight smile to her face. 'Clare was called away on urgent business,' Bea explained, a pinprick of worry at her friend's inexplicable and urgent departure pulling at her. 'Is there anything I can help you with, Mr...?' She let her question hover in the air, allowing him time to offer a name.

His brows knitted together, and every cell in his body exuded impatience. 'You must be mistaken. This meeting has been scheduled for weeks. I flew in this afternoon for this specific purpose.'

Bea's eyes opened wide. If that was true, then they'd bungled something—badly—and that ran contrary to every instinct she possessed. 'Oh.'

'Yes,' he clipped, crossing his arms over his chest and glaring—there was really no other way to describe his expression— at her across the space. The air between them seemed to grow thick with a tension that made Bea feel as though she was continually cresting over the high point of a roller coaster. She dug the fingernails of one hand into her palm, forcing her expression to remain neutral with effort.

'As I said, something urgent came up, otherwise I know Clare wouldn't have left you in the lurch.' She waved a hand in the direction of Clare's office, the lights off, door closed. 'If you give me a moment, I can try to get in contact with her, or log into her calendar and see if—'

He scowled fiercely. 'This is completely unacceptable.'

Bea hesitated, unprepared for this man's obvious frustration. When he was cross, like this, his accent grew thicker, more mysterious and honeyed.

'I do not have time to be messed around, nor to accept excuses from some secretary or cleaner or whatever the hell you are. I've worked with Clare a long time, but this is—'

Bea felt as though she were drowning. She'd only been with the London Connection for a few months but she knew what this company meant to her friends. Not to mention what it meant to her! This PR firm was important to all of them and, whoever this man was, she didn't want to have a disgruntled client on her hands.

'Yes, very disappointing,' Bea inserted, belatedly remembering that while she was relatively new to the firm she was also the head of the legal department, having been recruited across from her senior partner role in a top tier City firm. She wasn't accustomed to being spoken to as if she were the dirt on someone's shoe. Modulating her voice to project an air of calm authority, she met his eyes straight on, her spine jolting at the clarity of their steel-grey pigment. They were like pewter; she wasn't sure she'd ever seen anything like it before. 'Unfortunately, standing here firing scorn and derision at me isn't going to achieve very much, is it?'

His shock was unmistakable. His eyes widened, flashing with an emotion she couldn't register, and then his jaw moved as though he was grinding his teeth together.

'I am not—'

She expelled a soft breath as she cut in. 'Yes, you were, but that's okay. I understand you're disappointed. And I am truly sorry that you've flown to London from—'

He said nothing.

She waved a hand through the air. 'Wherever, only to find Clare not here.' She turned, moving towards her friend's office. 'You mentioned that you've worked with Clare for a long time, so obviously you're aware how unusual this is. I hope you're able to overlook this rare mistake.'

'I am not generally in the habit of forgiving mistakes, rare or not.'

A shiver ran down her spine at the steel in his words. She didn't doubt for a second that he meant what he said. There was an air of implacability about the man that she'd felt from the minute he'd arrived.

Bea had, at first, thought his accent was Italian, but as he spoke more, her appraisal changed. She was almost certain he was from Greece—one of her favourite places in the world. She'd spent a summer there during her degree, and had fallen in love with the sun, the water, the history and, most of all, the anonymity. When she travelled abroad, no one knew Bea as Beatrice Jones, daughter of Rock Legend Ronnie Jones and Supermodel Alice Jones.

'Then I hope you'll make an exception just this once,' she implored as she flicked Clare's screen to life, typing in her friend's password quickly. 'Please, have a seat.'

He glowered at her without speaking.

A dislike for this rude, arrogant man was forming in her gut. She knew she couldn't treat any client of the firm's with disrespect but the way he was acting was truly unforgivable! So Clare had made an unusual mistake. It obviously wasn't ideal, but nor was it the end of the world.

'Now, let's see if Clare's left any notes here,' Bea murmured, reaching for a pen and tapping it on the edge of the desk.

'Should you be doing this?'

She frowned, looking up at him.

'I cannot imagine Clare would want just anyone accessing her files. There'll be sensitive information in there, including financial documents.' Suspicion crept into his voice. 'What exactly is your role within the company?'

She double-clicked into Clare's calendar as she prepared to answer him but, before she could speak, all the breath whooshed out of her lungs. His name hovered on the screen before Bea, in black and white pixels.

Ares Lykaios.

AKA the firm's most important, gazillionaire, global tycoon client. This man had a finger in just about every corporate pie imaginable. From transport and logistics to airlines to textiles and telecommunications, as well as casinos and hotels, Ares Lykaios had been given the nickname 'Gold Fingers' at some point because, as the press liked to say, everything he touched had a habit of turning to gold.

He was also a man both Clare and Amy had pulled Bea aside to warn her about.

'He's intelligent, demanding, ruthless and loaded. Deep down he's a good enough guy, probably, but he expects top level service—and doesn't suffer fools gladly.'

'Should your path ever cross his, which it likely won't because he only deals with Clare, do whatever you can to keep him happy—we can't afford to lose his business.'

Bea gulped, her eyes straying to the man's stained shirt with renewed panic.

'Mr Lykaios.' Her voice was strangled in her throat, unwanted nerves robbing her of any confidence. She shook her head, forcing herself to project professional authority. She stood, wiping her palms surreptitiously down the sides of her pencil skirt. 'I'm Beatrice Jones, head of legal here at the London Connection. Allow me to apologise once more—'

'No more apologies.' His eyes, grey like the strongest steel, seemed to lance her. 'I am not in the mood.'

'Then why don't you allow me to organise you a drink—perhaps something to eat?—while I familiarise myself with your file. I don't have Clare's or Amy's experience, of course, but I'm sure I'll be able to—'

'I have absolutely no desire to be palmed off with someone who, by her own admission, doesn't have the skill set required to manage my interests.'

Bea's jaw dropped. 'Mr Lykaios—' her voice shook a little with indignation '—please don't misunderstand the situation. While Clare isn't physically here right now, she's as involved in the business as always. As is Amy. You're in very good hands, I assure you.'

'Really? Because it certainly doesn't feel that way.' He pushed his fingers through his hair, which was thick and dark, cropped to the nape of his neck. The action conveyed obvious irritation. Bea's eyes, though, were drawn to his torso; she couldn't help noticing the way his expensive business shirt pulled across his obviously taut abdomen, the spilled coffee highlighting the definition of his pectoral muscles.

For as long as she'd known them, Amy and Clare had pushed Bea, telling her she needed to be more assertive. To tell her parents how she felt. To speak up about the hurt rendered in her childhood, and to stand up to the partners who'd pushed their workload onto Bea's desk, all the while claiming the hours for themselves. Her best friends had pushed her to speak up about *anything*, and Bea always smiled and nodded, knowing their words were kindly meant—and definitely not something she would ever act on. Yet anger rushed through her suddenly, and for one ghastly moment she was terrified of unleashing it all on this man.

With no Clare and no Amy in the office—and Bea new enough to still be grappling with clients and staff—she'd had a demanding enough day already. Straightening her spine, she gestured once more to the seat across from her. 'Please, take a seat. Tell me what you need.'

'What I need is for my usual PR manager to discuss the launch of a seven-billion-dollar operation in Mexico and Brazil. Do you feel you can discuss the nuances of that, Miss...?'

'Jones,' Beatrice supplied and, despite the tension humming between them, she was glad he hadn't heard of her. Glad for some of that Greek anonymity to be here in this room.

'Well, Miss Jones—'

'Please, call me Bea,' she suggested, aware that she needed to break down his barriers—and quickly—if she was going to have any hope of defusing this situation.

Bea. The name was short and brief, jarring and unpleasant. He dismissed it, wondering why she had chosen to use this moniker instead of her actual name. In the back of his mind, Ares knew he was being a first-rate bastard. He could see the pretty young woman was close to snapping point and it was an excellent indication of the kind of day—scratch that, *month*—he'd been having that he didn't care.

But 'Bea' had raised an excellent point. He'd come to Clare Roberts about three months after she'd opened the firm a couple of years ago, and he'd never once wavered in his choice to support her fledgling PR company. He'd witnessed her go from strength to strength and had always admired the work she'd done for him. Surely she'd earned a little leeway from him?

Yes, she had, undoubtedly, but at the moment all of Ares's leeway was in use.

His phone began to buzz in his top pocket.

'Now, just give me a moment, and I'll see if Clare's made any—'

He held up a hand to silence her, reaching for his phone and swiping it to answer. He understood the look of displeasure that crossed Bea's face at his obviously rude gesture.

Another tick in the 'bastard' column for him.

'Lykaios,' he barked into the receiver.

'It's Cassandra.'

He closed his eyes, his stomach immediately sinking. The fact that the nanny he'd hired for his infant niece was calling yet again was definitely *not* a good sign. The last time it had been to beg off the assignment, telling him she wasn't equipped to 'cope' with the child. Danica was only five months old! How hard could it be?

'Go ahead.'

'I gave it another shot, I did, but honestly, she's impossible.'

He tossed his head back, staring up at the ceiling as he rubbed his fingers across his neck. 'Isn't that what you're supposed to be trained to deal with?'

'I'm a nanny, not a magician.'

He could have laughed if he wasn't already at breaking point. 'Your résumé and references are excellent,' he reminded Cassandra.

'Yes, I know. But I don't generally work with infants, and definitely not infants like Danica. She needs—'

'Whatever she needs, she can have. But right now, I need you.' He compressed his lips, the sense of flailing out of control horrifying him, so he stood taller, straighter, staring directly ahead at the wall across the room. 'Double the agreed salary, Cassandra. Just do your damned job.' He hung up before she could answer, confident the exorbitant pay he was offering would be too tempting to turn down.

It wasn't Bea's fault, but when he turned back to her, his mood had dipped into oblivion.

'You are telling me Clare thinks so little of my business she has disappeared into thin air and left only *you* to help?'

The insult hit its mark. He almost regretted the words. It was beneath him to treat anyone like this. But the look of fire that stoked in the depths of her eyes was fascinating and somehow compelling. He moved closer, bracing his palms on the back of the leather chair she kept trying to wave him into.

'I'm not sure what your implication is,' she murmured, her cultured English accent irking him far more than it should.

'Aren't you?' he drawled, a mocking smile curving his lips. He wasn't amused though. He was frustrated and angry, just as he'd been since his younger brother had checked himself into rehab—thank God—after too many benders to ignore, stranding the infant Danica with Ares, a man completely unsuited to being responsible for anyone, let alone a baby. All his life he'd been taking care of others, and failing them at the same time. His mother. His brother. And now his niece. Why wouldn't they see that Ares was a loner—not meant to be depended on by anyone?

He dug his fingers into the back of the chair until the flesh beneath his nails turned white.

'Look, Mr Lykaios, I appreciate how you must be feeling. This is so unlike the London Connection. You mentioned you'd flown into London for the meeting. Will you still be here tomorrow?'

'I wasn't planning to be.'

Her delicate jaw moved as she bit back whatever it was she'd been about to say. Goading her was giving him the most pleasure he'd felt in weeks. Irrational and stupid, he knew he shouldn't bother, yet sparking off this woman offered a kind of tension release.

'If you could perhaps see your way to changing your plans, I can spend tonight familiarising myself with the campaign proposal and meet with you again in the morning.'

'And can you promise you'll offer me exactly the same level of service and expertise Clare ordinarily would?'

'Well, given that I'm head of the legal department and I'm more comfortable wading through hundreds of pages of technical contracts than analysing public relations, I can't promise *exactly* the same level of expertise, but I think you'll find me sufficiently well-informed.'

They stared at each other across the desk; it was impossible to say who was more surprised. Ares for having succeeded in stirring her into the outburst, or Bea for having given in to the sarcastic flood of words.

She clamped a hand to her lips, shaking her head. 'I'm sorry; that was rude.'

'Yes, it was,' he agreed, brushing aside her words and still taking a perverse pleasure in making her sweat. 'I have already told you though: I'm not interested in apologies.'

Her eyes swept shut, her dark lashes forming two perfect crescent fan shapes against her creamy cheeks.

'As for your offer—' he loaded the word with as much condemnation as he could, in no mood to be messed around after everything else he'd been through '—I'll take it into consideration.'

She frowned. 'What exactly does that mean?'

'That I'll see how I feel in the morning. Do your homework, Miss Johns. If I'm here, I'll expect you to be prepared.'

She hadn't even corrected him on her surname! 'It's Jones,' she'd intended to snap, but the words had died on the tip of her tongue, as they often did when confronted with people who treated her as he had just done. Instead, she'd watched him stalk away through the offices, his pace long and feral, anger emanating off him in waves.

She sank into her chair with a worried expression, staring at Clare's computer with wariness. She was *not* a public relations expert and she wasn't interested in becoming one, but she would protect this business with every fibre of her being. And that meant fixing this monumental mess-up, or risk losing their biggest client.

Not on her watch. It would be a long night, but that was nothing new to Bea. For the sake of the company, she'd do whatever it took. Even suffer through another meeting with that arrogant bastard of a man.

CHAPTER TWO

ADDICTION WAS A beast of a thing. While Ares's younger brother had struggled with it most of his life, following in the footsteps of their drug-addicted mother, Ares had never found that this demon resided within him. It was one reason he could pour himself a measure of Scotch some time before midnight, aware that one measure would bring him the sense of mental tranquillity he craved—but that one small measure would be sufficient. Unlike Matthaios, Ares had never drunk to excess, nor had he indulged in a penchant for drugs. Being in control was essential for him, and he sought that feeling whenever and however he could.

Drinking to excess or taking mind-altering substances was anathema to him. Perhaps that explained why he'd let his brother down so badly. If he'd shared the same proclivities as Matthaios, maybe Ares would have been better placed to help him. He might have seen the path ahead sooner, foreshadowing Matthaios's unravelling after Ingrid's untimely death. The loss of Matthaios's beloved wife in childbirth, coupled with the burden of a screaming newborn, had obviously been too much for a man who'd struggled with addictive impulses all his life.

Ares's grip tightened around the Scotch glass, his eyes chasing the lights of London's renowned skyline. It was a view he drew little comfort from—he far preferred the outlook from his home on Porto Heli. Yet tonight he stared across the ancient city with a feeling that this was the only place he wanted to be in the world.

Or was it that his home was the *last* place he wanted to be? With the screaming, unsettled, demanding infant in residence, and a nanny looking to break the contract he'd had her sign before undertaking the assignment, Porto Heli had temporarily lost its charms. Every time he looked into little Danica's eyes he felt a suffocating sense of failure.

The baby deserved better than him. Just as Matthaios had deserved better than to be raised by Ares, just as he should have been able to save their mother and hadn't. It was history repeating itself over and over and Ares had no doubt he was out of his depth. Which was why he'd hired the best nanny he could find, a woman who came highly recommended by several sources. It was something he would never have dreamed of affording as a teenager. He and Matt had been on their own: poor, starving, alone, and Ares had had to do the best he could—and live with the fact that it had never been quite enough. But for Danica it was different. He could provide her with a nanny for as long as necessary, making sure she would always have what she needed.

Except that Cassandra, the nanny, had been threatening to quit for over a week.

If he wasn't in Greece, perhaps human decency would force her hand. Perhaps she'd decide the right thing to do was stay. Perhaps she'd bond with the baby and decide she couldn't leave her. And perhaps a drift of pigs would fly past his window right now.

He threw back the rest of the Scotch, cradling the empty glass in the palm of his hand.

The meeting this evening had been the last straw. Clare Roberts from the London Connection was someone he saw a few times a year and corresponded with marginally more frequently. She was incredibly organised, professional and detail-oriented and he'd been needing someone like that today. He'd wanted to walk in there and know that everything was in order in at least one aspect of his life.

Instead he'd got *Bea*. Her name bothered him less now than it had earlier. In fact, when he heard it in his mind, he saw her cupid's bow lips framing the word and almost felt the soft rush of her breath across his cheek.

Something like shame gripped him as he recalled their inter-action, everything he'd said to her slamming into him now, so he felt as though he'd taken out the hell his life had turned into on the first person he'd found he could blame for something. Yes, he'd used her to unleash his tension simply because he'd reached his limits, and that had been inexcusable.

Right before he fell asleep, Ares resolved to fix that—he'd been unreasonable, but he could undo whatever damage his tirade had caused. Tomorrow was a new day; perhaps things would look better in the morning.

'Mr Lykaios, please, take a seat.' Any hopes Bea had held that the arrogant billionaire might have become less good-looking overnight evaporated into thin air when he strode into the of-fice a little after midday. Wearing a dark grey suit with a crisp white shirt flicked open at the neck to reveal the strong col-umn of his neck, he was preposterously hot. Seriously, was it necessary for him to have *that* face, and *that* body? Wouldn't one or the other have sufficed? Strong features, chiselled jaw, eyes you could drown in, and a body that looked as though he could run marathons before breakfast. Bea's physical reaction was inevitable. Her mouth went dry and her stomach swooped, but she told herself the latter was owing to nerves.

After the disastrous 'meeting' the evening before, she'd spent most of the night reading every single thing she could on the man and his business, as well as swotting up on the current pub-lic relations undertakings the firm was making on his behalf. And that was no mean feat. He was a dynamo in the corporate world, with interests all over the globe. The London Connection was currently overseeing ten specific campaigns, as well as doing ad hoc PR work as the need arose. There were four staff members dedicated to him full-time, with Clare managing their work diligently, as—according to the file on Ares Lykaios, he preferred to have only one contact rather than needing to get to know 'new people'.

Strike one, she was out.

As with the evening before, he ignored the chair, striding towards Bea instead, his pewter-grey eyes latched onto hers in a way that made her tummy flip and flop.

'Miss Jones.' He nodded in greeting and her tummy stopped flipping and started feeling as though it were under assault from a kaleidoscope of over-excited butterflies. He held out a hand and she slid hers into it on autopilot, but the second his fingers curled around hers Bea's eyes flew wide, locking on Ares's in shock. Sparks of electricity seemed to be exploding through her, heat travelling from the pads of his fingers to the centre of her being. Her breath was burning in her lungs and heat stole across her cheeks. She dragged her eyes away; it did little to alleviate her physical awareness of the man. Great, that was all she needed: to be *attracted* to this mega-client.

Bea had a minuscule degree of experience with men, and had always been glad she was far too plain and dull to attract anyone's attention. That wasn't strictly true—she'd been asked out on dates before, but the very idea of a relationship had made Bea feel as if her skin was being scrubbed with acid and she'd always backed off. Meaning she'd never had first-date tingles or a blush of attraction when a man she liked looked into her eyes as though he might find the meaning of life in their depths.

Whoa. Hold on. She didn't *like* Ares Lykaios. He was a client first and foremost, and her ingrained professionalism and diligence prohibited her from thinking about him on any other level. But even if she were inclined to fantasise—which she definitely, truly wasn't—how was she forgetting the way he'd treated her the night before? She'd grown up with enough spoiled, entitled, arrogant people in her orbit to know that these were her least favourite qualities.

Their hands were still joined. She pulled away jerkily, wiping her palm on the side of her trousers. That did nothing at all to stop the tingling in her fingertips.

'I had some refreshments ordered in,' she offered politely, pleased when her voice emerged cool and crisp. She sounded far more in control than she felt. 'Pastries, fruit, sandwiches. Please, help yourself.'

His dark head dipped in silent acknowledgement, but he didn't reach for any food. Instead, she watched as he lifted the sterling silver coffee pot and poured a measure into a mug. His focus was on what he was doing, which meant she could watch him—unguarded for a moment. As he poured the coffee, his sleeve shifted a fraction higher, revealing the flicking tail of a tattoo—cursive script, perhaps?—running up his wrist. Curiosity sparked in her belly; she tamped down on it post-haste. This wasn't the time to be wondering about his tattoo, or his body.

Except…she found it almost impossible to stop.

He was tanned, as though he spent a lot of time outdoors. Given that it was only April, it suggested he lived in a warmer climate than London, which was just starting to see some clear blue sky and warmth thaw the ground. Bea had always hated the cold. It reminded her of long nights at boarding school when the blankets had never felt quite warm enough. Or perhaps it was more the ice in her heart, an ice that repeated rejections—first by her biological parents and then her adoptive ones—had locked in place.

His lashes were long and thick, the kind supermodels would kill for. As Bea knew first-hand—she'd witnessed her mother's attempts at enhancement for long enough to understand what went into procuring such thick and radiant eye furnishings.

Unexpectedly, he jerked his gaze to her face and heat spread through her. Guilt too, at having been caught staring. She looked down at the tabletop in a knee-jerk response.

'Coffee for you?'

She nodded quickly, taking up the seat at the head of the table. 'Thanks. I've already had three cups this morning but if it weren't for coffee I have no idea how I'd get by. I should have credited my law degree to the stuff.' *Stop. Talking. For the love of God.*

He was the opposite to her. Silent and brooding, pouring the coffee with his long fingers holding the mug mid-air, replacing the pot then striding to her side of the table. Close enough for Bea to inhale his intoxicatingly masculine fragrance. Her gut kicked. What the hell was happening? She'd made an art form out of ignoring the opposite sex. Why was she suddenly obsessed with details like his tantalising cologne and curly eyelashes?

To her chagrin, Ares Lykaios, all six feet plus of him, folded himself into the seat directly to her right, so close that if she hadn't moved quickly their legs would have become entangled beneath the table. Her pulse was in frantic overdrive at the very idea! She wrapped her hands around her coffee cup and stared at the swirling steam rather than look at him again.

'Try not to spill it on me this time.' The words were serious but she felt an undercurrent of amusement in their throaty depths. It unsettled her completely.

'Shall we begin?' She didn't sound remotely cool now. Her words were still crisp, but closer to being whispered, as though she were afraid of him.

Get a bloody grip, Bea!

She conjured an image of Clare on one side of her and Amy the other, their smiling, encouraging faces providing much-needed strength. But there was also the spectre of fear—what would happen if she bungled this and lost the firm's most important client? Clare had ploughed all her inheritance money into this place, and it had finally given her a sense of purpose and safety. Bea could never let anything happen to the London Connection on her watch.

'Soon.' The word dropped between them, shaking Bea out of her thoughts. She frowned, looking at him.

He was studying her now with the same intense curiosity she'd focused on him earlier. Bea *hated* to be looked at and actively did everything she could to discourage that kind of attention, but what could she do now? Tell him to stop? Tell him she didn't like it? When the truth was, a strange kind of warmth was bubbling through her blood and her lips were parted on a husky breath of surrender.

Why was he looking at her, though? Bea was under no false illusions regarding her looks. Her adoptive mother was a supermodel and her younger twin sisters had inherited their mother's looks, all slender and fine-boned, blonde and blue-eyed, with skin as translucent as milk and honey. She'd known from a very young age she didn't compare and, even if she hadn't understood that, the articles the press had run through her teenage years—when pimples and puppy fat had attached to Bea with gusto—had left her in little doubt as to her physical merits, or lack thereof. After suffering comparisons to her mother at the same age, and then the twins, Bea had eventually developed a thick skin, yet only after years of painful arrows had already hit their mark.

But who cared about that stuff anyway? she reminded herself staunchly. She'd never wanted to be known for her looks—how vapid and dull! That was just genetic lottery. Far better to build a reputation based on hard work and effort. Tilting her chin, it was on the tip of her tongue to say something to bring their meeting back on track, except he was staring at her mouth now, and logical thoughts were suddenly impossible. Self-conscious, she bit down on the edge of her lip, wiggling it from side to side. She stopped when she saw the way his forehead creased, his thick brows drawn together speculatively.

'I—' She spoke because the silence was like the beating of a drum, resonating in the air around them and deep within her, demanding action—inciting a physical response which was new to her. Her pulse was hammering in the same way, rhythmic and urgent, low and slow, echoing throughout her whole body.

But her attempt at starting a sentence seemed to rouse him. He shifted, reaching for his coffee cup, taking a sip before returning his eyes to hers. Sparks flew through her.

'I came to apologise.'

It was the very last thing she'd expected him to say.

'What?' She shook her head from side to side, a bemused expression on her features. 'I mean, I'm sorry?'

His lips twisted. 'You stole my line.'

Her smile was instinctive. 'But—what for?'

'You don't think my behaviour last night warrants an apology?'

She looked down at the gleaming conference table, unsure how to answer. She wasn't going to tell Mr Millions-of-Pounds-in-Revenue that he'd been incredibly rude. Besides, he evidently knew that already.

'It's fine, honestly.'

'It is *not* fine. The fact Clare missed our meeting was not your fault. I shouldn't have taken my displeasure out on you.'

Her pulse began to race for another reason now. His apology was limited specifically to her. The company wasn't out of the woods yet. Bea still had work to do.

'I'm a senior team member of the London Connection,' she said firmly. 'I should have known you were expecting to meet with Clare, and I should have been prepared. It was an oversight none of us has ever made before. It's I who should apologise.'

His eyes remained glued to hers as he took another mouthful of coffee, so a shiver ran down her spine. Not a cold shiver, though. More like that delightful sensation one experienced when sinking into a warm, fragranced bath on a cool night. Pleasure radiated through her. She jerked her eyes away, forcibly angling her head a little so there was no risk of meeting his eyes again.

'Then we were both at fault,' he agreed. 'But to different degrees.'

Something like amusement snaked through her at his determination to take the blame for their catastrophic meeting the evening before. 'You don't strike me as a man who apologises often, and yet you do it well.'

'I may have an ulterior motive to earning your forgiveness.'

'Oh?'

'There's an event tonight, and I need a date to accompany me.'

Bea's pulse ramped up. She quickly looked down at the iPad on the tabletop, trying to remember every detail from the files she'd read overnight. 'I—can't remember seeing that,' she admitted belatedly, curving her hands around her own coffee cup to stop them from shaking visibly. 'Is that something we usually arrange for you, Mr Lykaios?'

His eyes widened and then he tipped his head back on a laugh that reverberated around the room, rich in timbre and heavy in amusement. She sipped her coffee, simply for the comfort its familiar taste would bring.

'I am asking *you* on a date, Bea, not to act as an escort service.'

Now it was Bea's turn to be surprised. 'Just to be your escort then?'

The humour was gone. Something far more troubling flared in the depths of his eyes. Despite zero practical experience with men she'd still watched enough movies to recognise sensual appraisal. Her knees felt as though they'd been pumped full of water and she was grateful she was sitting or she might have fallen down.

'The event is high-profile and will be covered extensively in the press. I'd prefer not to arrive alone. Think of it as a PR service.'

Every fibre in her body screamed at her to say no. All the buzz words she'd learned to fear and hate were in that sentence. Press. PR. Event. High-profile. She stared at her coffee, sure her face must look whiter than a sheet of paper. 'Mr Lykaios, I'm afraid that's not possible.'

'You're involved with someone?'

Her heart thumped against her ribcage. 'No,' she said before she could think better of it, denying herself a simple explanation for her demurral. 'Not exactly.'

'What does "not exactly" mean?'

'I'm not seeing anyone,' she grumbled, biting down on her lip once more.

'Even if you were, it wouldn't matter,' he said after a pause. 'This isn't a romantic invitation, Bea. It's just work. A small way you can make up for the inconvenience of last night.'

His words were a form of torture. On the one hand reassuring, because she didn't *want* to go on an actual date with someone like him—or anyone. But the fact that he was taking such great pains to tell her this wasn't romantic speared her with unmistakable disappointment.

'Or,' she murmured thoughtfully, 'I can go through the information I ascertained about your PR concerns, and you can go through your no doubt extensive Rolodex of past dates and choose someone else to accompany you.'

Oh, my God. She lifted a hand to her lips again, her eyes drowning in his as the whip of her words cracked through the room. 'I'm sorry. Again,' she mumbled, shaking her head.

'I meant what I said last night. I do not have any interest in apologies.'

The hypocrisy of that stung. '*You* came here to apologise.'

'I was in the wrong.'

'I thought we just agreed I was too.'

He dipped his head. 'I'm asking you to show me you're sorry. That's far more valuable to me than empty words.'

'By going to some event with you?'

'Precisely.'

'But why?'

'I've already answered that.'

'Because you don't want to arrive alone?'

His eyes narrowed. 'In part, yes.'

'Then, as I said, perhaps you could consider—'

'Inviting someone else?' He brushed that suggestion aside. 'I'm asking you.'

'I don't understand why.'

'Because it's tonight, and you're here.'

'I'm here?'

'Yes. Available and in my debt.'

Her lips parted. 'I wouldn't exactly say that.'

His teeth were bared in an approximation of a grin. 'Wouldn't you?'

Damn him. He knew what he was worth to this business, and he knew she'd do just about anything to keep him happy.

And he was right. She sensed the jeopardy they were in, and no way would she do anything to worsen it. If going to some event with this man was the price she had to pay to keep him happy then she'd do it. She'd do it for Clare and she'd do it for Amy, even though it was the last thing she personally wanted!

'I'd have conditions,' she mused.

'I'm all ears.'

He definitely wasn't all ears. He was all hot, handsome face and Greek god body. That was a huge part of her problem. She'd never found a man it was harder to ignore.

'This isn't romantic in any way. Under no circumstances will there be any touching, kissing or flirting.'

'Agreed.' Why then did his droll smile feel exactly like flirtation? Inwardly, she groaned.

'It's only for one night. After which you'll drop me home and that's the end of it.'

'Isn't that covered by rule number one?'

'I'm a lawyer; what can I say? Specificity is my stock in trade.'

'Fine,' he agreed, his voice warm with amusement. 'I won't look to seduce you on a technicality then.'

Fire burst through her. She could no longer sit at the table, so close to him. Instead, she stood, pacing to the windows that overlooked the bustling streets of London. She wore a slightly oversized trouser suit but the sunlight streaming in through the window highlighted her slender silhouette. She was unaware of the way Ares's eyes lingered on her body, appreciating her shape—her breasts, the curve of her hips—or she would have sprinted from the natural light as though a tiger was on her tail.

'And you'll forget about yesterday completely,' she added.

She wasn't looking at him, and Ares didn't speak for a while. 'I can't do that.'

She gaped, turning to face him. 'It was a mistake, Ares,' she pleaded, forgetting momentarily to address him more formally, then wishing she hadn't when that same look of sensual appraisal appeared in his eyes. She was drowning, and there was no lifeline within reach.

'Not your mistake, though.'

'Yes, my mistake,' she rushed to correct him. 'I was here, and I should have—'

He stood abruptly, a warning in his gaze now as he strode towards her, fast and intent. 'I will not forget yesterday but I will forgive it, so long as you agree to accompany me this evening. Do we have a deal?'

Her heart shifted in her chest. He stood right in front of her, so close that if a gust of wind blew her forward by a matter of an inch or so they'd be touching. She took a stilted step back, an awkward gesture that didn't escape his notice, if his slightly mocking look was anything to go by.

'Not quite.'

'More details?'

Her lips twisted in wry agreement. 'Always. I don't need you

to forgive me or forget yesterday, but I do need you to promise to give the London Connection another chance. Allow me
to have this meeting with you now, seeing as I spent all night
preparing for it. Or to call in one of my colleagues, who actually does most of the grunt work on your case and would be far
better versed and able to answer your—'

He pressed a finger to her mouth and every cell in her body
began to tremble. Her lips were like lava, her face bursting
with heat.

'No.'

Her stomach dropped but Bea was unable to feel as much disappointment as she should have. Instead, her body was intent on
making her aware of just how nice it was to be touched by him.

'I can wait until Clare returns.'

'I don't know how long she's away for, but I'm sure she can
do a virtual meeting at the earliest convenience.'

'I will arrange this.'

Bea's heart thundered.

'I have some conditions of my own.'

His finger lingered on her lips. She was glad; already she
feared its removal, her own rules be damned.

'Yes?'

'This is a ball. You will need to dress appropriately.'

More heat stole through Bea. A ball was so far down on her
list of favourite ways to spend time, she practically classified
it as a torture technique. She gritted her teeth. For the good of
the company and all that. 'Fine.'

His finger drifted slowly across her lips, moving sideways,
travelling down to her chin and lifting it slightly.

'I have drawn a line in the sand under yesterday. We do not
need to discuss it again. Come tonight, be a charming date on
my arm and I can promise you there will be no ramifications
for the unprofessional mishap.'

She went hot and cold all at once. Bea had no doubt he knew
exactly what he was doing—incentivising her cooperation with

the most lightly delivered threat. But why would he care so much about having her accompany him?

His fingers stayed on her chin, the touch light, so she wanted more, and that very idea had her lips parting. 'You're already breaking rule one.'

Was it her imagination, or did Ares move closer? 'You think this is flirting?' he asked huskily.

Her heart skipped a beat. She nodded, dislodging his finger and telling herself she was glad.

He frowned. 'You're wrong. This is business, and it's best you don't forget it.'

CHAPTER THREE

AS HIS CAR pulled up outside the London Connection offices, Ares wondered for the tenth time that day why he'd insisted on doing this. He'd initially gone to Bea's office intending to apologise and draw a line in the sand, leaving the matter behind him. Overnight, his temper had simmered down and he could clearly understand why he'd overreacted. Since his brother's spectacular breakdown and admission to rehab, and Danica's entry into his life, Ares had felt as though he were lurching from one disaster to another.

Clare forgetting their meeting had been the last straw and he'd taken that out on her hapless business partner.

An apology had been called for, but once he'd made it that should have been the end of it.

But the way she'd looked at him had stirred something inside him, a curiosity he couldn't quell, and Ares was determined to get the answers he craved.

He stepped out of the car, then was striding towards her office with a confident gait, pushing the door inwards and hailing the lift. The doors opened immediately; he stepped inside, watching as the buttons indicating each level glowed as he passed. When the doors pinged open to the London Connection, he acknowledged he was actually looking forward to tonight.

It was unexpected but, given it was the first time in a month he'd felt anything other than a slight sense of panic, he wasn't going to question the emotion. Ares Lykaios had used to feel like this before. Before Matt. Before Danica. He liked women, he liked spending time with them, and for the first time in a long time he felt a rush of pleasure at the prospect of a night spent with a woman who was intelligent and interesting. There was nothing more complex than that behind this evening. He was scratching an itch, giving himself a reprieve, distracting himself from the dumpster fire of his life for a few hours.

It was just after five and the office was still a hive of activity. He announced himself at Reception and was directed to Bea's office. He strode towards it, pausing to read her name on the door: Beatrice Jones. Beatrice suited her better. He knocked twice then pushed in without waiting.

And froze.

She was looking out of the window, her expression—even in profile—taut, but he spared her face only the briefest of glances. Instead, his eyes roamed her body, cataloguing the effort she'd gone to—and the effect it had on him. Her hair, a soft brown, had been styled into loose, tumbling waves that fell over her shoulders and down her back. The dress was subdued and yet that didn't matter. Somehow even the fact it was minimalistic— a simple black with a halter neck and a full skirt that fell all the way to the floor—made her look elegant and regal. When she turned to face him her expression was troubled, but she smiled as he strode towards her and any doubts about why he'd committed to this course of action fled.

'You're stunning.'

Her lips quirked. 'That sounds a lot like something someone flirting with their date might say.'

'Only a fool would deny the truth.'

'Flattery will get you nowhere, Mr Lykaios.'

He shook his head. 'No. Tonight you will call me Ares, as you did earlier.'

Her lips parted and the regret was back. Not regret that he was spending time with Bea, but that it was to be at a ball, surrounded by other people. This was a woman he would have enjoyed spending time with—alone. Now *that* would have been an actual distraction...

'And I will flatter you whenever I see fit.'

Her eyes darted to his and then looked away again, as though she were actually panicked by the very idea. More questions.

She paused at the reception desk and Ares was aware of the eyes that were trained on them—curious staff members unused to seeing a senior member of the team dressed like this. Her cheeks grew pink at the obvious attention. 'I'll have my phone for anything urgent. Please call if you need me.'

The receptionist grinned, gesturing to the lift. 'We'll be fine, Bea. Have fun.'

'So what is this event, exactly?'

'It's to mark the opening of a children's hospital. My foundation was involved in the funding.'

'Ah.' She nodded, mollified by that, as it made it all the more obvious that this was, in fact, a work commitment. 'I read about your foundation last night. You do a lot of work with children's charities.'

'Yes.'

'I didn't realise you were involved in any in the UK though.'

'Our foundation has many partners. Often our work is indirect.'

'Silent philanthropy?'

'Attention isn't exactly the point. I do not support charitable acts because I'm looking for praise.'

'Don't you?'

The grey of his eyes turned stormy like the ocean. 'That's a rather cynical viewpoint to have.'

She laughed, unexpectedly caught off guard by that. 'You're right, it is.' How could she feel otherwise, though, given the way her adopted status had been brandished by her adoptive mother only when it suited her purposes? If she ever needed the world to see her as a Mother Teresa figure, out would come Bea, some photoshoot or other arranged to convince the world of the Jones family's altruism.

She looked towards the car window, her mood slightly dampened by the bitter reflection. 'You didn't say where we're going tonight.'

'No,' he agreed laconically. 'You're new to the London Connection?'

His change of subject was swift and she frowned, but reminded herself that he was the client and she couldn't afford to offend him again. It had nothing to do with what *she* wanted— if she had her way she'd be home bingeing Netflix, definitely not on the way to some swanky affair with this Greek god brought to life.

Before she could respond to his question, he reached for the skirt that covered her knees, lifting it a little.

Surprise had her dropping her eyes, and then, as she followed his gaze, wincing. He'd noticed her shoes. Red high-tops with their trademark white star on the sides, a little scuffed at the toe. Coupled with the sheer black stockings she wore, she was well aware they looked ridiculous.

'In case you need to run away from me?' he pondered, his smile the last word in sexy.

It was the kind of smile designed to melt ice, but Bea's frozen heart was unlike anything Ares had ever known. She offered a cool smile in return. 'Oh, absolutely. A girl never knows when she might have to break a world record.'

'Usain Bolt, eat your heart out?'

'You better believe it.'

'Seriously, though. Did you leave your shoes at home? We can stop and get them if you would like?'

Bea didn't want to admit that she'd chosen to wear these

shoes out of habit—that at five foot ten she always wore flats to avoid looking like a giraffe.

'Nobody will see them beneath the dress. I'll be fine.' She just managed to avoid adding 'Won't I?'

But when she looked at him he was scrutinising her thoughtfully. She uncrossed her legs and rearranged her skirt so the hem covered her shoes.

'You were telling me about your job at the London Connection.'

'No, you were asking,' she reminded him, relieved the conversation had returned to something less personal than her choice of footwear.

He waited, watchful in that unnerving way of his.

'It was a few months ago,' she relented. 'Though Clare's been asking me to join for years.'

'You've known her a long time?'

Bea's expression assumed a nostalgic air as she thought back to her teenage years. 'The three of us went to school together. They're my best friends.'

'You're very different to Clare and Amy.'

She was, but his perceptiveness surprised her. 'In what way?'

'Many ways,' he said, the answer frustrating for its lack of clarity. The car turned towards the river. She couldn't think of any hotels here, but it had been a while since she'd ventured this way. Perhaps they were going to a converted warehouse?

'Is being similar to friends a prerequisite to friendship?'

He put his arm up along the back of her seat, his fingers dangling tantalisingly close to her shoulder. 'I couldn't say. It apparently works for you.'

That drew her interest. 'You don't have friends?'

He frowned. 'I didn't say that.'

'You kind of did.'

It was his turn to laugh. 'You're reading between the lines.'

'Do you mind?'

As the car slowed to go over a speed hump, his fingers briefly fell to her shoulder. An accident of transit, nothing intentional about it. The reason didn't matter though; the spark of electricity was the same regardless. She gasped and quickly turned her face away, looking beyond the window.

It was then that she realised they had driven through the gates of City Airport.

She turned back to face him, a question in her eyes. 'There's a ball at the airport?'

'No.'

'Then why...?' Comprehension was a blinding light. 'We're flying somewhere.'

'To the ball.'

'But...you didn't say...'

'I thought you were good at reading between the lines?'

She pouted her lips. 'Yes, you're right.' She clicked her fingers in the air. 'I should have miraculously intuited that when you invited me to a ball you meant for us to fly there. Where, exactly?'

'Venice.'

'Venice?' She stared at him, aghast. 'I don't have a passport.'

'I had your assistant arrange it.'

'You—what? When?'

'When I left this morning.'

'My assistant just handed over my passport?'

'You have a problem with that?'

'Well, gee, let me think about that a moment,' she said, tapping a finger to the side of her lip. 'You're a man I'd never clapped eyes on until yesterday and now you have in your possession a document that's of reasonably significant personal importance. You *could* say I find that a little invasive, yes.'

He dropped his hand from the back of the seat, inadvertently brushing her arm as he moved, lifting a familiar burgundy document from his pocket. 'Now you have it in *your* possession. It was no conspiracy to kidnap you, Beatrice, simply a means to an end.'

Clutching the passport in her hand, she stared down at it. No longer bothered by the fact he'd managed to convince her assistant to commandeer a document of such personal importance from her top drawer, she was knocked off-kilter by his use of her full name. Nobody called her Beatrice any more. She'd been Bea for as long as she could remember. As girls, they'd formed a club: ABC—Amy, Bea, Clare, and the 'Bea' had stuck. But her full name on his lips momentarily shoved the air from her lungs.

'Why didn't you just tell me?'

He lifted his shoulders. 'I thought you might say no.'

It was an important clue as to how he operated. This was a man who would do what he needed to achieve whatever he wanted. He'd chosen to invite her to this event, and so he'd done what he deemed necessary to have her there.

'Your business is too important to our company, remember?' She was grateful for the opportunity to remind them both of the reason she'd agreed to this. It had nothing to do with the fact she found him attractive, and everything to do with how much she loved her friends and wanted the company to continue to succeed.

'And that's the only reason you agreed to this,' he said in a deep voice, perfectly calling her bluff. Was she that obvious? Undoubtedly. Her lack of experience with men meant she had no idea how to conceal her feelings.

Fortunately, the car drew to a stop at that point and a moment later a man appeared, dressed in a smart navy-blue suit, opening the door.

He spoke in Greek, and Ares responded in English. 'Miss Jones will be joining me. Please have champagne brought to us after take-off.'

Bea stepped out of the car, her jaw dropping at the sight of a gleaming white aeroplane emblazoned boldly with the word 'Lykaios' down the side in bright red letters.

'Of *course* you have a private jet,' she said with a bemused shake of her head.

'It's a practical necessity. I travel a lot.'

She refused to be impressed. 'You know how bad they are for the environment, don't you?'

He gestured to the steps. 'I offset my footprint in other ways. The reality is, my schedule cannot be made to fit in with commercial airlines.'

A flight attendant stood at the top of the steps, wearing a navy-blue trouser suit with a crisp white shirt.

'Miss Jones,' she greeted, word apparently having reached her of the unexpected guest. 'Good evening, Mr Lykaios,' she added.

'*Yassou*, Andrea.' He put a hand in the small of Bea's back, the touch light and impersonal, yet nonetheless doing very personal things to her insides. Large leather seats were on either side of the aisle, then there was a bank of four facing each other. He indicated she should take one, which she did, spreading her skirt over her knees to conceal her shoes.

He sat opposite, one ankle crossed over his knees in a pose that was sexy and nonchalant and drew attention to his powerful legs. She'd realised he was wearing a tuxedo, of course, but, seeing him sitting directly across from her, the full impact of his appeal hit her like a freight train.

'You're quite ridiculously handsome, you know.'

He burst out laughing. 'Thank you, I think?'

'It's not really a compliment,' she hastened to assure him. 'Just an observation. I mean, you'd be crazy not to realise that.'

'I always thought looks were subjective?'

'Sometimes, but some people are just objectively attractive. It's a bone structure thing.'

'Is it?' he prompted, teasing her with his eyes and his tone.

'Absolutely. But don't worry, I've never really thought good looks were anything to write home about, so I'm not going to break our cardinal rule.'

'I'm glad to hear it.'

For the briefest moment, despite her best intentions, Bea's eyes dropped to Ares's broad chest. Her temperature spiked; her tummy flipped.

Andrea arrived, proffering two glasses of champagne, but Ares waved his away. 'Coffee, *efcharistó*.'

Bea took hers gratefully. She needed something to soothe her frazzled nerves. 'Your first language is Greek?'

He dipped his head in acknowledgement.

'Yet you speak English flawlessly. Did you study here in the UK?'

'No.'

'How did you learn to speak it so well?'

His lips twisted in a smile that hid emotions Bea couldn't interpret. 'Speaking many languages was somewhat of a survival skill. I got good, fast.'

She quirked her brows. 'I don't understand.'

'No,' he agreed calmly, watching as she sipped her champagne.

She let out an exasperated laugh as the engines began to roar beneath them, the plane starting to move down the runway. 'So what does it mean?'

He stood suddenly, filling the void between their seats with his large frame and masculine aura. He reached down, his eyes holding hers as he buckled her seatbelt into place, fastening it so it sat low on her hips.

She was breathless, completely unable to look away. 'I could have done that.'

He took his own seat again, fastening the seatbelt just before the plane took off, a rush of adrenalin flooding Bea as it often did when she flew.

Once they levelled off Andrea returned, brandishing a tray. The aroma of coffee hit Bea squarely between the eyes. There was a small plate on the side, with crescent-shaped biscuits topped with flaked almonds.

'After my grandfather died, my brother and I spent some time on the streets. We made our way to Athens, where tourists were plentiful. At first we begged—' he said the word with disdain and her stomach clenched for him, the pain he felt at admitting just that palpable '—but once I had a decent command of English and Japanese I began to do odd jobs for the hotels. I earned a pittance—less than begging, most days—but I liked it far more.'

Bea found it hard to catch her breath. 'I had no idea. I presumed you were—'

'Go on,' he prompted.

She couldn't look at him. Shame at her preconception—her *mis*conception—made her mouth grow dry. 'I just presumed you'd had an easier journey to success.'

'You thought I'd been born into a wealthy family?'

'Honestly, yes.'

He laughed. 'Why?'

'Because you are *so* wealthy,' she said, gesturing around the plane by way of example. 'Amassing this kind of fortune, the empire you command, having come from what you've just described... How did you do that?'

'I was extremely well-motivated.' He lifted the plate, offering her the biscuits. 'Have one.'

She took a biscuit automatically. 'I love *kourabiedes.*'

'These are my pilot's grandmother's recipe,' he said with a smile that might have disarmed a less well protected heart.

She took a bite, moaning as the flavour infused her mouth. Almond essence, but not so much as to be overpowering, ran through her, sweet and addictive. The insides were a soft, melt-in-the-mouth consistency, while the top was crunchy, so the texture was a contradiction she longed to enjoy more of. The dusting of icing sugar on top was the *pièce de resistance.*

Closing her eyes to savour the flavour more fully, when Bea opened them it was to find Ares staring at her in a way that drove every thought from her head. The full force of his dynamic attention was focused on her lips, his own mouth held in a tight line, his pupils large in his stormy grey eyes, his body tense, as though holding himself absolutely still against his will.

She lowered the biscuit to her lap, her heart hammering against her ribs.

'You eat that biscuit as though you are making love to it.'

The husky words sent her nerve endings into overdrive. If he had any idea she'd never made love to anyone—man or biscuit—what would he say then? Panic flooded her body, awkwardness at her inexperience overpowering her. She dropped her eyes, staring at the floor.

'It's very good.'

'As all lovers should be,' he responded.

Bea wished the plane would somehow expel her onto a nice fluffy cloud she could hide out in and pretend that Ares Lykaios wasn't talking to her about lovers and sex.

'I'm sorry your childhood was so difficult.'

She risked a glance at him to find a speculative look in his eyes, as though she were a puzzle he wanted to make sense of.

'Another apology?' he murmured, but though it was in the tone of a joke, it wasn't. At least, humour wasn't flooding the air between them. Instead, there was a raw, sensual heat that pulsed with throbbing need.

'A turn of phrase, I suppose.' Her voice sounded strangled. She cleared her throat. 'What other languages do you speak?'

He sipped his coffee, his eyes holding hers. His hands were so powerful-looking, and the cup so delicate, she had to fight an urge to tell him to be careful he didn't break it. She imagined a man like Ares might drink from a goblet cast from stone, rather than pretty white porcelain with a fine gold rim. He replaced it on the tray, the action accompanied by a musical sound.

'Italian, French, Spanish. Some conversational Cantonese.'

She blinked at him, lifting her fingers and counting. 'Plus Greek, English and Japanese… That's six and a half languages.'

He crossed his legs, his foot brushing hers, sending arrows of desire through her body.

'Yes.'

'And you speak them fluently?'

'I couldn't write a novel in all of them, but I can hold a conversation like this.'

'You make me feel quite inadequate. I speak passable enough French to order my favourite meal in a restaurant, and that's about it.'

His smile sent butterflies into her belly. 'Which is?'

'Duck à l'orange.'

Something like approval glimmered in his eyes.

'I first had it when I was about twelve. I remember the trip so clearly.' She didn't go into the details—Paris Fashion Week, her mother's doting on the twins and their matching couture, Bea just growing into her hormonal body, feeling too big and too awkward, the photos the media had picked up of her bored, slouching, reading a book in the light cast by the stage. She pushed those sharp recollections away. 'We went to a restaurant and the waiter recommended it to my dad. He ordered one and so I thought I would too.'

Inwardly she grimaced, remembering her mother's displeasure. *'Darling, duck is incredibly fattening. And as for the sauce—'*

'It was so good. I made a point of ordering it from then on, whenever we ate out.' And not just to spite her mother, though that didn't hurt.

'If only we were going to Paris instead of Venice. I know the best restaurant, on a small cobbled street in Montmartre. It isn't famous, and has no Michelin stars or other plaudits, but the chef cooks traditional food as her father taught her to: each dish is perfection.'

'I'll have to get the name from you,' Bea said, more captivated than she cared to acknowledge by the image he was evoking.

'The restaurant is tiny. If you wish to try it, let me know and I'll arrange things. Ordinarily you have to book in months ahead.'

Bea hid a smile behind her glass of champagne. 'But, let me guess…for you, the chef makes an exception?'

He grinned that charming smile of his, pushing back in his chair and regarding her with all of his focus. 'Always. And therefore for you too, if I ask it of her.'

Bea had been to Venice a handful of times, always with her family, and when she was much younger. She'd been too caught up in the push and pull of their dynamic to enjoy the place fully, and certainly to appreciate its beauty. As the plane began to circle the curious, ancient water city with its glistening canals and baroque homes, she craned closer to the window, pressing her brow to the glass so she could see it better.

The sun was low in the sky, not yet disappeared but obliging with an incredible palette of golden lights. Rays of orange burst towards them, and she sighed, something like calm settling over her.

As the plane touched down, she avoided looking in Ares's direction for fear the sight of him might diminish even the beauty of the spectacular sunset.

CHAPTER FOUR

'PUT THIS ON.' He held out a fine silk scarf towards Bea, pale pink and turquoise, unmistakably designer.

Bea frowned, looking down at her outfit with a frown. 'Why?'

He focused on her hair then lifted the scarf, wrapping it over her head, letting the ends drape behind her. His hands fussed to ensure it was tightly tucked and then he nodded, stepping back to admire his work. 'So you don't get windswept.'

Bea turned to follow his gaze towards a low black speedboat.

Of course it made sense, yet, years earlier, her family had taken a taxi to the airport, not travelled by water despite being in Venice.

With a sensation of fluttering nerves, she put her hand in Ares's so he could hand her down onto the boat. A man stood, wearing jeans and a dark shirt, a lightweight cardigan over the top and a beret on his head.

'Enrico,' Ares greeted, following Bea into the boat with a lithe motion. The engine purred beneath them and the sun cast spots of gold across the water as it dipped nearer to the horizon.

It was a warm enough evening but, as the boat began to move, Ares shrugged out of his tuxedo jacket, holding it towards Bea. She shook her head instinctively, afraid to be engulfed in something that was still warm from his body, terrified of being wrapped in his masculine aroma. Ares, though, wouldn't take no for an answer. Perceiving the fine goosebumps on her arms, he slipped the jacket over her shoulders, his hands lingering there a second longer than might have been, strictly speaking, necessary.

Bea concentrated on remembering that he was the most important client the firm had, and he was annoyed at having been let down. *That* was the only reason she'd accepted this proposition.

'Would arriving alone to the ball really have been so bad?' she prompted, having to shout above the roaring wind.

His eyes probed hers, his smile a sensual lift of one side of his lips. 'I prefer having company.'

'You're the opposite to me,' Bea said with a small smile, turning away from him. She presumed the boat would swallow her words, but if she'd stayed looking at him she would have seen a speculative glint ignite in Ares's eyes.

Murano was recognisable first, the low-set red and brown buildings familiar to Bea from a long-ago trip to a glass factory there. A few minutes later and the boat tacked south, then swept into a wide canal surrounded on both sides by Gothic-style buildings, the Moorish influence apparent in the curved windows and ornate decorative screens. She held her breath as they passed beneath a bridge, tourists above it waving and smiling. She waved back then looked to Ares instinctively to find his eyes trained on her. He hadn't waved at them.

She felt gauche and silly, focusing instead on the view ahead. Enrico, the driver, reached the Grand Canal, pausing to allow a water taxi to pass, then several gondolas, before he pushed across, moving in a northerly direction. She didn't need to ask where the ball was being held. A few hundred metres away stood a grand old palace, peach in colour with white detailing and a red tiled roof. Several balconies were adorned with candelabras and musicians playing string instruments, so the sound of an orchestra filled the canal. A crowd had formed out the front, including a group of paparazzi.

Instincts honed long ago fired to life. She straightened her spine and squared her shoulders, but it did little to quell the flipping in her belly. How she hated the press!

Ares's hand in the small of her back didn't help. Enrico slowed down the boat, pulling in behind another speedboat which was disposing of its elegant guests, a similarly attired driver helping them onto the platform. Ares moved to stand in front of Bea, his fingers working at the scarf until it was freed, but he didn't move away. He stood in front of her, staring at her, reading her, watching her, so her lungs refused to work properly and all she could do was watch him right back.

'Am I—?' She frowned, painfully aware of how often she'd let her mother down at events like this, and not wanting to do the same to Ares tonight. 'Do I look okay?'

His face bore a mask of confusion. 'Okay? Have I not already told you that you are beautiful?'

She shook her head, brushing aside his praise. 'I'm serious, Ares. I haven't been to anything like this in years.'

'Why not?'

Heat infused her cheeks. How to answer that? 'There hasn't been the need.' Her voice held a warning note.

'You look almost perfect.' He dropped the scarf onto a nearby seat, then put his hands on her lapels.

'Oh.' Belatedly she remembered that he'd provided his tux jacket for her to stay warm. 'Yes, of course.' She shrugged out of it as he slid it from her, standing where he was as he replaced it on his body. His scent still lingered though, and he stood close enough that his warmth did too. Enrico lurched the boat forward as space became available and Bea almost fell—she would have done so, had it not been for Ares's lightning-fast instincts. He shot out a hand, catching her behind the back, his legs like two powerful trunks securing them both to the centre of the boat, his body rigid as he drew her to him. It was the work of an instant, a quick movement to steady her, then he stepped away again, giving Enrico space to throw some ropes to staff atop the platform. The action drew the boat closer, and then Ares was holding out a hand to help Bea off.

She felt strangely shy as she put hers in his, glad when she reached relatively dry land and could relinquish his hand. The pins and needles stayed. Ares practically leaped from the boat, his natural athleticism easy to appreciate.

The sight of him was distracting enough that for a moment Bea didn't realise the photographers' lenses were trained on them—or rather, him—but when they began to call his name she instinctively shrank away, seeking to put distance between them.

Except Ares was too quick for that. His arm curved around her waist, drawing her to his side, fitting her perfectly against the muscular strength of his body, so that, despite the horrible feeling of being photographed, she was reassured by his proximity. Her mother's voice crashed into Bea's mind.

'Smile, darling. But don't show your teeth—your jawline is very horse-like. Straighten those shoulders—never hunch!'

It was over blessedly fast. Another boat pulled up, carrying a bona fide Hollywood celebrity, so Bea and Ares were allowed to walk in peace towards the double doors at the entrance to the famous palazzo. Hewn from ancient timber, thick enough to withstand any number of attacks, they were held open and guarded on either side by staff dressed in white tuxedo tops and slim-fitting black trousers. As they crossed the threshold, Bea used the move inside as an excuse to put some space between herself and Ares. After all, this wasn't a date.

The look he threw her was laced with mockery.

'This way.' He gestured across the tiled entranceway to a room that had Bea gasping at its splendid beauty. Paintings adorned the walls, either late Renaissance or Baroque, swirling scenes with clouds and angels, rippling torsos and long white-bearded men brandishing golden spears to offset the panel framing, which was a lustrous golden colour. Candelabras adorned the walls and ceilings, the floor was a polished parquetry. The room was filled with guests dressed in the most incredible ball-gowns and tuxedos, so Bea was glad she'd dusted off the dress she'd bought for one of her parents' Christmas parties in the hope of fitting in.

'This is a lot of people,' she remarked grimly.

'Yes.' His eyes skimmed hers speculatively; trembles ran the length of her spine.

'I've never seen anything so beautiful,' she murmured as they moved through the crowd. He dipped his head closer to hers so that he could hear her better. People were staring at them. She felt a familiar prickling sensation on the back of her neck, aware that, as they cut through the elegantly dressed guests, heads were turning, scanning Ares first and then Bea, apprais-ing her in a way that filled her veins with ice. She moved a little to the side, putting even more distance between them.

She didn't belong with him. She wasn't good enough for him.

It was just like being with her picture-perfect adoptive fam-ily. Bea was an outsider.

A waiter passed with a tray of drinks and Bea swiped a glass of champagne from it, her large hazel eyes almost the colour of burned caramel in the atmospheric lighting.

'Why did you bring me here tonight?'

His expression was quizzical. 'We covered this. I didn't want to arrive alone.'

She waved a hand through the air. 'Fine. But surely there are dozens of women who would have jumped at the chance to be your date?'

His lips flattened into a line that spoke of disapproval at her questions.

'So why not ask one of them?' she insisted.

'Because I do not want any complications.'

She frowned. 'What does that mean?'

He lifted his shoulders in a laconic shrug. 'It means that I didn't particularly want a date on my arm, just a companion. No expectations, no promises. No…romance.'

She nodded thoughtfully. 'And any woman you asked would have expected more from you?'

He grimaced. 'There is always that risk.'

'So you don't date?'

He nodded once. 'I date. But not in the way you might expect.'

She laughed unexpectedly. 'How many ways are there?'

His look was droll. 'There is dating because you believe in the fairy tale, and there is dating because you enjoy companionship and sex.'

Heat burst through her. She found it impossible to breathe. 'And I only do the latter.'

Bea opened her mouth to say something but a man approached them at that exact moment, and she was immensely glad. It was clear that the gentleman—Ares referred to him as Harry—was intent on having an in-depth discussion with Ares about an investment in Argentina. Bea shifted sideways, more than happy to leave Ares be—and to get her head together.

Ever since he'd arrived to collect her, things had been spiralling wildly out of control and yet his assertion just now that he didn't welcome the complications of romance only served to reinforce the parameters of tonight. After all, they weren't dating in the hope of the fairy tale and she certainly wasn't going to have sex with him. Which meant this was business, pure and simple. She should have felt relieved by that, shouldn't she?

Ares had learned, with difficulty, to control his emotions. As a child he'd frequently felt lost, angry, hurt, damaged and broken, and as a teenager he'd been terrified but he'd known he couldn't reveal that to Matthaios, who'd depended on him for everything. He'd also realised that the more emotionally he behaved, the worse things got for them. He'd always been big for his age and the sight of a glowering, thundercloud-faced seventeen-year-old had hardly endeared them to the tourists they were depending on for small change. He could control his emotions with a vice-like skill, except recently.

Since Danica had come into his life he'd felt that control slipping, and tonight it was basically non-existent. He watched Bea walk away, catching the tiniest glimpse of her shoes as her skirts swished with her, and wishing more than anything that she'd stayed by his side. He'd liked the way she'd felt there, tucked against him, her softness the perfect antidote to his muscular strength. Instead, though, she weaved through the crowd; an irritating number of other women were wearing black so that, despite her height and natural grace, she disappeared from view far too quickly.

Between scanning the walls for the world class art and making sure she looked busy and distracted so as to avoid entreaties for conversation, Bea was also aware of a young girl with blonde ringlets and a pretty pale blue dress. She stood to the side of a gaily laughing group. From time to time she'd make a foray into the group, tugging on the skirt of one of the women, only to be rebuffed with a shake of the head and a pointed finger back to the wall.

'I didn't know there was going to be a real-life princess here!' Beatrice remarked as she drew closer.

The little girl—Bea would have guessed her age to be six or seven—had eyes that shone when they lifted to Bea's face. 'A real princess? Is there really?'

Bea feigned bemusement. 'Aren't I looking at one?'

'Where?' the little girl asked, craning her neck to see behind her.

'Here.' Bea gestured to the girl.

She looked surprised then shook her head. 'I'm not a princess.'

'Aren't you? You could have fooled me.'

Pink spots appeared on the girl's cheeks and then she was giggling. 'I'm American. We don't have princesses.'

'Hmm. Technically, I suppose you're right. Yet I could have sworn you were. Are you having fun, Your Highness?'

The little girl's smile brightened and then dipped away completely. 'Um…honestly?'

'Of course.'

'Not really.' She ran the toe of her shoe across the lines in the parquetry. 'I hate stupid balls. They're so boring.'

'They can be,' Bea agreed. 'Do you attend many?'

'Way too many,' the girl groaned. 'Dad's job means we always have to come and I hate them. There's never any other kids here and nothing for me to do but stand quietly and wait.'

Bea nodded sympathetically. 'I used to feel exactly the same way.'

'Really? My mom says I'm ungrateful. She says she would have loved to come to fancy parties at my age.'

Bea wrinkled her nose. 'Everyone's different, but I always found this sort of thing incredibly tedious.'

'Did you have to come when you were little?'

'Oh, yes, all the time.' Bea shuddered at the memories. 'To parties and shows and I would get bored and then so tired that sometimes I'd fall asleep on a chair in the corner!' she half joked.

'What happened?'

'They stopped bringing me,' she murmured, not mentioning that once the twins had been born she'd been shipped off to boarding school and only seen her adoptive parents a few weeks a year.

'I wish mine would stop bringing me,' the girl said a little too loudly, so her mother turned in preparation to scold her, pausing only when she saw Bea in conversation with the child.

'You know, I used to keep myself busy by playing maths games. Want me to show you what I mean?'

The girl nodded eagerly.

'Well, first of all, I'd count all the women wearing pink.' She frowned as she surveyed the crowd. 'There aren't very many tonight, so that won't take you long. Once you've done that, look for men wearing black shoes. Then women wearing tiaras, then men with ties versus bow ties. You'd be amazed at how it helps to pass the time.'

Having spent almost thirty minutes locked in conversation with Harry, expecting Beatrice to reappear at his side at any minute, he'd moved beyond frustration and onto irritation when she seemed to have simply disappeared into thin air.

He'd circumnavigated the room for another twenty minutes, being interrupted too many times to count to make short conversation with acquaintances and business contacts. As he'd scanned the room, his eyes had landed on something that made very little sense, and he'd drawn his gaze back.

A woman sitting on the ground at a ball was a strange sight indeed, so he knew somehow instinctively that it could only be Bea. Sure enough, as he moved closer, assiduously avoiding several more attempts to draw him into conversation, he saw that she wasn't, in fact, sitting so much as crouching beside a little girl, who was cross-legged beside her. They were staring into the crowd, a matching expression of concentration on their faces. Bea pointed at something and the little girl frowned as she followed the gesture, then she burst out laughing.

Something grabbed at his chest at the unexpected sight and his impatience changed gear. No longer irritated by her disappearance, he was now irritated by the fact that there were so many people surrounding them when he wanted to be all alone with her.

It was a warning bell he heeded. He hadn't brought Bea to be distracted by her. He'd been honest with her earlier when he'd explained that he didn't want any complications. Perhaps ending this night prematurely was the wisest course of action.

'Ares—' she smiled to cover the rapid beating of her heart as she stood up '—there you are.'

'You sound as though you've been looking for me, but I suspect this is not the case.'

A guilty heat stole along her cheeks. 'You were busy,' she explained, fidgeting her hands in front of her.

'Yes. Harry is a partner in a project—'

'In Argentina, I gathered.'

'Indeed.'

'Who's this?'

Bea turned to the little girl. 'Emily, this is a friend of mine. Ares Lykaios, this is Her Royal Highness Princess Emily of Connecticut.'

'Hello, Your Highness,' he volleyed back without missing a beat. 'I'm pleased to meet you. Thank you for keeping Bea entertained while I was talking to someone else.'

'You're welcome.' Emily grinned. She pointed to his shoes. 'Thirty-nine!'

Bea nodded. 'You're right! Well done.'

'Are you enjoying yourself?' Ares asked.

Bea smiled at Emily. 'We're having a good time, aren't we?'

Emily nodded. 'Much better.'

Ares compressed his lips. Children made him uneasy; they always had done. Bea, on the other hand, seemed completely at ease with this little person. 'We can leave any time. If you're ready?'

Bea's eyes lit up. 'Really? You don't have to stay?'

'No. I've made an appearance; that's all that was expected of me.'

She looked down at Emily apologetically.

'It's okay.' The little girl pressed her hand to Bea's. 'I'll be fine. I'm looking for wigs next.' Emily wiggled her pale eyebrows so Bea laughed softly.

'That's a delicate one. Make sure you don't point or count too loudly.'

Emily tapped the side of her nose. 'Promise.'

Ares's hand was firmly insistent as he guided Bea away from Emily. 'A friend of yours?'

'A new friend.' Bea sighed. 'A lovely little girl rather too young to be dragged to events like this.'

'It's not exactly a child-focused evening.'

'She reminds me of how much I used to hate this kind of thing,' Bea said with a shiver.

'Used to?' he prompted, and again she was struck by how insightful he was.

'You caught me. I still do, generally speaking. In fact, you'd normally have to drag me kicking and screaming to something like this, so you should take it as an indication of how important your business is to the London Connection that I'm here with you tonight.'

She wondered why the words felt slightly disingenuous. As if to prove that he knew she was lying, he lifted a hand, catching a thick wave of brown hair and tucking it behind her ear. A *frisson* of awareness shimmied down her spine.

She gulped, trying to remember what she was saying, desperately hoping her voice emerged with a semblance of control.

'As a child, I was made to attend so many functions with my parents. Parties like this, with fancy clothes and beautiful music, and I came to hate them. Everything about them. The food, the forced laughter, the social interactions.' She lifted her shoulders. 'Give me a good book and a quiet living room and I'm all set.'

'And do you wish you were in your living room now, instead of here?'

The challenge lay between them. She feared they both knew the answer to that...

'I...am having a better time than I anticipated,' she said unevenly.

It was like stepping off the edge of a cliff and into an abyss. She was in freefall, losing herself in the depths of his silver-grey eyes, with nothing to hold onto. He stared at her long and hard and turned away from her, but not before he uttered under his breath, 'As am I.'

CHAPTER FIVE

THE GONDOLA HAD been a mistake. He should have refused. But her eyes had been so hopeful as she'd looked out on the canal, watching the little boats bobbing past, and before he'd been able to stop himself Ares had heard himself say, 'Would you like to take a ride?'

Of course, he'd simply been being polite. She'd smiled awkwardly and for a moment he'd held his breath, thinking she'd say no, but then she'd nodded, a simple shift of her head.

It was tighter than he'd imagined in the boat, the seat designed for lovers, so they had no choice but to sit hip to hip, her body lightly pressed to his side, her warmth permeating him. 'You're good with children.' The words were cool, and he was glad. This wasn't a date—she wasn't a woman he was looking to bed.

'Thank you.'

Silence stretched between them, long and taut. He should continue it, ignore her, get this evening over. But again, almost against his volition, he asked, 'Do you have siblings?'

Her smile seemed to communicate something he couldn't understand. Uncertainty? Pain? 'My adoptive parents had twin girls when I was seven. Annelise and Amarie.'

'So you must have been given plenty of opportunities to

babysit?' The moon overhead was almost completely full, only a fingernail snippet missing from one side. It cast the canals of Venice in a glorious silver light, the water lapping gently at the edges of the wooden boat.

'I went to boarding school shortly after the girls were born. I really only saw them during the holidays—a few weeks a year at most.' Her words were robotic, as though she'd practised the line many times.

'How old were you when you were adopted?'

Her fingers fidgeted in her lap; she stared down at them, the matte black nail polish the perfect complement to her dress. 'Three.'

He waited for her to continue and was eventually rewarded with a shaky explanation.

'Ronnie and Alice tried to fall pregnant for a long time. Years and years of IVF and fertility treatments, all with no luck. Adoption was their last resort—definitely not the kind of parenthood Alice had envisaged, but better than nothing.'

Ares was very still, the rejection she was describing making him pity the little girl she'd been.

'The twins were a miracle. She was in her forties when she conceived, and without fertility assistance, after years of being told it would never happen. You can imagine how doted on the girls were.'

'And you felt pushed aside?'

Bea's smile was iced with years of pain. 'I felt that way because I was.' She fixed him with a gaze that was like steel, and yet it didn't deter him. He could see through it easily. 'Anyway, I don't really like to talk about my family.'

But he wouldn't let her turn away. His finger caught her chin, guiding her face back to his, and now he was so close to her, grey eyes morphing to silver in the moonlight reading her as he had been all evening. What the hell was he doing? She was pushing him away with her words, and he should let her do exactly that. Not caress her face and draw her towards him. 'Families can be complicated.' His voice was throaty.

'Yes.' Just a whisper, the word caught on the air, brushing across his cheek towards his ear. She was a beautiful woman, but he hadn't brought her to Venice with this in mind. Yet sitting in the gondola, his body so close to hers, he felt a drugging desire to throw sense to the wind and act as though she was any other woman. What harm could come from that?

'Amy and Clare are my family.' It was a strange thing to say. Was she simply explaining that she didn't need her adoptive parents and siblings? Or was she looking to remind him—and herself—of her best friends and business partners?

The gondola moved to the side to let another boat past, and some waves formed in its wake that caused the craft to rock from side to side, lurching Bea towards Ares. She made no attempt to resist the gravitational movement and he was glad.

Her hands lifted to his shirt; her face stayed tilted to his.

He stared at her, torn between doing the right thing and getting the hell back to Enrico and sending her back to London, or doing what he desperately wanted and closing the distance between them completely. His eyes dropped to her lips, staring at their pouting form, aching for her. She lifted one finger to her mouth, tracing the line his eyes were taking, her fingertip trembling at the intimate gesture. It was an invitation and an entreaty; what she wanted was blatantly obvious.

And so? Why fight this? He'd explained to her that he didn't believe in romantic relationships. He'd been explicit in telling her that all he looked for when he dated a woman was sex. If she was interested in him, and what he was offering, then he'd be a fool to resist. Right?

'Tell me, Bea, did you have a rule about kissing?'

Her breath hitched in her throat at his low-voiced question. She tried to think straight but it was almost impossible. 'We agreed no kissing.'

'I think you said no touching too,' he suggested, dropping the hand that held her chin to her knee, where he cupped her flesh there, sending sharp arrows of pleasure through her skin. She leaned infinitesimally closer to him, her skin lifting in a veil of goosebumps.

'And definitely no flirting.'

'Tell me, Counsellor, how does one go about revising the rules?' he asked.

Her mouth was dryer than dust. She was on the precipice again, nudging closer to the edge even when she knew she should turn and walk away.

'You're a client,' she reminded herself and him, saying the words aloud in a desperate attempt to bring sanity back to her mind.

'Not tonight.' His head dropped closer to hers, so close that if she pushed up she could take his lips for her own. Blood formed a pounding cacophony in her ears, an orchestra of need like a tidal wave she was cresting over.

'No? What are you then?'

She sucked in a gulp of breath but the stars in her eyes didn't go away.

'They are your rules,' he responded without answering directly. 'To break or ask me to abide by. I'm in your hands.'

The imagery conjured was too much. How could she explain to someone like Ares Lykaios that she was nothing like his usual companions? How could she explain to him that she didn't simply go on dates with handsome strangers and kiss them beneath the bright Venetian moonlight? How could she explain to him that she was, of all things, a twenty-nine-year-old virgin?

'I don't think this is a good idea,' she whispered. Because surely whatever happened next would be wildly disappointing for him—and possibly earth-shattering for her. The imbalance in their experience was terrifying. 'I'm really, really not your type.'

Despite the tension thickening between them, his smile

reached inside and calmed Bea's nerves. Her body was, if anything, moving closer to his.

'If you want to retain our original agreement, then I'll respect that. But make the choice based on *your* feelings, not what you believe mine to be. I know exactly what I want right now.'

Her heart lurched completely off-balance. 'And that is?'

He moved so close that their lips brushed and whatever willpower she had left to resist him disappeared completely. 'I want to spend the night with you.' His finger ran along her cheek, and she was trembling against his body, the desire he was invoking too much to resist. 'Just one night, nothing more.'

It sounded so simple! So easy! Sex, plain and simple—except nothing with Ares Lykaios would ever be plain.

'But I'm—' The words trailed into nothing.

Then, to hell with the rules, he was kissing Bea and she was kissing him back, their lips enmeshed in a way that blew all Bea's preconceptions of such a thing well out of the water. Unlike the passionless encounters she'd had in the past, every movement of his mouth stirred flame in her blood, so that she couldn't sit still. If she did, the fire would engulf her; she had to move.

The boat rocked from side to side as she pushed up into his lap, needing to be closer to him, so much closer than their clothes and public location allowed. His hands moved inside his jacket that she wore, wrapping around her slender waist, holding her there as he drove his tongue into her mouth, the rhythm fast and urgent, leaving her in no doubt as to just how badly he did, in fact, want her. One hand on her hip moved lower, cupping her bottom, and she groaned, flinching a little at the completely foreign contact but welcoming it too, needing it—and him—in a way that shook her to the core of her being.

She often felt too tall, too ungainly, but in Ares's hands she was dainty and petite, his size engulfing her, his strength dominating her completely as he shifted and by degrees moved her with him, so she was straddling him, the voluminous skirts

of her dress forming a circle around them, her fingers pushing through his hair and joining behind his neck, her breasts
crushed to his chest as his mouth continued to torment hers,
his expertise and experience meaning that the kiss alone had
the power to make her stomach swoop all the way to her toes.

But then he rolled his hips, lifting a little on the seat of the
gondola, so she felt something unfamiliar and unmistakable
between her legs, his hard arousal striking panic into her heart
even as ancient feminine instincts came to the fore, reassuring
her that she'd know what to do when the time came. Her hand
dropped to his shoulder, then lower still to his shirt, her fingers
curling into the fabric and squeezing, holding on tight.

He tore his mouth away but held her head steady where it
was, calling Italian words over his shoulder.

He was kissing her again before she could ask him what he'd
said, but the gondolier took a side canal, so she could only presume Ares had given a change of course. And, with any luck,
to a hotel!

Why was it that he, of all people, could affect her like this?
She'd spent her entire adult life believing she was immune to
the opposite sex and yet here he was, stirring her to a fever pitch
on a boat in the middle of Venice.

'To hell with the rules,' he growled.

His hand pushed under the fabric of her dress, resting on her
thigh. He kept it there, not pushing higher, as though he sensed
it was a limit for her, that she needed time to process that sensation first, to reconcile herself to the intimacy before he took
another. And God, she hoped he would take another and another
and another. Sparks of anticipation flew through Bea's blood as
she realised what was about to happen: Finally, she was going
to have sex. She was going to lose her virginity, so she could
have some understanding of what all the fuss was about. And
with Ares Lykaios she knew it would be a night to remember!

A low, throbbing noise was sounding in her ears, running
through her body, vibrating in her chest. She attributed it to her

heart until her brain kicked into gear. Pulling back from him and staring—dazed—into his hooded grey eyes, she pressed a hand to his torso. 'You're ringing.'

He looked as swept up by passion as she felt. He stared at her for a beat before the words resulted in action. He lifted his shoulders, pulling her closer. 'I don't care.'

She moaned softly as he parted her lips with his, sliding his tongue in more slowly this time, the enquiry gentle, but no less urgent. She rolled her hips, a primal wisdom beating in her heart, showing her how to answer her needs, how to act.

The throbbing began once more, vibrating through Bea's chest, so she pushed away, her breath laboured, her eyes sparkling. 'Answer it, then switch the damned thing off.'

His brows flexed and with a forceful exhalation he reached into his pocket. A frown crossed his face as he glanced at the screen, and then he swiped it to answer, his other hand still on her thigh, his thumb stroking gently over the skin there, as though he knew he could keep her in his sensual thrall with that slight contact alone.

'Yes?' Frustration emerged in the clipped tone, taking Bea back to their first meeting, when he'd spoken to her like that. She was glad not to be on the receiving end of his impatience any more, and pitied whoever had called.

They were in close proximity and she could hear the string of high-pitched words without being able to understand any of them, owing to the language in which they were being spoken. His thumb stopped moving; the weight of his hand on her thigh grew lighter.

He barked something into the phone in Greek, his eyes on Bea's face without, she suspected, seeing her. Ares was gentle yet insistent as he dislodged her from his lap, shifting her back to the seat at his side, his features looking as carved from granite as ever but harsher now so they were jagged and sharp. For no reason she could think of, a shiver ran down Bea's spine.

He said something short and then disconnected the phone. It

was the only movement he made; the rest of him was completely still. Shocked? She couldn't tell. It only lasted a small beat of time and then he was speaking to the gondolier once more.

'Ares? What is it?' Her voice was still husky, the passion flooding her veins slow to recede.

When he looked at her it was almost as though he'd forgotten she was there. 'Beatrice,' he muttered. Her heart lurched. She'd been treated as an inconvenience often enough to immediately understand his meaning.

'I have to return home, immediately. It cannot be delayed.'

Concern eclipsed her own feelings of rejection. 'Has something happened?'

A grimace was his only response. Mentally she derided herself for asking such a stupid question. *Obviously* something had happened. But what?

Everything felt different now. The buildings of Venice still sat on either side of the canal but now it was as though they were looming watchfully, bathed in too-bright yellow rather than a gentle gold, and even the lapping of the water seemed to inflame Bea's uncertainties and anxieties.

They had not travelled far and, using a series of shortcuts, the gondolier had them back at the speedboat a short time later. He pulled up to the pontoon, moving to help Bea disembark, but Ares was there first, his strong hand guiding her out of the boat even as his face bore an unrecognisable mask of stony intent. Another shiver spread through her as she shrugged out of his jacket and looked around behind her.

'You go.' She nodded towards the sleek black speedboat. 'I'll catch a water taxi to a hotel.'

His frown was just the slightest shift of his lips, then his hand was on her back, drawing her with him. 'I doubt any will have space available. Between the ball and the opera, Venice is packed.'

'Surely somewhere—'

'Nowhere reputable.'

She nodded, relying on his better knowledge of Venice at that point, stepping into the speedboat with him. At the airport, she could arrange a flight to London. Disappointment was a visceral ache rapidly spreading through her. She refused to think about where the night had been heading only moments earlier; she refused to think about the heat still pooling in her abdomen, demanding fulfilment. She refused to imagine Ares naked on top of her, and what the weight of his body would feel like over hers; she refused to go down that path even when it was dragging at her every second of the torturous, silent boat ride to the airport.

Relief flooded Bea's veins when they arrived; she wanted Ares more than she could say, but at the same time she desperately needed to get away from him so she could process what had just happened.

He walked quickly away from the speedboat and she had to take long strides to keep up. He was taking the same path they'd trodden earlier—a partly concealed sign declared *'Aerei Privati'*. Private Aircraft.

She stopped walking and, despite the fact he was marginally ahead of her, some sixth sense must have alerted him to the change because he halted and turned to her. 'Come. I must be quick.'

His accent was more noticeable, his words rushed with something like panic.

'You go on. I'll make my way to the terminal and see about getting a ticket to London.'

His brow furrowed, as though he hadn't expected that. 'There won't be any commercial flights at this time.'

Beatrice glanced at her wristwatch, groaning because of course that was true! It was almost midnight. She looked around with a growing sense of unease. 'Then an airport hotel—' She gestured to a low building in the distance bearing a familiar logo, associated with three-star hotels the world over.

'No.'

She startled at the word. 'I beg your pardon?'

He compressed his lips, turning to her in a manner that made Bea feel as if she were a recalcitrant child. She stood her ground.

'I do not have any time to spare, Beatrice. I cannot take you to that hotel, and I will not leave you to make your own way there. So you need to come with me.'

'Where to?'

'My home.'

'I don't even know where that is.'

'Does it matter?'

She glared at him with hauteur.

He sighed. 'In Greece. It is an emergency; I do not have time to argue with you.'

'Then don't argue with me,' she said quietly, practically on the brink of tears at how the night had turned out. 'You do your thing and I'll do mine. I'm a big girl, more than capable of getting myself to that hotel and checking in for the night.'

He shook his head. 'I won't have it on my conscience if something goes wrong, and I do not have the time to see you there safely myself.'

'We're going around in circles here, Ares, because I've already said I'll be fine, and you're saying you don't know that for sure. But I can see no reason to come with you, especially when something's obviously happened that requires your attention, so, short of kidnapping me, you're going to have to accept my decision.'

He stared at her, his bright eyes bitter; she could feel her skin burning under their assault. And then he moved, taking one step towards her and lifting her easily, as though she weighed nothing, hoisting her over his shoulder. She was too shocked to make a noise; he had already resumed his earlier path and taken several steps before she squawked in indignation, 'What the hell are you doing?'

'Kidnapping you.' The words obviously came from between gritted teeth. 'Just as you suggested.'

CHAPTER SIX

HE HAD TO give his flight crew credit. They acted as though seeing him arrive hauling a very cross woman over one shoulder was a totally everyday occurrence, running through all the normal pre-flight checks without batting an eyelid. For his part, Ares was grateful for their professionalism, and only slightly shocked by his own behaviour towards Bea.

It hadn't been about wanting to kidnap her and drag her to his home, even though such thoughts had been tormenting him all evening, so that he'd imagined her against the sheets of his bed, her languorous hazel eyes staring up at him, begging him to make love to her.

This had been a question of practicality alone.

The call from his housekeeper, Xanthia, had pushed all other considerations aside. Cassandra, the nanny, had walked out after hours of the baby's screaming. Xanthia, herself a grandmother, had sounded beside herself. What choice did Ares have but to go straight home and assess the situation?

His eyes drifted to Bea, who was sitting opposite him, a belligerent expression on her face that—at any other time—he would have been very tempted to erase from her pretty features using far from respectable methods. As if to torment him even further, his fingers tingled with the memory of her silky-smooth thigh beneath his palm, the way she'd juddered at the contact, her body begging him for more.

He'd held back, telling himself they had all night, that the pleasure was better savoured than rushed, but now he wished he'd ignored that impulse and let his hand drift higher, finding her sweet femininity and brushing her there, feeling her heat and watching as she exploded in his arms.

'I wish you'd tell me what's happened,' she said quietly. 'It seems like the least you could do.'

It was the first time she'd spoken all flight, and they were almost in Athens. He stared at her, the words locked deep inside. But he had to say *something*. She was about to walk into a scene that would make it perfectly obvious he'd been left—literally—holding the baby.

'Five months ago, my brother's wife died.' He spoke clinically, no sign of the ensuing trauma in his words. 'It was a complete shock—something went wrong during childbirth. Ingrid was delivered of their baby, a little girl, but then wouldn't stop bleeding, and the doctors could do nothing to save her.'

Bea gasped in that way she had, lifting her fine-boned hand to cover her lips.

'Now my brother is…not well…' he glossed over the nature of Matthaios's illness out of instinct to protect him '…and has left me with the care of his child while he seeks treatment.'

The sympathy in her eyes was unmistakable. Ares hated it. As a teenager he'd seen that look on countless faces and he'd sworn he'd show them. He was not an object of pity. Strengthening his spine, he infused ice into his bones. 'Naturally, I hired an exceptional nanny. My workload is hardly conducive to the care of a child, and young children particularly need a lot of care. Unfortunately, the woman I hired has been almost as much work as my niece since day one. My housekeeper just called to inform me that the nanny had walked out.'

'Cassandra,' Bea prompted thoughtfully.

'How did you—?'

'She called while you were in Clare's office.' Pink bloomed in Bea's cheeks. He looked away, controlling his body's response to the betraying gesture with difficulty.

'Yes, Cassandra.' He spat the name with derision, almost missing the way Bea's lips lifted a little at the corners. She was smiling at him? Trying not to laugh at him? It didn't make sense and Ares liked things to make sense.

'I have to get back there, to see what's going on,' he snapped.

Her eyes, clear pools of burnt butter, appraised him for several seconds and then she nodded slowly. 'If you'd explained this sooner I wouldn't have fought you at the airport.'

His lips tugged downwards. 'It didn't occur to me. I was too preoccupied.'

Again, sympathy crossed her face. It took Ares a moment to realise it wasn't sympathy for him so much as for the unknown baby, and the entire situation.

'Naturally, I'll arrange for you to fly back to London tomorrow.'

She barely reacted, yet in the depths of her eyes he was sure he saw something unexpected—something akin to disappointment? Or maybe that was wishful thinking: ego?

'Don't worry about me,' she insisted quietly. 'I can take care of myself.'

Bea's adoptive parents owned a grand old country home in the English countryside, the kind of place with rolling green lawns, a stream filled with trout, stables that had been empty for many years until the twins asserted a desire to learn to ride, and horses were therefore acquired from top breeders. The desire had lasted three weeks, the horses longer—they were now given free rein of the western paddocks and, from time to time, found their way into the orchard and ate their body weight in fruit, much to Alice Jones's displeasure. As an organic-only fruitarian, the orchard represented almost her sole source of food, so the horses' act had been seen as a declaration of war.

The house itself dated to the early Tudor period, though much modernisation had occurred in recent years, and now boasted ten bedrooms, each with its own bathroom, three swimming pools—one for diving, courtesy of Amarie's insistence that she was going to be an Olympic diver. The pool had been completed about a week too late—she'd moved onto playing the drums by then and, despite the fact that Ronnie had a full studio in the basement of the house, a separate drums studio was built for Amarie, perhaps to save Ronnie from the torture of listening to her murder the tempo of any more classic rock music.

So it wasn't as though Beatrice hadn't been surrounded by wealth. But ever since arriving at the airport in London and being ushered into Ares's private jet she'd felt as though she'd been exposed to a whole other level of extravagance. Upon touching down in Athens they were ushered to a limousine which drove them a very short distance to a gleaming black helicopter with darkly tinted windows. The upholstery was brown leather and the details oak. Her companion was as silent as a tree himself and his manner became colder, more intimidating with every minute that passed.

Bea distracted herself by staring out of the window, trying not to compare him to the way he'd been on the gondola. Then, she'd almost felt as though she could say anything to him, tell him anything, but now he was so distant it was impossible to think of him as anything except an incredibly successful self-made businessman who was also a very important client—a man whose business the London Connection needed to retain.

And, for some reason, all she could think about was the time she'd been sent home from school with suspected chickenpox and somehow the message had never reached her parents. The doors to the house had been locked—Bea never had a key of her own—and so she'd walked around to the drawing room, peering in through the windows. The sight of her parents and sisters having dinner together had made her heart ache in an unforgettable way. It had been easy to lie to herself until that night, to make excuses for why she was treated one way and her sisters another, but seeing them enveloped in the warmth of their home, the focus of such obvious parental love, had made the literal point to Bea that she was an outsider.

It had made her see that she had never had that. Not from her biological parents, and not from the parents who'd adopted her. No one had ever wrapped her into their warm embrace and made her feel as though she was special and irreplaceable.

She'd never looked to her family for affection again, nor did she seek it from anyone else. Being on her own was better, easier and infinitely safer.

The helicopter circled lower to the ground. The full moon shone on the coastline, showing the ocean as a shimmering expanse of black with a silver trail through its centre and, along the shore, set several miles apart, a handful of houses. The helicopter headed towards one that was boxy and modern, elegant lighting illuminating the sides in a warm glow that was somehow at odds with the stark white walls. A swimming pool was lit with turquoise lights, lending it the impression of a five-star resort. The helicopter came lower, confirming the fact that this was Ares's house, landing squarely on the rooftop.

The helicopter had barely touched down before he had unbuckled his seatbelt and was standing, moving to the door at the side. Bea couldn't take her eyes from him. He was completely absorbed, focused only on reaching home and finding out what had happened. She unbuckled her own seatbelt, the fierce throb of disappointment in her body not worthy of her in that moment. There were far greater things to worry about.

'What happened?' he demanded as he moved from the stairs and into the living room. He had to speak loudly to be heard above the infant's screaming. Every two seconds the little baby paused to suck in a gulp of air, then made a bubbling sound as she pushed it out, wailing into the night. If he allowed himself to feel fear he knew it would overtake him, so he refused to admit the possibility that something could be physically wrong with Danica. Not on his watch.

'She will not stop crying,' Xanthia said in Greek.

Despite the fact he'd barely spoken to her since leaving Venice, Ares was ever conscious of Bea just behind him, and switched effortlessly to English. 'What caused this?'

'Nothing.' Xanthia did the same, herself fluent in many languages, a prerequisite to the job as he required his housekeeper to oversee the management of his properties in various countries. 'She had a bath and then refused her evening meal. When Cassandra attempted to put her to bed she began to wail, and nothing could calm her.'

'Why?' he asked with obvious disbelief. 'Shouldn't she be tired?'

Xanthia pursed her lips and looked at him as though he were an idiot and, to be fair, in that moment he felt like one. But shouldn't this be easy? Weren't babies supposed to just need food and sleep?

He ground his teeth together, the sense of inadequacy overwhelming. 'For God's sake, has she been like this the whole time?'

'Yes,' Xanthia confirmed, rocking the baby from side to side, which only caused Danica to scream more loudly.

'You said she didn't eat—' the voice came from behind him '—could she be hungry?'

Xanthia's green eyes turned to Bea, appraising her quickly. 'She is only little. Dinner consists of some spoons of cereal and a bottle of milk.'

'Nonetheless,' Bea continued, moving towards the baby. Despite the screams, the gentle rustle of her skirts reached his ears, reminding him of the way they'd felt bunched in his hands. He formed a fist at his side, an act of determination, a refusal to be distracted by his body's base impulses. Bea lifted a hand to the baby's head, checking for a temperature.

'She's warm,' Bea said gently. 'But that's probably because she's so agitated.' She held her hands out. 'May I?'

Xanthia's jaw dropped. 'Oh, please. I have been holding her for hours. Please, yes, take her.'

'Would you go and prepare her bottle?' Bea prompted, taking the baby and barely flinching at the noise. Without lifting her attention from Danica's face, she addressed him. 'Ares, I think a cool facecloth might help to calm her. Would you get one?'

He stared at her, totally unprepared for this turn of events. He'd expected Bea to fade into the background at best, or, at worst, be something of an inconvenience if she'd continued to fight with him about coming to his home, but her cool manner and air of control knocked him sideways.

Even Danica seemed mildly less hysterical in Bea's arms.

'Yes, of course,' he said belatedly, turning on his heel to fetch what she'd asked for. He noticed as he waited for the cloth to dampen sufficiently that he wasn't wearing his tuxedo jacket. It was still wrapped around Bea's shoulders. The thought tightened his body, making him far more aware of her as a woman than was appropriate, given the circumstances.

He entered the lounge at the same moment Xanthia did, and both stopped walking and simply stared at each other.

Danica was silent. Not quite, he amended. She was making lots of little breathy noises, rapid and urgent, as she calmed down from so much screaming. Her cheeks were mottled pink and tear-stained, her hair damp from crying, her nose sticky with snot, but she was no longer wailing.

As he approached, he heard Bea's voice, soft and gentle, singing words in a language he didn't know, like English but different. Almost elvish, reminding him of Middle-Earth.

'Oh, my ears,' Xanthia whispered, smiling broadly, her dark grey hair piled high on her head in a loose bun, frazzled after hours of trying to console a screaming child.

He held out the facecloth to Bea but she shook her head.

'She's cooler now that she's stopped crying. Perhaps a tissue though?'

He nodded without moving, simply standing, awestruck at the sight of someone so completely *comfortable* with the child. Not since Danica had arrived at his house had he seen her actually seem halfway to peaceful.

Xanthia held the bottle out to Bea. She took it, returning to singing as she looked around. Her eyes momentarily met Ares's and something passed between them, something fierce and intractable, a magnetic force that demanded acknowledgement. He ground his teeth together, jabbing one hand into his pocket.

'The tissue,' she reminded him with a pointed look and the hint of a smile, jolting him into action.

'Right, the tissue,' he repeated, still reluctant to leave the scene. He bypassed Xanthia, pausing beside her. 'You should go to bed. Thank you for holding the fort tonight. I'm in your debt.'

'Of course, Ares,' she said with a shake of her head, switching back to Greek. 'The poor little dove simply couldn't be settled. Not until you showed up with the baby whisperer. This nanny shows much more promise than the other.'

He was about to correct her but, instead, Xanthia's words settled inside his chest, landing there with a soft thud. *This nanny.* He cast a glance over his shoulder.

It was easy to see why Xanthia would have made that mistake. Despite her formal dress, Beatrice was unmistakably at home holding the baby...

'Where's her nursery?' she whispered, stroking the darling little infant's shoulder with the pad of her thumb.

Ares had been standing, watching for the twenty minutes it had taken to feed Danica and rock her slowly to sleep. 'I'll show you.'

Bea stood slowly—it had been years since she'd held a baby, though it was surprising to realise how easily it all came flooding back. Memories of helping her friend Priti with late-night feeds and colicky tantrums filled her with confidence. This, though, was different.

Holding Danica, feeding her, lulling her to sleep, had caused something to flicker to life inside Bea that had caught her completely off-guard. A stirring of maternal instincts she absolutely didn't expect and definitely didn't want. She'd decided a long time ago that she was *never* having children.

She walked beside him and, without the ticking time bomb of a furiously upset infant, was able to take in the details of his palatial home. It was a temple to modernity, all crisp white walls, polished cement floors with Danish-style furniture. The only concession to colour came in the form of abstract paintings which hung in niches along the walls, lit with art-gallery-style spotlights. The stairs were highly polished wood. As Ares walked ahead of her Bea had a perfect view of his powerful legs and firm bottom and the sight of both made her mouth go dry.

She looked away, concentrating only on her steps, one after the other, holding Danica close to her chest so that she would stay comforted and warm.

Ares paused on the landing, pointing to an open door a little down the hall. Bea walked towards it, trying not to speculate on which of these doors might lead to his room. The nursery was a guest bedroom with a cot in the corner and a rocking chair by the window. Bea stood above the cot for a moment, singing 'Calon Lân' to Danica, gently lowering her over the sheet. She startled a little, so Bea placed her on the mattress quickly then held her hand on Danica's tummy, reassuring her she was still there, lifting her fingers lightly, gradually, until it was clear that Danica had settled. She turned to Ares and smiled, overcome with shyness now, uncertain what to say.

Nothing within the baby's earshot, that was for sure! What the poor little thing needed more than anything was a good night's sleep.

As she stepped through the door, Ares pressed his hand to her back, guiding her towards the stairs. The lightest touch made her nerves go haywire. She moved a little ahead of him on the steps, her own hand seeking the reassuring firmness of the railing.

In the lounge, he strode across the room, throwing open the glass doors and quirking a brow by way of silent invitation. Bea hesitated a moment, then moved in his direction, keeping her face averted as she brushed past him.

It was cool outside; she was grateful to still have his jacket on. Salt filled the air; the sound of rolling waves made a gentle background rhythm.

'You're good with kids.'

She turned to face him, a tight smile on her face. 'She was just overwrought. Babies don't always know how to calm themselves down; they need us to do it for them.'

He shook his head dismissively. 'The nanny I hired came highly recommended but she couldn't manage Danica. No one could.'

'I find that impossible to believe.'

'I'm not making it up.'

She tilted her head. 'I'm not saying that. It's just—she's just a baby, Ares. She's—did you say five months old?'

He nodded once.

'That's so little! And she's had a lot of change in her life so far. Babies are more perceptive than people realise.'

'And you are the only one who can calm her,' he said quietly.

'That's not true.'

'How did you know what to do?'

Her smile was tinged with the best kinds of memories—sweet ones, those that were solely good. 'When I was at university, my flatmate Priti fell pregnant. It was a one-night stand, completely unexpected. The dad wasn't in the picture. She really wanted to be able to keep studying and, seeing as we were doing the same course, we came up with a schedule for school work and baby-minding. It was a crazy time.' Bea laughed softly, recalling the madness of it. 'I'd go to lectures and record them for her, we'd cram over buckets of soaking laundry—nappies and bibs—and study while Nikki slept. She wasn't an easy baby. In fact, I'd say she was downright difficult. Some nights it would take hours to get her to sleep. *Hours*, no exaggeration. Some babies are just like that,' she said with a shrug.

When he didn't respond, she rushed to fill the silence. 'If it's any consolation, I can assure you that that difficult baby is now a confident, intelligent pre-teen who rarely has a temper tantrum and absolutely sleeps through the night, so it does get easier.'

Ares seemed to stiffen. 'Hopefully she won't be my problem for much longer.'

Bea's lips parted on a soft sound of outrage, her expression full of chastisement. 'That's no way to talk about your niece.'

He winced at the reprimand. 'Ever since she arrived she has been like this. Screaming. Red-faced. Angry.'

In spite of his words, Bea smiled. 'She wasn't angry. Misunderstood is a better way to describe her.'

'I paid a nanny to understand her.'

'It doesn't sound like that worked out very well.'

'Cassandra clearly wasn't the right choice.'

'Apparently not.'

The silence between them throbbed and every second that passed did something to Bea. She felt herself being pulled towards him, as though a ribbon was wrapped around her, dragging her closer. She resisted it, but the effort it took was monumental.

'My brother is likely to be in hospital for another few weeks.'

Bea frowned at the swift conversation-change.

'I need someone to help with Danica while she's with me.'

'Perhaps you can find a nanny who has more experience with unsettled babies? It's quite a specific skillset, but if you let the agency know—'

He shook his head, moving towards her with urgency. 'I'm not going to contact the agency again.'

Bea looked confused. 'Then how will you find someone?'

Ares pressed a finger to her lips, silencing her as he'd done in the office earlier that day. Had it really only been a day? 'I've already found her.'

Bea stared up at him, unable to think straight when he was so close.

'Danica is a difficult child, you're right. But you were able to calm her easily.'

'That's just experience.'

'It's experience I need.'

She stared up at him, her expression wary. He couldn't possibly be suggesting…? 'You do realise I have a job?'

His eyes glittered with ruthless determination. 'Unfortunately, *agápi mou*, you showed your hand too early.'

Bea was silent.

'We both know what my business means to the London Connection.'

Her heart stammered, her jaw dropping in surprise.

'And we both know you'll do almost anything to keep me happy.'

'Ares,' she whispered, a plea in her voice, 'I was happy to help you tonight, but I can't just walk out of my job—my real job—to play babysitter. No matter how cute the baby is.' Or how sexy the uncle, she added mentally.

'Unfortunately, I'm desperate. Otherwise I'd never think of blackmailing you into staying here for the month.'

'A *month*?' she repeated on a wave of something that was terrifyingly like excitement.

'My brother's treatment will take a few weeks, at least. Let's say a month, to be safe.'

'We can't "say" anything, Ares. I'm not agreeing to this.'

'Of course you are,' he dismissed easily. 'You have no choice.'

She shook her head.

He made a frustrated sound. 'I would prefer not to bully you into this, Beatrice. Stay because we—I—need your help. Because I must do whatever it takes to help Danica. Stay because it's the right thing to do, just like it was the right thing to help Priti finish her degree. Stay because I am desperate.' He moved closer, his body finishing the intoxicating job his words had started. 'Stay because you want to finish what we started on the boat tonight, and a month gives us ample time to do that.'

Her stomach squeezed on an exhilarating wave of hope and need, but her brain was reluctantly firing to life. Disbelief hit her. On the gondola he'd been offering one night, not a whole month of them... Alarm bells sounded at the intimacy of that. It was all impossible. 'It's not that simple. I can't just click my fingers and walk out of my life.'

His nostrils flared; it was obvious Ares Lykaios was not used to hearing the word no. She'd expected him to kiss her in an attempt to persuade her, or to throw money at her, or maybe even to remind her of the blackmail angle. Instead, he addressed the realities of making this work.

'I do a lot of work from here. I have office space to spare, with all the latest facilities and technology, excellent Wi-Fi, and if you're worried about how you'll manage Danica and whatever work you cannot pass off to someone else then we can work around that.' He paused a moment, lost in thought. 'Xanthia told me of a girl in the village who babysits. She can come and help during the days—so long as you agree to step in if there's a problem—so that you have time to yourself. Deal?'

She wanted to say no, just to thwart him, because he was moving the pieces of her life so effortlessly, showing such control and intuition.

But that ribbon around her chest was being tugged again, drawing her to him, showing her a glimpse of a more impulsive life. Weren't Amy and Clare always telling her to follow her instincts more? To listen to her gut? Well, both her instincts and gut were telling her to jump first, look later. They'd been telling her the same thing all night. And now Ares was making it easy for her to do just that.

'What is the expression about having cake and eating it as well?'

She lifted a hand to his chest, tempted beyond words. 'To have one's cake and eat it too,' she supplied, distracted.

'Exactly. Isn't this a way to do that?'

She sighed. 'It's...complicated.' The kiss they'd shared on the gondola felt like a lifetime ago—as though it had happened to a wholly different person. She couldn't believe how free she'd felt then!

'Why?'

Embarrassment rolled through her. She dropped her gaze, unable to look directly at him. 'I'm not someone who just casually...gets involved in relationships.'

He was quiet and, despite the fact they'd only known each other a short time, she knew exactly how he'd be looking at her, appraising her, trying to understand what she wasn't saying. Nerves flew like butterflies inside her belly.

'I mean, I never have before.'

She risked a glance at him; he was frowning.

'Been in a relationship?' he prompted. 'Let me reassure you, Beatrice, I'm not offering anything serious. This would be a strictly short-term arrangement.'

Her lips twisted in a half-smile. 'I don't mean that. I mean... I've never...' But she couldn't finish the sentence. She was twenty-nine and had never had sex. That didn't usually bother Bea, but now she found it mortifying to confess.

'What is it?' he pressed. 'Are you trying to tell me you're a virgin or something?'

Her stomach swooped but she knew there was no sugar-coating it. Tilting her chin defiantly, she forced her eyes to meet his. 'Yes. That's exactly what I'm telling you. I'm a twenty-nine-year-old virgin. Are you sure you still want to make sex a part of what you're offering?'

CHAPTER SEVEN

ALL THE AIR evacuated his lungs at once. He felt as though her words were rattling through his ears like a freight train on a looped track. It didn't make sense.

'You said you're twenty-nine.'

She fidgeted her hands at her sides, not meeting his eyes.

'And prior to taking up your role at the London Connection you were a senior partner in a law firm?'

'A top tier firm,' she confirmed, in that habit she had of babbling a little when she was nervous.

He nodded anyway, taking the titbit of information and filing it away.

'You are an intelligent, beautiful and kind woman. Twenty-nine years old. And yet you've never slept with a man?'

Her cheeks were bright pink and it was an unfortunate consequence of the situation that he found that mesmerising. His desire increased rather than doing what he wanted—and abating completely at her pronouncement.

But the way they'd kissed on the boat, the way her body had moved over his, her hips pushing down on his masculine strength, showing with her body how much she needed him... 'So you've never had sex with a man,' he said with narrowed eyes. 'But you've obviously had some experience with other elements of lovemaking.'

Her throat moved in a delicate knot as she swallowed. 'You want my dating résumé now?'

'I think I'm entitled to some explanation.' It wasn't exactly the truth—he didn't feel entitled to anything, but he *wanted* an explanation and he hoped she'd give one.

Her eyes lifted to his, her mouth parting on a small sigh before she bit down on her lower lip. 'It's not a big deal.'

'I beg to differ.'

Hurt washed over her features; he regretted the words instantly. Hell, he was out of his comfort zone by about a thousand feet.

'I didn't intentionally mislead you. I didn't go to Venice expecting anything to happen between us. It was just work for me, nothing more. The gondola ride...' Her eyes assumed a faraway look as she tried to draw in breath. His gut rolled with a desire to kiss her. He stood his ground, his body like stone. He couldn't—wouldn't—give in to his instincts now. Not until he understood exactly what he was dealing with. A reformed nun? A runaway cult member? The idea of a twenty-nine-year-old virgin in this day and age beggared belief.

'The gondola ride was a total surprise. Put it down to the magic of the moonlight or something.' She laughed uneasily, awkwardly. 'And, as you know, coming back here wasn't on my agenda. You kidnapped me, remember?'

He remembered every detail of the evening they'd shared, and he knew this part would be forged in his memory banks in particularly vivid detail. 'Was your intention to save yourself for marriage?'

Her face scrunched up in a visceral reaction to that statement, a reaction he would have found amusing under any other circumstances. 'Don't be absurd. I'm never getting married.'

'That makes two of us. So what then?'

She closed her eyes, tilting her head towards the ceiling at the same time. 'Do we have to talk about this?'

'Help me understand and then I'll let it go.'

He had no real right to make demands of her, and yet Ares knew himself well enough to know he wouldn't rest until he understood. He liked things to make sense and this, quite simply, didn't.

'Is it really that big a deal? I just never met anyone I wanted to have sex with, that's all.'

'You didn't go through puberty?' he asked sceptically. 'It's my experience that at a certain point in everyone's lives hormones take control.'

She spun away from him and his fingers tensed with the desire to reach out and grab her, to turn her back to him, to pull her against his chest and listen to the rest of her explanation with her breasts crushed to him, her breath warming his throat. He ignored those instincts, aware that they were part of what had got them here in the first place.

'I was studying my backside off at an all girls school,' she said stiffly, sounding ever so prim. 'I didn't have time for boys.'

Despite himself, he smiled. He could imagine her saying exactly that to any friends who'd tried to lead her astray at the time. 'At university then?'

'Same deal, Ares. I studied. All the time. Some people seemed to be there to socialise, but not me. I worked hard and in any spare time I did have, I was helping Priti with the baby. I graduated with a first, and was offered a graduate role to start that summer.'

'And you didn't date that whole time?'

Her eyes sparked with something when they met his. 'I wasn't *interested* in dating. I wasn't interested in men. I wasn't interested in being lied to, told I was the love of someone's life just so they could get me into bed. I've seen it happen enough times to my friends to know that's the drill. I saw the way heartbreak torpedoed their lives and chose to avoid that for myself. Men, frankly, suck.'

Her words whirled around him. It was a speech laced with bravado, but he heard the hurt that underscored it. 'Heartbreak and sex don't have to go hand in hand. I'm sorry you've missed out on something so wonderful for so many years, simply because you were afraid.'

'I'm not afraid,' she rejected, so quickly it was obvious she hadn't given it a moment's thought.

For Ares, it was all he needed to push home his advantage. He hadn't realised he'd been laying the pieces of a trap—he'd played to win without even intending to—and now it was set.

'If that is true, you'll consider my proposition more seriously.'

Her eyes widened; he could feel her temptation.

'I will not break your heart, Bea, because I don't want it. I will not make you promises, I will not lie to you. I'm offering only sex.' His lips twisted with a hint of mockery. 'Nothing more complicated than that.'

He could feel her wavering, her certainties eroding, but it was too soon to celebrate. Too soon to rejoice in the fact that he would make her his. A heady rush of adrenaline at the prospect of being her first lover flooded his veins, but it wasn't time to act on it yet. She was staring at him appraisingly, a battle clearly being waged inside her mind.

'I think it would be foolish to stay here,' she said stiffly, so whatever jubilation he'd been feeling a moment earlier evaporated. But Ares Lykaios intended to win and there were two objectives for him that evening.

'Oh, make no mistake about it, you're staying here, Beatrice. At least you are if you value my business at the London Connection.'

He knew it was beneath him, but desperation to find someone who could help with Danica forced his hand there.

'I don't believe you,' she whispered. 'One minute you're

asking me to make love to you and the next you're blackmailing me?'

'Not to sleep with me. Only to look after Danica,' he clarified, as though that made it any better. Since when had he become someone who stooped to this level? The answer was simple. On the streets of Athens, broke and starving, he'd done things as a teenager he knew to be reprehensible. Things that were against his strict moral code, all to ensure Matthaios's survival. He'd stolen food from grocery stores—not a lot, just enough to survive, but it had offended every cell in his body to do it. He'd hated that their impoverished state had required it of him. On one occasion he'd even stolen money from a tourist. A ten-euro note had been sticking out of her pocket, so close to falling. He'd walked behind her, waiting for it to drop and, when it hadn't, he'd brushed past her and taken it, aware that the money could make all the difference to Matt. He'd done what he'd needed to protect his brother, and now he was doing what he needed to protect Danica.

He didn't have to like himself for it though.

'Just to be stranded in this luxurious fortress for a whole month?'

He ground his teeth together. 'Think of it as an assignment.'

'I'm a lawyer. I don't get "assignments".'

'You're also a senior member of the London Connection, aren't you?'

'Stop banging me over the head with that,' she demanded haughtily. 'You don't need to keep reminding me of your importance to the company, and I'm well aware of the company's importance to me.' Her gaze clashed with his, cold anger stirring in their depths. 'But if you knew me, Ares, if you'd listened to anything I've said tonight, you would have known how unnecessary it was to go to such crude, bullying means to achieve your ends.'

He felt as though a boulder was pressing down on his chest, but didn't visibly react to her condemnation.

'I told you how I put my whole life on hold to help Priti with her baby. Tonight, at the ball, I spent an hour with a little girl I didn't know just because I felt sorry for her. You could have pleaded with me on Danica's behalf and won me over. You didn't need to show yourself to be such a callous bastard.'

She sniffed, a sound of anger not sadness.

Provoked into responding with total honesty, he spoke unapologetically. 'I had to be sure of your cooperation. I could have played on your sympathy, certainly, but then you might have said no. In my experience, people are always motivated by money.'

She laughed dismissively. 'It's not *money* that's motivating me, you idiot. It's basic human decency, and love. Love for Clare and Amy and the business they've built up. Love for the clients they take care of with every breath in their bodies.' She pushed her hands onto her hips, looking at him as though he were scum. 'Even *you*,' she said witheringly. 'To think, Clare works her butt off for you and this is how you behave!'

Strange that earlier that very same day she'd gasped any time she said anything approaching an insult, apologising profusely. There was no sign of apology in her face now, just scathing condemnation.

It stirred an ache in his gut he'd never felt before.

'I take it that means you'll stay?'

Her eyes swept shut, her features taut and skin pale. 'Obviously.' The word was seething with disgust. He felt every measure of it in the core of his being.

'But as for sleeping with you,' she said coldly, moving towards him, pressing a finger to his chest. 'That's something I no longer have any interest in doing.'

It was a split-second decision. No, there was no decision-making about it. He acted purely on instinct, the same instinct that had seen him steal out of desperation as a starving teenager—he wasn't proud of it; it showed his darker side—roared to life now. He took hold of her finger, moving her hand to their sides, his eyes flashing with intention before he acted, his mouth claiming hers. Not like on the gondola—this wasn't a kiss of gentle, moonlit exploration, with waves splashing at their side. This was a kiss of desperate anger, a kiss of dominance, a kiss designed to entreat submission. Other than his hand holding her finger, he didn't touch her anywhere else. His mouth ravaged hers and she moaned, her body swaying forward, her abdomen pressing to his arousal. She made a low, keening noise as he grew harder against her, a whimper, and then a plea in his mouth.

How easy it would have been to take it further, to undress her and show her the full extent of her dishonesty. But Ares knew his limits, and he'd already stretched them well beyond an acceptable level. He broke his mouth free, staring down at her with darkly glittering eyes.

'You can lie to yourself all you want, Beatrice. Tell yourself you do not want to sleep with me, if you like. But don't lie to me, or I will take great pleasure in showing you the truth.' He stalked across the room, picking up the airphone and speaking a few words into it. He had his back to her—time he desperately needed to cool his temper and put a halt to the raging blood in his body. When he turned to face her, shame washed over him. She was shaking like a leaf, so pale and fragile-looking. Regret chewed through him, but he refused to show any form of weakness. 'A member of staff is on their way to show you to your room. Goodnight, Beatrice.'

She wanted to strangle him. She wanted to put her hands around his throat and strangle him for what he'd done, but at the same time her anger was really all directed at herself. Her stupidity in kissing him back, in immediately begging him to make love to her. The way she'd pleaded with him, over and over, his name moving from her mouth to his, begging him for so much more than a kiss, wanting satisfaction and fulfilment as she never had before.

He'd been right about hormones. That was all this was. Some kind of pre-programmed biological response. Her oestrogen responding to his testosterone, causing a hurricane of desire she'd been unable to ignore.

All night she lay in the luxurious bed, staring at the ceiling, trying to work out if he'd carry out his threat if she were to leave. He was hugely important to the London Connection but it wasn't a one-way street. They were important to him too. He wasn't a man to suffer fools so, without knowing the details of previous PR campaigns and the ongoing management they did for his various business interests, she had to believe Clare was doing an excellent job for him. Surely he wouldn't rip his business away simply because she'd said no to helping him with a baby—a job for which, despite what he might think, she was manifestly unsuited.

Except, at the same time, Bea had to acknowledge there was a risk. Although the London Connection was fast gaining recognition for its client management, there were other firms out there that had been established for much longer, that had more resources, bigger teams, larger reach. How many of the London Connection's clients had come across to them simply because they had someone like Ares Lykaios on their books?

It wasn't just about losing Ares's business then, but about losing the prestige that came from his association with them. Beatrice couldn't be responsible for that, and yet she was sorely tempted to roll the dice and see what happened. Despite his words, there was a part of her that suspected he was bluffing. She couldn't say why, but she had an undeniable faith in his inherent goodness and fairness—it was incompatible with his threat, and yet she felt almost certain that if she were to tell him she was leaving his home—come what may—he'd let her go, and continue working with Clare regardless.

But being almost certain wasn't good enough.

She prevaricated all night, veering from one opinion to the other. She tossed and turned and, somewhere in the early hours of the morning, before the sun had started its ascent into the night sky over Greece's Argolic Gulf, she gave up on trying to sleep and pushed out of bed. Her ballgown was where she'd left it—hardly suitable attire, but for lack of other options...

She had a quick shower and as she reached for a towel she saw that some clothes had been left folded on the cupboard beside the linen. The trousers were a size too big; she had to knot them at the waist to keep them from falling down, but the shirt—long-sleeved and a pale yellow in colour—was a perfect fit. She finger-combed her hair and rubbed a scented moisturiser over her face, regretting that sleep deprivation had left two brown smudges beneath her eyes, then defiantly reminding herself she didn't care.

She moved through the house, intending to hunt down a coffee, but a noise stopped her. Crying.

Baby crying.

Her feet moved towards the sound quickly and silently, piecing together the route to Danica's room. It wasn't easy. The house was huge and she'd been turned around by everything that had happened after she'd put Danica to bed. The crying grew louder though, leading her there, and she pushed the door inwards without hesitation, without a pause for what she might find on the other side.

It certainly wasn't this.

Ares stood dressed in only a low-slung towel, his chest bare, his hair damp, the crying infant in his arms. A lamp had been turned on near the bed, casting them both in a warm glow.

Bea's heart thumped painfully at the sight. He turned to look at her, his dark eyes defensive and then utterly bleak.

The baby howled. Bea held her ground, unable to move.

'Beatrice...' His voice was thick, groggy. 'Please...stay. We need your help.'

CHAPTER EIGHT

BY LUNCHTIME HER HEAD was swimming.

Leave a baby to cry it out. Never leave a baby crying longer than a minute. Leave them to cry but stay in the room so they can see you at all times. Put toys above the bed to distract them and comfort them. Never over-stimulate a baby at bedtime: remove all toys from their line of sight.

So much contradictory advice, all from reputable-seeming parenting authorities, none of them particularly good at agreeing about how to soothe an unsettled baby.

'And you've definitely ruled out medical factors?' she asked, tapping her pen against the thick pile of pages she'd printed off the internet. Going back to her law school roots, she'd spent Danica's fitful daytime naps with a highlighter and notepad, intending to distil what she'd presumed would be a sort of parenting manual onto paper—a guide for both of them to ease Danica into a better routine.

'Cassandra had her checked over by several paediatricians,' he said darkly. 'None could find anything wrong with her.'

'Well, that's good,' Bea said, returning her attention to the pages because it was preferable to looking at Ares. She was still angry with him, she reminded herself, even when the image of him shirtless and comforting Danica was now imprinted on her eyeballs. 'With Nikki, it was just about routine,' Bea murmured thoughtfully. 'If we missed her naptime by even ten minutes, she'd be a nightmare for days. It was hard because Priti and I were both trying to study, but we ran the house like clockwork. It meant we could have a semblance of a normal life,' Bea concluded. 'I wonder if Danica is the same?'

Ares's only response was to lift—by a degree of millimetres—his shoulders.

Bea compressed her lips. 'Did Danica's nanny keep to a tight schedule?' she prompted.

Something flickered in Ares's face. 'I don't know.'

'Well, were her daytime naps all at roughly the same time? What about bedtime?'

'I am not someone who sticks to a strict routine,' he said eventually. 'The reason I hired a nanny who was so highly regarded was because I'm often away from home. Xanthia would be better placed to answer any questions about that.'

Bea shouldn't have been surprised. She tried to keep the judgement from her expression but unfortunately his remark hit way too close to home. How familiar that was to her! The notion of an adoptive parent outsourcing the parenting and consoling themselves with the fact that they'd hired 'the best'. Ares wasn't Danica's adoptive father but he was her uncle, and he was—for the moment—her closest family.

Ice chilled her heart as her own experience of familial rejection spiked through her, paining her all over again.

'I'll speak to Xanthia then.' She scraped her chair back, walking towards the door with a spine that was ramrod-straight. Unusually for Bea, she had the strangest sense she might cry.

'Wait.' His voice was commanding and insistent. Oh, how she'd have loved to ignore it! But that would be petulant and childish, and she refused to indulge either emotion.

She half turned to face him, her neck swan-like, her brown hair piled onto her head in a loose bun.

'What time will you put her to bed tonight?'

Bea had drawn up a schedule which seemed to contain a lot of overlap from the various parenting sites and books. 'Six-thirty. Why?'

'Once she is asleep, we'll go to Athens.'

She gave up on the half-turn and spun back to face him completely. 'What for?'

'You're here for a month. You'll need more to wear than a ballgown and Xanthia's husband's clothes.'

Bea looked down at the misshapen outfit with a raised brow. 'Really? I had wondered…'

'Meet me on the roof at seven.'

Bea pursed her lips, jolted back to the present. 'I can't do that.'

A scowl darkened his face.

'I don't know if she'll go to sleep straight away, and if she doesn't I'm not going to leave her to have another exhausting and traumatic screaming episode. It's not fair to Xanthia either.'

Tension arced between them, an argument in their eyes, and then finally he relented—after all, he could afford to lose the battle. He'd already won the war. 'I'll be waiting. Come up when you are ready.'

Bea should have been relieved that Danica went to sleep so easily. Surely that was a good sign that something about the routine she'd implemented was working? In the end, she'd followed her instincts. An early dinner, a warm, lightly fragranced bath, a calm book-reading in an almost dark room, followed by a bottle with Bea singing softly as Danica fed, a quiet cuddle and burp and then into bed. Bea kept her hand on Danica's chest lightly, as she'd done the night before, watching as the baby's beautiful blue eyes grew heavy and finally dropped closed, her breathing rhythmic as sleep swallowed her.

Xanthia was hovering on the other side of the door, her face lined with worry.

'She's asleep,' Bea whispered.

Xanthia's look of shock brought a smile to Bea's face. 'Already? But...how? It isn't possible!'

'She was tired, I think,' Bea said with a shrug. 'I've switched the monitor on. You'll keep an eye on her?'

'Of course, of course.' Xanthia was glowing. She looked as though she wanted to hug Bea. Instead, she clapped her hands together. 'Peace, at last! I have been so sad for the little girl—so much heartbreak and no one—' Xanthia cut herself off abruptly. 'I'm glad she has you.'

Strangely, so was Bea. Despite the fact it had only been one day, so much had happened that her London life already felt strangely distant. Almost as though she was looking at it through a sort of screen.

'Ares asked me to remind you he's waiting,' Xanthia added belatedly, as though just remembering the reason for being stationed outside Danica's door.

'Like I could forget,' Bea muttered. 'Please call if anything happens with the baby. I don't want her to be upset like she was last night.'

Xanthia nodded. 'Tomorrow morning, Ellen will come. A girl I know from the village. She has two younger brothers and three younger sisters, all of whom she helped raise. You'll like her.'

It had only been hours since she'd last seen him, but Bea still felt a jolt of something like awe at the sight of Ares Lykaios when she pushed open the door to the rooftop helipad some ten minutes later. He wore a suit that must have been made for his body, the darkest navy blue with a crisp white shirt open at the throat. He was designer, delicious and dangerous. Far too handsome for any one man.

Butterflies burst through Bea's belly and her legs were unsteady as she walked towards the gleaming black helicopter. As she approached, he lifted the aviator-style sunglasses from his eyes, hooking them in the top of his shirt and pinning her with a gaze that hollowed out what was left of her tummy.

'She's asleep?'

Bea nodded. She wanted to stay cross with him, to remember that he was palming off the care of his infant niece to a virtual stranger, and that he'd blackmailed her into being here, but at the same time images of him in just a towel, comforting Danica in the small hours of the morning, showed that to be a lie. He did love the baby, and he was doing what he could to care for her. He simply felt bewildered by the enormity of being thrust into the role of parenthood out of nowhere. Relenting, she offered him a cool half-smile. 'She seemed tired. Hopefully she'll sleep well.'

His relief was obvious. 'Thank you.'

And because she'd heard the helplessness in his voice that morning, when it had been just the two of them in Danica's nursery, she understood the depths of his gratitude.

'You're welcome.'

The air between them seemed to spark with awareness, or perhaps that was all coming from Bea. Close to Ares, alone on the rooftop, she wanted more than anything to feel the strength of his body close to hers once more, to lift her face to his and have him kiss her as though that were the most normal and natural thing in the world. And maybe it was—for other people. But not for Bea. She'd never wanted a relationship with a man, and even the kind of relationship he had suggested seemed fraught with danger.

Dragging her eyes away from his with determination, she realised they weren't in fact alone. A man in dark trousers and a pale shirt opened the door to the helicopter, smiling at Bea in an invitation for her to step inside. She took the same seat she'd occupied the night before, presuming Ares would do the same, but before he sat down he hovered over her, reaching for the straps of her seatbelt and fastening it into place, just as he'd done on the plane. Her breath held, her gaze was drawn to his face as if by magnetic force. She couldn't look away.

He pulled the seatbelt tight, his fingers lingering at her hip as he lifted his attention to her face and she had to bite back a moan. Awareness crashed through her like a tidal wave, a desire she'd never known before pressing bright sparks of light into her eyes.

His gaze roamed lower, landing on her lips, so she remembered every single sensation of having him kiss her the night before, the way he'd plundered her mouth with his, proving a point. And he had proved that point—she wanted to sleep with him, no matter what she'd thrown at him in the anger of their fight.

Desire stormed through her blood; she was helpless to fight it.

She surrendered a part of herself in that moment, acknowledging how much she wanted him. She was taken back to the way she'd felt on the gondola, when she'd been tempted to throw all caution to the wind and experience, for the first time in her life, what sex was all about.

'Ares—'

His name on her lips was a plea, drawn from deep within her.

And he understood. She saw it on his face that he knew how she felt, and what she wanted. So it made absolutely no sense when he stepped back, taking the seat across from her, his expression neutral as he buckled his own belt in place.

Her cheeks felt as though they'd caught fire. She stared at him in disbelief, then blinked, turning her attention to the window. Uncertainty and need were looping through her. She felt completely out of her depth, an experience Bea had always hated.

Before she could contemplate pulling the pin on the whole idea of a shopping trip in Athens, the helicopter's blades began to whirl, the engine noise cutting out any possibility of conversation as the craft lifted up into the sky.

For a moment the view distracted her. The night before it had been pitch-black, and she'd spent the entire day enveloped in baby-related research. For the first time, as the helicopter took the trajectory of an eagle over the coastline, Bea realised how stunningly beautiful it was. The sun had not yet set but was on its way, painting the sky a dramatic palette of fiery oranges and pinks; the ocean below them was a deep turquoise, enhanced by the dusk light. She could see how sparsely populated the coastline was too, each house spaced several miles apart, each luxurious and modern, though Ares's most of all.

'Champagne?' The throaty-voiced offer had her turning to face him. A recognisable label on a piccolo bottle was being held towards her. She stared at it a moment before nodding, watching as he curled his palm around the cork and lifted it, the sound muted by his hand's tight grip. He placed a straw in the top, handing it across to Bea, and she took it gratefully.

'How long have you lived here?' she asked, simply to fill the silence—a silence that was throbbing with a drugging awareness.

'I bought the house ten years ago.' His lips twisted in a way that suggested to Bea he was concealing something.

'For any particular reason?' she asked.

'I liked it.'

She nodded thoughtfully. 'You look as though there's more to it than that.'

Surprise briefly flashed in his features and he was quiet for a moment, thinking, before he shifted his head once. 'When I was a boy I used to live just over there.' He pointed across the glittering bay to a small town on the water's edge. Unlike the sparsely populated coastal region where Ares's mansion stood, this village looked full to the brim, tightly packed houses jostling for space. 'My grandfather was a fisherman, and I'd go out with him sometimes. There were barely any houses here then. Two or three enormous sprawling homes that—to my eyes—looked like palaces.'

Bea sipped her champagne, listening intently.

'When I made my first billion American dollars I bought one of these homes.'

Bea gaped. 'Your first billion?' She shook her head a little ruefully. 'Exactly how many billions do you have?' She grimaced, regretting the forthright question immediately. 'Don't answer that. I shouldn't have asked.'

He flexed a brow. 'It's a matter of public record. I have no issue with you knowing.'

'Oh.'

'Current estimates put my wealth around the hundred-billion-dollar mark. It fluctuates a little, depending on international markets and world events.'

Bea blinked. 'I can't even imagine what that's like.'

A muscle jerked in his jaw. 'The thing about money is that once you have enough to feed yourself and your family, buy a secure home, a warm bed, it doesn't really change that much. There's not a huge difference between ten thousand dollars and ten billion, to my mind.'

Having lived through homelessness and poverty, Bea supposed he was uniquely placed to comment on that.

'You must have felt pretty damned good walking in that door for the first time though,' she said, nodding back towards his home, now a distant speck far beneath them.

'I felt better when I bought our first home, actually,' he said quietly.

'Our?'

'My brother, Matthaios, and mine. He was still at school. Back then I'd amassed what I thought was a fortune—spare change now, really, but to me, at the time, it was a king's ransom. Being able to buy an apartment outright, to know that, whatever happened, Matthaios would have somewhere safe to live—that was the best feeling I've ever known. This was enjoyable, but nothing will ever compare to that.'

'He's your younger brother?'

He nodded but his demeanour shifted, so that he seemed closed off and distant. 'He's two years younger.'

'You're close?'

A terse nod.

'You said he's sick?'

Ares's eyes flashed to hers, dark emotions tumbling through their depths. 'Yes.'

'I'm sorry. Is it serious?'

'It's a…lifelong condition.'

She frowned, sympathy tugging at her heart-strings.

He sighed heavily. 'My mother was a drug addict. My brother inherited her…tendencies. I should have realised sooner what was happening.' Self-directed anger thickened his voice. 'As teenagers, we had no money—he couldn't drink or do drugs; it simply wasn't an option. But, once things improved for us financially, he found it easy to procure whatever the hell he wanted.'

Bea's heart tightened.

'I worked a lot. I didn't see what was right in front of me, despite having witnessed my mother's addiction play out for years. I should have known he was losing himself to drugs, alcohol—whatever he could get his hands on.'

She shook her head to dispel the blame Ares was laying at his own feet. 'You were working so you could support him,' she reminded Ares gently.

'That's no excuse. I should have realised.'

The helicopter changed direction, so that the ocean gave way to verdant land far below.

'By the time I saw what was happening, he was so far gone. It took years to convince him to go to rehab, and in the end I had to let him hit rock-bottom before he finally got there. You cannot imagine what that was like, Beatrice. Watching him self-destruct, knowing there was only so much I could do.'

Her throat shifted as she swallowed. Strangely, he didn't mind the sympathy on her face now.

'I could only keep him safe,' Ares admitted gruffly. 'I hired security to guard his house—and him—so that at least he was watched.' He shook his head angrily. 'They called me one morning when he wouldn't wake up. He'd come this close to an overdose.' He pinched his finger and thumb together.

'That's horrible,' she whispered.

He nodded. 'He spent two nights in hospital and then he chose to go to rehab. He begged me for help. I've never been gladder than I was in that moment.' He grimaced, because that happiness hadn't lasted long. As so often in life, a downfall had already begun to approach. 'He got sober, and turned his life around. He started an investment firm which did incredibly well, then met Ingrid and fell in love.' Ares's expression had assumed a faraway look and Bea knew that, though he was speaking aloud, he was really recounting the facts to himself, going over them as if he could make better sense of them somehow. 'Their wedding day was one of the happiest of my life. To know how far he'd come, to see the hope on his face, the love in his eyes... I felt...such immense relief, as though finally everything was going to be okay.'

'And then Ingrid died,' Bea said softly.

He lifted his eyes to her face, torment in his features. 'Yes. Ingrid died and my brother was left with a black hole of grief and a tiny, dependent child. I should have done more. I should have—'

Bea made a frustrated sound and leaned as far forward as she could, putting a hand on his thigh to draw his attention fully. 'You can't blame yourself for this.'

'Can't I?' he asked quietly, his voice still ringing with self-condemnation. 'I'd seen what he'd been through before. I'd seen my mother grapple with her demons for years. I knew how desperately he needed to blot out the pain. I should have done more to help him.'

'What more could you have done?' she asked logically.

Ares stared at her.

'He's a grown man. Your job isn't to live Matthaios's life for him, Ares. It sounds to me like you've done the best you can for your brother all your life, and you're still doing that now.'

'You don't understand. I should have seen what was coming. I should have predicted he'd turn back to drugs. I should have—'

'Kidnapped him to your mansion for all eternity?' she

couldn't help teasing, despite the serious tenor of their conversation.

His eyes flared, showing surprise at her quip.

'You couldn't chain him up until his grief passed. And you couldn't watch him twenty-four hours a day. Did you support him, Ares? Did you call to check on him? Ask how he was, how the baby was?'

His face paled. 'I spent a month with him, after her death. Then I had dinner with him several times a week. I hired security, as before, to keep them both safe. I hired nannies—he fired them. But still I thought he was doing well, given the circumstances. He seemed heartbroken but well, at the same time. I looked for signs of addiction. I checked his house when he was occupied with Danica, and I called at unusual times, wondering if I would detect something in his voice that spoke of drug use or alcohol abuse. I detected *nothing*. I missed the signs.'

'Or maybe he was holding it together and then something happened and he had a bad few nights. Or maybe he was just that good at hiding his behaviour from you...' She paused, frustrated that he couldn't see how much help and support he'd offered. 'But look at what you've done for him now. He's getting treatment and help, and you've stepped in to care for Danica, so that when he comes out his beautiful baby will be waiting for him. If you hadn't done that she would have ended up in foster care, Ares. Do you have any idea what that would have meant? It would have been far from guaranteed that Matthaios would be able to take Danica back when he was ready. You've given him a second chance to be a father—that's something to be proud of.'

His gaze shifted to her hand, still on his thigh, and he looked at it for so long that her fingers began to tingle and warm. She was about to retract it when his own hand came down on hers, keeping it right where it was.

'You were adopted.'

The statement shattered something inside her. A shame Bea

worked hard to rationalise away burst through her at the un-expectedness of his words, a shame that came from knowing how unwanted she was: by her birth parents first, by her adoptive parents ultimately. A sour taste flooded her mouth and she went to pull her hand away again, but he held on tightly, his eyes loaded with warning when they met hers. Under his intense scrutiny her pulse began to go haywire.

'So?' Her voice shook with defiance, dredged from deep within her soul. She didn't need anyone to love her; what did it matter that she'd been rejected by all the people who were meant to love her most? She'd worked herself into the ground to build her career, and she had Amy and Clare.

'I just wondered if you're speaking from experience.'

Her breath evacuated her lungs on one huge whoosh. 'No.'

She pulled away then and he let her. Bea tried to ignore the coldness spreading inside, and the fear that he was seeing more of her than she wanted him to—more than she'd ever let anyone see. To the world, Bea was an in-control lawyer, intelligent, bright and driven. No one needed to know the gaping wounds that existed in her heart, the feeling that there must be something inherently wrong with her to have been rejected so consistently. Her secret fear—that no one would ever love her or want her enough—was just beneath the surface, though.

She wouldn't let Ares know how broken she was inside. For some reason he was the last person she wanted to see beyond her façade.

CHAPTER NINE

SHE WASN'T LIKE any woman he'd ever known. She'd shunned the high-end boutiques his chauffeur had brought them to, wrinkling her nose up at the clothes the assistants had suggested, repeatedly walking out empty-handed, despite his insistence that he wanted to furnish her with a wardrobe to get her through the month they'd agreed on.

Had they agreed? He couldn't precisely remember. The night before had gone as far from his expectations as possible, and yet somehow he had taken the fact that she was still here as tacit consent that she'd remain.

He'd wondered if she was just being contrary to spite him, but as they'd passed a department store she'd stopped walking and pressed a hand to his chest. 'Perfect. Wait here.'

He'd ignored her suggestion, following behind as Bea whipped through the chainstore's women's fashion offerings. She scooped up clothes as she went. A pair of jeans, a denim skirt, some shorts, several T-shirts in the same style and different colours, before turning around and pushing the selection into his arms.

'Hold these.' Her eyes challenged him. 'Do not follow me into the lingerie section, Ares. I mean it.'

Oh, how sorely tempted he was to do exactly that! But her

innocence put him in an unusual position—torn between his desire for her and a need to tread gently, reminding himself that she wasn't like his usual lovers.

Oh, she was beautiful and smart, sophisticated and intelligent, but she was also a virgin, and for a man like Ares who'd only ever offered one part of him to the women he slept with—his body—surely that innocence made her off-limits? All the more so because he couldn't offer her more than a physical relationship. Sex. His temperature skyrocketed and in the middle of the department store his body grew hard, his arousal tight against the seam of his trousers so he lowered the bundle of clothes a little. What the hell was wrong with him? The fact she was a virgin should have been a huge red flag. He shouldn't be interested in being her first, but hell, he wanted her regardless.

He hovered on the edge of the section, determined not to look in her direction. Instead, he wandered, finding himself amongst Lycra swimsuits and picking several out simply to keep busy. The deep red bikini would complement Bea's complexion, but so too the cream with gold straps. He ignored the black one-piece even when he knew, somehow, that the bland, unflattering style was the one she would have gone for. He returned to the clothing section then, picking up a floral dress with a cinched-in waist and buttons down the front, adding it to the clothes she'd chosen, before Bea approached him, already carrying a plastic bag with the store's logo emblazoned on the front.

'Let's go pay for those,' she said, unable to meet his eyes.

His stomach clenched at her coyness. She'd bought the underwear already, rather than risk him seeing them? It was yet another reminder of how different she was to the kind of women he usually dated—women who would happily swan around semi-naked in silken lingerie.

He knew he shouldn't tease her, but he couldn't resist. 'Did you find what you were looking for?'

She nodded, reaching out for the clothes without looking, but he shook his head. 'I'll take care of it.'

'Then I'll go wait outside,' she said breathily, apparently desperate to escape.

He watched her make a beeline for the exit and then turned on his heel, heading back into the lingerie section. He had no doubt she'd chosen boring cotton panties and bras. That was fine. But Ares wanted to add something else to her wardrobe, something that she might wear and imagine him removing...

There was a meagre selection of sensual nightgowns in this family-friendly store, but he managed to find a slinky black negligee with lace detailing, and a matching pair of French lace panties. He whistled as he made his way to the checkout, unable to think of anything except Bea in sexy lingerie, against the sheets of his bed.

'We really should get back,' she said quietly, as much to herself as Ares. The truth was, she didn't want to return to his home just yet. Being in Athens with Ares, it was almost possible to forget what had happened the night before, the way he'd bullied her into staying with him, to help take care of Danica.

No, it wasn't that she'd forgotten. It was simply that the more time she spent with him, the more she understood him. She saw how motivated he was by his love for his brother, his desperate need to care for his family—and that included Danica. He'd move mountains to be sure the little girl was cared for, and last night Bea had represented the best chance for him to do that.

'We should eat,' he contradicted firmly, taking the bags from her hands and passing them to the waiting chauffeur. 'There is a nice French restaurant near here. Shall we see if they have duck à l'orange?'

His recollection of the small detail sparked something in her blood, something she found very difficult to suppress.

She wasn't used to anyone paying that much attention to her. Amy and Clare aside, and Priti when they were at university, Bea had never been important enough to anyone for them to care about the small things she said. It had been a throwaway comment, for goodness' sake!

But she wasn't important to Ares. That wasn't what this meant. He was just a control freak with an eye for detail. How else could he have achieved what he had in the business world?

'Danica...' she reminded him weakly.

'Xanthia would have called if there was a problem. I'm sure she's fast asleep.'

Bea bit down on her lip, tempted.

'A quick dinner, and then home,' he insisted, putting a hand in the small of her back, taking advantage of her prevarication.

'I suppose so.' And, despite the fact it was a suggestion of practicality, a burst of anticipation spread through her limbs, so she felt a smile crossing her face as they walked. It was dark now, the sky an inky black. The hand at the curve of her spine moved sideways, catching her hip and drawing her closer as though it were the most natural thing in the world. He held her close to his side, moulding her body to his, and she indulged a need for that closeness, lingering beside him, feeling the power of his steps as they moved through the cobbled streets of Athens.

'This is where you lived when you were a teenager?' she asked, partly to fill the silence and partly because she wanted to piece together everything there was to know about Ares.

She felt him tense and wondered if he wasn't going to answer. 'Yes. After my grandfather died we had nowhere to go.'

'Your mother?'

'She'd left us with him many years earlier. She disappeared; we didn't know how to contact her.'

'I'm sorry.'

He slowed down so she looked up at him, and their eyes clashed with a fierce strength of emotion that almost toppled Bea. She sucked in a gulp of air and turned her face forward once more, her skin prickling with goosebumps.

'We came here, thinking it would be easier to find work.

It wasn't. Hostels were often full, so more nights than not we were on the streets.'

Her heart was heavy, imagining the teenager he'd been then. 'You must have been terrified.'

'I was many things,' he said cryptically.

She tilted her face to his once more.

'The hardest part was the hunger. I'd never known anything like it. My grandfather didn't have much money but fish were plentiful, and he grew vegetables in pots. We ate well enough. When we came to Athens it was so hard. I will never forget trying to sleep through that dull, throbbing ache in my gut, knowing my little brother was feeling it ten times worse.'

Emotions throbbed in Bea's chest, sympathy chief amongst them.

'Having enough money to buy food became my primary concern. I used to watch people walk past in their expensive clothes and shoes, looking so happy and carefree. I promised myself, and Matthaios, that one day that would be us.'

His lips twisted in a dark grimace. 'Being carefree isn't something any amount of money can buy though.'

She jerked her head in agreement. 'There's no correlation between wealth and happiness,' she said softly.

'You have experience of this?' he prompted, leading them down a smaller alleyway. Buildings were tightly packed here, with bright flowerpots bursting with lavender and geraniums, some with small citrus trees, making the already narrow lane a tight squeeze, so he had to hold her even closer to his side.

'My adoptive parents had money,' she said quietly. 'But I don't know if I'd ever describe them as happy. My mother is... hard to please. In my experience, that's kind of the enemy to happiness.'

He nodded slowly, bringing them to a stop outside a brightly painted turquoise door. It had a glass panel and a moment later it was pulled inwards, so that any response Ares might have been poised to make was swallowed by the greeting of the waiter.

He spoke in Greek, addressing Ares as an old friend, pulling the door open wider.

'You come here often?' Bea prompted, feeling self-conscious now in Xanthia's husband's clothes and wishing she'd taken the time to change into some of the items she'd chosen at the department store.

'From time to time,' he replied, gesturing to a table by a window. A candle was set in a round wine bottle, with long tendrils of wax showing that various others had melted in the same bottle top well before this one.

He held the chair out for her, and as she took her seat his hands brushed across her shoulders, sending little flames scurrying through her veins.

'Was she hard on you, when you were growing up?'

It took Bea a moment to realise he was talking about her mother again. She never liked talking about her childhood, but she especially resented its intrusion now. She pushed a bland smile to her lips, reaching for a menu instead of answering.

'What do you usually order here?'

His long, confident fingers reached over and removed the menu, replacing it on the tabletop. 'I always let the chef choose. Answer my question.'

She blinked at him. She shouldn't have been surprised by his demand. After all, this was the man who'd point-blank insisted she remain at his home even when she'd told him she wouldn't. Ares got what he wanted, and right now he wanted to know something about her.

She swallowed past the bundle of nerves in her throat, relieved when another waiter approached their table, asking if they'd like a drink.

She remembered enough Greek from that long-ago summer spent in the islands to respond in his native tongue, asking for a soft drink. Ares opted for a glass of red wine.

'You speak some Greek?'

'Just a little,' she said. 'I travelled around the islands for a few months, back when I was in school. I picked up a bit.'

'I didn't realise you'd been here before. Where did you go?'

She listed the islands, smiling as memories of that time swept through her. 'I could be completely myself here; I loved it. The people were so welcoming—no one knew anything about my parents or me. There were no god-awful British paparazzi following me, looking for an unflattering photo, trying to turn me into some kind of B-grade tabloid fodder.' She winced, too distracted to care that she'd revealed so much of herself.

He immediately pounced. 'Why would paparazzi chase you?'

She waved a hand through the air dismissively. 'My mum was a supermodel, my dad a rock star. Despite the fact he hasn't been on tour since I was a young girl, in Britain he's still idolised, and Mum loves to "stay current", as she says. She has all the glossy mags do interviews with them every year; some come to the house for in-depth features. You know the kind of thing— "what life's like in the Jones family".' She rolled her eyes, wondering if the few sips of champagne she'd had in the helicopter had loosened her tongue so much, even when she suspected it was far more likely to be the effect of the man sitting opposite.

'Let me just say this...' She paused as the waiter appeared with their drinks, and so Ares could advise the waiter that they'd eat what the chef recommended.

'Do you have any allergies?' he asked Bea.

She shook her head.

Once they were alone again he reached across the table, putting his hand on hers. 'Go on.'

That simple gesture, as well as his prompting her to continue, warmed something that had been frozen in her chest for a very long time.

'Oh, just that what life looks like in the pages of those magazines is often a far cry from the truth.' A sense of disloyalty had her dropping her gaze. 'Or perhaps that's just being mean-spirited. I shouldn't have said it.'

'Is it true?'

Sparkling hazel eyes lifted to his. After a moment's hesitation, she nodded silently.

'Then you can say it.'

Nonetheless, perhaps sensing her reluctance to share further personal details, he moved the conversation to safer ground, asking about her studies instead, and her time as a senior partner, her career ambitions, and then her friendship with Amy and Clare, so, before Bea knew it, the dessert plates were being cleared and her stomach was full of the most delicious food she'd ever eaten.

'Oh, my goodness.' She stared at her watch with a look of panic. 'That wasn't a "quick meal"! We've been hours!'

'Yes,' he agreed, leaning back in his chair, completely confident and content. 'And while you were in the restroom earlier I checked in with Xanthia. Danica is still sleeping soundly. See? You are a magician.'

Relief and pride spread through Bea. 'I'm so glad. I hated seeing her as she was last night.'

'She has been like that most nights since she came to live with me.'

Bea tilted her head to the side a little. 'Babies are very intuitive,' she said thoughtfully. 'It's often believed that because they look helpless they are, when really they're capable of understanding so much more than we give them credit for.'

He waited for her to elaborate.

She chose her words with care. 'It sounds like Danica's life has already known no shortage of trauma and grief. The loss of her mother, her father's grief, and now his absence... It doesn't really surprise me that she's been struggling to settle.'

'So why were you able to calm her last night?'

Bea had her own theories on that, but she wasn't about to spout them to Ares. He hardly needed to know that Bea wondered if her own latent childhood traumas and grief had somehow spoken to Danica on some level, bonding them in a unique, unusual way, reassuring the little girl that she was in the company of someone who understood her pain.

'I don't know.' She shrugged. 'But I'm glad it worked.'

His laugh was unexpected. It spread like warm butter over her body. 'As am I.'

He ran his finger around the rim of his glass, his eyes probing hers in a way that sent shivers down her spine.

'I find it impossible to believe you've never dated before.'

The observation was completely unexpected and it roused her out of the heavenly state of relaxation she'd allowed herself to fall into. Sitting up straighter, she looked around.

'You must have been asked out?'

Bea bristled. 'I can't see how that matters.'

His smile was lightly mocking. 'Can't you?'

She looked down at her own drink, then his, mesmerised by the way his finger was moving.

She pursed her lips, searching for words. 'I'm twenty-nine. Of course I've been asked out.'

'So you've never said yes?'

She bit down on her lip, nodding warily.

'That makes no sense.'

'Apparently it takes a kidnap scenario to get me to go on a date,' she responded, only half joking.

Undeterred, he leaned forward, his legs brushing hers beneath the table. Her eyes widened. 'Haven't you ever wondered what it's like?'

'Dating?'

He shook his head slowly from side to side, not touching her, and yet heat spread through Bea's body as though his hands were on hers. 'No, *agápi mou*. Being made love to, slowly, gently, until you can barely breathe for how turned on you are.'

She gasped at the fever his words had incited.

'Or being made love to hard and fast because your lover cannot wait to make you theirs.'

Her lungs worked on overdrive.

'Have you never touched yourself, imagining your hands were those of a man you wanted? Touched yourself and wished it was your lover's mouth, worshipping you in your most sacred place?'

'Ares...' Again, his name was a plea on her lips. 'Please...' She didn't know if she was asking him to stop or begging him not to.

'I would like to show you what you're capable of feeling, *poulaki mou*,' he murmured. 'If only this were not so complicated.'

Oh, she wanted that too. She wanted it so badly she was terrified to admit her feelings. 'Why is it complicated?' she asked instead. 'I should have thought it's the most basic biological act.'

His smile was cynical. 'And yet you're a virgin.'

Her eyes dropped to the table.

'I do not sleep with virgins.'

She gasped. 'Is that a rule or something?'

'It might as well be.'

Disappointment speared her belly. She wanted to shake him, to tell him he was being silly. But then what?

Confusion, heat, need—all these feelings rushed through her like a live wire of electricity.

'Then...what...?'

When she risked a glance at him, he was appraising her silently.

She gathered her courage, forcing herself to speak her mind. 'Why are you flirting with me?'

His eyes were mocking, but was it directed at himself or her?

She waited, breath held, for his response, and yet she wasn't prepared for what was coming.

'Because I want you. Even though I know it's wrong, and that I can't offer you what you deserve, I look at you and feel as though I am fighting a losing battle.' Now his expression held a challenge, as though he were laying down a gauntlet. 'You've never had sex before and, despite what I just said, I find myself obsessing over being your first lover. I want to be the one who awakens you to the physical pleasures of intimacy. I have no doubt that's selfish of me, and yet here we are.'

Her breath wouldn't come easily. She stared at him in disbelief, her pulse racing, her mind blank. 'Ares…' But what could she say in response to that? He was offering her exactly what she wanted. She finally managed to suck in a deep breath, doing her best to think straight.

'I don't want more than sex.' She blurted the words out loudly and blushed to the roots of her hair, looking around to make sure that she hadn't been heard. 'Perhaps that's part of what's held me back from dating. The idea of a relationship is anathema to me. You don't need to worry I'll want more from you. Just… sex…is fine.' She cleared her throat. 'More than fine, in fact.'

What the hell was she doing? The water was up to her neck; she was about to drown. Or was she swimming? She couldn't tell. She knew only that it felt good and right to speak like this— two adults outlining a new set of rules, an agreement that would protect them both. There was comfort in the sanity of that when every other part of her felt disconnected from reality.

'It would change nothing between us.' There was wariness in his voice, but also the hard edge of control, as though he was on the brink of losing it.

'Fine by me.' A breathless agreement.

Their eyes met and it was like the signing of a contract. Without words, Ares stood, holding his hand out. Bea stared at it long and hard and then slid hers into his palm, fire zapping through her veins.

He didn't speak as they left the restaurant, but she answered him—and herself—nonetheless. 'I'm ready.'

CHAPTER TEN

HE'D TAKEN THE helicopter ride from Athens to Porto Heli thousands of times, but never quite like this. The tension in the helicopter could have been cut with a knife. She sat opposite him without talking, her hands fidgeting in her lap so her anxiety became all he could focus on. Not her anxiety so much as how he could alleviate it, show her that her body knew what it wanted and could be trusted to guide her. He knew that once they were home he could take charge, pleasuring her until all doubts fell from her mind.

There were no familiar landmarks beneath—it was too dark to see anything properly, but he knew—to the minute—the time it should take to arrive. He checked his watch, relief spreading through him when they reached single digits and then, finally, his home came into view. Her eyes were on him, watching, appraising, and anticipation spread through him. He ached to touch her, to feel her warm softness beneath his palm, her silky hair in his fingers, entangled in his grip, her beautiful body beneath his, welcoming him, losing herself to the heady rush of sensual euphoria.

The fact that he would be her first tightened his arousal to the point of pain. Now that he knew there was no risk of emotional entanglement, he could simply enjoy the pleasure of Beatrice Jones. The helicopter had barely touched down before he was moving, unclipping his own belt before attending to hers. Bea's fingers were shaking when he took her hand in his, but when she looked at him he didn't see what he'd expected to. There was no hesitation in her face, only the same blinding urgency that was exploding in his chest.

The night was cool and he held her close as they moved to the door, partly to keep her warm and partly because he was selfish and simply wanted to touch her, to feel her. Her body was slender but curved; he hungered to feel her in his hands. At the stairs, he dropped his arm, taking her hand in his as he led the way, pausing only briefly at the bottom, waiting for her to take the last step before he strode down the corridor, towards his bedroom.

Bea was right there with him. Until he opened the door and drew her through it, shutting them in his room, he didn't realise he'd been half terrified she'd change her mind. He turned to face her in the dimly lit space, just a lamp near the window casting the room in a gentle glow, and every rush of need that had been tormenting him since they'd left the restaurant burst through him now. His chest rocked with the torturous act of breathing, his body tense. He stared down at her and she looked up at him, and then he moved.

He'd kissed her twice before and this was like the second time, full of urgency, a kiss that overtook him with need, that seemed to happen almost without his control—something Ares would ordinarily despise. But anything that could bring his body to hers like this and have her dissolving against him in a soft, whimpering form of surrender had his approval. He took a step forward, pressing her against the back of the door, his tongue duelling with hers, demanding her supplication. Over and over she said his name, moaning it into his mouth as best she could, her hands pulling his shirt from his trousers, pushing at the buttons until her fingertips could touch bare flesh.

Her need to explore and touch was as real as his own. Despite her inexperience, she was guided by instincts and they were strong, so that if she hadn't told him she'd never been with a man he wouldn't have guessed it. Bea made a growling sound as she yanked at his shirt, separating it finally, removing it from his body as though she couldn't live another second without seeing him naked. He understood.

His hands completed the same task, removing the unsophisticated clothes she wore, stripping her down to her underwear and then dispensing with them so she was naked against him, her body warm and soft, just as he'd fantasised. Her hair was still up in a topknot; he pulled it loose as he kissed her, spilling her hair over her shoulders and down her back, before stepping back to admire her. The sound of their harsh breathing filled the bedroom, loud and demanding. He needed a moment though to commit her to his memory banks just as she was. Her cheeks pink, her chest too from his stubble, her pert breasts with peach nipples tautened by desire, her flat stomach and gently curved thighs.

He swore under his breath, holding out a hand. She put hers in it and he drew her to the bed, knowing he had to curb all his own selfish impulses—the desire to simply drive himself into her sweet sex and lose himself there, to take her hard and fast until they were both incandescent with pleasure. There'd be time for that—a month, in fact. A month to enjoy her sweetness and to teach her how great sex could be.

Tonight was about being gentle. Gradually introducing her to lovemaking without overwhelming her and, hell, without hurting her.

He scooped her up without warning, laying her down in the middle of the bed, kissing her as he moved his body over hers, still kissing as he extended an arm and lifted a condom from the bedside table. He discarded it near them on the bed—for later. First, he wanted to taste.

* * *

The sensation of his mouth on her breasts sent sharp arrows of pleasure-pain spiralling through Bea so she lifted her hips in a sudden, jerky movement. It was almost too much. Too intimate—too personal. He took one nipple between his teeth, rolling it there a moment before flicking it with his tongue, while his hand moved between her legs, brushing her femininity lightly at first, so she didn't know what to focus on, nor which feeling was more overwhelming. She knew only that she was coming apart at the seams in some vital, unmistakable way.

His hand between her legs was heaven-sent, but also not enough. She bucked her hips again, silently begging him for something she couldn't explain. He understood though; she felt him smile against her breast as he kissed his way downwards, his tongue swirling invisible circles around her belly button, over the plane of her stomach and low, teasing her hipbone before moving between her legs.

She groaned as his tongue touched her there, lightly at first and then with more intensity, more speed, more everything, delivering her towards a destination she'd never heard of, never even known about. She dug her nails into the bed first, then his shoulders, as her moans grew louder and louder and eventually she was tipping off the edge of the earth, pleasure swallowing her whole, changing her for ever.

But before she could recover she was dimly aware of the sound of foil and then his knee was parting her legs, his body over hers, his mouth kissing her softly as he pushed the tip of his arousal against her sex.

Despite the heavenly pleasure he'd already delivered, tension filled her. She whimpered, fear widening her eyes so she stared up at him for reassurance. His response was to speak in Greek, his words gentle and soft, words she didn't understand but which succeeded in reassuring her.

He wasn't gentle now. At least, not *so* gentle. He pushed into her, watching her the whole time as his arousal stretched parts of her previously untouched, his body possessing hers for the first time, breaking through an invisible barrier so that briefly she felt a sting of pain, a sharp, visceral response to his presence. It abated almost immediately, and she nodded, a silent encouragement to a question he hadn't asked.

It was then that he began to move. Then that Bea realised whatever pleasure she'd felt a moment ago, it was nothing to the overwhelming, all-consuming delight of this. His body mastering hers, his weight on top of her, the roughness of his chest hairs against her breasts, his hard erection deep inside her, being squeezed by muscles that were trembling in pleasure. Stars danced against the lids of her eyes; she was falling from heaven, or perhaps flying through it? She tilted her head back, capitulating to this madness completely, utterly lost and completely found all at once.

'How do you feel?'

It was a question with no answer. How could she describe how she felt in words? She turned her head to face him, her hooded eyes roaming his features with renewed speculation and interest. She felt a primal claim to him—as though he were hers in some vital, unchangeable way, and always would be.

Oh, it was a stupid way to feel. She recognised that almost immediately. No one person could belong to another and, even if they could, sex wasn't a gateway to possession. For someone like Ares, this had probably been a perfectly run-of-the-mill bout of sex. Just because the very parameters of Bea's world had been significantly redefined didn't mean it had meant anything to Ares.

He frowned, his finger lifting to trace her lips. She sucked in a breath, the small act somehow seeming intimate despite what they'd just shared.

'Fine.' She cleared her throat. The word was banal and inaccurate. She felt so much better than fine. She felt shiny and new. She felt desirable and sensual. She felt wanted.

The realisation had her smile dropping, just by a fraction. *Careful, Bea.*

She knew the inherent risks of that feeling. Being wanted was something she'd never experienced; it was a loss she'd had to accept in her life. She couldn't start looking to someone like Ares Lykaios to fill that vital void within her.

Sex was sex. Nothing more. They'd agreed on that.

The bath water was the perfect temperature and, as she sank into it, Bea acknowledged that she was a little sore. Parts of her body that had never been used made themselves known, so she winced a little.

He was watching, and a small grimace appeared on his own features in response.

'I'm fine,' she promised. And then, because he seemed genuinely worried, 'Better than fine, in fact.'

His smile was her reward. It shifted across his face, changing his features completely, so, for a moment, all she was capable of was staring. 'I'll be back.'

She was tempted to make a Terminator joke but he was gone too quickly. When Ares returned he was naked, holding two glasses filled with a pale amber liquid.

'Scotch?' She wrinkled her nose.

'You don't like it?'

'I've never tried it.'

'That seems to be the theme of the night,' he quipped, placing the glass on the edge of the bath before he stepped in, taking a seat opposite her. The tub was large—easily able to accommodate them both—yet their legs brushed and she was glad. The contact was a different sort of intimacy. She welcomed it and cherished it even as her own warnings swam through her mind. She knew she could balance the physical delight of his presence against the mental knowledge of his impermanence in her life.

Not just *his* impermanence. Everyone's. The unreliability of other people. Bea had sworn a long time ago that she'd never depend on another soul, certainly not for something as important as her happiness. She would enjoy this moment while knowing how fleeting it was. Convinced she could balance those beliefs, the germ of an idea flared in her belly.

'So, I've been thinking,' she murmured, reaching for the Scotch glass, her voice level despite the buzz of what they'd shared.

'Go on.'

His tone was cool, muted, and she hid her smile behind the glass.

'Perhaps I will stay here for a month.'

He tipped his head back and laughed, a deep noise that reached inside Bea and squeezed her tummy.

'I mean, not just because I really, really like what we just did,' she said with a lift of her shoulders.

'Of course not,' he murmured, mock serious. 'This would still be purely business.'

'Oh, absolutely. I might even have to call you Mr Lykaios from time to time,' she said, tilting her head to the side as she considered that. 'Or sir, if you'd prefer.'

He grinned, finishing his own Scotch before placing the glass on the edge of the bath and moving closer to her.

'As your self-appointed instructor in all things sexual, that does seem appropriate.'

'You mean there's more to learn?' she enquired with wide eyes.

'Oh, Beatrice, so much more. Where to start…?'

As always, he woke with a start, a sense of foreboding knotting in his gut that drew him immediately into consciousness. It didn't ease when he became aware of the warm, naked body at his side, her soft brown hair fanned across the pillow, stirring needs within him that should have been well and truly satiated by the night they'd shared.

On the streets of Athens he'd slept with one eye open, aware that danger could come at any point and that if it did it would be his responsibility to defend them both, to protect Matthaios. It was an alertness for danger that could only be eased in one way: control.

Ares didn't lose sleep about his business interests because he oversaw every single aspect of his empire. No matter was too small to escape his attention. In his personal life it was much the same.

Everything was on his terms, always.

The women he dated understood that—he made sure of it. Just as he had with Bea. He'd been crystal-clear.

Despite that, he felt a deep, dark worry that he might hurt her. He couldn't say why, but he had the strongest sense that there was something within Bea that needed protecting, a vulnerability she desperately tried to conceal, but which he nonetheless sensed.

He wouldn't hurt her.

They'd both acknowledged what this was, and he'd been open about the limitations of it. They'd even put an expiry date on her remaining with him. Surely that was some form of insurance?

Fighting a strong desire to wake her with the kind of kiss that would lead to so much more, he slid out of bed and dressed quickly, dragging on some low-slung jeans and a black shirt. If Danica woke he didn't want the crying to disturb Bea—she needed to sleep.

At the door, he took one last look at her. She was so beautiful and peaceful, so…trusting when she was asleep.

Despite the assurances he'd just given himself, the sense of foreboding was back, chewing at his gut. He pulled the door shut behind himself.

'Excuse me,' Bea apologised, stifling the fifth yawn in as many minutes.

Ellen's expression was sympathetic. 'The baby kept you awake last night?'

Heat suffused Bea's cheeks as she smiled awkwardly, looking away, infinitely preferring not to think about all the ways in which she'd been kept awake. Not by a baby, but by the sinfully sexy Ares Lykaios instead.

'Xanthia says you have a heap of experience with children.'

'I have lots of younger brothers and sisters,' the girl agreed, her round face dimpling as she smiled affectionately. 'And I have been hired as a babysitter since I was about nine years old,' she added.

'How old are you now?' Bea prompted.

'Twenty-one. I know I look younger,' Ellen laughed.

'Yes, you do,' Bea agreed, gesturing for Ellen to walk on ahead, into the lounge. Danica was set up in a playpen, lying on her tummy with a soft baby's ball in the palm of her hand.

Ellen made a little squealing sound of delight. 'Oh, she's so beautiful. May I pick her up?'

'Please,' Bea encouraged, interested to see how well Ellen handled Danica. The surge of protective instincts firing through Bea surprised her. As with the first night she'd held Danica, it was an almost maternal humming in her blood, a feeling that there was an invisible cord connecting the two of them, that she would fight to protect with her life.

Ellen spoke in Greek to the little girl, something that was wholly appropriate but which felt like a knife being plunged into Bea's heart. She felt excluded and unwanted. Old feelings spread through her; she turned away.

It took a moment for Bea to get her own emotions under control, and to remind herself that she had a life and a real job back in London. Despite the fact that Amy had been reassuring in an email—they had an excellent team of staff who would be able to continue to work to the high standards required by the London Connection's clients while Amy, Clare and Bea were away—she still knew she needed to get back at the end of the month. There was no guarantee Matthaios would be out of rehab by then, despite what Ares hoped. If Bea could leave Danica with someone like Ellen then she'd have the peace of mind of knowing Danica was being not just looked after—but loved.

'How often can you work?'

'Every day.' Ellen smiled sweetly, rocking Danica on her hip. 'I'm between jobs at the moment, so the timing is perfect.'

'Yes.' Bea's voice caught in her throat. She coughed to cover it. 'I really need help through the day, so that I can get some work done.'

'You're a lawyer?' Ellen said curiously.

Bea nodded. 'Not the kind that goes to court though. I think it sounds more exciting than it is.'

Danica made a little noise then, and one chubby arm extended, reaching for Bea. Her heart turned over in her chest, the sense of being wanted and needed by Danica making her ache.

For a moment, Bea resisted. The longing to feel wanted was always followed by the knowledge that she wasn't—and that would happen here too. While Danica seemed dependent on Bea now, she knew that when she left Porto Heli the baby would have Ellen and Ares, and then Matthaios. Her life would continue without Bea, whereas she would always think of—and miss—the little baby who had so quickly worked her way into Bea's heart.

She wanted to resist out of a need for self-preservation, but those damned maternal instincts had her crossing the room and taking the baby from Ellen's arms. Danica put her little head on Bea's shoulder.

'Why don't I give you a tour of the house?'

An hour later, all the terms had been agreed. Ellen was going to spend several hours a day with Danica, and more if needed. She was helpful, flexible and had a kind nature. Bea told herself she was glad, even when she knew that with the admission of Ellen into the household staff, Ares's need for Bea lessened dramatically. It was a very good thing, then, that she was keeping a level head and not allowing their insane sexual chemistry to make her want more than was on offer.

CHAPTER ELEVEN

'IT'S SO BEAUTIFUL HERE.' Bea sighed appreciatively at the colours lighting up the sky—pink, purple, grey and silver, as the sun dipped closer to the horizon, preparing to draw a blanket of stars overhead. But for now it was a stunning display of dusk, her favourite time of the day, and Bea's soul drank it in.

They'd watched a week's worth of sunsets together since the first night they'd shared. By unspoken agreement, a rhythm had formed to their lives. Ares worked long days, often in his Athens office, returning after Danica was in bed. Bea worked when she could; despite Ellen's presence, she tried to limit herself mostly to Danica's nap time, so that she could be involved in the baby's life, and be sure things were running smoothly.

There was no cause for concern with Ellen. The young woman was calm and enthusiastic at the same time, an excellent companion for an energetic baby.

Bea's phone buzzing caught her attention. She reached behind her, swishing the screen to life, her pulse firing up when she saw a message from Amy.

'Bad news?' Ares's voice was deep and husky.

Bea read the message, her frown deepening.

Sorry I've been MIA. Try not to stress about what you're seeing in the papers—I'm okay. It's nothing like last time. I'll explain everything face to face. Love you. X

She didn't have the heart to tell her friend—a PR exec—that she hadn't read a newspaper headline since she'd been in Greece.

'Not bad news, I don't think…' She shook her head, quickly googling her friend's name and gasping when she read the first headline that appeared.

Palace Scandal! History repeats itself with new Lothario-in-Chief!

'Oh, no, Amy!'

She skimmed the text, baffled by the revelation of Amy's relationship with the Prince of Vallia. Last Bea had heard, Amy was going there in a professional capacity. So what was going on? This wasn't exactly good PR for the prince. She clicked into another article, shaking her head, reminding herself that Amy's text had explicitly said she was okay. It went some of the way to assuaging Bea's worries. Besides, there was no way Amy would get involved with a guy like Luca Albizzi. Not after last time.

Nonetheless, she hit the forward button on her phone and sent the article to Clare. Speaking of MIA, she'd heard nothing from the third member of their trio, but Clare had said she'd likely be unavailable for a while, so that was hardly surprising.

Trying to ignore the *frisson* of worry, Bea brought herself back to the present, focusing on the warmth of the sun on her arms, the colours in the sky and, of course, the man in the pool.

Ares drew closer to the coping, his dark hair a wet pelt against his head. She watched the way the droplets rippled over his shoulders, admiring his tanned flesh and muscled arms.

'You're sure you won't join me?'

Her smile was wry. 'As I've told you every time you've asked, it's way too cold for swimming.'

He laughed. 'It's warm, I promise.'

On previous nights the evening had brought a chill breeze, but tonight there was more heat in the air. Though summer was still another six weeks away, the promise of its warmth surrounded them tonight.

'I'll compromise by sitting at the edge. Deal?'

He didn't say anything, simply watching her in that intense way of his as she stood, strolling towards him then sitting down. The denim miniskirt left her bare legs free to dangle in the water, the oversized tee required a pushing-up of the sleeves.

'How was work?' She reached out, ruffling his hair with her fingers, a jolt of anticipation running through her at the ease with which she could touch him, a man who had so recently appeared into her life and made her feel inadequate and powerful all at once.

His frown was infinitesimal. 'Busy,' he said, his eyes probing hers for a minute before he looked away.

Her heart skipped a beat as, for the first time in a week, she felt something akin to insecurity whisper through her. It was as though he was hiding something from her. As always, Bea was on the alert, looking for signs that a person she cared about was losing interest in her, ready to jump before she was pushed. How often she'd employed those skills with her parents—reading them intently, leaving a room before they could suggest she go and find something else to do, pretending occupation with a book so she wouldn't appear to notice the way they fawned over the twins, hanging on their every word.

'Ellen is doing well with Danica,' she said, to lay the groundwork for that possibility. If he wanted her to go, she wouldn't put up a fight. She'd make it easy for him, and walk away with her head held high. Worse than being unwanted, she'd learned a long time ago, was losing one's pride along with it.

'Yes.' The agreement was distracted, as though something important was on his mind.

Danger signs blared and, despite her intention to stay cool, panic gripped her heart.

'In all honesty, she could probably move in, you know.' *Say it, coward*, she urged herself. Clearing her throat, she forced an over-bright smile to her face. 'You could even release me from my kidnapping early.' She let the words hover between them, the suggestion that she would be completely fine with that.

'What?' His drawn-together brows showed confusion, as though it was the last thing he was expecting her to say.

'We agreed to a month before Ellen entered into the equation, and when Danica seemed much less settled,' Bea pointed out quietly. 'She's like a different baby now. You don't really need my help any more.'

The words were a form of acid in her throat. She tried to hold his eyes, to look brave and unconcerned, but she couldn't. She focused on the water instead, blinking several times to push back an overwhelming rush of emotion.

'We agreed to a month.' The words cracked around them harshly. 'I expect people I do business with to uphold their end of a deal. Are you trying to renege on our agreement?'

It was the reassurance she craved but in the strangest possible sense. This was so much more than business...wasn't it?

Doubts and uncertainties warred within her. She had no experience with men to compare this to, no idea what she'd wanted him to say. It was an indication that he didn't want her to leave though. Shouldn't that be enough?

'I'm not reneging,' she denied and, despite her best efforts, the words were softened by hurt.

He swore in his native tongue, coming to stand between her knees, looking up at her face intently. 'Do you want to go home?' he prompted, his own expression impossible to interpret. He was evidently far better at shielding his emotions than she was hers.

Home.

It was a strange word to employ, because it spoke of a sense she'd never known in her heart. Only as Ares asked the question did Bea realise she'd never actually thought of anywhere as home.

'I will not keep you here against your will.' The words seemed cut from glass, each sharp and cold, with the power to wound. But to wound who? His voice softened. 'And I will not sever my relationship with the London Connection. You do not need to stay because you're afraid of repercussions.'

It wasn't losing his business she was afraid of now; it was losing herself.

'Did you ever intend to fire the agency?' she asked quietly, moving her gaze to his face.

'Clare has managed my interests better than I can imagine anyone else doing,' he admitted finally. 'I never let my personal feelings enter into a business decision. Having made a single mistake in two years would have been a pretty poor reason to fire her.'

Bea's heart felt strangely light. 'So you were just using Clare's absence as leverage over me?'

He lifted his fingertips from the pool, dribbling a little water over her knee. 'I use whatever tools are at my disposal to achieve what I want.'

'And what did you want?'

'To get to know you better.'

Her ears were filled with a rush of noise like a tidal wave. 'Why?'

His frown was swift; she almost missed it. 'I can't say.'

'Why not?'

'I mean I don't know,' he corrected quietly. 'You were different, somehow.'

'Different to what?'

He braced his hands on the pool coping, pushing up effortlessly and holding himself there, a feat of abdominal control that even in that moment she didn't fail to notice. 'I was fascinated by you,' he corrected, brushing her lips with his, sending arrows of need through her body, arrows that almost drove all other thoughts from her mind. 'You were a contradiction and I wanted to understand that.'

He dropped back into the pool, resting his arms over her legs.

'And do you now?'

'No,' he answered immediately. 'If anything, the more I get to know you, the less sense you make.'

Her hazel eyes flared wide, surprised by that analysis. 'I think you're looking too hard. I'm actually very simple.'

His laugh was disbelieving. 'Liar.'

She dipped her fingertips into the pool, dribbling water over his shoulder before dropping her hand to his flesh, tracing invisible circles there.

'Stay the full month,' he said quietly, his eyes probing hers. 'So that I have more opportunity to make sense of you.'

It wasn't exactly what she needed to hear—no one had ever managed to offer Bea that—but it was enough. Enough for now to stave off her basic insecurities, to make her feel that he really did want her with him. He wasn't looking for an excuse to push her away; he wasn't counting down the minutes until she could leave. And even though he had Ellen to help with Danica, he still wanted Bea to be a part of their lives. For now.

'What is that song you sing to her?' Ares asked later that same night, when Bea was almost asleep. Her eyes were heavy and it took her mind a moment to wade back from the drugging proximity of sleep. Her body felt as though it was glowing, pleasure spreading through her limbs as the way he'd made her feel earlier set her pulse racing.

She hadn't been back to the guest room since the first night they'd made love. They hadn't discussed it; this had simply evolved out of a mutual need to be together at night, a desire to hold and touch, to wake up and reach for one another, satiating themselves over and over…

'Which song?' she asked sleepily. She flicked a glance to the bedside table. It had just passed midnight. Not terribly late but, given the way they were spending their nights, she was snatching sleep wherever she could find it.

His own voice was low and deep, so that when he hummed the familiar tune to Bea it sounded somehow mystical and different. She caught her breath, unused to hearing the song from anyone else.

'It's called "Calon Lân",' she murmured, turning in the bed so she could face him, resting her head on the pillow. 'It's Welsh.'

'You speak Welsh?'

'No.' Sadness etched her smile. She'd never told another soul why she knew that song, and yet the words bubbled through her now, pulling her towards him. 'I used to hum it as a girl—just a few lines, all that I could remember. For a long time, I didn't consciously know where it had come from, nor why I sang it. My adoptive dad, Ronnie, recognised the tune and played the full song for me.'

'Where did you learn it?'

Her heart skipped a beat. A pain that was almost too raw to speak of sliced through her. But Bea was nothing if not brave; confronting pain head-on was something she'd had to do enough times to be able to face it now.

'It's the only memory I have of my birth mother,' she said quietly. 'It's not even a memory,' she corrected, 'so much as a fog. A haze. If I think on it too hard it's like trying to catch soap in the bath—slippery and impossible. I can't remember what she looked like, and I can't remember anything about my life before…before I came to live with Ronnie and Alice—' her voice was rushed '—but I know she used to sing the song to me. She must have done it often, because it's kind of imprinted inside of me. And when I sing it I can feel her arms around me. I know that sounds strange.'

He shook his head once, just enough to disabuse her of that idea. 'Memory is a funny thing.'

'Yes.' She bit down on her lip. 'When I heard Danica crying, the words just came out of me. It's always comforted me, the song, and I thought it might do the same for her.'

'It appears to work wonders.'

She nodded, pressing her palm to his chest, feeling the steady rhythm of his heartbeat.

'What happened to your birth parents?'

She realised she'd been afraid of this question. No one had ever asked it. Amy and Clare had always instinctively understood that it was a no-go area. It was an almost impossible thing to reveal, because it was like admitting to someone that you just weren't very lovable.

'They didn't want me.' The words burned their way through her heart. She clamped her lips together in an attempt to stem any more.

A crease formed between his brows as he analysed that statement. 'For what reason?'

And there he'd found the crux of the matter. She laughed uneasily, flipping onto her back and staring at the ceiling. 'I was a difficult child, I guess.'

She couldn't look at him, so didn't see his reaction.

'It's fine,' she lied. 'They did the right thing and gave me away, obviously expecting I'd end up with a family more capable of caring for me.'

The silence that fell was barbed. 'And did you?'

Another question she'd never been asked, but this time because Amy and Clare had been able to see the truth for themselves. 'I grew up with everything you could want.' Her voice had a practised tone to it—the same one she'd used whenever people had enthused about how 'lucky' she was to have rock royalty for a dad and a bona fide supermodel as a mum.

'Why do I suspect that's not true?'

Damn him! She didn't want to talk about this. 'Are you kidding? Who wouldn't want to be raised by a couple of celebrities?'

'Lots of people,' he answered simply. 'And definitely you.'

Her throat thickened with emotion.

'You hate attention,' he said gently. 'And yet, given their fame, I imagine you received more than your fair share.'

His perceptiveness knocked her off-balance, so she turned her face to his, her eyes wide.

'It was a strange way to grow up,' she agreed, careful not to reveal more than was necessary. 'They thought they couldn't have kids, so I was spoiled rotten when I first came to live with them.'

Most people would focus on that, wanting the details of just how much people like Ronnie and Alice would give their daughter. People were, in Bea's opinion, always obsessed with the minutiae of a celebrity's life—how were they like 'normal' people and in what ways did they differ?

Not Ares. He wasn't so easily diverted by the mention of fame and fortune.

'And then she fell pregnant and everything changed for you,' he prompted, recalling their earlier conversation, on the night they'd arrived at Porto Heli.

'In many ways.' She lifted one shoulder. 'Anyway, as I said, I really don't like to talk about my family.'

'I let you get away with that once, but not again.'

She blinked, surprised.

'I want to understand you,' he reminded her. 'And I suspect this is at the root of your mystery.'

'There is no mystery,' she demurred with a quick shake of her head.

'Why did you decide to study law?'

The subject change was so swift it almost gave her whiplash.

'I was good at it.'

It was a throwaway comment but the expression on his face showed something else, as though he was sliding another piece of a puzzle into place. She angled her face, hating the sensation of being a bug beneath his microscope.

'I imagine you received a lot of praise for that,' he said thoughtfully.

Bea pulled her lips to the side. 'I don't know what that's supposed to mean.'

'You received accolades for your academic achievements?'

'I mean, I graduated with a first, so in that sense, yes.'

'And your parents? They were proud?'

The pain was as fresh as when she'd called to tell them her results and her mother had spoken over the top of her to announce that Amarie had started dating a Hollywood actor.

'We think they might get engaged soon! He's so delicious, darling.'

'Of course they were,' she lied.

Without even turning to look at him, she knew he didn't believe her.

'Are you someone for whom good grades came easily?' he asked.

'No.' Oh, how she hated the bitter tears that were flooding her throat. She swallowed desperately. 'I suppose I have a bent for the law—it came more easily to me than, say, mathematics did. My mind definitely works a certain way. But I studied hard, to the exclusion of everything else. I was determined to—'

He waited for her to finish the sentence.

'To do well,' she finished lamely, not wanting to admit to him that making her parents proud had indeed formed a huge part of her motivation.

'And you did,' he said gently. It wasn't praise. It wasn't congratulations. And yet hearing him say those words warmed some small part of her, so she blinked her eyes and smiled, a weak smile pulled from her soul.

'Thank you.'

He lifted a hand, running it over her hair, his eyes following the movement of his fingers. 'I used to look at people like you and think you had it all. I would jealously watch university students with their books and rucksacks, their easy lives, and wish more than anything that I could trade places. I desperately wanted to be able to study. I thought people like you had it so easy.'

'Compared to you, I did,' she murmured softly.

'I don't know if that's true.' He moved closer, his lips brushing hers. 'There are many things besides food that people starve for, *agápi mou*.'

CHAPTER TWELVE

BEA WAS BEYOND worried about Amy. The last time they'd spoken, everything had been fine. Sure, the conversation was rushed, but Bea had presumed Amy was just caught up with work. But now Amy was back in London and her first order of business had apparently been to send this email. Bea read it again, shaking her head at Amy's request: Fire me, before this scandal gets out of hand. It made no sense, and all Bea could think was that she needed to speak to Amy, to tell her she loved her and would always support her. There was no way anyone was getting fired, no matter what had happened!

'Where are you? When are you coming back?' Amy asked when Bea called to reiterate her support. But before Bea could brush the question aside and bring the focus back onto Amy's email, Amy had a text from her demanding mother and had to abruptly end the call.

Bea's placed her phone down with a growing sense of disquiet.

The following week was the first time Ares had been allowed to see his brother and the visit brought with it a maelstrom of emotion. Matthaios looked good, but still, it was impossible for Ares to shake his sense of anxiety, as though he might say or do the wrong thing and set Matthaios back in his recovery. He felt as though he must walk a mile on eggshells.

'Who's the woman in the photo?' Matthaios asked conversationally, pointing to the image of Bea on Ares's phone.

Ares's eyes were drawn to her face, the affection she felt for Danica obvious in every line of her body. From the way she cradled Danica so completely, to the look in her eyes as she stared at the baby's dimpled face.

'Just someone who's helping me care for her,' Ares hedged uncomfortably. After all, that was the primary purpose of having Bea at Porto Heli. Never mind that they'd also spent the past three weeks exploring each other's bodies and minds to the point where she was almost all he could think of.

Not that Ares would ever really let a woman have that kind of control over him. He was focused on his work, on Matthaios, and now on Danica. That was it.

'*Theós*, she looks like her mother.'

For a moment Ares thought Matt meant Bea, who bore no resemblance to Ingrid whatsoever, except, he conceded, for their slender frames. But Ingrid had been so Danish, with her white-blonde hair and sky-blue eyes. Belatedly, he understood. Matt only had eyes for Danica. He was staring at the phone so hard it was possible a hole might burst through it.

'I will ask your doctors if I'm allowed to bring her here,' Ares said firmly. 'You're doing so well, Matt. You seem like yourself again.'

Matthaios looked to his older brother, shaking his head slowly. 'Don't bring her to this place. It's bad enough that I'm here,' he muttered, dragging a hand through his hair. 'I don't mean that I don't need to be here. I know that I do. But I don't want Danica to see me like this.'

'She's barely six months old,' Ares reminded Matthaios. 'I don't think she'll mind that it's somewhat lacking in charm.'

'I'll mind,' he said.

'I think she misses you.'

'She deserves so much better.'

Ares's sigh was heavy, drawn from deep inside. He'd been reflecting on that lately—the bond between children and their parents or carers, the people put on this earth to keep them safe. For them, that had been their grandfather, and when he'd died they'd been cast out on their own, needing to fend for themselves. Their grandfather had died but the lessons he'd taught them remained. Ares knew that was where his resilience and determination had come from: mornings spent battling harsh weather and frigid temperatures, pulling ropes out of the ocean until calluses had formed across his palm, never once complaining or even remarking on the difficulties of that life.

'I think she's doing okay,' Ares commented.

'Thanks to you. Ares to the rescue, as always.'

But Matt was wrong. Ares wasn't coming to the rescue. He was simply cleaning up his own mess—fixing something that would never have been a problem in the first place if he'd done a better job of looking after Matt and Danica.

'Is she from an agency?'

Ares didn't immediately follow.

'I thought you said Cassandra was the last nanny they'd send you, after all the nannies I fired or shouted at.'

'No.' He shook his head. 'She's…a friend.'

'Oh.' Matthaios regarded the screen with more attention and now Ares wanted to flick the image away. A possessive heat ran through him. Not possessive of Beatrice so much as of what was happening between them. He wasn't prepared to discuss it; that felt like a betrayal. What they were sharing was inside a bubble, separate from time, and from their normal lives. Though they'd never agreed to keep it a secret, it just felt right.

'We've worked together. She saw how much I was struggling and offered to help out.'

'I see.'

Damn it, Ares suspected Matthaios *did* see. Having grown up so near in age and enduring most of life's adventures at each other's side, their relationship was very close, and Matthaios understood Ares better than anyone.

'Will I get to meet this friend of yours?'

'No.' The answer was swift and definitive. 'She must return to London next week. A month was all she could give Danica, I'm afraid.'

He ignored the swift stabbing sensation beneath his ribs.

'I don't know when I'll be out, Ares. Are you sure she can't stay longer?'

'Take all the time you need. Beatrice has hired a local girl who is also very good with the baby. Ellen dotes on her and will be available to help even when you return home. Someone who can ease you back into normal life.'

'And keep an eye on me, you mean?' Matt demanded sharply, briefly taking Ares back to the god-awful time shortly after Ingrid's death, when every question had led to an angry retort from his younger brother.

Matthaios winced apologetically. 'I know you mean well. I just hate…being here and having no…'

'Control,' Ares supplied, before his brother could even finish his sentence. 'I understand how you feel.' He could think of nothing worse than losing control of any situation, ever. 'What you have to realise is that in getting well you are taking control back. Control over the addiction that will chew through your life if you let it, just as it did our mother's.'

'I know that.' Matt's eyes fired with courage. 'I'm not going to mess this up, Ares.' He looked to the phone once more. 'She means too much to me.'

'You're very quiet.'

He regarded Bea over the rim of his glass. She was wearing the dress he'd chosen from the department store. He'd grabbed it simply because it had been nearby but, seeing it on her now, the colours were the perfect palette to draw out her complexion.

'Am I?' The question was designed to stall. She was right; he had been preoccupied since returning from visiting Matthaios.

'You've answered in monosyllables practically all evening.' Concern clouded her eyes. 'Is everything okay?'

He fingered the stem of his wine glass. 'I saw Matt today. My brother.' And then, as though she couldn't connect the dots. 'Danica's father.'

Her smile showed how redundant his second two statements had been. 'How is he?'

'Doing better,' Ares admitted. 'Frustrated that it's taking longer than expected to feel back to full health.'

'What do the doctors say?'

'That he should take as long as he needs, but that he's showing very promising signs for a meaningful recovery. It's never a smooth journey, though. It will require lifelong vigilance, so now it's about arming him with the tools to recognise when he's at risk of relapsing, as well as how to surround himself with people who are good for him.'

'What was Danica's mother like?'

Ares's smile came easily. 'An excellent influence. He adored her, and she didn't let him get away with anything. I abhor the idea of soulmates,' he said with an unintended shudder, 'but in this case I would willingly make an exception.'

'Are you so sceptical about love?' she asked, and although he knew she was determined to get back to her life in London he felt a natural throb of concern enter his bloodstream. This was the longest he'd ever spent with a woman. Ares always, without fail, left before things could get beyond the first flush of sexual chemistry. He had no interest in growing dependent on anyone, and even less in being needed.

If this time had proved anything, though, it was that he was stronger than he'd thought. Three weeks with Bea had flown by and while they'd been thoroughly enjoyable, he had no difficulty in accepting their affair was almost at an end. Oh, he'd miss her, but just in a physical way, and that wouldn't last long, surely.

'Love is fine,' he said with a careful smile. 'For Matthaios it was necessary. Ingrid changed him and even though her death destroyed a part of him, he is still a better man for having loved her.'

'But it's not for you,' she pushed, her own expression giving frustratingly little away.

'Love requires commitment and I have always preferred to be alone.'

'Why?'

'This, coming from you?'

Her grimace might have been an attempt at a smile.

'My career is my life,' she said.

He understood her drive and determination. He had always been motivated by a similar need to achieve.

'As a child, I knew that Matthaios's life was inextricably linked to mine. His success was mine to encourage. His failures landed at my feet. When my grandfather died, he left just the two of us, and Matt became dependent in a way that has haunted me ever since. I've let him down too many times, Beatrice.'

'I'm sure he wouldn't share your assessment.'

'Be that as it may, it's how I feel. I would never want anyone else to depend on me. Not a woman, not a child. No one.'

She reached for her own drink, sipping it slowly, her eyes showing she was lost in thought.

He couldn't say why, but he wanted her to understand. 'Dependence is…difficult,' he said with a shake of his head. 'My mother…' Was he really going to go down this path?

'Yes?'

His eyes locked on hers on a sigh of frustration. 'I couldn't help her. I loved her—I was just a kid and she was my mother—but it didn't matter what I said or did.'

Beatrice was frowning. 'What was she like?'

'Fun.' His grimace showed pain. 'When she was around, at least. She was full of energy some of the time, taking us to the playground at midnight or sneaking us in to see a movie, spontaneous and—' He sought the word.

'Erratic?' she supplied gently.

'Yes. Exactly. I realise now that this "spontaneous" fun usually coincided with her benders. Then the darkness would come—days of her being in bed, unable or unwilling to move. Sick, shouting at us to be quiet.'

'And so you took care of her?'

'As much as she'd let me.' He shrugged.

'And Matthaios?'

'Yes. I cared for him too. Someone had to feed him.'

Bea's eyes were filled with sympathy. He looked away, firming his jaw.

'So you can see why I'm sceptical about the whole idea of being needed by anyone. It's not healthy. I hate it.'

Bea's soft exhalation of breath eventually drew his gaze back.

'Anyone else might say that sounds kind of lonely,' she observed eventually.

Something strengthened in his chest. 'But not you?'

She shook her head slowly. 'No. Not me.'

For himself, he understood the decision, but for Bea, something inside Ares cracked apart a little. There was something completely unacceptable about the way she'd walled herself off from life and the experience of companionship.

He reached across the table, putting his hand on hers. 'I don't get seriously involved with the women I date, Beatrice, because I abhor the idea of relationships and all the emotional expectations that come from them. But I *do* date. I enjoy the company of women, I enjoy sex and intimacy. I appreciate the importance of human connection, even when I know I have my limits.'

Her smile was wry. 'I don't think that's any better than the way I live my life.'

'So when you leave here, is it your intention to go back to the way things were before? Avoiding men, avoiding dating, hid-

ing yourself in unflattering outfits lest someone actually rec-
ognises that you're a sensual, attractive woman?'

Her cheeks turned a vibrant pink, her lips parting indignantly.
'That's not—' She clamped her lips down on the denial. 'That's
none of your business.'

He laced their fingers together, squeezing her hand. 'You
deserve better than the life you're living.'

She pulled her hand away. 'I like my life.'

He didn't need to say anything to challenge her. His look
communicated his scepticism just fine. She huffed and stood,
pacing towards the pool. As the evenings had grown warmer
they'd taken to eating out here. Beatrice, Ares had learned,
loved sunsets, her affinity with this time of day something
he'd subconsciously begun to crave. He'd made sure he was
home in time to enjoy them with her—or, rather, to enjoy her
enchantment as the sky dressed itself in a different outfit each
evening. Tonight had been cloudless, so the sky had filled with
a gentle gradient, fading from purple at the horizon to gold and
peach. The ocean took on tones to match, a steely turquoise in
the lessening light.

He pushed his own chair back. Nothing he'd said had been
wrong, but upsetting Bea was intolerable. He prowled towards
her, standing at her back, his hands curving over her shoulders.

'It's your life,' he murmured gently. 'And in less than a
week you'll get back to it. I don't like to think of you leading it
alone—even when, selfishly, a part of me never wants you to
get involved with any other man.'

He felt her sharp intake of breath and laughed. 'Don't worry.
I'm not suggesting that we continue this. It's pure male ego.'

She exhaled slowly. 'What if...'

The words were so soft he barely caught them. 'Yes?'

She turned in the circle of his arms, her eyes looking deep
into his own, stirring something in his soul. 'What if, after this
week's over, we still...see each other?' The muscles of her throat
bunched delicately. 'From time to time,' she added quickly.

It was like being split apart by the stroke on an anvil.

There was danger here. Danger in the way Beatrice provoked him, spoke to him, pushed him—danger in the sweet little noises she made when they slept together, danger in the fact that he'd already spent more time with her than he had with any other woman. If maintaining control was the most important thing in his life, then Bea represented a very real threat to that.

He ground his teeth together, mentally distancing himself. 'That's not possible.'

He saw the hurt in her eyes briefly before she let them drift shut, her lashes forming two dark velvet fans against her cheeks. 'Why not?'

'Because it would just be prolonging the inevitable. I won't let you waste your life like that.'

'It's my life,' she pointed out defiantly.

'And my conscience to live with.' He regarded her warily, hating that she was trying to move the parameters of their safe agreement.

She turned away from him abruptly so he had no idea of her reaction to those words.

He had to drive his point home. 'Bea, I like sex. I like it a lot. These last few weeks have been…better than I could have imagined. But we both knew it would end.'

Silence grew thick between them. When she spoke, her voice was stiff like iron, but quieter than the whispering wind, so he had to lean closer to catch the words.

'This isn't a protestation of love. I'm just saying we could—casually—see each other when I'm back in London. If you want to.'

Why did he hate that even more? Why did he want to shout that a no-strings relationship like that wasn't good enough for her?

It was a double standard; if she wanted to limit herself to that kind of relationship—just as he did—then that was her choice.

But Bea was different to him.

Where Ares had grown hard and ruthless out of habit and necessity, Bea was soft and sweet, vulnerable beneath a thin outer layer that imitated coldness. She wasn't cold though, and she wasn't someone who was suited to live her life alone. She was just too scared to let herself love anyone.

He clamped his jaw, turning her gently and catching her hands, lifting them to his chest. She didn't quite meet his eyes.

'I want to enjoy the time we have left, and then I want you to leave my home and never look back. Don't think about me, don't think about Danica. Go home and start your life over— only promise me that you'll keep an open mind about companionship. You deserve better than to keep pushing everyone away, *agápi mou.*'

Pain was slashing through her. A pain that was familiar and intense.

He didn't want her.

He didn't want her.

The words kept circling through her brain, prickly and sharp, so she had to bite back a groan. Her insides were awash with acid but Bea wouldn't let him see her pain. Just like she'd learned to hide it from her parents, and from everyone else, she hid it from Ares now, flicking him a careless smile even as something inside her was shattering into a thousand pieces.

He didn't want her.

'I'll grant you most of what you've asked for,' she said gently.

He was very still and that stillness was all the confirmation she needed. He'd never want her. No one would.

'I won't think about you when I leave...' the words caught in her throat a little '...but Danica will always have a place in here.' She pulled her hand free and pressed it to her heart. 'I can't promise I won't think of her often.'

It wasn't just sunset that Bea loved; it was sunrise too. The bookends of the day that broke across the sky, rendering it with a sense of magic and newness, the promise of a new dawn and new hope.

The next morning she pushed back the sheets of Ares's bed and crept out silently, steeling herself to recognise that this was almost over. Soon there would be no more waking up beside him, no more pressing back against his naked body, teasing him with her proximity, silently pleading with him to make love to her again. There was only a handful of nights left to enjoy Ares, and then she'd never see him again. Because he didn't want her.

The sand was cold beneath her feet, and damp from the receding waves' kiss. She walked slowly at first, her arms wrapped across her chest, her eyes on the distant stars in the sky, each dwindling by the second, losing their sparkle as light permeated their backdrop.

Her first thought should have been of Danica. The little girl who'd lost her mother, and in some ways her father too, who'd been sent to live with an uncle who'd outsourced her care because he didn't know how to accommodate her in his life and heart. The little girl who had calmed at the first sign of real love and understanding. Her first thought should have been of the baby, but it wasn't. Though she would miss Danica like an absent limb, her feelings for Ares were so much more complex.

She could admit how she felt about Danica. She could understand every single emotion she had for the baby. The sense of affection, of protectiveness, her amusement at the little faces Danica pulled—everything there made sense.

She felt, Bea supposed, as one was meant to when confronted with an adorable, helpless, dependent, sweet infant. She loved her.

It was simple and made sense, whereas everything she felt for Ares was a Dumpster fire of doubt. Physically, she understood what she wanted. He was gorgeous and he made her feel as though she were floating. She could never have counted how many orgasms they'd shared, but that wasn't the whole story. This was more than just sex. It was the way his leg brushed hers beneath the dinner table each evening, the way he held her vice-like, clamped to his chest as he slept, as though he needed to exhale and inhale with the same rhythm she did. It was the way he reached for her hand when they walked, or watched her as she did something as banal as making coffee. It was the way she'd felt that first morning when she'd seen him holding Danica and a wound in her heart had started to stitch back together.

But beyond the physical it was all so murky and uncertain.

She knew she didn't want to do as he'd suggested the night before. She didn't want to walk away from him and forget he existed. She didn't want to live without him in her life.

The realisation made her gasp. She stopped walking, shocked into an inability to put even one foot in front of the other. It shouldn't have surprised her so much; wasn't that what she'd been suggesting last night? Hadn't she tried to find a way to maintain some form of relationship with Ares?

And he'd shut her down. Pushed her away. Oh, he'd done it so well, so beautifully, so *kindly*, as though he really cared about hurting her feelings, but the root cause had been the same. He wanted her to leave at the agreed upon time. He wanted her to leave and never contact him again.

He wanted her out of his life.

Her fist lifted and pressed against her mouth, blocking the sob that was welling in her chest.

Everything Bea had ever read about adoption had spoken of the total unwavering love and commitment an adoptive parent felt for their adopted child—the fact that most wouldn't make the distinction between biological and adopted. That hadn't been the case for her. Not only had her adoptive parents acted as though they regretted bringing her into their lives, her mother had frequently said as much. Not in so many words—Alice was too delicate for that—but she'd made it abundantly clear how she felt.

Like the time a photographer from a glossy magazine had come to the house to take photos to accompany an article they were featuring, and Alice had sent Bea to the study, suggesting it would be better with 'just the real family'. She'd been thirteen years old, home from school for a brief holiday, and the phrase hadn't made sense at first, then it had filtered into her brain like a thunderstorm at its peak, screeching and whirling with the force of a tornado. She'd gone to her room and cried, but out of those tears a determination had formed. She'd sworn she'd never let Alice hurt her again.

Oh, that hadn't been possible. Though Bea tried to be hard-hearted, she wasn't. Naturally she was soft and loving, and every insult and exclusion from the only people she thought of as family lashed her like a whip at her spine.

It wasn't only their cruelty that had cut her, though. It was their volatility. When Alice had wanted the world to see her as a compassionate, altruistic doyenne of charitable acts, she'd brought out Bea for everyone to see, disregarding Bea's natural dislike for cameras and attention. At those times Alice appeared to dote on Bea, and Bea, so starved for affection and warmth, had lapped it up, craving more, wondering what she'd done to deserve the sudden spurt of affection. It would dissipate just as abruptly as it had emerged, Bea packed off back to boarding school, and weeks would pass without a call or text message from her parents.

Her spirit broke so many times over the years, she thought it had been destroyed beyond repair.

She thought she'd got to the point where she would never again run the risk of being hurt. She'd pulled right back from her adoptive parents, deciding that she could play her part at Christmastime, visiting them for lunch and then speaking to Ronnie and Alice as equals—the less she expected of them, the better things went.

She'd grown out of wanting their love, and she'd told herself she'd never want *anyone's* love again. It was too dangerous, too likely to lead to emotional carnage, and God knew she'd suffered enough of that in her lifetime.

She sank down onto the sand; it was cold beneath her bottom. Staring out to sea, a wall of fear surrounded her, as vast as the ocean beyond this bay.

Despite everything they'd done to her, Bea loved her parents. She'd tried not to, but love wasn't something you could choose to feel or avoid. Love was as non-optional as breathing. And somewhere since meeting him, probably the night he'd stormed into the office, so cranky and unlike anyone she'd ever known before, Bea had fallen head over heels in love with Ares.

It was a disaster.

She knew without a shadow of a doubt that he would never love her back. And she knew intimately the pain that came from loving and not having that love returned.

If he felt anything for her whatsoever, he would have accepted her suggestion that they find a way to continue seeing one another, even after she went back to London. He hadn't. He didn't love her and that meant one thing and one thing only.

Bea had to escape.

CHAPTER THIRTEEN

HIS ARMS AROUND her waist were almost too perfect to bear. She allowed herself the weakness of sinking back into him just for a moment, one last sublime second of physical closeness, one last moment in which she could pretend that everything was just as it should be, before shattering the illusion with the truth.

Her heart stuttered in her chest, the enormity of what she was about to do dragging on her like a stone.

You could stay, a little voice in her head taunted. Stay for the rest of the week, enjoy the intimacy he was willing to offer, gather the crumbs of his affection for Afterwards, when he was no longer a part of her life and she needed to line her heart space with as many gold dust recollections as she possibly could.

At what cost?

Another sob welled in her chest and she pulled away from him, moving towards the corner of the kitchen, her palms pressed to the counter, her spine straight as she rallied every iota of strength she possessed. Fortunately, Bea had a lot of experience with difficult goodbyes, and even more with heartbreak.

'Beatrice?'

God, she loved how he used her full name. He was the only person who did, and the way he said it, with his accent, spiced with desire…

She swallowed, turning around and forcing her eyes to meet and hold his. She saw the speculation in them, and then the concern.

'Something's wrong.'

She'd asked Ellen to take Danica for a walk in the pram, having given the little baby a tight squeeze and a kiss on the tip of her nose, her heart breaking with the abundance of affection she felt for a child she had known for less than a month. So much for never wanting children! Never wanting to fall in love! What a fool she'd been to think she could dictate such basic human emotions.

'What is it?' He crossed the room, catching her hands in his, lifting them between them as he'd done the night before. It was a strange and fitting gesture, bridging their hearts in some way.

A thousand words swirled through her brain but she struggled to pluck the right assortment to form a sentence that would explain the realisation she'd had, and why that meant she had to leave immediately.

'When I graduated from university my parents sent their personal assistant to take photographs and give me a gift,' she said softly, recalling the delicate diamond bracelet in the turquoise box. 'The assistant was as awkward about it as I was devastated. He took the photos, gave me the gift and left as quickly as he could.' Her throat felt as though it were closing in on itself. 'I was so angry, Ares. It was a simple graduation ceremony only an hour's drive from their house, and they couldn't even make it. They didn't want to.'

He frowned, nodding slowly, though the reason for Bea divulging this obviously made little sense to him.

'My life has been filled with this horrible feeling of loving people who'll never love me back. Of knowing that nothing I do will ever make them proud, or even really make them aware that I exist. They supported me financially—they gave me anything I wanted materially—but they had, and still have, no idea who I really am. And yet I love them, because they're the closest thing to parents I've got.'

Her eyes swept shut as so many memories and hurts battered her, swelling within her, demanding to be shared.

'I know what it feels like to live in a void of uncertainty. Loving and not having that love returned is a horrible way to live, so I swore I'd never risk it. Why would anyone love me, anyway?'

His hands squeezed hers. 'Stop that. You know what an incredible woman you are. Any man would be lucky to have you.'

'Don't.' The word whipped between them, fierce and furious. 'Don't lie to me. Don't placate me with empty words.'

Surprise etched its way across his features.

'You say that but, as I've learned, words are cheap. It's easy to say one thing when you feel exactly the opposite.'

Something like proud defiance lit his eyes. 'I never say what I don't feel.'

'But you don't love me,' she challenged him.

His features grew taut, his lips tight.

'You say any man would be lucky to have me, but you don't want me. Are you not "any man"?'

'Beatrice…' He said her name like a plea, and her gut ached because this was all too familiar. How often she'd been made to feel guilty for complaining. Oh, not recently, but as a young girl, before she'd learned to accept the reality of her situation, when she'd still thought there could be an explanation for the inequities of her parents' treatment of her versus the twins, she'd argued for her cause, only to be made to feel as though she were being overly dramatic.

'Don't gaslight me,' she snapped, earning herself a look of complete shock.

He pulled his hands away, lifting his palms to her. 'I'm not. I'm simply trying to understand—'

He didn't finish the sentence. His brows drew together as he scanned her face, as though he might find answers there.

'What I suggested last night, about us seeing each other again after this week—it wasn't just because I enjoy having sex with you. I like being with you. I like spending time with you and getting to know you.' She shook her head with frustration. 'No, not getting to know you. I feel like on a soul-deep level I know everything there is to know about you. I feel like if it's possible that one person could be designed to fit perfectly with another person, then you're *my* person.'

His jaw shifted as though he were grinding his teeth together; he said nothing.

Bravely, she pushed on, her voice soft now, thick with emotion. 'I lied to you last night, Ares, but only because I've been lying to myself. It turns out I gave you my heart the first night we met, and I want you to keep it for ever.' She only became aware that a tear had slid down her cheek when it landed on her wrist.

'I can't believe this.' The words were short, his own emotions colouring the sentence so it emerged with obvious disappointment. 'I was so clear—'

'I know you were,' she agreed, a part of her withering at his clear-cut condemnation of how foolish she was being. 'But did you really think that would be enough?'

His eyes flared wide and something sparked in her chest. Hurting him felt good. What was wrong with her? How could she want to hurt the man she loved?

Because he was hurting her, and she was so tired of that. So tired of being hurt and ignored by the people she loved.

'Did you think that telling me I couldn't love you would mean a damned thing when you *invited* me, every single night we spent together, to do exactly that? Your words told me not to care but your body made it impossible not to.'

'That's just sex,' he said, but his voice was uneasy, guilt evident in every line of his face.

'Wow.' Now it was Bea's turn to feel pain—more pain than she'd known. 'Just sex. Good to know.'

'Beatrice, that isn't what I meant.'

'I thought you didn't say things you don't mean.'

He compressed his lips. 'Stop trying to trap me. I'm attempting to explain—'

'But that's just words again,' she interrupted, panic making her voice high-pitched. 'You say I can't love you, but do you even stop and think about whether or not you love me too?'

He wore a dismissive mask, his eyes glittering grey. 'I do not need to think about it.'

Her chest ached. Tears caused her throat to sting. 'So you don't love me.'

A muscle flexed near his jaw. 'I've said this from the first night.'

'Yes, yes,' she groaned. 'You did. But that was almost a month ago. Do you really still feel that way?'

He stared at her for several seconds and then nodded. 'Yes. It's exactly how I feel.'

He was being so clear and emphatic. Only a fool would continue this conversation when it could result in just one thing: more hurt. More rejection. Yet still she stood there, allowing the screws to be tightened, a glutton, apparently, for punishment.

'I came here wanting to hate you for kidnapping me, and then I saw you with Danica and I saw you with me and everything changed. I fell so completely in love with you, Ares.'

'Stop.' He shook his head. 'Stop saying that, Beatrice. It's a betrayal of everything we agreed. I don't want your love. I don't want you to need me. For God's sake, I don't want anything from you—got it?'

His outburst surprised them both. His words were so much more certain than she'd expected. She'd hoped for a hint of doubt. For a sign that on some level he might be torn, or starting to comprehend his true feelings. But this was adamant and determined. No one who felt even a hint of love could speak like that.

She angled her face away from him, the enormity of their

situation and her error, first in loving him and second in telling him, spreading through her.

'Hurting you is the very last thing I wanted.'

She nodded slowly. 'Then why are you?'

'Do I have an alternative?'

She looked deep into his eyes, trying to fathom his meaning.

'I don't love you, Beatrice. Should I lie to you, just to avoid
making you cry?'

Even now, his words were so cutting. Devastation wrapped
around her. It wasn't only from what he was inflicting on her;
it was the culmination of every feeling of worthlessness she'd
ever known.

He cupped her cheek so gently that it was a lie in and of itself. His touch spoke of such tenderness and affection, yet he
didn't feel those things for her.

'I don't love you, but not because you're unlovable, *agápi
mou.*'

She dipped her eyes downwards, focusing on the floor between them, fresh pain scoring her heart. 'Then why not?'

She felt his gaze burning the top of her head and waited for
an answer, an explanation, anything he could offer that would
lessen the sting of this rejection.

'Because I'm not capable of it. And because it's not what I
want.'

You're not what I want. So simple. So final.

She blinked rapidly, trying to clear her eyes of tears and her
brain of the tangle of emotions. 'I have to get out of here.' It
was a whispered resolution at first. Then stronger. 'I have to
go home.' Home? What a farce.

'Yes.' His agreement was the final straw. She spun away
from him just in time; her sob escaped with enough warning
to muffle it completely. 'I'll have my jet fuelled up.'

'No.' It was an immediate visceral reaction. 'Not your jet.'
She swallowed furiously. 'If you can just get me to Athens, I'll
organise my own flight home.'

'Beatrice, be sensible. I have a plane on standby. It's no trouble.'

'No.' She shook her head to underscore how serious she was. Everything about his private jet would only remind her of him. She couldn't do it. 'I want to do this myself. Please.'

His eyes warred with hers. She felt he was about to argue and held her breath, reserving her energy for exactly that. But, to her surprise, he dipped his head in agreement. 'When would you like to leave?'

'I'm ready now.'

His eyes glittered, something like rejection in them, and a fierce dismissal of that, but again he nodded. 'I'll get Danica so that you can say goodbye.'

'I've already done that. Ellen's taken her for a walk.' Heat flushed her cheeks. 'I didn't want them to overhear our conversation.'

His eyes narrowed and she felt ice run the length of her spine. 'You've thought of everything,' he remarked with stony reserve.

'Don't you dare make me the bad guy here.'

He stared at her, something tightening in his features before he sighed. 'I'm not. I'm well aware that title is completely mine.'

She could only stare at him, her heart in tatters at her feet, her soul withering deep inside her.

'Meet me on the roof when you're ready. I'll be waiting.'

It was an unconscious echo of the words he'd said on the day they'd gone shopping. So much had happened since then, he hadn't consciously evoked that time. But he'd thought of it again as he'd waited by the helicopter, watching her walk towards him holding only a garment bag which contained, he presumed, her ballgown. She brought no other bag, none of the clothes she'd accumulated whilst staying here.

He was both glad and sorry. Sorry because it showed how deeply he'd wounded her that Bea wasn't even able to take her own clothes, and glad because these physical items would serve as some kind of reminder of her. So that when he woke up at night and wondered if it had all been a dream, he'd see the clothes and know that, no, for a little while, he'd had Beatrice in his life.

And he could have her for longer, he argued with himself as she approached. All he had to do was ask her to be patient. To let him see if he could love her.

But he knew the answer already.

This wasn't about whether he could love Beatrice; it was about whether he wanted her to love him. To depend on him. To rely on him for her happiness and safety. There had been someone relying on him since he was a young boy, and without fail he'd let them down. His mother, his brother, now Danica— he hadn't even been able to hire appropriate staff to care for her. The idea of Bea depending on him, only to realise what a terrible idea that was...to see her life turn to ashes as he failed her in some vital way?

No.

He couldn't bear that.

He'd let her go and, despite what she might think now, she'd get over him. She'd move on and because of the experience they'd shared she'd be more open to love with the right sort of man next time.

'Armandos will take you to the airport,' he said when she was almost level with him. 'Unless you would like me to come with you?'

She bristled visibly, moving her head to the side. 'I'd prefer to go alone.' Her smile was brittle. 'Thank you.'

Ever polite, he thought with a harsh twist in his gut.

'Beatrice?' He had no idea what he was going to say, but he knew it didn't feel right to let her leave like this.

'Thank you for everything. With Danica.'

Her eyes shifted to his shoulder. 'I loved spending time with her.' Her lower lip wobbled and he moved quickly, opening the door to the helicopter, understanding the small kindness he could show her now. She just wanted to escape. Trapping her here to talk was further proof of his inability to be the man she needed.

'Let me know when you're back in London,' he requested. 'So I know you arrived there safely.'

She grimaced. 'I'll be fine, Ares. You can start forgetting about me right now.'

What could he say to that? He'd practically boasted to her about that being the wise thing to do. He couldn't deny it now, or she might read something into it. But as the helicopter lifted off, becoming a distant, gleaming speck of black against an azure blue sky, he knew he'd never forget Bea, and strangely he was glad of that.

Bea was in a fog. She managed, somehow, to buy herself a ticket on the next plane leaving for London, and to contemplate sending Amy a quick text to let her know she'd be home soon. Except Bea didn't want to see Amy or Clare. For the first time in her adult life, Bea truly felt that she didn't want to talk to her best friends. Not about this. She simply needed to be alone.

Amy would know within seconds that something serious had happened, and Bea couldn't lie to one of her best friends. She had to be stronger before they had that conversation.

If Amy had been a less worthy friend it would have been possible to presume she'd be too wrapped up in her own life to notice anything amiss with Bea. But Amy was loyal, kind and compassionate and she'd likely take one look at Bea and realise that her heart had been shattered. Hell, she'd probably insist the London Connection drop Ares as a client after this, and Bea knew they couldn't afford that. She had to heal a bit before she saw either Amy or Clare again, knowing their loyal streaks would be invoked. No one was expecting her back in London for a few more days. She'd sneak home to her apartment and lie low, just until she was ready to drag her brave face back into place.

Decision made, she went through Security and waited near the boarding gate, trying not to think about Ares, about Danica, and about how much she was already missing them both.

It was a stunning sunset. All the colours streaked across the sky, the deepest oranges and reds with a shimmer of gold, purple glowing from behind the scant covering of silvery clouds. Ares stared at it and felt a gut-punch of sorrow. He was sorry that Bea wasn't with him; she'd have loved it. Sorry that they weren't going to see another sunset together.

Sorry that he'd hurt her so badly.

Sorry that he'd never see her again.

Just horribly, regrettably sorry.

She never texted or called to let him know she'd arrived in London but, given the lack of news about a plane crash or the kidnapping of a twenty-nine-year-old executive, he had to presume she'd made it there and chosen not to contact him. A wise decision, but he yearned to hear something from her. Just to know she was okay.

As a child, his grandfather had told him often that 'time heals all wounds', and Ares had generally felt there was truth in that. But the more time that separated him from Bea, the worse he felt. Danica was unsettled and, two days after Bea left, Ellen moved into a guest room so she could be available to help around the clock.

Ares took that as an opportunity to leave Porto Heli, where everything, everyone and everywhere, reminded him of Bea. He needed to get away from her, any way he could.

CHAPTER FOURTEEN

'OH, MY GOD.' She stared at the rapidly spreading stain of milky coffee against a broad chest, her heart in her throat as her eyes lifted higher to ascertain that, yes, somehow, surely in an alternative universe, Beatrice Jones had once again managed to spill her coffee all over Ares Lykaios's chest.

It made no sense. Her brain struggled to translate what she was seeing. She'd barely slept since returning from Athens four days earlier. She was living on a strange combination of Netflix and coffee from the coffee chain beneath her apartment. She didn't even have to order now; when the baristas saw her walk in they began to prepare her drink, so all she had to do was tap her credit card and grab it when it was ready.

And in the case of this, coffee number four for the day, slam it into the chest of the only man she'd ever loved.

'I swear I put on the lid.' But the fact that it had burst open the instant she'd bumped into him might make him beg to differ.

Oh, God. She looked terrible. She couldn't remember the last time she'd showered. Her hair was scraped back into a ponytail, her shirt had a stain on the sleeve and she'd abandoned make-up for the sheen of takeaway noodle fumes.

'Beatrice.' He growled her name from somewhere deep in his throat and goosebumps ran across her skin; her stomach flipped. She looked at her watch for no logical reason except that time would tether her—she hoped—to reality. It was almost five in the afternoon. Of what day?

'What are you doing here?'

Of all the questions running through her brain, that was uppermost.

'I came to see you.'

Obviously. Why else would he be in this exact part of London? 'Is it Danica?' she asked quickly, concern for the little girl momentarily eclipsing anything else.

He flinched. 'Danica is fine. She's…at home with Ellen.' His lips were a grim smudge on his face.

'Oh. I'm glad.'

'May I come in?' He gestured to the security door to her building.

Bea stared at it, panic gripping her heart. She shook her head instinctively.

'Just for a moment.' There was something so imperative and commanding in his tone that Bea found herself sighing and moving towards it. She could control this situation. And she could definitely control how much she let him see of her pain. She had pride and she would use it to strengthen her resolve until he finally left. At the same time, she acknowledged that she desperately wanted him to stay. Seeing him under any circumstances was better than not, and oh, how hungry she was for the sight of him, the feel of him.

'How did you find out where I live?'

'It wasn't difficult.'

Of course it wasn't difficult for someone like Ares Lykaios. Somewhere during the time they'd spent together in Greece, she'd come to see him as a mere mortal, simply a man she'd fallen in love with, but he wasn't anything so pedestrian as that. He was powerful and could do whatever the hell he wanted.

She buzzed open the security door then gestured to the door

at the top of the stairs, a shiny black with a golden number four emblazoned on it.

'There are two apartments downstairs,' she explained as she averted her gaze from him, knowing she couldn't watch as he walked up the stairs or desire would undo every effort she was making to hold onto her pride. 'But no apartment number three. I've always wondered if the original builders thought it was unlucky or something.' She clamped her lips together, aware she was filling the nervous silence with babble and hating herself for that.

At the door of her apartment she hesitated, her eyes darting to his before returning to the lock.

'Two minutes,' he commanded, and when she still didn't move he reached out and took the extended key from her fingertips and inserted it, pushing the door open with an expression that was inscrutable.

Bea's heart was in her throat, emotions running rampant. She wasn't prepared for this. She'd wondered if she'd ever see him again, but had presumed that she'd at least have time to brace for that, to prepare herself for the mental hurdle of being near him once more.

This was *hard*.

She fought ingrained good manners, pointing to a chair without offering him a drink. Despite the dark patch spreading over his shirt, she refused to do anything to accommodate him. She'd had enough of being trampled. Enough of putting her heart out there and having it unceremoniously refused.

Bea's apartment had a large open-plan kitchen and lounge area. She kicked off her shoes then padded into the all-white kitchen, depositing the almost empty coffee cup into the sink and washing her hands before slipping a pod into her own machine. The muscle memory of the task was reassuring and somewhat calming; his eyes on her as she did something so simple was not. The machine whirred as dark coffee began to run into the mug.

When she turned around, he was staring at her intently and her breath slammed through her. She wanted to stamp her foot and she realised her temper was running away from her. How dared he come here with no warning, looking so damned perfect? As though nothing in the world was bothering him. As though his life was continuing completely as normal.

'What are you doing here?' Pride be damned. The words were a husky groan, a plea for him to disappear again so she could continue getting over him.

His lips compressed. The coffee machine stopped whirring. 'I can't sleep.'

She stared at him, the words making no sense.

'Then you should go see a doctor. See if they'll prescribe you something.'

'It wouldn't help.'

'I'm sure it would.'

He shook his head. 'Every time I close my eyes I see your face on that last morning in Greece. I see the way you looked at me when you told me you loved me and I didn't say it back, and I feel as though something is being twisted in my chest, the blade of a dagger, I don't know. And then I'm wide awake again. I just…need to know that you're okay. That's all.'

Her heart stuttered. She turned away with the pretence of reaching for her coffee, cradling it in her hands, taking a perverse pleasure in denying him the same courtesy. It was childish, yet she didn't care.

'I'm fine.' Pride came to her rescue. She'd begged him to love her once. She wouldn't do it again.

He nodded slowly, his eyes scanning her face.

Please go. She couldn't handle this much longer.

'Fine.' He dragged a hand through his hair. 'Good.' He frowned. 'I'm…glad.'

He turned towards the door and took two steps in that direction then made a deep noise of frustration, pivoting to face her. His eyes pinned her to the spot, his features a mask of something she couldn't fathom. He stared at her long and hard, so the air between them became thick with unspoken words, and then he swore, a dark, throaty curse in his native Greek, a word that reverberated around her kitchen again and again.

'Damn it, Beatrice. I can't do this.'

She wasn't capable of speaking.

'I can't be the man you want me to be. Do you have any idea how much I want to give you what you want?' He strode towards her and she braced for that as best she could, but it wasn't enough. She wasn't prepared to be so close she could see the flecks of silver in his grey eyes, breathe in the scent of his alpine cologne, mingled with her spilled coffee.

'It's not that I don't love you.'

She almost choked on her breath.

'It's that I don't want you to love me. I need you to stop. Tell me you made a mistake and that you were wrong. I can't bear to think of you feeling that way about me.'

He waited, staring at her, his chest feeling as though it had been cracked in two. His eyes pleaded with her to give him what he needed. He couldn't live in a world where Beatrice loved him. The thought of disappointing her, of letting her down in some vital way, was the worst thing he could contemplate.

Hell, he'd already let her down. He could see the hurt in her face even now, days after that disastrous conversation.

She wasn't okay.

And he didn't know how to make her okay.

'There was no mistake.' She blinked at him, as though just realising something. 'And there are no regrets.' He was unprepared for her hand lightly brushing his chest, the flatness of her palm against his heart, as though she couldn't resist feeling him there. 'I'll always love you and, even though that hurts like hell right now, I'm grateful. I never thought I'd fall in love.' Her lips twisted in a poor imitation of a smile. 'I wouldn't trade the experience of falling in love with you for anything. The time we spent together was honestly the best weeks of my life.'

Her words rang with courage. He closed his eyes against it, wondering at the way the world was shifting beneath his feet, old certainties seeming to erode in the face of her determination.

'Don't you see, Ares? You're off the hook; don't beat yourself up with guilt here. You don't have to love me back. Just spending that time together was a gift.' She sniffed and he fixed his eyes on her face in time to see a single teardrop fall from the corner of one of her beautiful, expressive eyes. 'I'm not okay right now, but I will be. The pain will fade, and then I'll just have those memories. Good memories, almost all of them.'

Her heart was open to him, beautiful and forgiving, if only he'd get over his own fears and accept it. But life had made him cautious. Her heart might not have been broken, in spite of what she'd been through, but he feared his was.

And yet she was being so brave! What must it have taken Bea to face her feelings? To confide the truth of them to him. Didn't she deserve as much in return?

He ground his teeth together, his stomach unsteady as he tried to find words without overthinking them.

'I've never known anyone like you. I'd planned to fly out of London after my meeting with Clare, you know. I wasn't meant to remain here, but then I met you and you suggested I come back the next day, and I invented every excuse in the world just to see you again. You bewitched me from the start.'

Her eyes were wide but awash with disbelief. 'You were unimpressed.'

'No, I was...fascinated. Why do you think I demanded you accompany me to the ball?'

'So you wouldn't arrive alone,' she reminded him. 'So the media wouldn't get a photo of you appearing solo.'

'I go to events on my own all the time. My ego isn't so fragile, Beatrice, that I can't handle being photographed without a glamorous woman on my arm. No, it was never that.'

'So why then?' she pressed, removing her hand from his chest and curling it around her coffee cup again. She sipped it, dropping her gaze from his, pushing him away a little. He could feel that she wanted to keep him at a distance and sought to close it.

'I just wanted to be with you. I wanted to sleep with you.' He threw the words at her, needing her to understand that he was *that* kind of man. Someone who liked to seduce women he barely knew and then move on.

No mess. No emotional confusion.

'And if Cassandra hadn't quit, we would have had sex and you'd have forgotten me a week later?'

Despite what he'd thought a moment ago, he contradicted himself with a shake of his head. 'I don't think so. You were already so far under my skin, *agápi mou*. When I look back at the way I spoke to you that night, the way I threatened you—I was terrified of losing you. I'll never forget what you said to me: that if I'd simply asked, you'd have stayed. I'd never known anyone like you before. So kind and good and compassionate. So full of love, Bea, you were aching to give it.'

Her sob was almost silent, wrenched from deep within her chest.

'You loved Danica instantly and I wanted to be a part of it.' He grimaced, the full truth of his actions spread out before him. 'Do you remember what you said, the morning you left Greece? You told me I made you fall in love with me, and you're right. Not consciously, but I was so selfish. It wasn't enough for me to have your body. I wanted all of you, everything you had to give, and that included your heart.'

She shook her head frantically. 'Don't. I can't—'

He didn't know what she was going to say, but he was getting so close to understanding his own actions. He lifted a finger to her lips, silencing her as he searched for what he'd felt and why.

'Nothing good has ever come from loving me.'

Her eyes swirled with contradictions, but she stayed quiet.

'I've loved you since that first night we met, I think, but I have no idea how to love you. I have no idea how to be a man who deserves you and, *Theós*, you deserve so much. I am being selfish again, coming here, telling you this, when the best thing for you would be if I had just let you walk away.'

Her sob was softer this time, and then she was leaning forward, pressing her forehead to his chest, her gentle sobs filling him with emotions he couldn't comprehend.

After a moment she pulled back to look up at him, shaking her head slowly. 'You're such an idiot.'

He lifted his brows.

'How do you not see yourself as you really are? How can you be so disillusioned?'

He frowned.

'You keep thinking that you let people down, but I see the opposite. I see a boy who had to parent his mother, and raise his brother. Even now, as a man in his thirties, you're picking up after Matthaios. You are good and kind and honourable, and I've got news for you, Ares.'

He waited.

'You're full of love to give as well. I watched you with Danica and saw the way you felt about her, your big, beautiful heart exploding with a need to protect her and care for her. You want to know how to be the man I deserve?'

His lips parted on a roughly expelled breath.

'By doing this! Exactly what you're doing right now. You came here today and you told me the truth about how you feel, even though that's kind of terrifying. Love isn't just an isolated emotion. It's held up by so many others! Trust and respect, kindness, humour, intention. I trust you to do the right thing by me—and that doesn't mean I'll never get hurt again. It doesn't mean you can protect me from anything bad ever happening in my life. It means that, whatever happens, I want to go through it with you.'

'But what if—'

'What if—what?' she interrupted quietly. 'Life is full of

"what-ifs". The only one that matters right now is this: what if you walk out of here today and we never see each other again? Will you be able to live with *that*?'

Everything inside him froze. He stared at her, revulsion barrelling through him. 'Absolutely not.'

Her little laugh was tremulous but happy.

He groaned as realisation finally settled around his heart.

'You're right. I'm an idiot. I can't—won't—live without you. My first instinct that night was to kidnap you, take you to my home and keep you there as long as I could, and it was the right one. Please come home again, Bea. I love you.'

Her heart exploded, the word 'home' exactly what she'd been ruminating on for days. How Porto Heli had become a part of her soul without her realising it, all because of the man who lived there.

She didn't hesitate; there was no need. Bea didn't have a single doubt in her mind as to where she was meant to be, and with whom.

'I will,' she agreed, smiling up at him, her heart full. 'But not right away.' She laced their fingers together. 'I have to break it to the girls that I'm moving to Greece...'

'Oh.' He nodded. 'Then we can live here. I don't care.'

Bea laughed. 'I do. I want to come home.' The word cracked with emotion, and his expression grew serious, wondrous. 'Give me a week, okay?'

A lot changed in a week. Beatrice wasn't the only one whose life had taken an unexpected shift—Amy and Clare had revelations of their own, and excitement about their futures overlapped with frantic business meetings and staff hiring, rearranging the corporate structure to ensure the London Connection could continue to grow even with the best friends living in different cities around the world.

Of one thing they were certain: their commitment to the

business—and their loyalty and love for one another—would never change, no matter how far apart they were geographically. They were friends, sisters of the heart, and always would be.

EPILOGUE

'IT'S A PLEASURE to meet you.' Matthaios smiled as he drew Bea into a warm hug, kissing her on both cheeks before releasing her. His exuberance was understandable. After several weeks in the rehab facility he was clean and sober and completely committed to living a sober life. Between them, Danica squawked, lifting her hands towards Matthaios, and at the same time the little girl burst into tears, shaking with the force of her emotions.

'Aw, she's so happy to see you.' Bea's own eyes sparkled with emotion as Matthaios clutched Danica to his chest.

He spoke in Greek, low and soft, smiling as he hugged Danica as though he'd never let her go. Ares came to stand beside Bea, his arm around her waist drawing her close so that she fitted at his side perfectly. He was warm and he was home. She was home.

'She can't stop crying,' Matthaios said anxiously, without taking his eyes off the baby's face.

'She's just a little overwhelmed,' Bea reassured him. 'She has no other way to express how she's feeling, so she cries. They're happy tears, I promise.'

He nodded, kissing Danica's head, brushing their cheeks together. 'I've missed you too, little one.' He lifted his eyes to Beatrice's face, then sideways to Ares. 'Thank you both. I promise I won't let her down again.'

'I believe you.' Ares nodded. 'But we're always here for you, any time you need us.'

Bea smiled warmly, underscoring Ares's sentiments.

Later, when Danica was settled for her afternoon nap, Matthaios held a coffee cup in his hands, staring out at the idyllic ocean view. The day was warm, the water still, so Ares was already planning an evening swim with Bea, who'd gone to get changed.

'It's serious between the two of you?'

Ares turned to his brother, nodding. 'What do you think?'

Matthaios's grin was knowing. 'I think you're besotted and I'm glad. I've never seen you like this before.'

'I've never been like this before,' he said with a lift of his shoulders. 'I love her.'

'I can see that.'

Saying it felt right—and having Matthaios's quick acceptance meant everything to Ares. 'What I said before, Matt. I'm here for you. Whatever you need.'

'I appreciate that, but I've already needed you more than enough. It's time for you to live your life without worrying about me.'

'I'm not worried,' he said truthfully. 'I'm proud. Facing your demons is hard, and you've done it twice. I think you're a superhero. But even superheroes come unstuck sometimes, and if that ever happens you know I've got your back.'

Matthaios nodded, sipping his coffee. 'I know, but this time is different. I feel different. And I'm not going to risk hurting Danica ever again. I'm not going to be like Mamá.'

Ares thought about that—their mother's repeated benders, her hangovers, her disappearance.

'I'm keen to get on with my life. Get back to work. I have to be someone Ingrid would have been proud of—I owe that to her.'

'Yes,' Ares agreed, because he finally understood what it

meant to love someone with all your heart, and how that love changed you. 'You do, Matt.'

'Excuse me.' Ares turned at Ellen's interruption. Matt's eyes glanced over at the young woman. 'Bea said you wanted to be told when Danica was awake. It's her bath time.'

'And you are?' Matt prompted, standing, his manner assessing.

'This is Ellen,' Ares explained, getting to his feet. 'I told you about her.'

'I remember.' Matt extended a hand. 'Thanks for everything you've done. I appreciate it.'

'It's been my pleasure. Danica's adorable. I will be very, very sorry to see her go.'

As the two of them disappeared into the house, Ares stayed on the balcony, staring out to sea. Life was full of unexpected twists, and he could never have foreseen this. A chance meeting, an inconvenient scheduling mishap in the midst of one of the most stressful weeks of his life, had led to him finding the woman of his dreams. It was a piece of good fortune he feared he didn't deserve, but one that he knew he'd live the rest of his life being grateful for.

The sun was low in the sky but the water was still warm, lapping against Bea's sides. She clung to Ares, her legs around his waist, her arms at his neck, and she smiled because she was happy, as she'd been more often than not since coming to live with him.

Her parents had shown more than a passing interest in them as a couple, though Bea suspected that was because there was something newsworthy in her relationship with a man like Ares Lykaios, rather than being genuinely happy for her. She made a mental note to be on the lookout for pesky paparazzi, who would, no doubt, be sent by her mother, hoping for pictures to grace the pages of the tabloids. Even the thought of that couldn't dull Bea's happiness.

'They seemed so good together,' she said, thinking about Matthaios and Danica. 'He was really comfortable with her.'

'I noticed that too. I'm glad.'

'He knows he can stay with us as long as he wants, doesn't he?'

Ares nodded. 'He's keen to get back to Athens, to resume his life. His own business has been looked after by his chief financial officer, but that cannot go on for ever.'

'Let me guess. He shares your control freak gene?' she teased, kissing the tip of Ares's nose.

'I hope that's not a complaint, Beatrice Jones?'

'Absolutely not.' She blinked at him with wide-eyed innocence. 'I happen to like it when you take control.'

'I'm glad to hear it.' He emphasised his point by kicking back a little in the water, so that it was too deep for Bea to stand. She kept her legs wrapped around his waist, perfectly safe and utterly content.

'You know, when we first met, I remember you telling me that you had no intention of getting married.'

Bea tilted her head to the side, the throwaway comment one she had no recollection of making. 'Did I?'

'At the time, I paid it little attention. I thought I felt the same way.'

Her stomach lurched. 'And you don't?'

He shook his head slowly, his eyes boring into hers. 'No. Meeting you made me realise I feel the complete opposite.'

Bea's heart skipped a beat.

'I have been wondering if there's anything I might say or do to change your mind,' he said, running his hands down her back.

She sank her teeth into her lower lip, the man she loved staring at her so intently. 'To what end?'

'So that we can stand in front of our friends and family and agree to spend the rest of our lives together. What do you think?'

'Are you proposing to me?'

'Yes.' The simple response rang with determination and she

laughed because she suspected he would do or say whatever it took to assure himself of her agreement. And, while her heart was already saying yes, she couldn't resist the chance to tease him a little.

'It would require a new contract,' she murmured, but her eyes showed her delight.

'Indeed.' He nodded. 'I wouldn't have expected anything less. What terms this time?'

'Hmm.' She tapped her fingers on his shoulder thoughtfully. 'Coffee in bed every morning?'

'Done. What else?'

'A lifetime of happiness?'

'And togetherness,' he tacked on.

'As little time spent with my family as possible.'

His laugh was gruff. 'Just every second Christmas.'

'Excellent. And lots of time with Danica and Matthaios.'

'And Clare and Amy.' He nodded.

She stared at him, her heart skipping a beat.

'And one day children of our own?' he suggested carefully, as though he was surprised to find himself wanting that.

Bea felt the same—it was something she'd ruled out for so long, but now she knew what she wanted, and it was more than a life with Ares. It was a life with him and a family too, children who would grow up surrounded by their love. 'Definitely.' Her voice cracked a little. 'You know, I've spent all my life feeling unwanted, and like I didn't belong anywhere.' She shook her head wistfully. 'I just didn't realise that the place I was meant to be, and the man I was meant to be with, weren't in my life yet.'

'I've been waiting for you,' he agreed quietly, 'and I didn't realise it either.'

A powerful look of understanding passed between them.

'I'm taking this as a yes,' he said as he dropped his head to hers.

'Oh, it's a yes,' she sighed, kissing him slowly. 'In fact, it's a thousand of them, and then some.'

The sunset was spectacular once again that evening, but neither of them noticed the colours in the sky. That didn't matter, though. There was a lifetime of sunsets awaiting them—every evening for the rest of their lives.

Two years later...

'You didn't have to come. I know how busy you are!' Bea fussed, reaching a hand out to Luca and Amy, smiling from ear to ear. Ares had never seen anyone so beautiful as his wife in that moment. Her face was still pink from her exertions, her hair pulled up into a loose ponytail, and all he could think was that he wanted to photograph her like this, so he could always remember her vital, incredible strength.

'As if I'd miss it,' Amy squawked.

'As if she'd let me,' Luca joked, but he showed he wasn't serious by bending down and kissing Bea's cheek before extending a hand to Ares. They shook like old friends—appropriate, given that they'd become very good friends in the intervening years, even working together on a wind turbine plant in South Africa.

'This is for you.' Amy held out an enormous box of Bea's favourite chocolate truffles. 'I know, they're probably the last thing you can think of right now, but later tonight you might want some spoiling.'

Tears sprang to Bea's eyes—a hazard of her current emotional state. 'Thanks, Ames. They're perfect.'

'I wanted to get the bear,' Luca said with mock disappointment.

Amy rolled her expressive eyes. '"The bear" is a six-foot-tall bright blue teddy bear that would take up half of this room. Trust me, take the chocolate.'

'Oh...erm... I think we've got all the bears we need,' Bea said with a crinkled nose.

'Where is he? Where's my godson?' Clare swept into the room, all fabulous glossy brown hair and glittering blue eyes.

'*Our* godson,' Amy corrected, hugging Clare tight. Dev entered a step behind Clare.

'He's over here,' Ares said, turning to the little bundle who was sleeping, swaddled up, in a small crib to the side of Bea's bed. His heart jerked at the sight of their infant, and a love so powerful he felt as though it might swallow him burst through him.

'Lemme see, lemme see!' Clare clapped her hands together, her heels clipping across the linoleum floor. 'Oh, my goodness, he's utterly perfect, Bea. You did good, Mamá.'

Bea relaxed back against the pillows, her eyes heavy, her smile permanent.

'He is very handsome,' Dev remarked, shaking Ares's hand. 'Must get that from his mother.'

Ares laughed. 'I hope he gets just about everything from her. If he does, then our son will be perfection itself.'

Clare and Amy shared an amused look, but Bea only had eyes for her husband.

'I ran into the twins downstairs,' Clare said, moving closer to Bea.

'Which twins?'

'Your sisters,' Clare prompted.

'Oh.' Bea's eyes skittered to Ares's. 'Mum must have told them I'd gone into labour.'

'Do you want me to ask them to come back tomorrow?' Amy asked gently.

Bea thought about that, then shook her head slowly. 'Honestly, no. They're here, and that's something I never would have thought—maybe today's a day of new beginnings,' she said with the kind of optimism that could only come from the euphoria of having given birth.

'They were just ordering coffee when we passed them, so I'd say you've got some time before they visit.'

'I'll tell them not to stay long,' Ares said, coming to place a hand on Bea's shoulder. 'You must be exhausted, and you've already had Matt here.'

'It *has* been a rather busy morning,' Bea said, but she didn't mind. Seeing Danica with her little cousin had been so heart-warming. She loved their son with all her heart, but Danica would always hold a very special place in her affections. She continued to spend as much time with her niece as possible, and knew she always would.

'On that note, we should let you have some rest,' Amy offered.

'Oh, no, please don't go,' Bea complained. 'I haven't seen you both in weeks!'

Amy nodded. 'We'll come back tomorrow.'

'And stay for lunch?'

Clare wrinkled her nose. 'Only if we can bring it. Hospital food is—'

'Totally gross,' Bea agreed. 'Deal. Dim sum?'

'Done.'

A moment later they were gone, and in the precious moments that followed, Bea allowed herself to feel completely, utterly at peace. Her heart was full and her future bright.

'I love you,' she said to her husband as her eyes drifted shut.

'And I love you.' Ares kissed her head then returned to the sleeping baby's side, his eyes trained on the infant their love had created. For so long, he'd lived in fear of being depended on by anyone, and now he could think of no greater honour than this—being needed and valued by two people as precious as his wife and child. He considered himself a very lucky man indeed.

* * * * *

The Playboys 'I Do' Deal

Tara Pammi

Tara Pammi can't remember a moment when she wasn't lost in a book—especially a romance, which was much more exciting than a mathematics textbook at school. Years later, Tara's wild imagination and love for the written word revealed what she really wanted to do. Now she pairs alpha males who think they know everything with strong women who knock that theory *and* them off their feet!

CHAPTER ONE

Hiding out from thugs who'd kidnap her in a heartbeat and cart her off to marry some beer-bellied, gold-toothed creepy old man who gave out loans in exchange for *desirable assets* wasn't how Clare Roberts had imagined her life playing out.

Not even as a girl with the extraordinary imagination that had been needed for transforming her feckless father, who'd dumped her at her unwilling aunt's doorstep when she'd been five, into an emotionally available superhero for years.

But just when she thought she'd hit rock-bottom, life decided to show her the green icky stuff beneath the nasty pond scum.

Desirable asset...the very phrase made her want to throw up.

To escape Goon Number One, who had made it clear he'd collect her instead of the money she owed his Mob boss—because when her dad had borrowed money from them he'd used *her* as collateral and then died before he could pay it back—the only option left to her was hiding out on board the superyacht of the man she'd slept with not a month ago. While the night had been everything she'd hoped for and more, the morning after had been entirely too awkward. Her one-night stand had neatly deleted her from his life as easily as spam email.

Served her right for taking an imprudent dive into the roller-coaster world of sex and romance with CEO and unapologetic bachelor playboy Dev Kohli. A former gold-medal-winning swimmer who had gone on to create the world's most contemporary sports brand Athleta. A billionaire before he'd turned thirty and a self-made man, the latter quality being something Clare had admired enormously for a long time after she'd first met him at a PR event she'd organized for one of his friends. As well as his wide shoulders and rock-hard abs, that was.

She should've known her own PR company, The London Connection, might do business with him in the future. After all, he was a man who was reputed to be more loyal to his clients than his lovers.

While Clare completely agreed with the sentiment for a business-only relationship, it pricked a little when, as an ex-lover, one fell into the former category. Not that she was still moping after him.

But the heart wanted what it wanted…or in her case, it was her lady bits that had done all the wanting, after being firmly denied until the ripe old age of twenty-eight.

A hysterical giggle—fueled by the two glasses of champagne she'd guzzled in panic—escaped her mouth. Her two best friends and business partners Amy and Bea would've teased her no end if she'd said "lady bits" within their hearing. Well, Amy definitely would. Bea would've simply fallen into giggles. But they were both on the other side of the world at that moment, trying to keep their business afloat. Apart from the odd text, they'd hardly heard from one another recently.

God, she missed them like an ache in her champagne-sloshed belly. Desperately wanted to hear at least one of their voices. Tell them what her dad had done to her and then have a cry while they cursed him to hell and back. He'd known he was dying and had sent her money to start The London Connection, which had gone from strength to strength in the last two years. He'd only lived for days afterward, and she hadn't even fully processed what it meant to discover now that, far from thinking her father had finally done something good for her, he'd actually betrayed her in the worst possible way, just to salve his own conscience for having ignored her for her whole life.

But contacting them while she was on the run from a mobster who was intent on kidnapping her and dragging her off to his cave was definitely not a good idea. What if he threatened Amy or Bea because he couldn't locate Clare? After all, anyone who'd done even a bit of digging into her life would know Amy and Bea were her true family. The only people who cared about her in the whole wide world.

No, she couldn't take the risk of endangering their lives too. So she'd decided it was better for them if neither of knew where she was—or who she was with. Her friends knew how determined she could be when she was on the scent of a new client, so she figured that when they didn't hear from her for a while, that's what they'd assume she was doing.

What her friends also didn't know, and Clare wasn't about to tell them, was that their new client was the same man she'd had a one-night stand with recently. She'd never shared his identity with them, feeling a strange sense of protectiveness about that night. Also, because if she talked to them, then she'd have to own up that she'd mostly failed at abiding by the most important rule of one-night stands—keeping it strictly casual. Especially as Dev had clearly had no such problem doing that himself.

Athleta was far too big a fish for Clare to walk away from just because its CEO hadn't proclaimed that he'd love her forever. And tonight had been her one chance to impress on him that her small PR firm could clean up his recently tarnished image.

Only the mobster's goons had trailed her all the way from London to a conference in New York and then to São Paulo, and it was terrifying. Today the mobster's intentions had been made crystal clear. He intended to simply...*take* her in lieu of the money he insisted she owed him.

For two weeks, she'd lived in terror of being snatched from wherever she was.

She'd been meaning to hightail it back to her hotel room

when she'd spotted Goon Number One with a drink in hand on the main deck of the superyacht this evening. The short, blond, chubby-faced man had smiled angelically—clearly his cheerful appearance was a useful tool in nabbing unsuspecting women. It was the same man she'd seen leaning near the newspaper stand on the street where The London Connection's offices were located, looking up at the sole window. The very same posh and supposedly secure street that they paid astronomical rent for.

He'd even bumped into her late one evening when she'd been rushing to catch the Tube after work. Apologized profusely. When she'd then seen him lounging in the foyer of her New York hotel, she'd wondered if she was hallucinating.

Now, he was here, aboard Dev's yacht. Looking just as posh as the rest of the designer-suited men. Wearing an affable smile, chitchatting away. He'd almost touched her. Tried to talk to her as if they were long-lost friends. She didn't have time to wonder how he'd got on board. She needed to hide. Now.

She ran her hand over her hips, contemplating the rounds the uniformed security guard was making. The emerald green silk skirt she was wearing had been a gift from Bea, and it gave her some much-needed courage. Without looking back, she stepped gingerly down the spiral staircase—who knew yachts could have staircases like this one?—and tried to not trip in her four-inch heels.

The champagne sloshed around in her belly again as she passed door after door. Peeked into one expansive lounge after another. Even in her panic, Clare couldn't help marveling at the airy, contemporary spaces, the chic stylish interiors. The click-click of her stilettos on the gleaming floors sounded like a sinister countdown.

Heart pounding, she walked into the biggest cabin. For a second, she was thrown at the sheer size of it. A large bed with a navy-blue duvet looked so welcoming that she took an involuntary step toward it longingly.

It was the feel of the luxuriously soft cotton underneath

her fingertips that made her realize she was pawing it. Her eyelids felt heavy, her entire body swooning with exhaustion. She'd been traveling nonstop for a week. Hadn't slept a wink ever since that ghastly man had started following her. But she couldn't sleep now. Not if she wanted to remain undetected until after the party wound down.

After one last wistful glance at the bed, she shook off the lethargic fog that threatened to engulf her. She was crashing from the shock of seeing that mobster's henchman again. Moving like an automaton, she walked into a massive closet.

It was about the size of her bedroom at her tiny flat. A faint scent of sandalwood and something else reached her nostrils. Her belly swooped, with a more pleasurable sensation this time. The memory of Dev's hard body driving into hers, the feel of the taut, sweat-slicked skin of his back under her greedy fingers... Clare couldn't help but cling to the memory of the utter feeling of ecstasy he'd brought her to. That moment of sheer intimacy when he'd looked into her eyes and simply...*seen* her. All of her vulnerability displayed on her face. And he'd just held her tenderly and kissed her temple.

The sense of well-being that arose from that memory suddenly calmed the fear brewing in her belly.

She sat down in the vast window seat and looked at the ocean. The expanse of blue was a symbol of how far away she was from her home, her friends and the business she'd built up with her own blood, sweat and tears.

But also on the other side of it was the man who claimed he owned her as if she were cattle.

Clare kicked off her heeled sandals and pulled her knees up to her chest. Leaning back against the plush upholstery, she closed her eyes and waited for her heart to slow its pounding beat.

For the party to be over.

For the yacht to start moving.

Every inch of her rebelled at the idea of traveling to a destination unknown with a man who'd walked away from her without a backward glance after the best night of her life. Who'd told her in no uncertain terms that while it had been pleasurable, their...association was over.

But the billionaire playboy meant safety for now. Even if that meant she'd be clinging to him like an unwanted piece of flotsam.

"Promise me you'll make it to the wedding, Dev. Please."

Dev Kohli pressed a long finger to his throbbing temple, his mild headache becoming aggravated by his twin sister's shrill pleading.

But since Dev didn't lie to himself—it was the only way he'd been able to survive in the military school environment his father had placed him in—he acknowledged that it was guilt that was turning one of the worst months of his life into something much...worse.

"You haven't even met Richard. I mean, Rich and I've been engaged for eight months and my twin brother hasn't met him yet. That's a bit much, even for you, Dev. Don't you want to make sure..."

Diya went on, without needing any more response from him than his grunts peppered throughout the conversation.

The fact that his sister—younger than him by a whole two and a half minutes—was piling on the guilt didn't mean that it was unwarranted.

He hadn't been back to his family's home in California since military school. He hadn't seen Diya in eighteen months. But, even throughout the nearly two-decades-long rift he and Papa had sustained, he'd always made it a priority to see his siblings. Even if all his attorney general older brother and renowned pediatric neurosurgeon older sister did was try to talk him into coming home.

It was Diya who had always been the one to check on him. Even when he'd turned his back on all the rest of them, Diya had been his only connection to his roots. His estranged family. To the one person he'd loved and lost—their mama.

"When's the wedding?" Dev asked, just to interrupt the barrage of English and Hindi building up momentum, spewing at him from across the Atlantic. He'd stared at the date for long enough in the last few weeks.

"You know exactly when it is," Diya snapped.

"This isn't the right time for me to visit California, Diya," he explained softly. "You know what I've been facing in the media. This sexual harassment scandal that's threatening my company's name is not a trivial matter.

"I've got people working around the clock to make sure something like that never happens again. And if I show my face at the wedding right in the middle of this...messy scandal, you know what *he* will say."

His sister didn't need to ask who "he" was.

"The last thing I need right now is to hear his negative voice preaching at me," Dev said, bitter even now. After all these years. Even after he'd proved his despotic father wrong on so many fronts.

"Dev, you can't let the past—"

"I just don't have the bandwidth to sit through another episode of family drama. If I stay far enough away, we can continue to pretend that we're the embodiment of the wealthy, successful Indian American family he's always wanted to be. Do you want to have your wedding upstaged by one of our dirty fights?"

Diya sighed. "If I have to spend every minute leading up to the ceremony keeping you and Papa apart, then I'll do it. In fact, I'll recruit Richard to play referee between you two. Papa adores Richard."

That little fact came at him like a bolt he hadn't even seen coming, lodging painfully in his chest. Dev wanted to bang his cell phone against the glittering glass bar and forget all about the wedding. Of course, his father approved of Diya's investment banker fiancé.

And at twenty-nine, here he was, still envious of something a stranger had—his father's admiration. As if he was that pathetic twelve-year-old boy again, desperate to please his father and utterly failing.

"I'm so sorry, Dev."

Dev sighed. "Not your fault, D."

No one understood how deep the scars of his childhood were, not even Diya. Not his obediently perfect older brother or his genius older sister either. It was like they'd had a father different from the one he'd been given.

Sometimes, he resented them all so much. But mostly for expecting him to just…get over it. To forget that he'd always felt like an outsider among his famous family's overachieving members. Especially after Mama had died.

No, he'd been made to feel like that. By Papa. Until he'd been sent away to the military school at twelve—which had turned out to be a blessing in disguise—Dev had been yelled at by his father, bullied into believing that he was nothing. That he was a cuckoo in a crow's nest.

And that was something he could neither forgive nor forget.

"I promise you, Dev," Diya said, launching into dire warnings now, "if you don't show up for my wedding, I'll…forbid you from seeing your future niece or nephew. Cut you out of my life. There will be epic poems written about the estranged uncle." Dev could hear the calming tones of a man speaking in the background, undoubtedly Richard. He smiled, despite the tightness in his chest.

He wondered what kind of a man had willingly signed up for a lifetime with his firecracker of a younger sister.

Damn it, this wasn't how it should be. Him thousands of miles away from his brother and two sisters and nieces and nephews. Mama would've been immensely saddened by this family rift that had left him utterly alone. She'd have wanted so much more for him than this solitary, nomadic lifestyle.

"Let me sort through the mess my company's in right now,"

Dev said, making up his mind, "and I'll be there at your wedding."

"You know that we all have faith in you, don't you? Whatever those trashy websites said about you knowing that female executive was being harassed... We know you'd have never tolerated something like that." He had no idea how she'd known, but Diya had just said the one thing that Dev had so badly needed to hear.

"Now, clean up the mess, Dev. And show up at my wedding with your billionaire halo all freshly polished."

Dev smiled.

"Also, it would be awesome if you could bring a date to the wedding."

The sudden image of silky dark brown hair and intelligent blue eyes boldly holding his gaze as he moved inside her was so vivid in his mind that for a moment Dev stayed mute.

Diya whistled. "So you've met someone! Who is she? What does she do? I can't wait to tell Deedi—"

The excited tone of his twin's voice sent alarm bells ringing in his head. "No one out of the ordinary," he muttered, feeling horrible for saying it.

Clare Roberts had been so far out of the ordinary that he hadn't quite recovered yet. He'd tried to tell himself during the last few weeks that she'd been just the same as his usual one-night stands, but he hadn't quite managed to convince himself of that yet.

"Continuing with the *love them and leave them* policy then, huh?"

"Don't push it," he warned her.

Diya giggled. "Fine. It's on your own head when you show up all single and handsome... Seema Auntie's been asking about you."

Dev groaned. Seema Auntie had been Mama's oldest, dearest friend and the most notoriously ambitious matchmaker on both sides of the Atlantic. With a horde of daughters, she regularly embarrassed eligible men without discrimination.

He quickly hung up after promising to update Diya on his plans.

Talking to his twin always left him feeling restless. As if he was back in his unhappy childhood. As if he hadn't achieved enough, conquered enough. As if he still didn't have enough. The feeling had been returning more and more frequently, and now it had been amplified by the man he'd trusted most using and betraying Dev's name in the worst possible way and endangering the company he'd worked so hard to build.

With a sigh, Dev looked around at the stunning sight of his yacht leaving the Port of Santos behind. He been visiting the nearby city of São Paulo, but he never stayed anywhere longer than a month. His sports merchandise was manufactured all over the world, and he preferred not basing himself permanently in one place.

In his heart, he knew he didn't really want to miss Diya's wedding.

Which meant he had no choice but to hasten the mass cleanup he'd already instigated in the company. There was no way he was showing up in front of his father with a harassment scandal weighing him down.

He was going to show up with his halo shining so bright that even Papa would be blinded by it. Preferably with a gorgeous, accomplished woman on his arm to ward off Seema Auntie, at least. As if waiting for the slightest signal, his mind once again instantly conjured the image of the woman he had determinedly pushed aside from his thoughts for the last three weeks.

While their night together had resulted in one of those rare connections that even the cynic in him had noticed, his behavior the morning after had been less than impeccable.

All the toxic rubbish that had been written over the past three weeks about his company and him at the center of it—a billionaire playboy who treated women with less care than he did his luxury toys—stung sharply when he thought of how he'd behaved toward Clare Roberts.

Granted, his company's name had just been plastered all over the media when he'd woken up that morning with *her* wrapped around him. He'd barely untangled her warm limbs before switching on his phone to find hundreds of messages from his PR team and board of directors. The female executive who'd not only been harassed but then hounded into leaving his company, had released an interview that had gone viral overnight.

A disaster of epic proportions had ensued.

Dev couldn't forgive himself for not realizing what had been going on under his very nose. He'd immediately launched an investigation, firing the man responsible for the harassment within twenty-four hours and offering a rehiring package to the female executive. But it was nowhere near enough.

He'd messed up big time.

He'd been so busy with launching the next product, chasing the next billion-dollar deal that he'd been distracted from his responsibilities toward the people who worked for him. It was the one thing Mama had tried to instill in all her four children.

That with privilege and power came responsibilities.

Dev had completely failed in taking care of his employees. He also knew that the solutions he'd already implemented were not enough to save his company's reputation. And that's where Clare Roberts was supposed to come in.

Walking through his empty yacht, he wondered why she'd disappeared tonight without approaching him. Especially after she'd hounded his secretary for an appointment to see him this very evening. When the initial request had come forward that the CEO of the PR firm The London Connection wished to see him, he'd done his own research.

He hadn't exchanged anything beyond first names with her that night. So, it had been a surprise to see that intelligent face stare back at him from her company's website.

For a second, he'd wondered if she meant to prolong their... association. Hot and memorable as it had been, the last thing

Dev needed was a passionate affair distracting him. But he had pushed the arrogant assumption away.

The London Connection was a small firm that had made great strides in the last two years. It had a reputation of being one of the foremost, woman-led companies that conducted PR for big brand names. Also well-known for their charitable efforts and female entrepreneur empowerment initiatives.

Dev had instantly known it was the kind of company he needed to reinvigorate Athleta's reputation. Clearly, Clare had seen the potential in the opportunity too.

Then why disappear before he'd even had a chance to greet her?

Why make all the effort to fly to São Paulo from New York, travel out to the Port of Santos where his yacht was moored, and then leave without even speaking to him?

Dev finished his drink and walked into his closet. Thanks to the call with Diya and now this woman not turning up for their meeting, his skin hummed with restlessness. He needed a vigorous swim. Even as a young boy, swimming had helped him work off the frustration he couldn't verbalize to his parents. He had felt free, as if he could communicate with his limbs instead of his words.

As an adolescent carted off to military school, his athleticism in the pool had been his saving grace.

He discarded his shirt. He was about to grab a towel from the neatly folded pile when he spotted a bright piece of emerald silk fluttering at the back.

He was very sure he didn't own a piece of fabric in that striking color. He also remembered thinking how well the emerald silk highlighted Clare's deliciously round bottom.

Was she here—still aboard his yacht, in his closet?

He walked past the rows and rows of suits and looked down.

Shock held him rooted for a few seconds, followed by a gamut of emotions he couldn't check. Anger, disillusionment, even humor traveled through him, ending in pure disbelief.

What the hell was she doing here?

She was curled up neatly in the window seat, her white hand-bag clutched to her cheek and completely...asleep. Her hair made a shiny mess around her face. A curly lock blew away from her face every time she exhaled. Her wide, pink mouth—perhaps a little too wide for her small face—was slightly open.

Dev reached out and gently shook her shoulder.

The last thing he needed was a mishap with another woman—even though she was the one invading his privacy and hiding in his damned closet.

Especially a woman he'd slept with...and hadn't been able to get out of his mind.

CHAPTER TWO

IT WAS A lovely dream.

Naughtily lovely and just what she needed to escape the nightmare reality of her life.

It featured a man's taut buttocks—the kind that athletes had—round and hard. The kind that spawned internet memes. The kind that Clare wouldn't mind sinking her teeth into. And thighs that would have no trouble holding her up against a wall making her sex damp with the raw muscular power in them. And, oh, Lord…that nicely defined V of muscles at his groin and the happy trail that lead to it…

Clare was desperate to hold on to the dream. She knew exactly who she was dreaming about.

Dev Kohli of the tight butt and the broad shoulders and the charming grin and the surprisingly kind eyes.

A loud curse and a hand on her shoulder ripped open the flimsy curtain between dream and reality. Clare sat up jerkily. Jarred into wakefulness, her limbs protested, after having been cramped tight into the window seat.

She looked up to discover Dev Kohli staring down at her with murder in his eyes.

Well, not quite murder precisely, but something close to it.

Clare swallowed. Blast it, had she actually fallen asleep in the man's closet? This was so not how she intended for him to find her. She'd meant to wait until the party was over and walk out and present her case to him like a rational woman.

He stepped back from her as if she was demented. And she couldn't really blame him. In quick movements, he grabbed a shirt and slipped it on.

If one could burn of embarrassment, Clare was sure she should be a steaming pile of ash on his lush carpet.

"Would you like to tell me what you're doing here?" Ice had nothing on his voice. "Or should I call security to handle you?"

Clare rubbed her palm over her temples. "I'm so sorry, Mr. Kohli," she muttered, straightening her skirt awkwardly. Her head felt like it was stuffed full of cotton wool and her belly ready to eat itself in hunger. Yet despite that, there was that prickle of awareness under her skin at his nearness.

"Why are you here, *Ms. Roberts*?" he asked, a wealth of meaning buried in how he said her last name. A little mocking. A lot annoyed.

Clare met his gaze without hesitation. "I promise, I don't usually go about sneaking into men's cabins. I had the most unbelievably horrid day and then I just... I can't believe I fell asleep. I think it was the scent of you that did it," she said, inanely pointing to rows and rows of Armani shirts.

"I have no idea what that means," he said, the scowl not lessening in intensity.

"I was terrified for my life. And the scent of you in here... I think, it lulled me into thinking I was safe. Because it's familiar, you know. After that night..." She flushed and sighed. "I'm making this worse, aren't I?"

"With every tall tale you're spinning to justify this intrusion, yes. Much, much worse."

"I'm not lying."

"I really doubt that."

It was the disdain in his voice that did it. That made her usually even-keel temper explode. "You think a lot of yourself, don't you? You think you're such a *studly stud* that no woman can stop herself from throwing herself at you? That no woman can keep her clothes on or maintain her dignity around you? That we're all falling over ourselves to get at that tightly packed muscular body of yours?"

Damn, girl, she could hear Amy's admiring laughter in her head.

Her face heating, Clare readied herself to be thrown out of the very window where she'd been hiding. It was shock, she told herself. Shock was making her mouth off like this.

Into the stunned silence came his laughter. Deep, low laughter that enveloped Clare like a comfortingly warm blanket. His face had broken into attractive grooves and lines, the flash of his white teeth rendering him even more gorgeous. If that was possible.

She looked away, needing a respite from all his irresistible masculinity. The dark hollow of his throat made her belly somersault. She had a vivid memory of burying her face there when she'd climaxed. And he'd held her afterward, as if she was precious to him.

The taste of his skin—sweat and salt and so deliciously male—practically hovered on her tongue.

Slowly, praying that her thoughts weren't betrayed on her face, Clare met his gaze. There was chagrin and impatience and more than a hint of humor lurking in the brown depths.

"That wasn't what I'd intended to say."

"Clearly. But that's probably the most truthful you've been just now, huh?" he said, agreeing with a grace she wasn't sure she deserved.

Clare couldn't summon a smile. "Just give me a minute to gather my bearings, please. I'll explain everything properly. And then—" she swallowed the fear "—if you still want to throw me out, you can just toss me into the ocean. It's probably safer for me anyway."

"Two minutes," he said, moving away.

He returned with an opened bottle of sparkling water and Clare took it gratefully. His gaze didn't move from her as she finished the bottle. It wasn't…roguish or obvious but she had a feeling he'd done a thorough sweep of her, from her bare feet to her short dark brown hair, still in disarray.

She fiddled with the empty bottle for a few seconds and then cleared her throat. "I'm not usually this unprofessional. I've had a really bad day, Mr. Kohli and—"

"Dev," he prompted.

"What?" she said, blinking.

His jaw tightened. "It's silly to insist on calling me Mr. Kohli when you've snuck into my yacht, into my bedroom, no less. Ridiculous to pretend that we don't know each other. On a level that strangers don't."

"That night has nothing to do with…today. Or now." At least her tone was steady even if her heartbeat wasn't.

He raised a perfect eyebrow. The man was more articulate with one gesture of his face than she was with all her words today, apparently. But then, it wasn't every day that Clare found herself riding a roller coaster of emotions, swinging from fear to betrayal to sheer lust.

"I'm having a hard time believing that."

Clare straightened, her hackles rising. "If you think I stowed away so that we could get…so that I can…" She could feel her face heating up again and cursed herself. "You've got this all wrong."

"Do I?"

"Yes. Absolutely. That night was a…one-off. I didn't hound your assistant for this meeting just so that I could wait for you in your bedroom. I'm not some sex-obsessed—"

"Then why are you here?" he hastily cut in.

"You need me," Clare said firmly. "That's why I'm here."

He stilled. "Excuse me?"

If she weren't stuck in a ridiculous predicament that threatened her very life, Clare would've found the outrage on his face hilarious. As if the world had turned upside down for him to need her.

"I need you?" he repeated, pushing his fingers through his hair.

Clare forged on, determined to keep his attention now that she had it. "What my company can do for you, I mean. This was supposed to be a business meeting tonight."

He shrugged. It caused all those delicious muscles in his chest to move in perfect harmony. The man shouldn't be allowed to wear his shirt open like that without a warning sign. "That's what I thought too," he said in a dry voice. Wary distrust was written all over his face. "Look, Clare. The last thing I need is to muddy the line between business and pleasure after what's happened to my company recently. I should've shut this meeting down the minute I realized we'd slept together."

She flinched.

"This—" he moved his hand between them, all masculine grace "—over."

And with that, he simply turned and walked away.

For a few seconds, Clare just stood there. She'd never been dismissed with such finality before. At least, not since she'd built The London Connection and made a name for herself in the world of PR.

After the cold indifference with which her aunt had welcomed her when her dad had dumped a five-year-old Clare on her unwilling doorstep like unwanted baggage, she'd made herself tougher. Grown a thick skin out of necessity. Day in, day out, she'd poured all that hurt and loneliness into getting good A-levels and then a business qualification. Into getting away from her aunt's long-suffering attitude.

And yet this stung.

Maybe because he was the one man Clare had ever let her guard down with.

Maybe because she wanted to see admiration and respect in those beautiful brown eyes of his, rather than contempt.

The last thing she wanted after her father had abandoned her was to run after another man who didn't care about her. Who thought she amounted to nothing.

The self-disgust turned to much-needed anger. That fresh burst of emotion propelled her forward before she realized what she was doing. Her hand landed on a warm, hard shoulder.

Clare pulled away abruptly, feeling as if she'd been electrocuted.

He turned, his frown morphing into a full-blown scowl.

Clare raised her palms and backed down. But not before the scent of warm, male skin invaded her nostrils and filled her with that strange longing once more. "Look, Dev," she said, ignoring his expression, "I know this looks bad, okay? But I had a reason for invading your privacy and hiding here. Stepping off the yacht tonight was literally the most dangerous thing I could have done. If you can give me just a few minutes, I'll explain everything."

"I'm not sure—"

"I took a chance on you. I went with my gut instinct instead of listening to what the rest of the world's saying about you right now. At the very least, you can afford me that same chance."

His jaw tight, he rubbed one long finger against his brow. As if he was at the end of his tether. "Explain yourself. About taking a chance on me," he said, as if it was the most outrageous thing he'd heard so far out of her mouth.

"I pitched for a meeting with you even though the entire world's gleefully painting you as a no-conscience, sexist monster who created a toxic work environment for women. Because I thought you should be given a chance to present your side too."

Despite the tension in his face, his mouth twitched at the corners. "So this is an altruistic effort on your part to save my backside?"

Clare shrugged. Trying very hard to not think of the backside in question. The very same one she'd so recently been dreaming of. "Not altruistic, no. I want my company to take over Athleta's PR on this side of the pond. I want a long, nicely padded contract that will put The London Connection on the map in North America. It will be a mutually beneficial arrangement."

A mutually pleasurable arrangement...that was what she'd said when she'd propositioned him that night.

The moment the words left her mouth, Clare knew she should literally have put it any other way. From the flare of awareness that lit up his eyes, he remembered it too.

After months of lusting over him from afar, she'd finally made her move at the charity gala for Women Entrepreneurs. They'd crossed paths a few times at parties and conventions before that, but he'd always been with a different woman on his arm. Despite that, she'd heard about his reputation as a fair and kind man through the grapevine. On that night, Clare had won an award and had been feeling on top of the world. When she'd gone to get a drink, he'd been there. Offering congratulations with warm eyes and that mobile, laughing mouth. Taking her in.

"You don't know who I am, do you?" she'd asked laughingly. "Or what I've won the award for."

He'd dipped his head in acknowledgment. "No, sorry. They were giving out those awards faster than glasses of pink champagne."

She'd swatted his shoulder with her clutch. "Hey, mine was a shiny gold plaque, you know. The others were only silver."

"Well of course, that puts you a cut above the rest." The devilish charmer that he was, he'd batted those eyes at her. He had ridiculously long lashes and pretty eyes for a...well, for a man. Hand pressed to his chest, he'd mock bowed. "Not that the award isn't deserved. I've just had a long week and the details are a little fuzzy right now."

"Ahh...as long as you aren't seeing multiples of me," she'd quipped, shaking her head as the uniformed staff walked by with a tray of champagne. She'd already had bubbles in her belly and a pounding heart thanks to the man bending down to her from his impressive height.

Her belly had swooped even though his shoulder barely touched hers. He was so broad that he'd filled her entire view. His gaze held hers, front teeth digging into the way too lush lower lip of his. "Why do I have a feeling that it would be even more delightful to have multiples of you?"

Clare had blushed then. "How about you make it up to me for mocking my award?"

He'd finished his drink and turned to her. Shining the full blast of his attention on her. That gaze of his had turned perceptive and thoughtful. Less roguish and more...curious. Even admiring in a way that had sent tingles up and down her skin. "I don't remember your firm's name. But I did hear the emcee say you're a self-starter. A woman who forged her own path, despite an initial struggle. No one can take that away from you, can they?"

She'd been absolutely glowing by then. Inside and out. "No, they can't. As a self-starter yourself, you also know then that we have to milk every opportunity to the max. As I know who you are, but you don't have a clue about me, I have the upper hand between the two of us, right now."

"You're bloodthirsty," he said, leaning closer.

"Does that scare you?" she said, raising a brow, feeling a thrill she'd never known.

Another heart-stopping smile. "On the contrary, I have a weakness for a bloodthirsty woman who goes after what she wants."

"So?"

"So, your wish is my command, my lady," he'd said finally.

"Dance with me," she'd said boldly.

To her eternal delight, he'd taken her hand in his and led them to the dance floor. He'd asked her about the initiative that had garnered her the award. Her views on women in high positions and the obstacles they faced in a company's hierarchy.

With his arm warm and solid around her, his questions peppered with real interest, Clare had never felt so wanted. So... seen for herself.

A successful, moderately attractive woman who could hold her own with a brilliant, self-made entrepreneur. A man who could laugh at himself. A man who could admit he was wrong, apparently.

High on her success, determined to see if the attraction she felt was more than one-sided, Clare had wrapped her arms around his nape. And then she'd asked him directly, the words coming out of her mouth as if the torrent of desire couldn't be denied.

"Are you interested in taking this further?" She'd been so forthright, so honest.

His fingers had tightened on her waist, just a fraction. Sending an arrow of pleasure straight down to her belly. "How much further, exactly?"

"One whole night further."

There'd been a few long seconds where he'd just stared at her. Clare had felt as if she was standing on the cliff-edge of the entire world, ready to jump into the unknown with this man. "No strings?" he'd eventually said with a raised eyebrow.

"No strings," she'd confirmed with a bright smile.

And that had been it. No more words had been needed. At least not until he'd brought her to his suite and had asked her one tormenting question after the other about what she wanted. How she wanted it. When and where and how slow...or how fast or how deep...

Her wish had been his command, literally.

Clare didn't regret it for one moment. Not even now, when he was looking at her so suspiciously. He'd made their night together spectacular on more than one level—he'd been gentle and exploratory and funny...the perfect man. Just what Clare had needed.

Which was why she kept flinching at his nearness. It was a

little hard to separate that perfectly wonderful man from this distrustful stranger who doubted her motives for being here.

But in spite of the wariness in his eyes, the knowledge of that night shimmered in the air around them. How hot and hard he'd been under her questing fingers. How he'd used those wickedly clever fingers to learn her rhythm. How deliciously heavy he'd felt over her when he'd ground his lean hips against hers.

A slow hum of heat built up under her skin but Clare ignored the feeling. Whatever had been between them was definitely over. This was all business now.

"Why are you so ready to help me?"

This she could answer with a certainty that had stayed with her despite how awkward things had become between them. "Because I saw how devastated you were when you looked at your phone that morning. How upset you were that something so awful had happened right under your nose." Even though she'd been hurt by his cold dismissal of her, she'd seen on his face the devastation the news had caused. That he was a man of integrity, just as she'd always known, made his ability to walk away from her so easily that much more...cutting.

When his gaze met hers, Clare rolled her eyes. "In the few moments before you threw me out of the hotel room, that is."

"I never threw you out. I said I was leaving."

"It was your suite," Clare said tartly, and then took a deep breath. "After I asked, in the most pathetic voice, if I had done something wrong." Heat flushed her neck and face, but Clare was determined to have it all out in the open. "You said it had been 'nice' but that's all it could be."

Dev rubbed a hand over his face, looking pained.

"The point is that...in those few minutes, before you replaced your mask of jaded billionaire playboy, I saw how genuinely shocked you were. I've followed the story as it exploded all over the media. The harm that was caused happened under your leadership. Everything you've said publicly since that interview, you've never once tried to get out of the fact that you'd failed your employee. Which made me believe that you should be given a chance to turn this around."

"And you're the one to do it?"

When it came to business, Clare never second-guessed herself. She'd built her company to be the best. "Your current PR firm sucks. I can do a much better job. The London Connection has a reputation of women empowerment initiatives. A good record of dragging draconic policies into the twenty-first century. Making companies equitable for all."

"How would this benefit you?" he asked, his gaze pinned on her face.

"Launched our North American branch with a bang? Built our reputation? Turned a big ship like Athleta around and made it a better place for women to work? Take your pick."

Irritation flickered in his gaze. "I don't need you to teach me how to fix this."

"No. I believe you've already implemented several measures."

"How would you know that?"

"Because, as I said, ever since that morning, I've kept an eye on you. You've hired an independent agency to comb through your HR. You've already promoted three different female executives into more senior positions. You've got an equality and diversity agency doing a private audit on your board of directors."

Again, one brow rose. Clare stared right back. She may have started this meeting on the wrong foot, but she'd never been second-rate when it came to her job.

"But you still need me to put a good spin on it. To make everyone, especially women, believe that Athleta will never make those mistakes again. In simple terms, I will validate your efforts. Isn't that why you finally agreed to see me, Dev?"

He leaned against one wall, his gaze thoughtful. "I'll give you points for thorough research."

Clare shrugged. "But you still don't trust me?"

He shook his head "It's not you in particular that I don't trust."

She waited patiently. If she landed this contract, it would be a huge win for The London Connection. Both for their bottom line and their reputation. Not to mention that, right now, she had nowhere else to go. Literally.

When he finally spoke, tight lines bracketed his mouth. The shock and stress she'd seen in his face that morning three weeks ago hadn't left him yet. "The man who harassed and hounded Ms. Lane out of the company, I've known him for fifteen years. He mentored me when I started in this business. He was one of my first seed investors.

"I... I delegated so much of the everyday operations of the company to him and the team he brought in. Mostly corporate bigwigs. Which meant their power and reach in the company was—" a nerve vibrated in his temple "—far more extensive than it should have been. Unchecked, even. Because I was too focused on the next deal, the next product launch. If you'd asked me a month ago, I'd have staked my reputation on the fact that he'd never abuse his power like that with a woman—with anyone. *Never*... And yet he did. While he worked for me." A curse fell from his mouth, echoing around the cabin. Full of anger and disgust and something more. "Trust is very thin on the ground for me right now. No matter who it is. He..."

"He made you doubt your own judgment," Clare said gently, picking the thread up. Knowing exactly how he was feeling right then. "You're wondering if you can ever get it back... that trust in yourself. You're not sure where else you might have made a mistake. You're struggling to come to terms with why you didn't see it when it was right in front of your eyes."

"Do you have a degree in psychology too, Clare?" His gaze shone with reluctant admiration. And despite the frustration on his face, that hint of humor peeked through. "Or are you gleaning all this from my expression too?"

Clare laughed. Because it was easier to laugh it away before the pain set in. Before she was forced to consider at length what all this meant and how it shattered the very foundation of her life. "No, no degree in psychology. Just a lot of life experience. Believe me when I say I perfectly understand where you're coming from." She took a step forward, intent on making him understand. "I'll prove to you without a doubt that I didn't hide in your bedroom just so I could seduce you all over again. Like I already told you, I have reasons of the life-threatening kind for invading your privacy."

"Fine. I'll ask the captain to bring us back into port, and you can explain that rather bizarre statement to me. We'll—"

"Why take us back into port?" she demanded, her thoughts in a panic again.

He stilled. "I'm en route to Rio de Janeiro, and then heading on to my remote villa in the Caribbean. I'm sure the last thing you want is to be stranded there with me for several weeks."

"I absolutely do want to be stranded at some remote villa in the Caribbean with you," she contradicted him urgently. "In fact, right now, that sounds like a heaven-sent solution to all my problems."

He raised a brow, not so much wary as leery of her motives now. "So you're admitting that you wanted to be stranded with me?"

She sighed, knowing that she was doing a horrible job of this. "Not stranded with you in a romantic setting but more stranded on an island where Mob bosses and their cheerful thugs can't get to me. I heard you say during the party that you were going to be sailing around, or whatever the hell you call it, for the next couple of weeks or so. That's the reason I stowed away."

That distrustful look was back in his eyes again. Not that she could blame him. Frustration and that familiar resentment sat like a boulder on Clare's chest. She'd slogged for so many years, carefully building her life so that she didn't need anyone in it. With one move, her father had negated everything she'd

achieved. She was going to sound like a certifiable loon for saying what she was about to say.

"Explain, now," Dev said, in a hard tone that did wonders
for the quagmire of self-pity that was threatening to engulf her.
"And no more beating about the bush. Give it to me straight."

"Straight, right. Here goes... I'd like you to kidnap me."

He rolled his eyes. "Now I know you've lost your mind."

"No, I haven't," Clare said with a laugh. It was the hysterical note in it, she was sure, that finally convinced him. "I'm the
original damsel in distress, stuck in one of those ghastly fairy
tales that I used to love. It's not really hoots and laughs when
you have to depend on someone else to rescue you, you know?"
she said, her words full of a bitterness she hadn't even known
was festering inside her. "I need to hide out with you until I can
figure out how I can avoid becoming the wife or mistress of
some Mafia boss. So much for all the women's empowerment
I've been a part of, eh?"

CHAPTER THREE

DEV STARED AT the glittering sheen of tears in Clare's eyes. Like a mirage in a desert, the wet shine disappeared as he moved closer to her, despite his resolve to treat her as nothing more than a business colleague. If not for the tightness around that lush mouth of hers, he'd have thought he'd imagined the gleam of tears. If not for the stark fear that was palpably radiating from her—that made him want to wrap her safely in his arms—he'd have called her crazy and thrown off his yacht, ocean or not.

But as wary as he was currently feeling about his ability to judge someone's character, Dev had a feeling she was telling the truth. Or at least the truth as she believed it to be.

He reached out his hand, then pulled it back.

This is not a good idea, Dev, the rational voice in his head said. The one that had tried so many times to curb his wild behavior. The one that was most in touch with his innermost feelings, so to speak.

But, as much as he'd grown a thick, impervious skin over the past almost two decades—thanks to his military school discipline—he wasn't quite the uncaring bastard the media had so recently accused him of being. Or that he sometimes wished he could be, whenever he found himself caring too deeply, about anything. Especially when he was confronted with a woman like Clare Roberts and all the unwanted feelings she evoked in him.

What they both needed was to take a step back and regroup after this strange meeting, in his closet of all places. "Why don't we move this discussion out of here?" When she shot him a wary glance, he said gently, "You look like you need a drink. I definitely do, after getting yelled at by my twin."

"Oh, you have a twin?"

The twinkle in her eyes had him nodding. "Yes. She's incredibly bossy and she's getting married in about a month. She's just warned me that she'll cut me off from any future nieces or nephews she may give me if I don't make it to her wedding. So the deadline to clean up my image just got even tighter."

"Because you don't want the cloud of this scandal to disturb the wedding atmosphere?"

"No, because I can't go if…" Dev checked himself. Big blue eyes watched him curiously. "Doesn't matter why. It's just important to change the narrative on my company before the wedding. If I want to make it, that is."

She nodded, lifting that stubborn chin of hers. "Then our plan needs to be aggressive too."

He still didn't know why she was here. "I'd also like to have this talk while I'm not still standing half-undressed in my own closet and you don't look as if someone's done a thorough job of…mussing you up," he said tightly. For all his numerous girlfriends, he hated the idea of mixing business with pleasure. Even though the pleasure had been in the past in this case. "I trust most of my staff, but there's no guarantee of anyone's loyalty if there's a nice price tag attached to a juicy story."

Her mouth fell open. "You think someone might tell the press that you've trapped me aboard your yacht with the intention of having your wicked way with me?"

She looked so delighted at the prospect that Dev felt his mouth twitching. "You sound like that's not a bad thing."

"Not a bad thing at all, if I was, in reality, a willing partner," she said dreamily, her gaze suddenly far-off.

"Is this one of your fantasies then, Ms. Roberts?" he said, trying and failing to sound serious.

Her gaze swept over his chest, naked longing shining in it. If he wasn't just as hungrily tracing every feature of her face, he'd have missed it. The woman had no idea how arousing her transparent desire for him was. He was both amused and a little annoyed by it.

No, mostly annoyed, he corrected himself.

Because, he was right in his initial estimate of her. It had been sheer madness—accepting her proposition that night. In his defense, she'd looked incredibly sexy and pretty and had been so earnestly direct that he'd found her utterly irresistible.

Clare Roberts—for all she tried to pretend to be a femme fatale—was very much an innocent from the top of her head to the soles of her pretty feet. The kind he usually avoided like the plague.

"Clare?" he said, and cleared his throat. Desire was a constant low thrum under his skin that he had to get used to—because it couldn't be indulged in again.

"What?" she said distractedly, still only half present.

"Maybe this isn't the time to act out one of your fantasies?" Dev suggested, suddenly realizing he was grinning. It was just too much fun to bandy words with her. More fun than he'd had in a long time. "However, you might want to check what my interest level is after we finish our business dealings though."

She drew herself up to her full five feet three inches, glaring daggers at him. "You really think I'm standing here daydreaming about being kidnapped by you, don't you?"

He shrugged, laughing. "Well, there's nothing wrong with kidnapping when we're both consenting adults, is there? And who am I to stand in the way of a woman's sexual fantasy? Thirdly, you're the one who got all dreamy and soft when I mentioned it."

"I was considering it as a story that could be carefully directed so that it reached the right ears, yes. Not getting all hot and bothered about you having your wicked way with me," she denied hotly.

"That's me put in my place then," he said, with a sigh. "As for a story about you and me being stuck together, Clare, forget it. The last thing I need is any unwelcome scrutiny on my love life."

"But what if it serves my purpose?"

"It doesn't serve mine," Dev growled, realizing she was serious. What the hell was she talking about now? "Do you want this deal with my company or do you want salacious stories about us in the media?"

"I want both."

Dev frowned. Maybe he had been too quick to trust this woman. "I think you'd better tell me the reason you're here first," he said. "Everything else can come later."

He saw her take a deep breath.

"I have a Mob boss after me. His hired thug was here, aboard your yacht this evening, watching me. It was why I had to play hide-and-seek in your closet."

"What?" Dev said, incapable of any other response. He arrested the stinging denial that rose to his lips. The stark fear in her eyes couldn't be a lie.

"The same man was camped outside my office in London. Then I saw him when I flew to a conference in New York. Then again here. When I spotted him up there tonight," she said, pointing to the upper deck, her entire body shivering at some invisible draft, "I just had to hide. I'm sorry for thrusting this all on you, especially when you have your own problems, but I had no choice. I'm stuck in a really bad situation."

"I know the man you're referring to. I signaled to my head of security after I saw him approach you. He was definitely not on the guest list. When I checked again, he'd disappeared."

Clare simply nodded. "I had a call from his boss as I arrived here tonight. He told me that he was going to have me, no matter what. That no one's going to stop him, because he owns me outright."

Dev saw her shiver again and fisted his hands. "You're safe here. My security escorted his henchman off the yacht."

"I'm safe for now," she corrected.

"Why is he after you?"

Her lashes fell down in a curtain, suddenly hiding her expression. "I took money from a man I shouldn't have trusted."

Dev couldn't help sounding incredulous. "You took a loan from a known Mob boss? Why?"

Pink scoured her cheeks. "I told you it was…a bad decision. I was desperate to establish my business. I didn't look closely at who I was trusting."

Dev raised a brow. "So wait, you took out a loan with yourself as collateral? How can a woman specializing in PR not understand what she was signing?"

"Please don't use it as a measure of my efficiency. Let's just say I found myself tricked. Those weren't the terms that were spelled out when I accepted the money. I was just so happy to have a running start on establishing my business. I…" She rubbed her temple with her fingers, her gaze anywhere but on him. "It doesn't matter why or how this happened, okay? That damned man thinks he owns me now."

Clare Roberts was a perplexing combination of innocence and sophistication, with a good measure of idiocy thrown in. Or had she been that desperate to launch her business? To establish her self-sufficiency? To prove her own self-worth?

Because those feelings of desperation were very old friends to Dev.

"I just need some time to figure a way to get out of his clutches. Somewhere he and his goons can't reach me. The last thing I want is to become the prized possession of some Mafia boss who'll delight in punishing me by lending me to his lieutenants whenever he feels like it."

"And how would you know he'd do that?" Dev asked, his mouth twitching again.

She looked at him and away, embarrassment shining in her face. "I binge-watched a show where the main character did that. Fairy tales and fantasies are not really what you'd associate with a practical businesswoman like me, are they?" A bitterness he knew only too well twisted her mouth.

"We all have our guilty pleasures, Clare."

"Like you and your never-ending array of bed partners?" she retorted. But before he could answer her, she shook her head regretfully. "Let's pretend I didn't just say that. And no, I don't need rescuing by anyone. I just need time to rescue myself. So?"

"So what?" he said, wondering what he was signing up for here.

"Will you let me stay aboard for a little while?"

Dev studied her. With her mussed-up hair and clothes, she couldn't have looked less like the CEO of her own PR firm. She looked like trouble. Of the kind that he didn't usually touch with a very long pole.

The last thing he needed right now was another headache. And yet, he couldn't just throw her out, could he? Not when he'd seen the very man she'd mentioned eyeing her like a particularly juicy steak. Not when stark fear at her plight had rendered her so distressingly pale.

He'd already let down one woman who'd been under his protection. Had failed in what he considered to be one of the most important aspects of his own personality—defending those who couldn't defend themselves.

Those who were deemed lesser or weaker, just because they didn't fit a certain definition of perfect or normal. He had been that kid once, with no champion to defend him. With no one to understand how he'd felt being cut off from the world of the written word. Especially not after Mama's death.

How could he ignore Clare's plight now, knowing that her

life might be in danger? He didn't want any more women on his conscience.

He looked down to find her gaze resolutely staring back at him. "All I'm asking for is a place to hide. Whether you hire me or not to clean up your image, you can decide that based on my proposal."

More than pleasantly surprised at how fast she'd turned all that emotion into something far more constructive, he impulsively said, "Fine. We'll figure out a way to get you out of this predicament."

He wondered who was more shocked by his ridiculous promise. Playing the hero had never been his forte. Emotional grandstanding of the kind that his father excelled in had always made him wary. So why was he spouting these words to her?

Thankfully, Clare apparently had a lot more sense and gumption than he had given her credit for.

She shook her head. "Now, Mr. Kohli, don't go making promises you can't keep. Even when I buried myself in fairy tales and stories, I knew enough to not think myself the heroine. To not lose my grip on reality." She sounded like a woman who had never had anyone to depend on. She sounded exactly like him. Dev wondered if that was her appeal for him. "This is a problem I'll solve for myself. As I've always done. All I ask is that you buy me some time."

"Are we really back to being Mr. Kohli and Ms. Roberts again then?"

"I think it's safest, don't you? Especially now that you might be one of my biggest clients."

Dev grinned. There was something about the sudden, starchy formality that she was insisting on that made him want to unravel her. Just a little bit. "Afraid you might not be able to resist me while we're stuck together, are you?"

She laughed. "You think this is being stuck together?" Her arms moved around to encompass the vast yacht. "Aboard your gigantic yacht. It's so ridiculously huge that one might be tempted to think the owner was overcompensating for something..."

Dev took a step forward. One step. There was still a lot of distance between them for him to reach her. Her mouth clamped shut. "You're being unfair, Ms. Roberts."

"How?"

"Making wildly absurd claims that I can't rebut without making statements that could be construed as innuendo? You're baiting me, knowing that I can't play along. You're having your own sweet little revenge."

She blushed and looked away, and he smiled in satisfaction.

"As long as we're clear on the fact that this is not some kind of invitation to re—"

"Yes, yes, I know it's not." She cut in, rolling her eyes. "I'm not stupid. Also, I'm not into skittish playboys who have to be convinced what a treasure I am."

"Did you just call me skittish?" Dev let out an outraged growl and now it was her mouth that twitched.

Her blue eyes widened as she considered him. "I'm not going to crimp your style by being here, am I?"

"What do you mean?" he demanded, feeling surly. Because there was that hum of desire under his skin again. Suddenly the idea of being stuck with this woman for however long— without being able to kiss that lovely mouth—was nothing but pure torment.

"Do you have anyone else on board, Mr. Kohli?"

"Other than my staff, no," he said, wondering where she was going with this.

"A girlfriend? An ex? A bunch of guests waiting to participate in an orgy?"

He pursed his lips. "No."

"Good, then I don't have to disillusion some poor girl looking for a good time?"

"Is that comment in general or specific, Ms. Roberts?"

"Both. We have to be really careful about who you choose as your next playmate."

"Ah…so you were bothered by my behavior that morning then?" He had no idea why he was pressing the issue. No idea why this particular woman had been so stubbornly stuck in his thoughts for weeks.

To give her credit, Clare didn't look away this time. Dev thought she was incredibly brave because her eyes shimmered with a truth she didn't give voice to.

He knew he had hurt her that morning. But it wasn't something he could change or even regret. Better she understood the truth about him now rather than build any ridiculous expectations of this…partnership.

It had to be strictly business.

"That's because I wasn't used to the morning after protocol," she said, all dignified effrontery. The twist of her mouth was both a challenge and something more…something that made Dev want to taste and absorb into himself. "And it was quite a hard landing after the ride you took me on that night. A girl should be forgiven for floating about on an endorphin rush. She needs a little time to recover from seducing you."

Dev burst out laughing. "For the sake of honesty, you didn't seduce me. I seduced you."

Clare was shaking her head and advancing on him suddenly. "No way. I had a plan, and I implemented it to perfection." When his eyes twinkled with a wicked mirth, she stopped.

Dev had no idea how she continually opened doors he didn't want to see through. But she did. "Of course, you had a plan." He shook his head, laughing. Remembering how she'd taken the chance he'd given her. How she'd neatly cornered him into a fascinating conversation and then a whole lot more.

"Why do anything without doing it well?"

He met her gaze again. But Clare looked away, as if that one moment of honesty had been indulgent enough. Reality intruded on them, bursting the bubble of awareness.

Clare knew she should be glad. But there was something about this man that made her not only feel hot and bothered but also naive and foolish. "Anyway, that night's done with. We need to move on from it."

But even now, as she studied his hard jaw, there was a part of her—that foolish part again—that wished he'd tell her that despite what he'd said to her that morning, he'd actually wanted to take her in his arms again. That he'd wanted to see her again afterward.

"Do I have your word that this won't become awkward between us?" he asked, interrupting her reverie with a nice heaping dose of reality.

"Of course you do," she said with extra vehemence. "I told you the reason I snuck in here. And now we've cleared that up, I can absolutely assure you I have no romantic notions whatsoever about you, Mr. Kohli. However, not hiring my company to clean up your image just because we slept together is its own kind of..."

His frown turned into a ferocious scowl. "What?"

"Unfairness," she said, amending her words. "Our sexual history shouldn't affect my career, Mr. Kohli. I shouldn't be penalized for going to bed with you."

"I agree with that a hundred percent," he said, releasing a sigh. He clasped his jaw in his palm, tension radiating from his frame. And then he looked at her. Clare braced herself. "You'll have to forgive me if I'm being extra distrustful of everyone right now," he said honestly, taking the wind from her sails yet again.

"I understand."

They eyed each other carefully—not exactly adversaries, but not friends either. But... Clare couldn't help thinking there was also a certain level of trust between them, even though he'd tried to be all cold and calculating about his decision to work with her. How could there not be a certain warmth between them when they'd been as intimate as they had? When whatever had pulled them together was still tangibly in the air, crackling into life every time they were within touching distance?

She might not have a whole lot of experience with men. But she knew what desire looked like on this particular man's face. She knew him a lot better than he thought, or she liked.

"I promise you that you won't regret taking me on, Mr. Kohli. I'll have my proposal ready for you by first thing tomorrow morning."

Dev shook his head. "Let's make it a bit later in the day. I have a lot of things to get through tomorrow. Why don't you at least take the morning off?"

"And do what?" She looked so dumbstruck by the suggestion that Dev laughed.

"Just lounge about. Recover from the stress of fleeing that man. Take a bath. Catch up on sleep. We'll meet later tomorrow afternoon some time when I'm free."

She nodded. But he knew it was a reluctant acquiescence. "Okay."

Dev stepped aside to let her pass. When she reached the doorway, he called her name, feeling a strange tightness in his chest.

"Yes, Mr. Kohli?" she said, her gaze steady.

"If you want my help getting out of this predicament you've landed yourself in, I'll need the entire truth from you."

And just as Dev had expected, she colored immediately, confirming his suspicions. He knew there had been something wrong with her story.

Her gaze turned stubborn. "There's nothing more to say. I trusted a man I shouldn't have. I…let my heart rule my head and made a stupid decision. I'm willing to help you clean up your mess. All I ask is that you give me a little time to clean up mine."

Dev had never met a woman who could turn the tables on him so well. And she was right. He knew firsthand the price of letting one's guard down. The price of fighting your battles alone. "Fine. We're partners, Ms. Roberts."

"Perfect, Mr. Kohli. You'll see you're right to trust me in this."

With that parting shot, she walked out of his cabin. Confirming his second suspicion that Clare Roberts was anything but the uncomplicated woman he'd thought her to be when he'd taken her to his bed.

CHAPTER FOUR

DURING THE TIME until their meeting—which to Clare felt like an eternity, since she'd been working without a break ever since she'd graduated from university—she explored Dev's gigantic superyacht. She couldn't help but be impressed, even though she'd teased him about the sheer size of it.

Even if she hadn't already known it after their night together, the more she researched his company, and the man himself, the more Clare learned that Dev Kohli didn't have any need whatsoever to prove his masculinity to anyone. So his yacht, other than being a supreme symbol of his success and stamina, was definitely not just a possession to be strutted in front of the world.

In a perverse way, it would have been so much easier to deal with the man if he'd neatly fitted into a preconceived mold.

Playboy—only cares about bedding women, not keeping them safe from evil henchmen.

Billionaire—cares about nothing except making his next billion.

Playboy billionaire—balding, beer-bellied old man with no humor lurking in his brilliant brown eyes.

But it seemed the man was a trendsetter in this too.

Following his advice, Clare had indulged herself last night with a long soak in the huge tub in her cabin's en suite bathroom, consciously reminding herself that she was safe. For now. At least from external events and Mafia villains. Physically, she was safe.

Emotionally...well, she'd survived for years on indifference, using her big dreams to propel her forward. And that's what she was going to do now too—turn this calamity into an opportunity and move forward with nothing but sheer determination.

Simply because there was no other choice except survival. If she had to be on the run, she'd prefer it to be on the luxury yacht of a man she trusted.

Snuggled in a thick robe that dragged on the lush carpet under her feet, she'd arrived in her bedroom to find hot soup and warm, crusty tomato and cheese sandwiches. Luckily, no one had been around to hear the loud growl her stomach had emitted. She'd tucked herself into another window seat that offered a gorgeous nighttime view of the blue ocean and finished her bedtime snack in a matter of seconds.

Digitally blacked out windows and cool, dark navy-blue furnishings had helped her fall asleep in minutes, all thoughts of kidnapping villains dissolving like mist.

When she'd jerked awake the next morning, warm in the nest of soft bedclothes, Clare realized she'd slept for ten hours straight—a miracle in itself. Not counting how normal and in control she felt after another quick shower.

Clearheaded and alert for the first time in days, she wished she'd done her hiding in a different bedroom and not faced Dev yesterday, when she'd been afraid for her life. She'd made a right little numpty of herself.

She hadn't built The London Connection by acting like a witless fool or a dreamy-eyed twit. The future of her company was even more paramount now than it had been before. Since, thanks to her father, she apparently owed a huge amount of money to a mobster. There was no margin for messing this up with Dev. She needed to keep her focus on it being all business between them, as he'd said.

Ten hours of sleep did wonders for a girl. The stern talking-to she gave herself as she blow-dried her hair boosted her confidence. She made do with the lip-gloss, concealer and mascara in her handbag.

Having enveloped herself in another thick towel, she spent the next twenty minutes, looking through the large but mostly vacant closet attached to her cabin. Luckily, she, Amy, Bea all made it a policy to carry spare underwear and all kinds of paraphernalia in their bags for any PR emergency. But she had no clothes.

As she eyed the almost empty wardrobe, she thought of her travel bag sitting in her hotel room in São Paulo, now all but lost. There was no way she could have sneaked it past security onto the yacht last night. For a few seconds, she indulged in the idea of wearing last night's skirt and blouse again. But then she remembered that before she'd got into that lovely warm bath, she'd dropped them into the conveniently placed laundry basket, which was now, of course, empty.

Apparently, the man's yacht ran as efficiently as his sportswear empire.

In the end, Clare ripped the packaging off one of Dev's dress shirts. Apparently, the man had designer dress shirts lying around in all the cabins. Savile Row deserved better, but she didn't care right then. Thinking for too long on why she was here on a stranger's yacht, sailing away to some idyllic island with her company's fate and her own hanging in the balance might lead to falling into the pit of despair and fury she was somehow keeping at bay.

With the shirt hanging almost to her knees, Clare used a belt and turned it into a dress. Back on went her leather stilettos, and she looked halfway decent. Or at least that's what she told herself.

After getting lost in a service elevator and ending up in a theater room, and discovering a neatly stowed away seaplane on the top deck, it began to dawn on Clare that the yacht was also the man's home. And that while he had invited her to explore, it had been mostly a polite response to a distressed and wild-tale-weaving woman he'd found in his closet. Not the welcome mat precisely.

With each space she invaded, it became clearer that he was a man who absolutely protected his privacy at all costs. Because for all the features in the media detailing his jet-setting life and fast girlfriends, no journalist had ever been allowed access to this yacht.

This was where Dev Kohli, former gold-medal-winning swimmer and billionaire playboy, retreated to when the alternately adoring and punishing world's media became all too much.

Like the man himself, while the exterior was all gleaming confidence, the interior had depths she couldn't plumb in a year, much less a day. There was none of the gold accents and veneer, or the traditional nautical motifs she'd imagined from peeking at antiquated travel magazines her dentist had lying around the office.

Up and down, Clare went, fascinated by it all. After getting lost again, she armed herself with a schematic map and a picnic basket from the galley—apparently, they had been given express instructions to look after Mr. Kohli's guest properly—and shamelessly explored the yacht.

Admiring this example of twenty-first-century engineering was definitely better than pondering one's fate as an owned woman. Or even worse, daydreaming about a man's happy trail. In the end, Clare settled into a lounger on the main deck, her picnic basket by her side, her laptop on her knee. The noonday sun glinted off the water in brilliant golden sparkles, while colorful coastal towns were visible in the distance.

If a man was disposed to moving from place to place, disinclined to put roots down...then clearly, Dev Kohli did it in style.

But, she mused, if all this wealth was at her disposal, the last place she'd want to be was on the sea. There was a temporariness to moving from place to place that didn't appeal to Clare. Even having been disillusioned again and again by her dad's unending lies over the years, that he would come for her and that they would be a family again, and by her aunt's indifference toward her, Clare had always wanted a permanent home.

A grand home and an even grander family of noisy sisters and brothers and nieces and nephews, celebrating birthdays and festivals together, prying into each other's business and making up after silly fights and all that sort of thing.

But with each year rolling around and her dad not showing up, it had become increasingly distant. Then he'd given her the money she'd used to start up her business, just before he died. She'd thought he would have been proud to know she'd used the money so well, but even that daydream had turned sour. Because the man her father had borrowed that money from had finally discovered her father was dead and couldn't pay it back, and so he'd come after Clare.

She was truly alone in the world and couldn't escape the knowledge that to put her in such danger, her father had never really cared for her at all.

She still couldn't wrap her head around that bit of news. Couldn't get her jumbled feelings to make any kind of sense. They just sat in the pit of her stomach like a knotted lump. For years, a foolish part of her had believed that he'd somehow turn into an ideal father one day. When he'd sent her the money, she'd thought her faith in him had finally been validated. That he had loved her in his own way.

But once again, she'd lied to herself.

Her laptop screen blurred in front of her eyes and Clare blinked hard.

No, she couldn't let the past muddle her future. Her vision cleared when she saw a social media photo turn up in her search results. She stared at the tall, gorgeous brunette—a model, of course, who had just revealed her...association with Dev. Clare's mind instantly did a quick calculation of whether she herself had come before or after this model, in his life.

The very idea of being just another night of transient pleasure to him grated on her nerves. But that was who he was. Dev Kohli was clearly allergic to relationships that lasted longer than a couple of weeks—if that.

She'd do well to remember that simple fact.

Pursing her lips, Clare added a bullet point to the list of things she needed to discuss with him.

It was going to take all the finesse she possessed to make sure Dev understood what he needed to do. So Clare once again pushed away the sorrow and grief that was crouching inside her chest and instead poured her energy into outlining the proposal for saving Athleta.

Focusing on her business, on tangible targets and not naive dreams, had always been her lifeline.

Clare blinked and opened her eyes as a short man in a pristine black-and-white uniform informed her that Mr. Kohli was waiting to see her now in his study. She sat up and straightened her shirt, aghast at the fact that she'd fallen asleep again after only a few hours' work. God, what sort of strange inertia and exhaustion had her in its grip?

Before the uniformed man disappeared to wherever it was that people seemed to hide on the monstrous yacht, she begged him to point her in the direction of the study.

Even with his instructions, it took her ages to find her way to there. It seemed the very universe was constantly conspiring to make her look unprofessional in front of the one man she wanted to impress with her smarts and sophistication and efficiency.

Laptop and a folder in hand, Clare walked into an expansive circular room with a dizzyingly high ceiling. Light filtered through the skylight in the center of it, casting a golden glow over the floor-to-ceiling shelves of books. Rows and rows of books were filed with almost military precision. Clare let out a soft sigh, the idea of spending hours and hours lost in the library in this study would be pure heaven to her.

The sound of a throat clearing jerked her attention away from the world of rare first editions.

In a sunken seating area, in the midst of the airy space, was Dev. Looking for all intents and purposes like a king sitting amid his priceless treasures. Except his treasures, it seemed, were books. Clare instantly knew that this space was different from everywhere else on the yacht. That this room somehow reflected his true nature. That if she wanted to know more about Dev Kohli—the real man beneath the billionaire playboy persona—this was where she would find him.

Not that it was something she did want, she told herself.

Still, she felt a totally unnecessary and unbidden spark of excitement at being given a view of his inner sanctum that he hadn't allowed anyone else.

Dressed in black trousers and a white dress shirt that was unbuttoned at his throat, he looked elegant and masculine and somehow edgy at the same time. His carefully cut hair was rumpled and not quite perfect today. He reminded Clare of a restless predator she'd once seen on a documentary. As if there was a constant hum of energy beneath that sleek brown skin and taut muscles. As if at any moment, he might leap up from the beige leather sofa and launch himself into...

"Ms. Roberts?"

The deep timbre of his voice made Clare start. "Yes, Mr. Kohli?" she replied tartly, irritated with her own woolgathering. Neither did she miss the affected formality in the way he said her name.

"I asked if you were unwell." His gaze swept over her face and body. Had been doing so for a while, she realized. From her hair to the shirt—his shirt that she'd styled into a dress—to the belt and stilettos, he took in every little detail about her. She felt the quick scrutiny like a warm caress, pooling in places she didn't want to think about right now. "We can do this another time if you're still feeling the effects of—"

"Of course not. I'm perfectly fine. Thank you for asking." Her response sounded chillingly polite to her own ears. A bit too chilly, in contrast to the laid-back humor she saw in his eyes.

Suddenly, she had a feeling that he'd caught her napping on the main deck. Her chin lolling against her chest, with drool pooling at the side of her mouth, most probably.

"I've been ready for this meeting for a while." She sighed. "Only I had no idea how to reach you or any other human on this boat. "Did you get a chance to look at the initial contracts I emailed you?"

"No, it will take me to time to get to them. And it's a yacht, not a boat."

"On this oversized yacht," she parroted obediently, something under her skin humming awake at the twitch of that gorgeous mouth. The man often seemed to be on the verge of laughing. At the world, instead of with it, she suspected. And then of course, that thought led her to unwisely mutter, "Are you laughing at me, Mr. Kohli?"

He shook his head, but the mirth in his eyes remained. "Should I find something funny about this?"

"No. That's what I meant to point out. Nothing about this predicament is funny and yet—"

"Of course it's not. But you have to afford me some allow-ances when you turn up here, your nose high in the air, deter-mined to find something or other about me to disapprove of."

"That's not at all what I was thinking," she hotly denied.

"Then tell me what is it that you don't like about my yacht," he asked, surprising her yet again.

"What's there to not like?" she retorted, trying to keep her tone steady. Dev was so dangerous in how easily he could read her thoughts. "Like I said, it's big and beautiful."

"And yet, you just called it oversized, implying it's osten-tatious."

"That was uncalled for," she said, forcing regret into her voice. Why did the man care so much what she thought of his damned yacht?

"I sense that you don't usually make uncalled-for statements, Ms. Roberts. Or that you say anything at all unless you mean it."

Their gazes held, his probing and lazily amused and hers... resisting the pull of his. It seems she was always resisting something or other about this man. Except the one time she'd stopped resisting and given in to desire, it had been glorious. She desperately hoped she wasn't wearing the jumble of her thoughts openly on her face.

"You're right, of course," she said, acquiescing. *Pick your battles, Clare*, came something that sounded very much like Bea's voice in her head. "It just seems like a lot of room for only one man."

"Ahh...you're going to lecture me about the environment and such? In my meager defense, I do travel with two personal assistants, three lawyers, a personal trainer and stylist, two chefs and a variety of other personnel—"

"Who I'm sure all contribute toward the larger-than-life image of you that mere mortal men can only aspire to."

"There it is again, Ms. Roberts." He raised an eyebrow. "That faint whiff of disapproval."

"Even though I've had a glimpse into the jet-setting lifestyles of certain celebrities while I've been working, I still find myself in awe of how much social media conceals from our eyes. How one-dimensional we want our celebrities to be. Nothing personal, Mr. Kohli."

His brows drew close as he regarded her thoughtfully, no quick response forming on that gorgeous mouth. That she had surprised him was clear by the sudden silence. But the buzz under her skin that was still there regardless of what he said or did...she so badly wished she could completely smother that involuntary reaction to him.

"You sound disappointed in me." He sounded comically

confused. As if it was impossible for any woman to not delight in him!

"Something like that," she said, thankful that he was so far off the mark. It wouldn't do to cater to his giant ego. She had to keep this attraction purely inside her own head. "So you have a veritable army of servants," she said, refusing to let him unsettle her with that silent scrutiny, "who are of course paid to be neither seen nor heard. I can be forgiven, I think, for imagining us to be practically alone on board."

He ran a hand through his hair, looking slightly uncomfortable.

She scrunched her nose. "I wasn't actually intending to lecture you, you know."

"No?"

"I read the interview you did a while ago for that lifestyle magazine. You run a billion-dollar empire that has offices in five different countries. You have eleven thousand three hundred and seventy-six employees around the world. Not counting the personnel you employ here on the yacht and across the two flats, three estates and one palace you have dotted around. What was it that you said…you've created *an economy all on its own*? So all of this luxury is simply a place to rest for a man who gives livelihoods to so many. You called it your kingdom. And you said your mother taught you that a king has both duties and privileges. That was a nice personal touch," she added dryly.

"What, that I have duties and privileges?"

"No, mentioning your mother."

A hardness entered his eyes that transformed his face from having an easy charm to a powerful remoteness. "It wasn't scripted to manipulate my audience, Ms. Roberts." His voice could cut through ice.

Clare nodded pacifyingly. Clearly, his family was a sore topic of conversation. She braced herself for the battle ahead. He wasn't going to like her plan one bit if he was ruffled at the mention of an old interview in which he'd referenced his mother.

"I never said there wasn't any truth to your interview." She eyed him as he sprawled on the circular leather sofa, surveying her with those long-lashed eyes. "You certainly do live like a king, Mr. Kohli."

One arm stretched along the sofa. The folded cuffs of his white shirt displayed a smattering of faint hair over strong forearms. Everything about the man was clean lines and masculine elegance. "You remember a lot about that interview."

Clare tried to not bristle at the inherent teasing in his tone. "I've always had a good memory for details. And it was clear that journalist came to you with an agenda."

"What do you think that might have been?"

"To lump you in with the current crop of spoiled, rich billionaires who don't give a damn about the state of the world. And you disarmed her very easily."

Far too easily, if you asked her. There was a unique quality about Dev—and she didn't just mean his astonishingly good looks—that put women at ease with him. But an inherently welcoming sense of safety and fairness he extended, probably without knowing it himself.

Of course, he wasn't a saint by any means. He rarely dated anyone more than a few times, but Clare didn't blame any woman for succumbing to the fantasy of being this man's lover. Of hoping that she might be the only woman he wanted in his bed, the only woman he allowed into his life. And heart.

Which was definitely a fantasy, all right. But she…she was made of sterner stuff. More importantly, she'd already had her one fantasy night with him, which was apparently all he was going to deign to allow her.

"So what is it in particular that you don't like about the yacht? Or was it just me who riled you up when you walked in just now?"

"I just…fine, yes, it's a lovely yacht. Airy and light—and don't think I haven't noticed in the information brochures about how it's built with recycled wood and other environmentally friendly materials. But it seems so empty."

"Empty?" he said, his gaze shifting to encompass the furniture around them.

"It's just a personal thing."

His elbows dropping to his thighs, he leaned forward invitingly. "Tell me."

"All this wealth on open display…it seems counterintuitive to what we're all supposed to be pursuing, isn't it?"

He frowned. "And what is that?"

"Happiness. Peace. A place to belong."

"And you think that's what we're all looking for?" He didn't sound quite put off by her opinion, but it was clear that he didn't like it much either.

"You did insist on hearing my explanation, Mr. Kohli," she said pointedly. "I just meant that it feels somewhat isolated. Designed to be cut off from the world. The home of a man who doesn't want to put down any roots."

A bleakness entered his eyes then, and Clare was sure she'd crossed some imaginary boundary she shouldn't have. Trespassed where she wasn't invited, much less wanted.

"Ahh…then it's a good thing that you don't know me quite as well as you think you do," he said, that momentary vulnerability disappearing with a slow, lazy blink.

"I quite disagree," she added, something inside her pushing her on. "The thing is, I've spent quite a few hours recently deep diving into your life, and what's in the media does paint quite a cold, clinical picture of you. Flashy affairs that end faster than people change their car tires and business deal upon business deal where you always emerge the winner. In fact, you appear to lead what looks to the outsider like a very…solitary, selfish kind of life."

"So you're telling me you don't approve of my lifestyle?"

"Not at all," Clare retorted. "I admit that I do try to avoid men who tend to forge their own path and leave people behind along the way, yes, but this isn't about me. There's a world of difference between what you've allowed the world to see and what you're really like beneath all that shine and glamor."

"Despite your…deep dive—" his distaste for the term couldn't be clearer and his nostrils flared with a rare show of temper "—into my life, you still don't really know me. I'm not interested in pursuing all those things you mentioned. Why tie yourself to one place when instead you can have the freedom to explore the entire world?" He moved his hand between them dismissively, as if the things she mentioned were totally unimportant. "Belonging anywhere is overrated, Ms. Roberts. The only time the world listens to you is when you dictate to it. On your own terms."

He was drawing clear boundaries, and it would be wise for her to follow them. And yet she couldn't help feeling this impression he was giving right now, of a man who wanted to conquer the entire world, was just a mask he was putting on.

A facade he had to display in public.

But whether her suspicions were true or not, it wasn't her business, Clare reminded herself. The man was telling her who and what he was, and she should stop searching for qualities in him that weren't present. She'd done this with her dad too. Year after year, she'd convinced herself that he would come back for her one day. When the truth was, he'd barely even bothered ringing her on her birthday or at Christmas.

Clare gave her assent with a nod. "Fine, Mr. Kohli. As you say."

"Toeing the line now, Clare?"

She shrugged. "It's not my job to moralize to you, is it? It's to make you look perfect in front of the world. To give this shiny veneer of yours a human element. And for the most part, I'm glad to have followed my instinct about you."

"Which instinct is that?"

Clare lost her patience. "That you aren't the villain the world is calling you, Mr. Kohli," she said sweetly.

He grinned. "So how are you going to improve my image? And for heaven's sake, please can you stop calling me Mr. Kohli in that prissy voice?"

"Fine. Your love life...it's a trail of broken hearts and short affairs that don't paint a homely picture of you."

"I didn't realize we were trying to find me a bride."

Clare rolled her eyes. "This isn't funny, Dev. For example, did you know that one of your exes, Sahara Jones, has taken to posting old pics of you and her on her social media this past week? Apparently, your breakup three months ago didn't suit her. She's got seven and a half million rabid followers who're all dying to know if you're back together as she's been hinting at and who'll turn into an angry mob at just one word from her. Is Ms. Jones going to brew more trouble for you in the coming weeks?"

"What do you mean?" he asked, surprisingly slow for a man who'd cut such a swathe through the worlds of competitive sport and then business with a dangerously irresistible combination of charm and smarts.

"Is she the type to drag your name through the mud? Plaster private information about you all over social media and make you look horrible? Because, right now, your reputation can't take any more hits."

"Of course not."

"And yet I'll point out that she was here on board your yacht last night—I recognized her. Presumably she was there without your knowledge?"

"You miss nothing," he said, jaw tight. Grudgingly.

"I don't. Neither did I miss that you had her escorted out by security with very little ceremony and that she didn't look very happy about it. So details, please."

"Excuse me?"

"I need details of your breakup so that I can gauge the possible consequences for myself."

His muttered something under his breath. "Sahara and I dated for just over two weeks. I ended our relationship, such as it was, when I realized she had no intention of respecting my privacy.

"On our second date, she sprung some talk show host on me so that we could both discuss all the disadvantages we'd each had to overcome to succeed. She was in talks with her agent about writing a book about our relationship. As you know, she's a model, but not massively famous and she had to jump through a lot of hoops to get there."

"And?" Clare prompted.

"She thought she'd ride the wave to stardom with me as her golden ticket. But I wasn't interested in a woman who was trying to probe into aspects of my life that were none of her business."

"What kind of salacious details did she manage to uncover?"

His jaw tightened. "There were no salacious details, Clare. She had no business thinking she could sell my life story as some romantic journey we were on together. I told my lawyers to sue her if she so much as whispers anything about me again. After the show she put on last time, she was fired from her latest contract. She was here last night to convince me that it had never been her idea in the first place. To help her land a different contract."

"Are you going to help her?"

Dev rubbed a hand over his face and sighed. "Yes. I'm not a callous bastard, Clare. I've already put her in touch with a friend of mine. Even though Sahara should've known better than to drag me into her drama."

"So I should count the matter as being resolved for now?"

"Yes."

"Why?"

"How do I know she won't create more trouble?" The frost in his eyes sent a small shiver down her spine. "Because she got what she wanted from me."

Clare nodded, biting back the question that lingered on her lips. "Can I suggest then, Dev, that until we make sure the world is firmly on your side, that you give up…women?"

The dratted man laughed. A full-bodied, rollicking kind of laugh that made her breath hitch in her throat. That transformed his face from a collection of perfectly symmetrical features to something altogether beautiful. A dimple sliced the hollow of his cheek and his eyes shone. "I don't think I've ever been ordered around quite so strictly in my life."

"Not even by your mother?" Clare added, enjoying the beauty of his smile and the warm fuzzies it aroused in her belly far too much.

He sobered instantly, but the warmth in his eyes lingered. "No. Not even by Mama. Not even when I made her life hell. Not even when I frustrated her no end and caused her grief." He gave a sigh that seemed to rock through the solid core of him. "My mother was one of those souls that was all love and patience and kindness itself."

"The point is," Clare said, wanting to chase away the shadows that crossed his face at the mention of his lovely sounding mother, "that when it comes down to it, hiring me to clean up your image is exactly like being in school with a very strict headmistress. This might never work if you balk at every—"

"Ah... I can see now why your company's so successful, Clare."

"Can you?" she said, having forgotten what she was going to say.

"I have no problem whatsoever imagining you as a strict headmistress."

He delivered it very tongue-in-cheek, his dark eyes full of an easy geniality. Clare couldn't blame him for teasing her, but she still flushed all over at his comment. She took a deep breath, hoping a fresh burst of oxygen would clear the miasma of longing that seemed to take over her brain and body.

A timely reminder to herself that Dev wasn't really the hero she was making him out to be in her head.

"I'm not going to apologize every time I have to advise you about your...sex life. In fact, to be on the safe side, I'd say, just don't have any. For a good, long while," she added feeling perversely petty.

Clare had never thought of herself as wicked, but the idea of policing Dev's sex life—because clearly the man was as distrustful of love as she was—filled her with delight. Whoever said there was a silver lining to every cloud was absolutely right.

CHAPTER FIVE

"EXCUSE ME? Did you actually order me to curtail my sex life?"
Dev repeated her words, even though he'd heard her perfectly
well. More importantly, he also agreed with her 100 percent.

The last thing he wanted or needed right now was to get em-
broiled with another woman.

He should have expected Sahara to show up after she'd told
him she was in São Paulo. To network, she'd said, citing a renowned photographer that Dev was friends with. He had felt a
little sorry for her when she'd lost her contract. But he couldn't
help wondering if she'd felt anything for him at all. Or had he
simply been a rich, powerful, good-looking walking, talking
cardboard cutout of a man for her to drape herself over?

Can you blame her for that? a voice whispered inside his
head. *When it's exactly what you want from your flings, when
you pursue exactly the kind of woman who has no interest in
you except your sexual prowess, your fame and your money?*

"Yes, I did," declared the woman in front of him, dragging
his attention away from the kind of thoughts he hated. Con-
science-stirring thoughts that made a man weak and useless if
he listened to them too much.

Clare continued. "As horrendously novel as this might seem
to you, I'm the boss of you right now, Dev, until we fix this

scandal and your image. Until we show the world that you're a wonderful, conscientious man who cares about women in the workplace, especially yours. I should decide who you see, who you talk to and who you kiss…" she declared, looking diminutive and delicate and decidedly ignoring the pink blush that crept up her neck.

Although there was nothing delicate about the steel in her words or the way she radiated a sort of resolute competence.

Even as she looked ridiculously cute in a makeshift dress styled from his shirt and belt. She was so much shorter than him that the hem of the shirt, thankfully, reached her knees.

Dev moved until he was standing at the foot of the few steps to the sunken seating area while she stood at the top. Her face still only came level with his, just. The wide-open collar of the shirt betrayed the rapidly fluttering pulse at the base of her neck. A prickle of awareness hummed to life under his skin. He studied the sharp curve of her jaw, the straightness of her nose and the blue shadows under her eyes that made them sparkle even more.

Her hair, cut precisely to enhance the line of her jaw, looked decidedly rumpled right now. His mouth twitched at the thought of the ever professional and polished Ms. Roberts sputtering away at the indignity of not being able to don the mask of ruthless efficiency she usually portrayed.

Once he'd had confirmation that there were some truly dangerous men chasing her—his head of security had even mentioned talk of a bounty on her head—he'd felt an immediate urgency to ensure for himself that Clare, with her larger than life smile and prickly demands, was kept safe from harm.

So instead of waiting any longer, he'd gone in search of her. And stared at her sleeping form for a full ten minutes like a horny teenager who was gazing at his first crush. She'd looked so fragile napping on the main deck, her mouth soft and lush in repose. Except Dev never normally felt the need to pursue women. Not since he'd shot up to his height of six two at the age of sixteen. They'd done all the chasing.

And he wasn't going to begin now.

It was just that there was something deliciously delightful about riling up Clare Roberts for the simple fact that her blue eyes widened and her lovely little mouth gaped and a myriad of expressions crossed her equally beautiful face. All the while she processed her frantic thoughts and inevitably arrived at an affected indifference that even she herself didn't quite buy.

"So you're going to be like a twenty-first-century chastity belt," he added.

She scrunched her cute nose at the thought, reminding him of a proud, pretty little bird sticking its beak up into the air. But Dev didn't miss the quick sweep of her gaze over his lower abdominal region, as if wondering how such a contraption would work on him.

His nether regions, suitably impressed by her avid perusal, perked up with interest.

"Not quite, but if it helps you get the idea, I say run with the image."

Dev grinned. "I think you're taking your role in my life too far," he added, holding up his hand for her.

After a few seconds' hesitation, she took it. A jolt of sensation clamped him instantly, the memory of those delicate fingers tentatively exploring his body sneaking upon him suddenly. He let go of her hand as soon as her stiletto-clad feet hit the carpet.

"I'm absolutely not. Rich playboy billionaires are just as accountable to the verdict of the masses as we normal people are, thanks to the power of social media. Even a hint of one more scandal right now could be enough to start a domino effect. Believe me, Dev, if there's one thing I know, it's how to manage reputations."

"Fine, I'll try not to attract too many women. Especially if I have to disappoint them with a no access message to—" he moved his hand over his chest "—all this."

Just as he expected, her blue eyes widened and her lush mouth gasped with indignation.

"Shall we get back to the business at hand?" she asked pointedly, her chin lifting.

"Absolutely," Dev said, grinning.

Celibacy might not be such a hard concept with the enchanting Ms. Roberts to entertain him. Clare was so full of complexities that Dev couldn't help but be amused by her. As he settled down on the opposite side of the couch from her, he knew that she was precisely the right woman to fix both his personal image and that of his company.

To bring Athleta back onto the right path.

For all that he'd occasionally caught her gazing at him with a flash of desire, he believed that she would be all business. He could trust her. Dev had known that, even the first night he'd met her at the charity gala. Like all the big decisions he'd taken in life, he'd gone with his gut on that one.

It was why he'd broken his own rule and taken an unknown woman to his bed. Why he'd indulged himself so thoroughly when—despite all the spectacular stories the press wrote about his supposed indiscreet affairs with any woman he pleased—he never usually gave into his desires with such little forethought.

And while Clare fixed his image problem, he was determined to take a good hard look at the choices he'd been making for the last fifteen years.

That the man he'd trusted the most had been able to abuse not only Dev's trust but that of a woman in his employ was a direct consequence of the choices Dev had made years ago, while at military school.

Fueled by resentment and rejection, he'd set a goal for himself. And in the pursuit of that goal, he'd become bedfellows with a number of men whose principles he didn't always agree with.

Now he had achieved success and wealth beyond his wildest dreams. Maybe enough to even impress his arrogant father, with his ridiculously extravagant expectations for his children. As if they were all trophies and achievements to be polished and put on display instead of breathing, living people with flaws and dreams of their own.

And yet Dev had to admit to himself that somewhere along the path he'd chosen for himself, he'd lost his way.

He'd surrounded himself with people who courted success and wealth while trading in their principles. That had never been him—whether in his personal life or in business.

Which meant this was his chance to find the right path this time—he'd continue to build Athleta into the biggest and best sports brand in the world, but he wasn't going to do that at the cost of losing himself.

"What else is in your plan," he said, nodding at the glossy folder she held in her hands, "other than curtailing my..."

"...extracurricular activities?" Clare finished his sentence, picking up the thread of the conversation again. "Yes, of course."

She had no idea why she was this flustered. Dev wasn't even a difficult client. She'd had to put up with much worse, especially before The London Connection had yet to build the solid reputation it had now. And yet it was only Dev who again and again, tripped her circuits, for want of a better term.

Dev leaned back into the luxury leather seat, a devilish glint in his eyes.

"Right..." Clare opened her laptop and clicked onto the notes file she'd prepared earlier. "I'm just going to pull up this spreadsheet I created of the assets and liabilities we have to work with."

At that, he got up and took the seat next to her. The couch she was sitting on was large enough to provide ample space between them, and yet it felt as if the very air she was breathing was charged with the vitality of the man.

It took Clare a few seconds to focus on the list in front of her. She cleared her throat and then caught him trying to peek at her spreadsheet. "There aren't any secrets here, Dev."

"Oh, I know that. But it's interesting to see one's life so neatly reduced to two columns. I'm especially curious about the liabilities list."

Clare rolled her eyes. And thanked the universe for giving her the sense to remove that list from this sheet. "Don't worry. I'll handle your masculine sensibilities delicately. I know a thing or two about the male ego."

He laughed at that and the sound enveloped Clare. "Absolutely not, Ms. Roberts. Since you have curtailed any and all of my usual entertainments, this could be the only highlight of my week. Or even the month."

"What?"

"Getting dressed down by you for all my various sins."

Clare bared her teeth in a mockery of a smile. "No one was more disappointed than me at the blatant lack of those sins. I might have to write to the ruthless playboy billionaire club and have your title revoked. Instead of shadows of shady deals, all I could find was a veritable halo, which just needs a little polish." Clare didn't wait for him deny it. "We need to shine a light on the charity programs and drives that are sponsored by Athleta."

That mobile mouth narrowed into a straight line. "I don't give to various charities for publicity," he announced in an almost regal way. As if he expected it to be the beginning and end of the matter.

Clare frowned. Usually, with most of her clients—those with either old money or new—she had to work very hard to convince them that not every small bit of charity was something that could be used for PR. "Whether you give all these large amounts of money," she said, pointing a manicured nail at the figures, "for publicity or not doesn't matter anymore. The pertinent fact is that you do. *Give*, that is. Believe it or not, Dev, you're going to be one of my easiest clients."

With his arm snaked over the back of the couch, and his long legs stretched in front of him, she couldn't help thinking he reclined like a maharaja. The corners of his mouth twitched and that dimple—that damned dimple of his—winked at her again. "I do believe that that is the highest compliment you've ever paid me."

Clare snorted. "Don't go strutting around just yet. But, yes, it is. I don't have to manufacture reasons to show you in a good light. Or convince you that your charity work needs to be more than just a sop to your conscience. I've closely followed Athleta's charity work. It's why I wanted to work with you."

"You have made it more than clear that it's only the job that's important to you, Clare. For the record, I'm no longer under any kind of misconception that you hid yourself on my yacht to seduce me."

Clare couldn't quite meet his gaze then. Knowing that he would see how horribly she was still attracted to him. Not that he probably didn't know.

Still there was a difference between him guessing and being given that information explicitly. "The world needs to know that Athleta is not rotten all the way through. That you, at the core of it, are still sound. That it was just one limb that was diseased and you quickly cut it off."

Any hint of humor disappeared from his face. "And I also severed everything that limb influenced," he retorted instantly. "Isn't that enough?"

Clare gentled her voice. Not just to appease the hint of bitterness she heard in his tone but because she understood where it was coming from. There was something very deep and complex going on with him, however much she wanted to continue believing that he was nothing but another shallow pool. "Would you give your trust back to someone once it was broken so easily?"

He looked away, his jaw tight. But as she'd known already, Dev was a man who faced the truth, always. Whether it painted him in a good light or not. Hand pushing roughly through his hair, he turned to face her, his dark brown gaze full of shadows that she couldn't see past. "No. I would never give my trust back once it was lost."

She'd meant to persuade him that it was going to take time and a little effort to convince the public, because he'd already, and had always done, the things that mattered most for a company's image anyway. But the vehemence with which he talked about his trust being broken… It found an answering echo within Clare.

"The various charities you give to—girls' education and empowerment through Asia, funding learning disabilities research in the US, youth scholarships for inner city kids… All these are things you and your company should be enormously proud of. It's not enough to do good, Dev. Especially now. It's also necessary to set an example. All the public normally sees is that you're basically living a life of extravagance and luxury and that you're this hot, athletic, aspirational figure that every average Joe wants to be and that every average Jane wants to be with."

Clare patiently waited for his laughter to subside. It wasn't a hardship because the man was insanely beautiful, and she was no better than the average Jane she'd just mentioned.

"You have such a way with words, Clare. You're very good for a man's ego."

Clare shook her head. "I'm not pandering to your ego at all. I'm trying to tell you that it's time to show people, especially your female employees, that you're more than some oversexed playboy billionaire."

He winced. "Oversexed playboy billionaire…is that how you see me?"

Clare pursed her lips. Did the man intend to jump on every little thing she said? "How I see you doesn't matter at all. We're going to drip feed as much information about Athleta's various charity activities as we can. Take this recent visit to São Paulo, for example. What the world thinks is you're here to party with some rowdy friends of yours. And yet I know you came here to work with a designer who uses recyclable materials for a new kind of sole for running shoes and that you attended a conference that's addressing the preservation of the rain forest."

"You really have done your research," Dev replied, surprise in his tone.

Clare felt a pang of satisfaction. "I told you, I'm very thorough when it comes to my job. The next item on the agenda... We need to do an interview with Ms. Jones," she said, mentioning the woman who'd exposed the harassment at Athleta with enormous courage.

"That's out of the question." Dev looked as if someone had punched him. "I'm not going to hound the poor woman into giving a statement just to make myself look better in front of the world."

Clare leaned forward, determined to persuade him to see reason. "But what if she agrees? What if—"

"You've already contacted her, haven't you?"

Clare stilled at the outraged look in his eyes. "I'm not going to apologize for doing my job."

He sighed. "Fine. But I don't want Ms. Jones to be pressured in any way that she's not comfortable with. She's been through enough. Is that clear?"

"I understand."

"What do you suggest I do next?" he said, his brow still twisted into a scowl.

"We're going to do a couple of interviews on a sports channel and a major network channel with your sisters."

If she thought he'd been angry before, it was nothing to the fury that etched his face now. This emotion was not hot like before. This was icy cold, brittle, hard, turning his features from simply stunningly handsome to harsh and rugged.

With a curse, he pushed up onto his feet and moved away from the living area. She craned her neck up, her gaze hungrily trailing the economic efficiency with which he moved. The black trousers he wore clung to his powerful thighs, the white shirt highlighting his broad shoulders and lean waist.

She took the time to simply study him. He'd been blessed with inordinately good looks, and yet it was the energy with which he occupied a space that fascinated her.

It was several minutes before he turned back to face her, his temper firmly under control. "I was ready to agree to your suggestions because one of my employees wronged an innocent woman. But the responsibility for that lies with me, as CEO. There is no need to drag my family into this."

"But an illustrious family like yours can only be an advantage," Clare retorted, and then instantly wanted to pull her words back.

It seemed that her ill-thought words had only pierced anew whatever wound Dev was determined to ignore.

"Let's not get into the advantages and disadvantages my illustrious family has afforded me. It's above your paygrade."

The dismissal was clear and cold. She hadn't been lying when she'd told him that she'd handled a lot of difficult clients in her time. And yet Dev's dismissal stung her deeper than any other. It shouldn't have, considering their "business-only" relationship.

But she refused to let him railroad her, not in this. "I have no interest in digging into matters you deem forbidden, Mr. Kohli," she said haughtily. "But neither will I be told how to do my job. During my research, I discovered that your older sister is a world-renowned neurosurgeon and your younger sister is a state diplomat. We need to show the world that you're not intimidated by powerful women."

"Doesn't the list of women I've dated show that? I've dated several influential, wealthy women in their own right."

"No. That just shows that you're allergic to commitment and that you're pickier than a five-year-old when it comes to what he wants for dinner."

That shut him up promptly. Clare bit her lip to stop smiling. "At this point, it's not just that you and Athleta are being roasted everywhere. But have you wondered why your invitation to the Ethics and Equity in Sports panel has been canceled?"

"How the hell do you know that?" he said incredulously. "It's only just happened!"

Clare shrugged. "I have my sources."

"You don't have to remind me why I hired you," he said dryly.

"Then stop being so difficult, Dev. If you want to bring about change in your company, it has to start with you. No one said it was going to be easy."

"Are you charging me extra for the motivational speech?" he quipped. Humor was his default setting, Clare was beginning to see. But it didn't mean he wasn't hearing what she had to say.

"I'm just as excited as you are by the changes you want to make. I've been out there, in the business world. The glass ceiling is very much alive and thriving, Dev. It's encouraging to see powerful men want to do their part in fostering an equitable environment for women."

"You're quite the force to be reckoned with, aren't you?"

"Why is there a question mark at the end of that?" Clare said, feeling as if the ground was being stolen from under her. It wasn't a bad sensation. Just a floaty one.

He frowned, his gaze sweeping over her features, as if he was searching for something. "Because there's one piece that doesn't really fit."

"What?"

"Why such a smart woman like you would make a deal with an unscrupulous Mafia boss. Even for much-needed capital. With your asset and liability columns and what little I know of you, I just don't see you taking a horrible risk like that."

Clare swallowed and gathered the papers she'd spread out on the coffee table in front of her. The unvarnished grain of the oak table felt like an anchor steadying her. She didn't know why she was hiding the truth from him.

Even Amy and Bea assumed she'd inherited the money after her dad had died, because the two things had happened so close together. She didn't know if it was her own fault for having foolishly trusted her father when he'd said he wanted to help her.

She wasn't sure if it was shame or grief that sat like a boulder on her chest every time she thought of herself so full of hope and happiness when her dad had called her and she'd realized she'd be able to start her business.

She just couldn't.

"I told you. That was a naive decision I made." She switched off her laptop and picked it up. She was glad for the steadiness of her tone as she walked up the steps and faced him. "Both your sisters have already got back to me saying that they would be delighted to do it. I'll arrange for the interview through a virtual channel. I imagine that would considerably lessen the stress you're feeling at the prospect?"

He didn't quite give her the smile she wanted but that warmth flooded his eyes again. Clare felt as if she'd won the biggest lottery jackpot.

"Yes, thank you. Make sure any personal tidbits my sisters might mention are edited out. You're going to have a hell of a long conversation on your hands."

She nodded, intensely curious about his sisters, his family, everything about him. "And the contracts? Have they been looked over by your team of lawyers?"

An instant shutter fell over his expression. "Not yet. Don't worry, Clare. The contract is yours." He went on then, as if he wanted to fill the silence. "I'm having dinner in Rio de Janeiro tomorrow evening." His gaze did a quick survey of her, but didn't linger. "It might be a good idea for you to do some shopping in Rio when we arrive."

"Yes, please. Running away from a Mob boss and his thugs is the one disaster scenario I didn't pack for."

"Perfect. Then you can join us for dinner."

Clare's heart did a thump against her rib cage. "Join you? For dinner? You mean, as your partner for the evening?"

He shrugged. As if the matter didn't require further scrutiny. "I'm meeting an old friend and his wife, who's a notorious gossip. Showing up in front of her as my partner is like taking a front-page ad out that we're together."

"Together?" Clare asked, a totally unnecessary, girlish flutter in her chest region. "Like a couple together? Or like a playboy and his PR guard dog together?"

Laughter lines crinkled out from the edges of his eyes as he threw his head back and roared. It was fast becoming one of her favorite sounds. "Your imagination needs to be put to better use than these scenarios you keep thinking up for us."

Clare straightened her shoulders. "If this friend's wife is such a gossip…"

"Then it's not a bad idea to fake it in front of her to help my reputation. A little smoke to start up a rumor that I'm falling head over heels with the mystery lady tucked away on my yacht…" He sighed when she didn't respond. "I thought being linked to me was what you wanted."

"For safety's sake, yes. But pretending in front of an old friend of yours is a completely different matter. Do you want me to flutter my eyelashes at you and simper?"

Dev grinned. "I'm sure you'll be found out in two seconds if you act all sweet and sugary toward me. Just be yourself—your starchy I'm-making-him-a-better-guy self who frequently likes to dress me down and keep my ego in check. Give your spiel about all the charity programs Athleta runs."

"To your friend?"

"I've been asking him to come on board with Athleta for a long time. This might be the push he needs since he's at a crossroads in his life too. I want to snatch him up before someone else does. He's a footballer and a world-class athlete."

Of course, business was at the center of everything for Dev Kohli. Still, Clare felt a flutter of interest at getting a bona fide glimpse into his personal life. "If he's a good friend, won't he know that we're just…faking it?"

"No, he won't. Especially once he meets you."

"And what does that mean, exactly? That I'm not up to the

usual standard of your stunning girlfriends, so you must have lost your mind over me?"

Dev lifted his palms, a smile tugging at the corners of his mouth. "Are you fishing for compliments, Clare?"

Her face heated, but she refused to leave it alone. "Of course not."

"Fine. You're just…different," he admitted.

"Different boring?" she pressed.

"Different…complex, okay?" His words had an edge to them now that Clare wanted to spend the rest of the evening teasing out. But that way lay nothing but trouble with a big *T*.

"Fine. I'll talk you up to him. It shouldn't be that hard. Although I don't see why you can't do it yourself."

"Is there anything worse than a man so pleased with himself that he won't stop boasting?"

Clare nodded, a shaft of pain hitting her in the chest. Her dad had been like that—he'd hardly ever called her, but on the few occasions he had, he'd never asked her about her own life. He'd always gone on and on about his next miraculous venture. Forever blowing his own, tarnished horn.

"I can have the chauffeur bring you back to the yacht after your shopping trip instead of joining us for dinner at the hotel, if you're afraid?" he taunted when she didn't respond.

"Of course I'm not afraid," Clare snapped, and the devilish man looked satisfied. He'd neatly cornered her into agreeing. "So are we going to stay overnight in Rio de Janeiro?"

"Yes. The next morning, we'll leave for St. Lucia."

"Okay. I'll meet you in the lounge for dinner."

"Can't wait to get away from me already?"

Clare sighed. "I'm not ungrateful. I just… I need to catch my breath. Can you understand that?"

"Yes."

"If one of your staff can get me a map of the city for to-morrow—"

He was shaking his head even before Clare finished her sentence. "That's not a good idea."

Something about his tone put her back up. "I've no idea when I'll get a chance to see Rio de Janeiro. I'm just going to play tourist. I won't be late and miss the dinner with your friend."

"I don't think you should venture out by yourself."

Fear gripped Clare. "Why? What have you heard?"

He shook his head again, but Clare had a feeling he wasn't telling her the complete truth. And that sent a spiral of fear and anger through her.

"I haven't yet figured out a way to solve your predicament," he said gravely. "Until I do, I'm...responsible for you, so I'll go with you."

She reached out to steady herself, her heart thumping dangerously loud in her chest. "I don't need anybody's protection. I certainly don't—"

"I can tell you're worried." His voice was curt, commanding, and Clare held on to it. "You have dark shadows under your eyes. If you won't talk to me, talk to someone else. Family, or a friend...someone. Or you're just heading for a—"

"I don't have anyone to depend on, okay? I...don't want to worry my friends as they have enough on their plates right now keeping the business going without me. It's just me." Clare fought the sob building in her chest. She knew if she told her friends they'd leap to her defense and might get hurt themselves. They were better off out of it. But with his careful concern for her, Dev was determined to unravel her. "It's always been just me." Suddenly, she felt dizzy.

"Breathe, Clare." Dev's voice was hard in her ears, an anchoring point. "Focus on me, sweetheart."

Clare looked up. His brown gaze held hers—steady and reassuring. His hand reached out and took hers, enveloping her small one. The thump-thump of her heart felt a little slower now, as she focused on the line of heat his thumb traced on the back of her hand. The familiar scent of him wound around her, like a comforting blanket.

As panic misted away, Clare's first instinct was to snatch her hand away from his. The concern in his face, the gentleness of his touch...felt strange. Alien, almost. She wanted to shake it off and hide. To reject his simple kindness, which sent a lump swimming in her throat.

"Tell me what it is that you're hiding. And I can help you even more."

Her head jerked up. "Why?"

He looked adorably confused as he frowned. "What do you mean why?"

"Why do you want to help me? Other than the fact that I've thrust myself into your life as an unwanted stowaway on your yacht. The last thing I want is your pity. I need something real right now. Like I've never needed it before."

Clare didn't even realize she was speaking the words until she heard them. Until she felt him react by tightening his hand on hers. "God, I sound pathetic, don't I?"

"No," Dev replied. "You sound like someone who's struggling. Who's wary of leaning on anyone other than yourself. You sound..." He released her hand then. And Clare felt only desolation at the loss of his warmth. Long fingers squeezed her shoulders before he moved away from her. As if he needed to put physical distance between them before he did something he regretted.

"There's something in you that reminds me of...me," he said finally. "That's why I was drawn to you that night at the gala. It's why it felt like more than just another one-night stand. And why I had to walk away from you the next morning. Is that real enough for you?"

Clare stared at him, feeling a surge of something powerful in her chest. Her gaze traced the arrogant nose, the high cheekbones, the mouth that was always ready to laugh...his face was as familiar to her now as her own. She nodded automatically, hugging those unexpected words to herself. Still processing them... "I hope you're not pacifying me because you feel sorry for me."

He smiled and her world immediately felt centered again. "There's nothing about you that evokes pity in me, Clare. Exasperation, yes, but definitely not pity."

Clare laughed then, and if she'd had a better handle on herself, she'd have hugged him. Instead, she dipped her head, hoping to swallow the tears in her throat before they escaped. "Thank you. I've had a lot of distressing news of late and it..."

"Catches you out and brings you to your knees just when you thought you had a handle on it?"

"Something like that, yes," said Clare, stunned by his perception.

"Being strong doesn't mean you lean on no one, you know."

She scoffed. "This coming from a man who cuts himself off from the world on a gigantic boat?"

"Yacht," he corrected loudly, and then grinned. "It sounds like I've met my match in you," he said, regarding her with those brilliant brown eyes, as if he could easily see into her soul. One brow raised, and he muttered, "Come to me when you think you can, Clare, and tell me what fills your eyes with such grief. I swear it'll be our secret."

And then he bid her good-night. Leaving her alone in that warm, wonderful library of his. Giving her something that she hadn't even known she'd needed. The temporary respite from fear.

CHAPTER SIX

HOTEL FASANO—the latest playground of the uber-rich in Rio de Janeiro—kept its promise of the understated luxury and elegance that Clare had heard of and never thought of stepping foot in. The sparkling crystal blue of the ocean and the jutting peaks of the mountains calmed something inside her.

It was only when they'd alighted from the helicopter and Clare could breathe in the air that she'd realized how caged she'd been feeling. It wasn't Dev's fault or his yacht's. It was running from her own life that she detested.

If anything, Dev had only made her feel safer and more secure than she'd felt since she'd first seen the mobster's henchman dogging her steps in London. But the problem was, there were other things Clare felt compelled to run from. Dev, for instance.

Something about the concern and warmth in his gaze that felt far more dangerous to her well-being than any thug—her heart's naive longings that there could be more between them.

Clare flinched internally, aghast at her own thoughts and at the same time wishing she'd asked him to share more of his feelings about their night together. Wishing she'd delved deeper into the meaning of his words.

He was, she was coming to learn, quite a considerate man,

for all that he tried to show the world only the shallow surface of himself. But just because he might be curious enough to know what secrets she was keeping didn't mean he had any special interest in solving her problems or healing the wounds inside her soul that never seemed to quite go away.

So she didn't like to give up control. Who did? Who was brave and foolish enough—in equal measures— to trust a stranger with their innermost fears? With their silly dreams that they should have long given up by the time they'd reached twenty-eight? Who poured out their inexplicable longings to a man who was stuck with her through no choice of his own?

Last night on the yacht, she'd snuggled into the sofa, not wanting to leave that library.

It was the one space on the entire yacht that had retained any of Dev's true personality. As if all the books remembered him. As if he'd left a warm imprint of himself behind after all the hours he'd spent in there. She hadn't wanted to be alone in her expansive cabin, adrift on the sea.

So, clutching a book to her chest, Clare had curled up and read and dozed. Noticed somewhere in that state between being awake and asleep that every book on the shelf also had an audiobook. Even some really old titles on subjects ranging from science and philosophy to Indian mythology.

On an impulse, she'd reached for a book on Hinduism and once again, there was its accompanying audiobook. Clare flipped through the book only to find that it was absolutely pristine. Each page still possessed an unmistakable crisp newness as if they hadn't ever been turned.

She'd examined older copies of some of the classics and it was the same. While the pages in those books were more yellowed, with the faint scent of aged paper emanating from them, it was apparent that they'd also hardly ever been thumbed through.

And yet, Clare sensed Dev's presence here—almost as if the books could tell her more about the man than he ever would.

Dev Kohli was anything but a one-dimensional playboy. At

some point, Clare fell asleep, pondering the fact that it would be quite something to actually get to know him. Not that she could afford to.

She'd jolted awake to find herself cradled in strong arms, the side of her chest crushed against a harder one. And the delicious scent of taut skin covering even tighter muscles invading her nostrils.

He smelled like Clare always imagined warmth and security to smell like.

Sleep heavy in her eyes, she'd looked up. Only to drown in that unfathomable gaze of his. Not even for a second had fear of a strange man holding her touched her. Even before her mind could completely grasp it, her body had recognized his. The strong line of his jaw, the wiry strength of his arms, the breadth of his shoulders…they had after all starred in her fantasy night.

And yet Clare knew it wasn't just her body that had recognized him, but her heart too.

She wondered if the thudding beat she heard was his heart or hers. Wondered how even in the slightly illuminated shadowy corridors through which he carried her, he could make her feel secure.

As she lay now, on a luxurious lounger next to the hotel's infinity pool on the eighth floor, looking out onto the beautiful Ipanema beach, supposedly glad to be escaping Dev's perceptive attentions, Clare was anything but escaping her own thoughts about the man.

Last night, as he'd carried her, she'd simply clasped her fingers tighter around his nape when it had felt like she was slipping out of his grasp.

"You have the habit of falling asleep in the most awkward places, Clare," he'd muttered, his voice husky and touched by sleep too.

A thick lock of hair had fallen forward onto his forehead. With no thought, Clare had pushed it back. Even after she'd done it, she'd felt no awkwardness. No regret or shame. Neither had his steps faltered even one bit. It had felt natural—her touching him so familiarly as if she had every right to do so.

Had he felt the same or had he simply not imposed that cold distance back between them because she was half muddled by sleep?

"I didn't want to be alone," she'd said, all her defenses down. He had seemed like a knight, come to take her away to a place of safety.

Clare cursed now, a flush claiming her skin. Where had her filter disappeared to?

"And the library is full of people?" he'd asked, a tiny line drawing his brows together. "Strange. I've always found it to be full of people's voices clamoring at me to hear them. So much to say, so much to teach…and always beyond my reach. It's like hearing the echo but never reaching the true source."

Clare frowned now, wondering at that cryptic statement he'd made.

"No, I don't think that, but it's not empty or soulless either," she'd said softly. "It's obviously the room you love most. Your presence lingers there."

His nostrils had flared, an enigmatic expression awakening in his eyes. "I don't know if I would quite call it love, Clare. I've always felt strongly about that room, yes. But it's not love," he'd said, a hitch of something—grief, pain—in his words.

Clare desperately wished she'd remembered more of the nuances now. She had this urgent feeling that he'd shared something extremely significant about himself. Something he wouldn't say in the daylight, in the absence of the intimacy and cover that the dark night and her sleepiness had provided.

She'd glanced up at him, his words puncturing a little more of her exhaustion. "Whatever it was, I didn't feel alone in there. Or afraid. I felt…safe."

His arms had tightened around her, more voluble than that gorgeous mouth of his. "I wouldn't think less of you if you'd simply admitted that in the first place, Clare." A soft smile crinkled the corners of his eyes. "In daylight, I mean."

She shrugged. "Care to show me how?" He was moving up steps now, and she was much more firmly held against his solid chest. If she hadn't been so intent on not disrupting the tidbits of himself he was tempting her with, she'd have nuzzled her nose into all that deliciously warm skin. "Because I learn best by example."

He'd thrown his head back and laughed then. And Clare had the weirdest wish that he would simply keep on walking forever and she'd continue to exist in that half-awake, half-aware state forever so that he would keep holding her and talking to her.

Which had prompted her to say, "Why did you come for me?" Hope and curiosity tied a knot in her belly. Hope that maybe he'd wanted her company too. That maybe he'd thought their night together had been remarkable.

"One of my staff heard you as they were coming to tidy up in there, and came to get me, rather than disturb you. You were having a bad dream. You kept saying, 'How could you?'"

And then he was walking into a bedroom and her heart fluttered like a bird caught in a cage.

"You're not alone, Clare," he had whispered then, gently placing her on the bed in a different cabin than she had been initially shown to. He had sat on the edge of the bed and held her hand—his large, calloused one enveloping hers like his body had done to hers once—and in that deep voice of his, commanded she go to sleep.

The traitor that her body was, it had immediately complied. She'd fallen asleep marveling at the novel quality of someone being there to comfort her, holding her hand to remind her that she was safe. Someone caring enough to say even those few words.

Mercifully, as far as she could remember, the night had ended there.

* * *

She'd woken up this morning in the vast bed, sunlight slanting onto her face. A quick look through the cabin had revealed the fact that she was now in a room that shared a door with the master cabin. Dev's cabin.

He'd taken her sleep-mumbled words seriously and kept her close by all night.

When she'd faced him this morning, Clare had refused to make eye contact. Embarrassment and something she couldn't define suffused her. That he had seen her like that…at her most vulnerable…it was a very uncomfortable feeling.

As if all that raw longing she sometimes felt inside was now on the outside for him to see. Her deepest, darkest dreams suddenly displayed in all their multicolored gaudiness.

But her fears that he might mock her or worse turned out to be unfounded. Because of course, Dev was the consummate gentleman.

He had perfectly followed her cue this morning, not even hinting at what had happened the previous night by raising his famously expressive brow. He'd simply asked her if she'd slept well. To which she'd focused somewhere over his shoulder and nodded.

So professional, the both of them.

When they'd arrived at the hotel, she'd gone straight to the boutique on the ground floor. Uncaring of the astronomical price tag for once, she'd bought a white two-piece bikini, as she'd forgotten to purchase one during her shopping trip beforehand. She'd desperately needed a little time to herself. Away from the shadow of the man who was beginning to pierce through her armor like a most determined arrow.

With her laptop in hand, she finished a number of administrative tasks and sent off a questionnaire to Athleta's newly revamped HR department. Looking through the interview questionnaire she'd prepared for Dev himself, she frowned.

He'd sent it back to her with a request to provide audio files of the questions. It wasn't that unusual a request, in the scheme of ridiculous requests that Clare had fulfilled for her clients.

But it made her think of the audiobooks she'd spied in his library aboard the yacht. How he'd said he couldn't immediately read and sign the business contract she'd put together for him based on the usual format she, Amy and Bea kept at the ready. How Clare had thought he was balking at the high price she'd quoted.

When she'd inquired if he was hesitating at how much her firm charged, he'd looked at her seriously. "Underestimating their own worth is often one of the biggest, most frequent mistakes women make in business."

Clare had nodded vehemently. "I learned that very early on in my career. And I never undercharge."

He'd just looked back at her steadily. "Good to know."

Clare had sighed and said, "That's not why you're not signing immediately then."

"No," he'd confirmed in a hard voice that didn't encourage further discussion. "But the contract is yours, Clare. Do you doubt my word?"

Clare had shaken her head. Knowing that to probe further was less than professional.

It had been a couple of hours before the straightforward contracts had been signed and returned to her. At the time, she'd thought he was just being very thorough with the vetting process.

Now, as she pulled out her phone and dictated the questions into it so she could email the audio file to him, Clare thought she was beginning to see the pieces of the man fall into place.

How and why he'd always played up the whole playboy role that the media had created for him. Why he'd trusted the man who'd betrayed him with so much power...

By the time late afternoon started edging into early evening and she needed to go get ready for dinner, Clare realized that however hard she'd tried to thwart her interest in Dev, it didn't make an iota of difference.

The more she learned about him, the more she wanted to know. The more she wanted to make this business partnership into something far more personal. But that way lay madness and hurt.

The sun was streaking the sky in shades of gold and orange, offering one of those unparalleled Rio sunsets that the city was so famous for.

The rooftop restaurant where she and Dev were going to entertain their guests, with its vintage retro lighting and buttery soft leather chairs and red brick facade, created an easy, intimate atmosphere. From the moment Dev had knocked on her door to escort her looking dapper in a casual jacket over tailored trousers, Clare knew she was going to enjoy the evening.

Neither had she missed the short but thorough appraisal Dev had given her sleeveless white sheath dress and suede pumps, and she'd had her hair styled at the hotel salon. Another expensive extravagance, but the warm admiration in his gaze was worth it.

"My friend has messaged to say they've been slightly delayed and we're to start without them."

After her hasty shopping trip when they'd arrived in Rio and the work she'd done poolside, Clare discovered she was ravenous once they'd been seated. She attacked the appetizer with a gusto she couldn't quite hide.

She looked up to find Dev's eyes on her. With his arm slung lazily over the back of her chair, he hadn't needed to bend too far to murmur, "I'm sorry if I embarrassed you, Clare. I was just…admiring your enjoyment of your food. You looked as if there was no pleasure greater."

The convivial atmosphere and the yummy food and that feeling of being free of thugs and fear—even for one evening—went straight to her head. And because some naughty imp was goading her, she murmured back, "There isn't. Except maybe the delicious weight of a man pressing down on..."

The sudden flare of heat in his eyes told her he knew what she'd been about to say. And yet Clare didn't feel any shame. Which was progress in her mind.

Dev was good in bed. He knew it. And more importantly, he knew that she knew it. It was high time she acted like an adult about it. Instead of looking like a blushing prude or imagining there was some sort of power play going on here.

Dev had never behaved as if this was a game to him. Even at his coldest. Which meant she needed to stop acting as if she was giving something away when she admitted how much that night had meant to her.

"Well, you know what I mean," she added in a breezy voice to cover up the sudden silence.

He didn't have to say anything as his phone pinged just then. "They're not coming."

"Oh..." Clare said, feeling a pang of disappointment. "Is everything okay?"

Dev shrugged. "Marriage problems I'd say. His wife can be a lot to handle sometimes."

Clare snorted. "Is that just conjecture? Or is there any truth to it?"

He sat back in his chair. Moonlight gilded the sharp planes of his features. "You doubt my word?" he said, mock affront lighting up his eyes.

"As a founding member of the playboy club, absolutely, yes. You might be the authority on everything else, but your commentary on marriage...sorry, but you're not likely to be an expert, are you?"

"I'll have you know I'm not against the institution of marriage, per se."

Hand on her chest, Clare pretended to gasp, "I don't believe it."

"I'm sure marriage is a healthy arrangement for people who

want that kind of comfortable companionship and children. It's just not for..."

"Just not for you, of course," she said, rolling her eyes. "Why settle for one meal when you can have the whole buffet?"

He smiled, but when he spoke, there was something far from humorous in his eyes. "Those are your words, not mine. And please for all my sins, I'm not so bad as to declare there isn't a woman out there who's good enough for me."

"Then what is it?" Clare asked, unable to keep that question to herself. For too long she'd been wondering about him, and now, finally, here he was, the true Dev Kohli.

"Love requires something from me that I can't give. It's that simple."

Their gazes met and held, in a silent battle of wills. The breeze from the beach, the star-studded sky, with soft jazz playing in the background made for a beautiful night. But Clare knew it was this gorgeous man and the way he looked at her that made every cell in her body run wild. That, despite his professed inability to love, made him still so fascinating to her.

"Should we return to our rooms and finish some of the interviews maybe? If they're not coming, that is," she asked into the gathering silence. Just to bring herself back to earth. Just to cut through the warm cocoon of attraction wrapping around them. "There's still a lot to..."

"Or we could just enjoy the rest of the evening? You're a hard taskmaster, Clare." He raised a hand and their next course was discreetly placed in front of them.

Clare took a sip of her refilled glass of wine, to give her time to get control of her thoughts. "Then you'll have to tell me a little about your swimming career."

"Don't you know enough about me yet?"

"Like I said, I'm building a profile of you for a few magazines. And I don't just want the stuff that everybody already knows. I want the real gold."

"And if there isn't any gold?" he asked curiously.

"Let me be the judge of that. Also, Dev?"

"Yes?"

"You have to trust me enough to know that I won't release anything you consider private information."

She saw him process that. Could imagine him loosening the boundary he held so rigidly around him. "What do you want to know?"

Clare leaned forward and smiled as she speared a baby carrot on her fork. "Tell me how you went from being a world-class swimmer to a billionaire CEO."

"That spans several very boring years."

"I've got time," she retorted.

He told her while they ate the rest of their meal. Peppering the details with funny anecdotes, self-deprecating humor, and more than a hint of anger and pain when he talked about the mentor in his company who had been the instigator of the sexual harassment.

"What about your father? I had a call from his secretary about doing a joint profile on the two of you. As a head of the local chamber of the commerce, your father brings a lot—"

"Absolutely not," Dev said, immediately shutting her down.

"But he—"

"He never had a hand in making me, Clare. Except by forcing me to become a stranger to my own family. In making me doubt myself at every turn. He was instrumental in molding me into the cold, selfish man you have frequently called me. So, no, but I don't need his help in making me look good to the rest of the world, thank you very much."

The sudden silence in the wake of those impassioned words resonated in the air around them. Clare couldn't rush to fill it. Not when she recognized and understood the depth of anger and pain in them.

"I didn't mean to—"

"Don't apologize. That you eventually raised the subject of my father was inevitable. I should've just told you right at the start that he falls firmly into the category of forbidden topics of discussion."

"What will happen when you see him at Diya's wedding?"

"He'll finally see who I've become." The hardness receded from his gaze as he considered her sympathetic eyes. "And I have a plan to defuse any surplus interest in my family dynamics."

"Let me know how I can help," she offered automatically.

Clare saw a sudden flash of something move across his face. As if he was momentarily stunned at an insight he'd just had.

She had the most intense urge to ask him why he was staring at her like that.

She wanted to ask him about the audiobooks. She wanted to kiss him and ask him to kiss her again. She wanted to see those brown eyes turn infinitely darker as his passion was aroused.

She wanted to...

But she couldn't. He'd made it very clear that he didn't want the traditional dream of home and family that she still did. That he didn't believe in love or that he was even capable of it.

Clare shivered, even though the evening was far from chilly. In the next second, a jacket descended on her shoulders, smelling of his delicious warm male skin.

"Do you want to walk along the beach by the hotel?" Clare asked, turning toward him. "I recorded some questions for you about the press interviews," she added hurriedly. The coward that she was, she didn't want him to think she was asking just to prolong the evening with him. Even though she was.

If he thought she was acting strangely, he didn't say so. "Of course," he said, his brown eyes twinkling. "Won't do for me to forget that you're only putting up with me for a paycheck."

Clare had no chance to answer as their lift door opened onto the expansive lobby of the Fasano where there was a tall, brown, insanely beautiful woman waiting in a peach-colored evening gown that clung to every curve.

"Dev? I thought that was you!" the woman exclaimed. "Oh,

my God, I can't tell you how glad I am to have bumped into you…" She swanned across the marble floor toward them, the thigh-high slit in the gown showcasing toned legs that seemed to go on forever and ever.

Dev's mouth split into a stunningly warm smile. "Angelina… what are you doing here?"

He must have braced himself as she approached because he barely exhaled when she threw herself into his arms. Dev held her with what Clare could only call open affection. Angelina clasped his cheeks and kissed him, and Dev let her.

A strange buzzing filled Clare's ears. For which she was immensely thankful because it meant she couldn't hear the gushing words they said to each other.

She knew she should look away, or paste a polite, but inquiring smile on her face. Or just leave. But she did none of those. She simply stood there like some village bumpkin and stared at the bronze goddess, who must surely be a model, feeling as if someone had punched her in the middle.

Had she imagined a one-night stand, followed by an unwilling pity rescue from a nightmare situation, and one evening of pleasurable playacting at dinner equaled the beginning of something more meaningful?

Hadn't she learned her lesson yet about relationships and foolish dreams—the consequences of which she was still dealing with?

This was not her life, she reminded herself. This was a bubble she was living in until she figured out a way to escape the terrible fate that was threatening her.

Without a word, Clare turned away from them. If she could have sprinted to the lift as she was sure Angelina with her endless, graceful legs could have managed, she would have done so. Alas, she had to attempt to convey a dignified retreat on her wobbly, short legs.

"Clare, wait," Dev called behind her.

And since she couldn't just act like she was having a tantrum—even though she really wanted to—Clare turned around. A polite smile shimmered on her lips in its full fake glory.

His arm around the woman, he said, "I'd like you to join us for a coffee."

"Oh, must she, Dev?" The woman pouted, barely even glancing in Clare's direction. "It's not like you'll remember her name a week from now. I was hoping you and I could have a private chat."

"Clare's not one of my..." Dev suddenly stopped, staring at Clare, arrested. As if he couldn't find the words to describe their relationship. "She's..."

Their gazes held, an arc of electricity practically sizzling between them.

"She's what?" Angelina demanded, turning her curious gaze on Clare.

"What I am is very tired. I'm turning in for the night," Clare said, determined to remain polite in the face of the woman's horrible rudeness. After all, why should she be surprised? This was how Dev Kohli lived his life. "My body clock is still all upside down."

He nodded, and the suspicion that he'd only asked her to be nice was confirmed for her. Dammit, what the hell was wrong with her?

A thoughtful frown crossed his face as Clare met his gaze and then skittered away. "Okay. I'll see you tomorrow. We'll leave right after lunch."

Clare bade him a cool good-night.

And yet, as his broad shoulders disappeared into the lift with the woman still clinging to him, all she wanted was to go back and demand answers from him. Answers she had no right to. Because he wasn't hers.

Dev Kohli wasn't the kind of man who could belong to only one woman. Men like him and her father...they needed larger-than-life dreams, variety, constant thrills to challenge them. So maybe he wasn't the shallow, ruthless playboy that she'd initially thought him to be. But neither was he the kind of man who would settle for anything as pedestrian as marriage and children. And as much as she'd tried to bury all her dreams, somehow they always took root again in her heart—dreams of a man loving her forever, of building a family with him, of living the rest of her life surrounded by people she loved.

The thought of following the couple in the lift made Clare want to be sick. Instead, she squared her shoulders and stepped out into the night. At least a walk might clear her head of her heart's foolish notions.

Dev Kohli wasn't the man for her.

CHAPTER SEVEN

THE REPETITIVE BANG of a fist on the door to his suite brought Dev's head up. He put down the glass tumbler of whiskey he'd poured himself and opened the door.

Her face pale, trembling from head to toe, Clare stood at the entrance to his suite. She looked as if she'd been running for her life. "I'm sorry for interrupting your...date, but can I come in?"

"Yes, of course, you can, Clare," Dev said, pulling her inside. He slammed the door and leaned against it, his own pulse racing at the terror on her face. "What's wrong?"

"I... I went for a walk after you left with...her. Down to the beach. I wanted to clear my head... I..."

She swayed where she stood, and Dev reached for her. Clearly, she was in shock.

He slung his arm around her shoulders seconds before her knees gave way. That she didn't immediately protest made unease curdle in his stomach. He half carried her to the bar, hitching her against his side.

A burst of laughter from her mouth made him look at her, tucked neatly under his arm. There was a near delirious look in her eyes. "You should've been a football player. American football, I mean," she said.

Dev didn't know whether to smile or call for a doctor. "I

considered that as a career for a while. I was told I was too small for it."

Another laugh. Less delirious but still with a slight hysterical edge to it. "You were too small? You…" Her gaze swept over his shoulders and his chest and trailed downward. And then back up again. She giggled, a sound that was very unlike the practical Clare he knew. "For what it's worth, in my opinion, you're very much not a small man."

Dev knew that fear had completely wiped away the cloak of control she usually deployed like some kind of invisible shield. Usually, he'd have preened at her admiring glance.

Picking up the drink he'd just poured himself, he held it to her mouth. She didn't quite sag against him, but he could feel involuntary shivers running up and down her spine. "Drink this," he said in a voice that didn't invite argument.

Scrunching that adorable, all too arrogant nose, she shook her head. "I hate whiskey."

"I don't care," he said, that tightness in his chest releasing a little. The matter-of-fact way she'd spoken meant whatever had terrified her was slowly releasing its grip. "You've had a shock and you look…horrible." The pale cast to her skin, the whiteness around her mouth, it was as if all blood had fled from her face.

She grimaced. "Just what a girl likes to hear from the mouth of the man she's lusting over."

His gaze warmed with a heat that was never too far away when she was near. "I can see that shock is having other effects on you."

"I'm tired of acting as if I don't want you."

He laughed and pulled her closer. "Come on, Clare. For once, give in. The whiskey will warm you up, if nothing else."

She didn't argue further. Her fingers shook as she tried to take the tumbler from him. Dev didn't let go. He held the base of the tumbler as she tilted it up and took a couple of resolute sips.

She coughed almost delicately and gave the glass back. But

he was glad to see some color climbing back into her face. His own pulse started slowing down from its former erratic pace.

"Now, tell me what happened."

Tears filled those blue eyes and spilled over as she raised them to his face. With a gasp of indignation, she wiped them off her cheeks. As if she found them beneath her dignity. "I think... No, I know I saw him on the beach, so I ran straight back to the lobby immediately and jumped in the lift."

"Who?"

"He got there just as the doors were closing." She closed her eyes, and sagged against the counter, as if her legs were giving out again. Dev tightened his hold on her. "That sweet smile of his... God, I'm going to see it till the day I die."

"Clare, who are you talking about?"

"Goon Number One, of course."

Dev didn't mean to laugh. Not when she looked like she'd shatter if he breathed too hard. But the way she'd said "Goon Number One," with distaste curling her lip, and her courage vying with her fear...he couldn't help it.

He was so surprised by the curse she spat out that it took a few seconds for him to react, and by then she'd slipped from his grasp.

Without having to turn all the way, he shot his arm out and pulled her back toward him. She landed against his chest, her forearms caught between them, blue eyes flashing daggers at him. "Let me go, Dev."

The fierce way she said his name made his pulse leap with excitement.

"Not so fast, darling," he said, adding an extra drawl to the endearment.

"I'm not going to stand here and let you make fun of me while I..." She shivered, as if on cue again. "I shouldn't have come to you at all."

Something about her reminded him of himself. She was clearly terrified and yet determined to hold her own. This

woman was a fighter, just like him. No wonder she kept tripping him up.

Dev tightened his arms around her waist just as she fidgeted
inside them. He pressed his mouth to her temple and she instantly stopped struggling. Her chest rose and fell, her breaths
labored. He took his time, wanting to do this right. Knowing
she needed exactly the right words from him just then.

Holding her like this, he could feel the strength of will it
was taking her to prevent complete hysteria from settling in.

The scent of her skin—warmed by her signature lily-of-the-
valley perfume—filled his lungs as he took a deep breath. "Take
a moment, Clare. If you want me to let you go, I will. But right
now, you need to be held. You need to know that you're safe.
You need human contact—preferably male and large and able to
provide at least an illusion of security. Ergo, someone like me."

Her laughing snort vibrated against his chest.

"I'll happily be the bad guy and hold you prisoner until you
decide that it's okay to lean on me."

She whimpered then, and his muscles clenched as she pressed
her open mouth to his biceps.

"For once, trust your instincts, Clare. Not your rational mind.
You came to me because, despite the fact that you hate my guts
sometimes, you knew you could trust me."

He knew firsthand how hard it was to be vulnerable in front
of someone else. To let people see you in pain, lost, direction-
less. To hope that a kind word would be offered instead of
humiliation or a tongue-lashing. And he fully understood her
reluctance. From the very beginning, he had seen the similarities between them, the need to be strong in front of the world.

"I can't," she whispered, and the grief in her voice made
him swallow.

"Of course you can." He pulled her in tighter and closer until
her breasts were crushed against his chest, her legs tangled with
his. Until he could rest his chin on top of her head and there

was no gap between their bodies. "But until you can, let's just agree that I'm encouraging you to lean on me."

"Why are you being so nice to me?" she asked in a small voice that reminded Dev of himself on one of those bleak nights when he'd felt all alone in the world.

"Oh, didn't you guess already, sweetheart? I thought you had my number."

"I did," she whispered then, and he was glad to distract her. "But you keep shifting on me. I can't quite pin you down."

He smiled then, glad that she was too preoccupied to look into his eyes. He didn't like that she saw so much of him that he usually kept hidden from the world. From even his twin.

Slowly, ever so slowly that it felt like an eternity, the stiffness dissolved from her frame. Her breathing relaxed its harsh rhythm.

And then he heard the sniffle. The soft gasp that she swallowed away before he could fully hear it. He didn't let go. Only gave her enough room to adjust her head until her cheek settled against his chest and he could feel the dampness of her tears soaking through his shirt to his skin. For a man who'd always avoided emotional entanglements, he felt no urgency to restore the distance between them or to redraw their professional boundaries.

He had no idea how long he held her like that. He didn't care if an eternity passed. There was something about Clare Roberts that had appealed to him from the first moment he met her. And the more he got to know the different facets of her, the more he found her irresistible.

Eventually, the sniffles stopped and she let out a small sigh. But she made no move to tell him she wanted him to release her. So Dev didn't.

Slowly, seconds cycled to minutes and the air around them began to fill up with something else.

Dev became more and more aware of the soft press of her breasts against his chest. Of the heat radiating from the line of her spine as he rubbed his thumb up and down her back. The dip of her waist and the flare of her hips under his other palm. Of how small and dainty she was in his arms.

Sensation began to crawl back into his limbs and muscles, in the wake of that awareness. She shifted against him—rubbing her soft belly against his muscled one, and a dart of pleasure shot low into his abdomen.

"I wasn't laughing at you, you know," Dev explained, clearing his throat. Needing to puncture the building heat between them, he gently nudged her shoulders back until she wasn't touching him, so he could think straight again. "When you said Goon Number One, it felt like we were stuck in a..."

She didn't look up, but he felt her mouth open in a smile against his arm. The warmth of her breath felt like a brand on his skin through the thin material of his shirt. "In a nightmarish B-list horror movie? Believe me, I know exactly how that feels. Until I remember that man's smile and everything becomes all too real again."

"He's not going to get you, Clare. I'm not going to let him."

"I want to believe you. I do believe you. I just... How though? How long am I going to have to keep running? How am I going to—"

Dev tipped her chin up. After the tears, her eyes gleamed brightly. As if she'd come out on this side stronger and more determined. "You're sure it's him you saw tonight?"

"Absolutely. I'd give anything to be told that it wasn't."

Dev nodded. He had no reason to doubt her belief that the henchman had tailed her this far. Not when all his sources said the crime lord that Clare owed money to was a seriously dangerous man. Which meant it was time for action.

"You'll stay here tonight. In my suite. We can't take the risk of him nabbing you right out of the lift or even from your own suite."

She opened her mouth as if to argue and then closed it. With a resigned sigh, she nodded. Stepping back, she looked around his suite. Dev didn't miss the wariness that crawled back into her eyes. He knew she was looking for Angelina.

"I... I know that it's inconvenient for you to have me here tonight but I'll keep quiet as a mouse."

"I'm not sure if I can stay quiet however," some devil goaded him to say. "As you very well know, I'm quite voluble when it comes to..."

Her palm pressed against his mouth. "You're playing with me."

Dev tugged her wrist away. "Am I?"

"I jumped to conclusions, yes. The thing is I've never done this before."

"Done what?"

"Tell a man that I want to be the one he kisses. Well, except for the last time. With you. Which was my first time."

He couldn't help but feel slightly shocked. She'd been so responsive he'd never guessed. "I know it's far too late for this, but I hope I...fulfilled at least part of your fantasy that night."

"You did," she said simply, and Dev knew she'd given him something precious and priceless. Something he wasn't sure he deserved.

It was just that every tentative smile and admiring glance that Clare threw his way had to be earned. It felt like he was constantly winning a prize—precious parts of her that she was reluctant to part with.

"Angelina is absolutely not my current squeeze, Clare. You ran away before I could clarify that. Plus, do you think I'd dare break the law laid down by you?"

"It's not funny," she said, coming closer.

His every muscle tightened with want as the scent of her reached him afresh. There was no hesitation or anger or reluctance in her gaze or in her steps just then. She looked as if she was determined to claim something for herself tonight. As if fear had washed away whatever kept her caged, instead of doing the opposite. She looked at him as if he was a prize. And yet he was nothing close to that.

"No, it's not. But you're determined to see me as some kind of rogue."

"You *are* a rogue. You're just not..." She looked away and back at him. There was a new light in her eyes, and Dev knew he should cut this conversation short right now. Knew that things were spiraling out of his control.

But damn it, the woman was irresistible. Even when she was busy thinking the worst of him—again.

"So she isn't your lover?"

"Nope."

Pink flushed her cheeks but she didn't shy from his gaze. His own humor came flooding back as he saw the inherent challenge in the lift of her stubborn chin. "It's just you did promise me that you wouldn't take any chances with your reputation right now."

Dev stared at how easily the damn woman shifted from terrified to assertive.

"So ask me," Dev said, lobbing the ball back at her. "You know you're dying out of curiosity. Ask me who she is, Clare."

If he thought she'd lift her nose into air and tighten that upper lip in fake haughtiness, he wasn't wrong. She did all those delicious things that made Dev like her so much. But she never ceased to surprise him.

Head held high, she demanded, "Who was that woman, Dev?" She looked like she meant to say more, but to his disappointment, she locked those words away.

She was standing so close now that he could see the pulse fluttering away at her neck. Could see the resolve glinting in her eyes.

"That was my best friend Derek Lansang's wife. The one that should have come to dinner with us. Not that I've ever gotten involved with a married woman, I hasten to add."

"She was very possessive of you."

Dev grinned, wondering if she knew how she sounded. "Angelina acts like that with every man she knows. It drives Derek crazy, but it's part of the woman he married. Despite their frequent spats, they do love each other. And I have some scruples, Clare. Just not as many as you."

Her shoulders ramrod straight, her gaze didn't budge from his even when she was in the wrong. Like Mama had done so many times. "I'm sorry. I shouldn't have jumped to that conclusion."

"No, you shouldn't have," Dev repeated, enjoying seeing her squirm.

Had she been jealous? Clingy, drama-creating women had never been his favorite kind, and yet there was something about being wanted by Clare that shredded his control.

"So that was Derek Lansang, the football player's wife," Clare mused. "I thought she looked familiar."

Dev nodded.

Blue eyes met his and held. "I was jealous," she said simply, and Dev wondered if he'd misheard her.

He had released his arms from around her, but her palms still clung to the material of his shirt.

"I... I had a lovely time at the dinner, playing your partner and I...got caught up in the fantasy of it. And when she appeared and you went off together like you were her knight in shining armor, I had this...most distasteful feeling in my belly. I know we laid down all these rules, and I have no right to feel jealous, but—"

Dev had never thought himself a man particularly prone to having an unruly heart. And yet something somersaulted inside his chest as he looked into her blue eyes. The lashes were still tinged with wetness and her straight nose was red; she should have looked ordinary. But the resolute strength of her character made her beautiful instead.

"But what, Clare?" he prompted, his voice hoarse.

"As I stood in that lift, I realized how sick I was of being afraid. How out of control my life has been ever since that man...started dogging my footsteps. How I've been just counting each day, longing for it to be over. How I've always tried to be the quiet, good girl who never demanded anything. Of herself or anyone else." And then she came closer and Dev could see the tremble in her lush pink lips. "I'm so angry. I'm furious about how much this bloody mobster is cheating me out of. I might escape him again tomorrow, but having this shadow always hovering over me, it's really not making much of a difference, is it? I could escape him every day for the rest of my life but still never be free."

"And that makes you mad?" Dev asked.

"That makes me...crazy," she said. And then her gaze focused on the now. On him. Dev felt his heart kicking like a mad thing against his rib cage again, and desire ran thick and heavy in his veins.

"So I've decided I'm not going to be scared anymore. I'm not going to simply lie down and give up. I'm not going to let every moment be consumed by fear. I'm going to seize the damned day."

"How?"

"For starters? I'm going to kiss you very thoroughly, as I've been wanting to ever since I woke up in your closet." Thick lashes flickered up and down his body before she met his gaze again. "If you're willing, that is."

Dev exhaled a long breath. Damn it, did the woman have any idea how arousing her artless honesty was? "Assuming I was—"

She cut his words off by trailing her fingers all over his chest. His heart pounded under her palm. The anticipation of a single kiss lit a fire in his blood like never before. But then something about Clare—that irresistible combination of honest, innocent passion, made his nerves sing.

"You are willing. That's all that matters to me. Yes, I already know your usual disclaimer. I don't care what this leads to or how long it lasts. I just want to feel this moment, live in it. Before all I remember about it is that I ran away from it. Before the only thing that will stay with me about this beautiful evening in this beautiful city is that...that bastard contaminated it for me."

She didn't leave it to chance. No, she hedged her bets to the highest, by tightening her fingers at the nape of his neck, going up on her toes until her breaths were crushed against his chest and she was burying her face in the hollow of his throat.

Dev's pulse pounded when she boldly touched her tongue there. Every muscle contracting on a wave of pleasure as she gently nipped the skin between her teeth. Every intention and rule he'd ever laid down for himself forgotten when she blew softly on the tiny mark she'd given him.

His hands on her hips tightened without conscious thought, and then he was pulling her even more tightly against him, until he knew she could feel his growing erection against her belly. She was gasping against his chin and then there it was...her luscious mouth against his—finally.

A stab of pure lust coursed through him as he dipped his head and pressed his lips to hers. Her moan fired up every nerve ending as he licked at the seam of those lips, suddenly voracious for more.

He reached for the round curve of her bottom with his fingers and hitched her higher against him. "Yes, please," she whispered against his mouth, and Dev lost the last bit of good sense he possessed.

As he delved deeper into the warm cavern of her mouth, as he tangled his tongue with hers, pressing her against the wall and drinking her in hungrily, the shape of the future—at least the immediate future—seemed to coalesce in his brain.

She needed his help. He couldn't turn away from the fact. So why not marry their problems and come up with the perfect solution?

He could show the world that he was settling down and changing his playboy image, and here was the perfect woman to do it with. If he felt a momentary doubt about whether he should be further involved with a woman who saw far too much of him all too clearly, it evaporated in the heat of their kiss. And anyway, not being tied down to any woman—even one as complex as she waswas his true nature. He'd be able to walk away afterward, just like he always did.

CHAPTER EIGHT

CLARE HAD LONG forgotten what it meant to feel vulnerable. If she'd ever known it as an adult, that was.

Once she'd been dropped off on her unwilling aunt's doorstep, she had, for the most part, learned to bury any emotional needs. She'd learned to keep her head down, work hard; in essence to be a quiet, good child with no demands. Either of her aunt or herself.

All the silly dreams she had kept building about her dad returning, though, she realized now were just those—something to sustain her through a barren childhood. As she had turned into an adult with little contact with him, she'd learned to foresee any need or want that might not be fulfilled and crushed it.

The need to be loved—unconditionally, of course—had to be the first one to die.

Vulnerability, she had realized long ago, was a costly thing for her. Her aunt had been the embodiment of the British stiff upper lip, and after a while, Clare had seen the value in it. But today, as she had walked away from Dev, while Angelina had wrapped herself like a vine around his broad shoulders, Clare had been drenched in a surfeit of emotions. As if everything she'd ever denied herself was determined to fill her up.

When Dev had opened the door to her, even through the

spine-chilling fear, she'd felt the urgency to snatch what she could from life. To stop spending it burying herself in pros and cons. To put herself out there and live.

As Dev held her for his devastatingly hot kiss, fingers plunged into her hair, her body sang with spiraling pleasure. If only her every act of vulnerability could be rewarded in such a delicious way...

In the passionate depths of his kiss, she felt as if she was rediscovering the dizzying sense of being alive again. As if she was shedding layer after layer of all those sterile restrictions with which she'd caged herself. As if she was finally seeing the core of her own self on glorious display for the first time in years.

This had the potential to be as vivid and soul shaking as the fear had been. Except this was something she was choosing. This was something she wanted and needed and deserved.

This man and this moment and this...unparalleled, total joy in a kiss.

Pleasure suffused through her every nerve, deepened by a giddy sense of power that he was just as mad for her taste as she was for his.

The shocking carnality of his kiss, because with Dev—a kiss was far more than just the slide of their mouths—it was a hungry, sensual exploration, a prediction of what their bodies could do for each other, and it rocked Clare to her soul. Every sweep of his tongue against hers, every nip of his teeth into the trembling flesh of her lower lip goaded her on. Every groan he let out filled the void she'd knowingly carved into her own life.

No more, she told herself. She was done hiding from life. Once she made up her mind, Clare had never been a passive participant.

The fabric of his shirt bunched satisfyingly within her grip. She snuck her fingers underneath, finding warm, delightfully taut skin. His powerful body shuddered when she raked her nails gently down his chest.

A fresh burst of desire bloomed low in her belly, urgent and grasping.

She set her fingers trailing up and down his chest and down to his abdomen. The clench of the hard muscle, the rough groan that fell from his mouth, the tightening of his fingers over her bottom…everywhere he touched, new pockets of sensation opened up.

There was already a familiarity to how they touched each other. A languid understanding of what the other craved, a rhythm to the give and take they engaged in. Clare delighted in this knowledge. And she used it ruthlessly, no longer bound by her own confining rules.

That first night they had spent together a few weeks ago, she'd let him take the active role. That was nowhere near enough for her anymore. She loved the light dusting of hair on his chest. She wanted to lick the hard slab of his abdominal muscles.

Why had she denied herself the life-affirming sight of that happy trail?

She wasn't going to let the mobster win. She wasn't going to let her father's cruel neglect of her or her aunt's cutting indifference define how she lived the rest of her life. "I've wanted to do this again," she said against his mouth, "ever since I woke up next to you that morning. And now I can't think of one good reason why I denied myself. I wrapped myself up in so many layers of protection that I lost myself. No more."

His hands moved up from her hips to her shoulders with a possessive thoroughness that pinged every cell in her body. Slowly, with a long, rough exhale, Dev pulled back from the kiss. "No," he agreed, his thumbs tracing over her cheeks in an almost tender gesture. "Nothing has ever tasted as sweet as you, Clare. Or been as full of surprising depths."

"Are you complaining?" Clare said, burying her face in his throat again. She loved the rough, bristly texture of his skin there, the taste of him, the scent of him. It was beginning to feel like her safe space. But of course, he wouldn't appreciate it if she said that.

He wouldn't like it if she took this interlude as anything more than what it was—a fragment of time where he was letting her set the pace and tone of this.

One kiss. Not that she'd had any doubts about his desire for her.

His fingers edged into her hair at the nape of her neck, his thumbs rubbing in mindless circles. "Not at all," he said. "Nothing but admiration here."

"Lower please," she said, in defiant demand.

His laughter vibrated through his body, transferring to hers. "Yes, my lady." He obediently moved those clever fingers down her neck and onto her shoulders.

Clare groaned when he pressed them into the tight knots he found there.

He was unraveling her, she knew. On more than one level. But she had no energy to resist. No wish to erect her silly defenses.

"Why?" she asked, wanting to know everything he thought of her.

Now his fingers were gently kneading her arms and her back muscles and reducing her to a blob of good feeling and nothing else. "Why what?"

"Why admiration? Because I kissed you better than I did last time?"

Again, that laughter. It was low and warm, and it made her chest feel full of a comforting quality. Clare wanted to roll around in that sound forever and ever.

"Why not? You took sheer terror for your life and transformed it into passion and determination. You didn't let it diminish you. You used it to find a new you…that, lovely Clare, is cause for admiration and celebration."

Clare clung to him, no inhibitions or reserve left in her. She'd worked hard all her life with no boyfriends or thought to the future except establishing her own business. The money her father had "given" her before he died—at such cost—had finally allowed her to do that. But the driving force had been her determination to build something for herself.

"You know something about dwelling in fear and forging something out of it, don't you?" she said then, knowing that she was crossing that invisible boundary she'd always sensed around him. Knowing that he might put those walls back up again in the beat of a breath and shut this interlude down.

But she was tired of being circumspect. Of settling for less than what she wanted.

She was also aware that patterns built over a lifetime of abandonment couldn't be broken overnight. Sooner or later, she was going to revert to her old habits. To being circumspect with her emotions. To becoming one of life's spectators once again.

But in the meantime, she was simply going to look at this as a forced, but much-needed vacation. And the main feature of her vacation would be doing deliciously wicked things with Dev Kohli.

Pupils darkened, mouth swollen, hair in disarray, the man looked scrumptious. There was none of that suave, unruffled playboy right now. This was a man in the throes of hard lust. She liked seeing him like this—all gorgeously rumpled, thanks to her hungry kisses.

If she could throw off her shackles for anyone, it had to be this man. Who, she was beginning to suspect, was quite the package—inside and out.

There was a sudden pause, but he didn't push her away and tell her that asking such a question was above her paygrade. Or that their devastatingly sweet kiss didn't give her a right to delve and probe.

Instead, he drew in a long breath and Clare felt the echo of it in the rise and fall of his chest. "Yes, I do know what it feels like when no one hears you. Or sees you. I know what it feels like when the only definition you have of yourself is set by others."

Clare gave up all pretense then. She threw her arms around his waist and held on tight. His large hands moved over her back—in an act of appeasement or need, she had no idea—and then he pulled her close.

"You're a witch," he said gruffly, but his fingers were gentle as they clasped her cheek, and then he was kissing her again.

This kiss was not gentle or sweet or exploratory. It was a fierce taking. It was a toll he demanded for giving a piece of himself. His fingers clasped her bottom, holding her firmly against his hard body, his erection a brand against her belly. Clare felt the most overpowering need to touch herself between her thighs, or beg him to. The ache that built there was so insistent.

"I want more," she said brazenly, determined to ride this high for as long as she could. She could feel a flush climbing her neck at her pouty request, but she didn't care. "I want a repeat of that night."

His sudden curse ripped through the air.

Hands on her shoulders, he gently put her back from him. "Let's think this through for a moment, Ms. Roberts. For one thing, you're in shock. For another..." His brown gaze zeroed in on her lips, and he seemed as though he'd forgotten what he was saying.

Clare licked them, wanting to feel the swollen sensitivity everywhere else too. "Lost your train of thought there, Mr. Kohli?"

"I think first we both need a cold drink and then... I suggest we wait." Another sweep of his eyes over her body, and it was almost like those big hands had stroked her all over again.

Her gaze dropped down. The outline of his erection was clearly visible. An incredible rush of female empowerment hit Clare in her belly. She flicked her gaze up to meet his eyes. Saw desire etched onto his sharp features. "Why wait? I told you, Dev, you don't have to worry that I'll ask for more."

A flush streaked the sharp blades of his cheekbones. "It's

not that. We need to discuss something important first. I think I've come up with a way to get you out of this."

"Out of sleeping together?"

A smile split his mouth. "No." He rubbed a hand over his face. "I think I've already made my peace with the fact that you and I'll end up in bed again soon enough."

"That confident of your studly prowess, huh?" Clare interjected, wanting to be miffed but not really succeeding. She couldn't pretend anymore that he was simply a man who looked at women as conquests or mindless entertainment. Neither was she going to turn him into perfect relationship material with her overactive imagination.

The present was all she had, and she was going to revel in it each day she could.

He shrugged. "Not my studly prowess so much as chemistry like ours. It doesn't happen all the time, and this is the strongest I've ever felt. Does that answer satisfy you?"

His tone glinted with humor and challenge, and Clare nodded regally. The answering warmth in his eyes made her heart feel too big for her chest.

"Do you get the sense that our roles are being reversed?" she said then, pulling away from him.

But he didn't let her hand go. Clare's heart jumped at the small gesture that had nothing to do with desire or lust and everything to do with something else. Something she didn't want to define. If she gave it a name, there wouldn't be the chance of an escape. "What do you mean?" he asked curiously.

"Like I'm becoming this devil-may-care woman and you're—" she smiled, loving how he tilted his head and stared at her hungrily "—turning into some kind of honorable man trying to keep me out of trouble."

Dev laughed. "Am I? Don't worry, Clare. This whole honor thing will wear out soon enough. Just listen to me, first."

Clare nodded, a trickle of apprehension diluting the heady sense of excitement that had filled her. She didn't want to face reality just yet. She didn't want to turn into boring old Clare again.

She liked this new, fun, to-hell-with-everything Clare she got to be with Dev. There was something about him that had made her want to push herself, from the first moment she'd laid eyes on him.

A smile creased his cheeks and that damned dimple flashed at her. "Don't look so worried. This should get you out of the Mafia thug's hands permanently."

Her pulse zigzagged through her body. "How?" she demanded.

"We'll simply get married."

Simply get married...

It had sounded simple in his head but as he watched how his suggestion landed on Clare, Dev wondered if he'd made a big mistake. Not about wanting to protect her. One way or another, he was going to get her out of this predicament.

He'd always had an affinity for the underdog. Seeing that he'd been one himself. Or at least he had before his transformation into an...*an oversexed playboy billionaire*, as she'd called him.

His mouth curved at the title.

While he still didn't understand how a smart woman like Clare could have made such a bad error in judgment by borrowing money from a known mobster, he couldn't hold it against her. His company wouldn't have been in this giant mess if he hadn't made a ghastly one himself.

But...given the way all humor fled her face at his words, and the way she stared back at him, he wondered if he'd just made another error.

By assuming that she'd take his idea in her stride. That she'd see it only as a solution to her problem and not something else. Something more.

When several minutes passed and she still didn't say anything, Dev felt more than a hint of irritation. "Do you have a boyfriend tucked away in London who might object to this idea?"

He knew it was the most ridiculous question the moment he heard it. She'd never hinted at any prior relationship, and he'd gotten the sense that Clare kept her relationships carefully vacant of too much attachment. But...the words had stemmed out of jealousy. From a place he didn't even know existed.

Which was ridiculous. Because it wasn't as if he was asking for anything from her, during their proposed arrangement. Nothing that wasn't inevitable anyway.

The very inelegant snort she let out told him the same. "Of course I don't." Then she straightened and he could see anger building in her face. "Do you think I'd be...cavorting around with you if I had someone I loved back home?"

"Cavorting?" he said, raising a brow, hoping to deflect her attention away from his stupid question.

"Don't think you can distract me, Dev," she said, putting paid to that tactic.

"Then what's the problem?"

She took in a deep breath. "The problem is that marriage is a big step. I...it means a lot of big things like trust and fidelity and..."

Dev reached out and rubbed a finger over her cheek. "I do trust you, Clare. Which is why I'm not hyperventilating."

She looked him up and down. "Are you the type to hyperventilate?"

"If the topic of conversation is marriage, yes. Does that make me less manly?"

"Nothing makes you less manly, Dev," she snapped, with more than a bite to her tone.

"Ah...so the hyperventilation would be a symptom of the underlying condition of not wanting to commit, is it? I forgot that you're the founding member of the bachelor playboy club, allergic to all things long term."

He scrunched his nose in distaste. "You make me sound like

I have a disease. But no, a traditional marriage isn't in the cards for me." He pushed a hand through his hair, annoyed that she kept making him ponder things he'd never...well, pondered before. Like marriage. And fidelity. And long-term relationships. And how it would feel to have someone permanent in your life who knew you inside out. Who would make you laugh and want and push you to be a better version of yourself.

Who would also have complete control of your emotional health? Who could destroy your self-worth with one well-targeted barb? the sanest part of his brain pointed out.

No woman was worth opening himself up to that kind of risk again. Yes, that meant sometimes his life was lonely. But it wasn't exactly a choice he'd made so much as a defense mechanism. A way he could survive intact. The only way.

"And while, yes, this is bigger than anything we've both done, it is to our mutual benefit."

"How?"

"Firstly, it should stop this mobster from just...taking you. As my wife, you'll be so much more high-profile, and there will be permanent security in place around you. He's unlikely to just kidnap you, which gives us time to negotiate and see if paying off his loan is going to satisfy his desire for vengeance. As for me, it provides me with instant respectability. A distraction for the media to focus on while I sort out Athleta. It's getting tiring hearing my competitors using this scandal to try and get ahead of me. My twin called and told me both my sisters have had paparazzi chasing them. Diya's also had to put up with my dad's lecture about how I'm casting a shadow over Bhai's shining reputation."

"Bhai?"

"My older brother," he explained. It had been only a matter of time before Dev heard his father's opinion on this matter. It didn't mean he'd ever been prepared for it.

"I told you those interviews with your family were important," Clare said, mercifully interrupting the spiral of anger and frustration he got pulled into whenever he thought of his father. "People need to see your face alongside theirs. They need to see different sides of you."

"I agree. And this way, they will see not only a loyal brother, but a happily married man—head over heels in love with his wife. Two birds with one stone... It seems to me like it's the best stopgap measure."

She laughed and Dev sensed the ache she couldn't hide in her words. "I never imagined I'd hear the words 'stopgap measure' in a proposal."

"Does that mean you've imagined getting a proposal?"

He thought she'd shrug and laugh it off. He needed her to. He didn't want to discover at this stage that Clare was the romantic type.

"In a faraway future kind of way, yes. I'm a businesswoman through and through. But it doesn't mean I didn't harbor the hope of a husband and a family someday. I want to be a wife. And a mum." She swallowed and looked away. When she turned and look back at him, her blue eyes glittered in a way he'd never seen before. "I want to belong. To someone. To something. I've always wanted more than just a career."

If she'd kicked him in the chest, Dev would have been less surprised. He didn't know why. He'd heard her talking about her best friends. He'd seen the hurt on her face the morning after their incredible night together when he'd told her they were done.

But somehow he'd thought she'd be more like him. More disinclined to take the traditional path in life. The idea of Clare marrying some stranger and having his children did strange things to his insides. Things he didn't want to dwell on.

He had to make one thing clear. "You're only in your twenties. All those things are still possible for you, Clare. This marriage is only a temporary solution to both our problems, and it doesn't mean you'll have to give up any of your long-term dreams."

"Making sure I know the score?" she said, the earlier ache in her voice gone. "Making sure you're in the clear? Don't worry, I understand."

He should have been glad that she could so easily shelve her hopes for the future. That she could keep that part of herself mostly hidden. Instead, Dev only tasted a perverse bitterness that she'd so clearly decided that he wasn't going to be included in that particular dream.

Even though, that was exactly what he'd already warned her.

He shrugged. "Earlier, on our way to the foyer after dinner, I spotted a photographer from a popular lifestyle magazine watching from behind one of those giant trees in the courtyard when I was giving you my jacket. I have a feeling the shot he took was quite an intimate one."

She gasped. "Why didn't you stop him?"

"It was too late," Dev said with a shrug. "I'm sure that photo of us has already hit the internet. There'll shortly be rabid speculation that I have a new woman. In a day, they'll know it's you. This way, we're staying ahead of the curve and dictating the news. We could get married at my villa in the Caribbean, and by the time we've sailed back to California for Diya's wedding, the news of our own private, top-secret wedding will be all over the news. As I've already said, hopefully, it will at least make your mobster think twice about snatching you openly. Between us all, my family has a lot of clout."

"He's not my mobster."

"You know what I mean."

"And it will only be an arrangement of convenience?" she said cautiously.

Dev nodded. "It can be whatever you want it to be, Clare." He pinned her with his gaze. "Do you trust me?"

"I do." Her instant answer calmed the furor in his head. Dev kept seeing the damned image she'd created in his mind—Clare marrying some staid accountant type. Clare running behind two children. Clare in bed with this boring old accountant who was nevertheless extremely good in bed.

Or was that himself he was imagining in her bed now?

Dev cursed.

Her gaze held his, a question in it.

Dev shook his head.

"I have a few conditions," she said after what felt like a weighty silence.

"Whatever makes you more comfortable," he said.

"I would like for us to have a prenup."

Stunned, Dev stared at her. It was something he'd fully intended to work into the conversation. With wealth like his, they were as common as summer homes in warm places. But it had felt somehow wrong discussing one with Clare. As if he was questioning her character.

"I'm glad I can still shock you," she said with a small smile.

Dev said nothing.

"I...when this is all over—however long it takes—I'd like to part as friends, Dev. I... I don't have a lot of those but the ones I have, I like to keep them. A prenup guarantees that our divorce will be straightforward, and we'll be more likely to keep in contact, right?"

"If I'd thought otherwise, even for a moment, I wouldn't have suggested this."

She nodded. "I'm realizing that."

"Is that all?" he said, uncomfortable with the look she sent him. It wasn't exactly gratitude. It was the same thing he'd seen in her eyes that morning. And the night when he'd carried her from the library on the yacht.

It was an emotion that Dev didn't know how to accept. Or even how to feel it himself, much less return it.

"Will you have loads and loads of marital sex written into the prenup?"

Dev didn't laugh. Because as sure as he was that she was

serious, he was also beginning to understand that this was no small matter. He held out his hand to her.

She looked at it without taking it.

"Come, Clare. Let's get you to bed. You're in shock and I shouldn't have sprung this on you."

She shook her head stubbornly.

"You're angry with me, I get it. We can talk this over after you've had a good night's sleep."

"I'm not angry with you at all. You're going above and beyond for me. It's just... I have a hard time being dependent on anyone. I don't want to be beholden to you, Dev. At the same time, I don't think I can quite act per some guidelines written down on paper. It would be too much of a farce. It would make it as much of a cage as that mobster was wanting to thrust me into."

Dev held her loosely, her fierce need to be in control of her own destiny striking an echo in him. "What can I do to make this better for you, sweetheart?" he said, pressing his mouth to her temple. "What can I do to make this less a punishment and more of your choice? Other than the lots and lots of sex that we're going to get to have during this marriage, that is."

She laughed then, and he felt as if he'd won a gold medal again.

As if for the first time in his life, there was perfect alignment, perfect harmony between him and another soul.

It was also the first time in his life he'd laid himself open and offered to give someone else everything he could. Emotionally, that was.

CHAPTER NINE

DEV KEPT SURPRISING HER. In a good way. In a fantastic, knee-buckling way. In a come-trust-me-with-your-heart kind of way.

Clare was so tired of freeze-locking her heart. Of pretending it didn't want more. That it hadn't already started thawing in this man's presence a while ago.

She was so tired of pretending that she wanted more out of life.

She looked into Dev's eyes, something solid and immovable lodging in her throat. She kept expecting so little, and he bowled her over every single time. A strange swooping sensation began in her belly, as if she was perpetually in flight. She drew a deep breath. "I need this to be more than just a...sterile agreement on paper."

He curled his upper lip in a deliberately lecherous way. "You mean all the sex won't unsterilize it? Because if I remember rightly, it was explosive."

Clare laughed and tucked away a lock of hair that fell onto his forehead. There it was again—that floaty feeling. It felt like the most natural thing in the world to laugh with him like this. To touch him like this. "Like you said, we'd have done that eventually whether we got hitched or not."

"True," he said with a nod. He sat down on the sofa and

pulled her onto his lap with an effortless poise, as if he couldn't go too long without touching her. "Let's see then." His palm was big and broad against her back, and Clare wanted to melt into it. "I prefer to sleep in the center of the bed. And I hog all the sheets."

Clare slipped her arm around his neck and settled in. "I would have found that out anyway."

He grinned. And tangled his fingers with hers in her lap. "So this is like a toll I have to pay then?" His thumb rubbed at her pulse on her wrist. "For you to marry me?"

They were both smiling and he was touching her so casually, and yet Clare could sense that invisible boundary tightening around him as he spoke. But she wasn't going to give in and let him keep his distance from her.

It had nothing to do with their getting married either. It had everything to do with the fact that she wanted to know more about him. That she wanted him to share in her own life too. That for the first time, she wanted more from life itself.

The strength of that urge sent a shiver of fear through her. An almost familiar echo from when she'd so patiently waited for her dad to show up, although he never did. But Clare pushed it away.

"How about I share something first?" she prompted, not for a game of give and take but because she wanted him to know. Because he'd earned her trust. By giving his own to her.

He looked at her and knew. Just like that. He knew from her face that it wasn't a small or silly thing. "Clare, it doesn't—"

She pressed her finger against his lips. "I want to tell you this." She swallowed the ache in her throat. "I haven't told a soul since I found out. But I want to tell you, Dev."

His fingers tightened over hers. "I'm not going anywhere, sweetheart."

"I didn't borrow the money from that crime lord. In fact, the first I heard of him owning me—" she shuddered, and Dev's arms came around her like a cocoon "—was when that goon of his accosted me in London. I didn't take the money, Dev. I didn't even know who he was."

His finger under chin, Dev tilted her face up to his. "Then why does he think he owns you?"

Shame filled her chest but Clare pushed on. "My father passed away a few years ago now. We...we were not a normal family."

"Is anyone's family normal, Clare?" he said, and Clare heard the answering ache in his words. It made it so much easier to go on.

"I have no memories of my mother. When I was five, my father dropped me off at my aunt's. With loads of promises of coming back. Of traveling around the world, making his fortune and treating me like a princess."

Dev nodded, encouraging her to go on.

Clare laughed, feeling that hope and disappointment in her chest like it was yesterday. "My aunt was not happy, to say the least. But she gave me shelter and food and for the most part, she was indifferent to my existence. But I hung on to my father's promises. I believed that one day he'd come back for me. It sustained me...that hope."

"But—"

"If you say it was foolish, I'll never forgive you. So please don't."

"I won't," he said with emphasis. "I won't say anything you've done is foolish, Clare. Or wrong. You're a survivor. That's all that matters."

Clare thought she might have fallen a little in love with him then. "I studied hard, got a scholarship to go to an excellent private school. That's where I met Amy and Bea. I found a job I liked, but I always wanted to be my own boss. So one day, Dad contacted me to tell me that he'd discovered he was dying, but that his hard work had finally paid off. That he was sending me a sum of money that I would have inherited after he passed away anyway. He said it was his gift to me—reparation for all the birthdays and holidays he'd missed. I was overjoyed to hear from him after so many years, and devastated he didn't have long left to live. I was foolish enough to think my faith in him had been validated. It was a lot of money, and I used it to set up The London Connection."

Dev's brows pulled together into a ferocious scowl. The tension in him was immediate. "Wait, so he sent you that capital? He took the money from the mobster and gave it to you?"

Her eyes prickling with heat, Clare nodded. "I wondered how that even works, in this day and age. Yes. And of course he died without paying it back. So the mobster eventually discovered what happened to him, and turned his attention to me. How could a man use his own daughter as collateral? Did he think a major crime lord would never find me?"

"I'm so sorry, Clare." His hand around her arm, his mouth pressed to her temple, Dev held her tight. As if he was determined to stop her from falling apart.

"I keep thinking with each day that passes, it'll hurt less. That I'll understand why he did this. That something will make me see the whole thing in a new light. But the cold, hard reality doesn't change. When all his other schemes failed, he took the easy way out. He only sent me that money before he died to salve his own conscience for neglecting me my whole life, and he even managed to mess that up in the worst possible way."

I took money from a man I shouldn't have trusted.

Her words came back to Dev. She'd meant her father, not the mobster. How could anyone hold that against her?

Dev fisted his hands by his side, fury filling him slowly. What the hell kind of a man jeopardized his daughter's life like that? He banked the fury knowing that it had taken Clare everything to tell him that much. Knowing that she needed comfort just then and nothing more.

She didn't want a champion; that much had been clear from the start.

But this... Dev now understood the fear, the need to be in control, the strength of will it had taken her to not only manage her emotions but to use the opportunity to pitch her firm to him.

Having always lived in the world of overachievers, Dev was full of admiration for this woman who'd withstood so much and still remained strong and fierce. All the while retaining a sense of joy in life.

"It's not your shame. Or even your burden, Clare. It's his. It doesn't matter that he repeatedly broke your faith in him. That he betrayed you in the worst way possible. None of it is your fault. You know that, right?"

"I do know that. But I've moved on from anger and hurt. I have to."

Dev frowned. This woman was forever going to surprise him. "What do you mean?"

Clare shifted her head and met his gaze. "If I let it, what he did will become a poison inside of me. It will corrupt my business, my life, my heart. And that isn't something I can afford to allow to happen. I have to choose to forgive him. Or it will become the thing that will consume and corrupt me." She took a deep breath. "So I'm going to try to let it go. I'm going to focus on getting out of this mess. On moving forward with my life. And that means I'll marry you and help polish your tarnished halo—" she scrunched her fingers through his hair, and his scalp prickled with sensation "—playing the part of your adoring wife for a while...and then go back to making The London Connection even better than it already is. There, now I feel mostly in control of this situation."

Pleasure and pride wound through Dev like a rope that couldn't be untangled. At the same time, he also felt a perverse resentment at her inner strength. Of how bravely she was making the choice to not let her father's betrayal ruin her.

He clearly didn't possess the same strength. He didn't have the generosity of spirit that she possessed. Even worse, he had no intention of forgiving anyone for anything.

Holding her like this, watching her choose joy and happiness over resentment and anger, he felt more than a little jaded. At twenty-nine, he felt as if he'd already lived through ten lifetimes of anger and resentment. All his choices in life now looked like they were tainted too.

Because he'd allowed the poison of his childhood to run rampant inside him for his whole life.

"Thank you for listening to me, Dev," she said softly, pulling him back to the present. "For just about everything."

"I didn't do it for your gratitude, Clare."

"No, you did it because it was the right thing to do. Thanks to you, my faith in men isn't completely dashed."

Dev shook his head. "Don't, Clare. This will benefit me too. So don't make me out to be some kind of hero." He pressed on. "But I know how hard it must have been to lay yourself open like that, so thank you for trusting me with the truth."

She looked up then, and the piercing quality of her gaze pinged through him. "I couldn't let you think I was that foolish anymore. It was fine when I thought you were just another only-in-it-for-a-good-time playboy."

He grinned at that. "I love these titles you keep coming up with for me."

"But none of them truly fit, do they?"

Dev frowned. "What do you mean?"

"I mean that I've seen more of the real you than you show the world, Dev. But there's still a lot more lying hidden. What was it you called it? Paying a toll? I don't want you to tell me as if it's a toll you're paying. I want you to want to tell me. I'd like to get to know the part of you that you don't show anyone else."

No one had ever asked him that. No one had ever cared enough to know. Not even his twin knew it all. But to confide in Clare meant something he wasn't prepared to admit to. "You're mistaking me for a deep lake. I'm a shallow pond, remember."

She pushed out of his arms and looked down at him. "All lies. But it's okay, Dev. If my pathetic excuse for a dad has taught me one thing, it's that you can't demand things from people —loyalty or love or even confidences—that they're unwilling to give. But I'd like you to know that I want more from you. From this partnership. More than orgasms, that is," she added candidly.

Dev had no idea how she did it—making demands of him he couldn't fulfill one minute and making him laugh the next. But there was no point in letting her think this was more than it was. His tone was grave when he said, "I've given you everything I'm capable of giving, Clare. Does that help?"

She scrunched her nose and smiled. A sad smile. As if she understood even though he didn't say the words. "Not really. But I'll take that as a win for now. And now, I'm going to shower, eat a tub of ice cream and then your spare bed's got my name on it."

When she'd have slipped away, Dev pulled her back to him. He felt a strange reluctance to let her go, even though she'd be in the next room to his.

For the first time in his adult life, he felt an acute need for companionship. For more whispered confidences. For more of a connection with a woman than just a sexual one.

For all of those things with this particular woman.

And yet he didn't want to fight it. Or shove it away. Or call it a temporary madness.

In this moment, he felt all of that resentment and distance that forced him to stand alone in the world fall away. In this moment, he felt perfectly aligned with the universe and with Clare.

Her arms came around his neck as he pressed his mouth to the upper curve of her breast. He could taste the salt of the ocean, smell the sea breeze and her own distinct floral scent on her skin. Desire thrummed through him as she responded instantly. Her nails raked over his skin, and a shudder went through her.

Dev licked at the thundering pulse at her neck. He let his hands run rampant, caressing the dips and valleys of her body. He didn't even need this to go any deeper than it was right now. There was a sense of contentment in just holding her and in stoking the fire of their mutual desire higher and hotter.

With a muttered curse, she tugged his face to hers and kissed him fiercely.

Laughter and something else he didn't want to name held him in its grip as she devoured his mouth as if there was no end to her hunger for him. Dev had never been appreciated so thoroughly in his life.

When she let him go, he was rock hard, panting and desperate for more.

"Good night then," the minx whispered, a wicked glint in her blue eyes.

The dark shadows under her eyes tugged at him. "You don't have to go to bed alone tonight, Clare." When she smiled slowly, he held up his palm. "I'm not talking about sex. I'm concerned that nightmare you had on the yacht will be back."

"If it does, then you'll pick me up and bring me to your bed, won't you?"

She didn't wait for him to deny her. Not that Dev would have. He had a feeling he wouldn't have to share anything with her. Because the damned woman had seen and knew everything about him already.

More than he felt comfortable sharing with anyone.

"You're putting a lot of trust in me that's not warranted, Clare," he warned. "I'm no hero."

"Ha! Believe me, Dev, the last thing I need is a hero. Because they don't really exist, do they? If there is such a thing, it's people like us who live their lives, day after day, even though they've been dealt a bad hand."

"Then what is it you think you know about me, Clare?" he asked. He suddenly wanted her opinion. He wanted to know what it was that she thought of him.

"I think you're a man who wants more than he realizes. A man who doesn't have as much as he thinks he does. A man who has a lot more to give."

With that parting, perceptive shot, she walked away.

Making Dev wonder and question and doubt all the things he'd always thought were unshakeable truths about himself.

She was getting married in a few minutes.

As she looked at the knee-length, cream A-line dress she'd picked up during the short shopping jaunt that Dev had allowed her back in Rio before they'd spent several days sailing to his villa on St. Lucia, Clare wondered how many times she'd have to say it in her head for it sink in completely.

She was getting married to a man she would have preferred to like a little less than she did, even if that sounded more than a bit twisted. She was getting married without either of her best friends present. At the thought of Amy and Bea, her throat filled up.

The feel of the delicate silk under her fingers gave her something to anchor herself with, instead of focusing on the looping thoughts inside her head.

"He's really a catch, you know," Angelina Lansang continued her chatter without missing a beat. "Everyone that knows Dev is going to go crazy to discover he's secretly got hitched. The press, the media…" The tall woman laughed, a little bit inanely. As if this was the best thing about Dev getting married.

Do any of them actually know him? Clare wanted to ask. *Do they know that he's kind and far more complex than any interview or article could ever capture?*

But Clare didn't say anything of the sort, because sweet as Angelina had been during the time it had taken to sail to the island, she couldn't betray the fact that this was a fake wedding.

For a few, fleeting seconds, Angelina considered Clare thoughtfully before smiling again. "I hope you're ready for all the attention you're going to get, my dear." Clare resolutely kept her mouth closed.

Not only did she not know Angelina well enough, she didn't trust her own thoughts. Several days of pondering this every which way hadn't untangled her thoughts any better.

Since the other woman was waiting for a response, Clare smiled. "I can't thank you enough for everything, Angelina."

Angelina nodded, and returned her smile.

Ever since Clare and Dev had met up with Derek and Angelina the following day in Rio and he'd introduced Clare as his fiancée, asking them to join them at his villa and witness the ceremony, Angelina had completely changed her attitude. Not that Clare wasn't grateful.

It was, after all, thanks to Angelina's insistence that Dev had reluctantly agreed to Clare shopping for a suitable bridal outfit before leaving Rio. Not that Clare couldn't have fought that particular battle herself.

Even if the agreement between them was that this wedding was nothing but a mutually beneficial arrangement, she'd had no intention of marrying him wearing a trouser suit more suitable for business than pleasure.

Even if it was a designer suit.

It had been while they were having that discussion that Clare had finally lost the battle of pretending that this wedding mattered as little to her as it did to him.

Yes, this was a convenient arrangement that would benefit both of them. But it didn't mean that she couldn't feel some sentiment. That she could treat it as just any other normal day.

The wedding was only a technicality. She had silently recited that fact so often, it was as if it were her life's mantra. But looking at herself in the mirror, dressed as a bride, Clare knew no mantra was going to work on her.

Foolish or not, naive or not, she'd always dreamed of this day.

Because she was marrying Dev, Clare didn't even have to build her castles on the empty promises of a charming man who was all glitter and no substance. And it was this fact that kept tripping her up.

"You look beautiful." The surprise in Angelina's tone brought Clare back to the present.

She knew it didn't really matter how beautiful she looked.

This marriage was only temporary and there would no doubt be countless other, far more beautiful women in Dev's life after she'd exited it. The thought darkened her mood, the pit of her stomach suddenly hollow. And that, in turn, flipped her mood back again. She was determined never to operate out of fear or loneliness ever again.

So what if she and Dev weren't going to promise to love each other for the rest of their lives? So what if their marriage came with a short shelf life?

She liked the man she was going to marry. She also very much liked what he was capable of doing to her with one playful glance from those twinkling eyes, with those clever fingers and with those sculpted lips. She wasn't going to pretend that she could be all matter-of-fact and cold about this. This was no fantasy she had concocted while waiting to escape from under the indifferent roof of her aunt.

This was her life.

Clare adjusted her hair and stared again at her reflection in the mirror. The dress was classy and elegant, but sexy enough as it clung to her curves. Her skillfully styled hair helped highlight her features. Her lipstick—a vibrant red—made her mouth look full and pouty.

She looked beautiful, she was getting married and she had the serious hots for her husband-to-be.

As she turned to leave the room, Clare told herself it was okay that this wedding felt real to her. It was the most real thing that had ever happened to her. And she was going to make the most of it.

"It's just a PR ploy," he'd said when his best friend had asked him what the hell he was playing at the night before his wedding.

"Like hell it is," Derek had said with a deep laugh. "You're in deep trouble, my man."

Now, as Dev watched his intended walk toward him in his

airy Caribbean villa, he felt Derek's words reverberate within his chest.

Clare looked nothing like some cheap participant in a PR ploy and everything like deep trouble poured into an enticingly petite frame. Just for him.

She looked stunning and elegant and beautiful in a cream-colored dress. Far too much like a real bride with her smile glowing and her eyes bright and generally radiating a serene kind of joy.

It reached Dev like a wave of emotion, intent on pulling him under.

He'd never given marriage much thought, except for knowing that it wasn't for him. He'd been far too busy building an empire.

But as he stood there, waiting for Clare to reach him, "PR ploy" felt like the most inadequate nonsense he'd ever uttered.

"You're in so much trouble, man," Derek whispered again with a pat on his shoulder.

Whatever retort he wanted to throw back at his friend died as Clare reached him. As he looked into the blue eyes of the woman he'd promised himself he'd look after. He hadn't, when he'd originally suggested the idea to her, thought to paint himself in the role of her hero.

For a long time, even into his adulthood, thinking himself as anything more than a failure had been hard. Even gaining Derek's friendship at military school and then discovering his talent for swimming, he'd struggled to see himself as anything but a disappointment to everyone around him.

Old patterns were hard to break.

It was only after he'd made his first million that Dev had felt a sense of achievement. Which was all kinds of messed up, he knew. Equating wealth and fame and power with self-worth was going down the same poisonous line of thinking Papa had employed when he'd scoured layers of Dev's self-esteem as a child with his harsh words.

You'll amount to nothing if you continue like this.

And the harshest cut of all: *Your mama's lucky to have gone before she saw you like this.*

By the time he'd realized that he'd started measuring himself by the same toxic yardstick as his father had done, it was too late to change. Plus, Dev had never been a hypocrite. He had enjoyed all the fame and wealth and power that his achievements and success had brought him.

Meeting Derek —who was six foot six and had weighed three hundred pounds as a sixteen-year-old, who was constantly viewed as a threat just because of his size and skin color while in actuality, the gentle giant possessed a heart of gold—had taught Dev a lot about how to manage people's perceptions.

So Dev knew there was a good reason Derek was calling him on his nonsense about his marriage being a PR ploy.

But it *was* saving his reputation too, he reminded himself. This was letting up pressure on him, his family, his company and hopefully salvaging Athleta's reputation. They would both simply walk away from this in a few months with their problems solved. He hadn't told Clare yet, but he'd already had his security chief make contact with the mobster to start negotiations to try to pay off her debt.

This would be yet another satisfying business arrangement with a few pleasures thrown in as enjoyable extras. And he knew it wasn't just him thinking about sex.

But, as he glanced at the woman now standing beside him, Dev kept hearing Derek's sarcastic laughter inside his head.

Deep trouble, man...

It wasn't that her simple but stunning dress made her skin shimmer. It wasn't that she was holding a beautiful bouquet of lilies of the valley as a bride usually did. It wasn't even the platinum ring she'd produced in contrast to the plain gold band he'd selected at her suggestion.

It was the look in her blue eyes.

She didn't look at him as if this was a business arrangement. Or as if she was putting on an act. She simply looked as if she were gloriously happy to be marrying him. In that easy, let's-turn-Dev's-world-upside-down way that only she had.

From the first moment they'd met at that charity gala, she had seen him.

Him. Only him.

Dev Kohli. Not the shallow playboy, not the ruthless billionaire, not the *studly stud* as she'd called him, but just him.

It didn't matter that he hadn't given her what she'd asked for. It seemed as if she'd taken a part of him anyway, even without his permission.

As they stood there saying their vows, culminating with him bending his head and taking her mouth in a kiss that sealed her fate with his—at least temporarily—Dev had the uneasy feeling that he'd gone a step too far with this marriage. That he'd tangled himself into something he didn't quite understand.

Because no kiss had ever shaken him to his core like this one did.

Sweet and familiar, her lips molded to his in the exact way he needed them to. Her body pressed against his with that wide-open generosity of hers, her heart thudding against his own.

She felt like she belonged to him. In a way nothing and no one else ever had.

And, as he pulled away from her perceptive gaze, and laughed at some joke that Angelina cracked, his heart beating faster and faster, Dev wondered how he was going to fight it. How he was going to maintain any kind of distance when all he wanted was to steal her away for himself.

How he was going to walk away from her when all this was over.

CHAPTER TEN

"ARE YOU DRUNK?"

Dev looked up from the open book in his lap he'd been flicking through for the last hour. The letters and words jumped and leaped on the page. Even more so than usual since his concentration was shot to hell.

He simply stared at Clare for a few seconds. Wondering if she was the cause or the means of escape from this torture.

She was standing with her back against the door to his bedroom. On the inside, he clarified for himself. The high walls and ceilings of his villa and all the skylights he'd had his architect install meant she was bathed in moonlight. Her freshly washed hair shone, and her eyes glittered with bright curiosity and something else as they swept over his naked chest.

Desire…and she didn't bother hiding it.

Awareness slammed through Dev.

She was his wife and he was her husband. He'd figured that a piece of paper with their signatures on it didn't really stand for much in the greater scheme of things. But he'd found that it did. He was discovering that maybe he was a traditional man at heart, after all.

A man who believed in marriage and family and all the things Mama had believed lay firmly at the center of human existence.

But with that realization also came the acute feeling of inadequacy that he didn't like. It left a bad taste in his mouth. Reminded him of how he'd struggled with it for too many years. What if he wasn't any good as a husband?

This discovery about wanting things that he couldn't have, wouldn't be any good at, bothered him. After years of being a physically perfect championship-standard athlete and then his unprecedented success in the business world meant he'd forgotten how it felt to be bad at something. As a result, he was in a roaring bad mood. Which was really rare for him.

He shook his head. "No."

Arms folded against her chest, she rolled her eyes. "Good."

"What's good?" he asked, knowing that he was winding her up but enjoying it anyway. They were hitting that rhythm again. Bandying words while heat built around them. This was something he was exceptionally good at.

"Well, to start with, it's good that Derek and Angelina seem to be getting through this rough patch," she said.

"Why is that good?"

"It's clear that you allow very few people into your life. Derek's happiness matters to you."

He grunted in response. Really, the last thing he wanted to talk about was Derek and Angelina's marriage. He didn't want to talk at all.

He wanted her. Desperately. He wanted to be inside her. He wanted to scratch this itch—as many times as required—and be done with it. He wanted to get rid of this sentimental nonsense that had taken over his head ever since he'd slipped the ring on her finger.

"You're not in a talking mood," she said, licking her lips.

"No."

"If anyone could see us now," she said, her eyes glinting with challenge, "they'd think I was the feudal lord and you my blushing bride."

He raised a brow. With each teasing word, she dispelled his

dark mood. "And yet you're the one plastered to the door." He pushed the duvet down and patted the space next to him on the bed. "Care to try that theory by coming closer?"

Dev found his gaze eating her up, any remaining discontent washed away by curiosity and that simmering hum of desire.

"What the hell are you wearing?" he asked hoarsely.

She raised a rounded shoulder and one thin, almost nonexistent strap fell down. "This was the only thing I could find in the little time I had."

It was unlike anything Dev had ever seen, outside of maybe a period drama. It was all white and made of fine cotton. But without any ghastly ruffles.

The V-shaped bodice and the floaty hem that barely touched her knees stopped it from being plain. But, unlike silk that would have hugged her petite curves, this nightgown fluttered in the breeze through the open French doors, hinting at the dips and valleys of her body.

"You disappeared from dinner too soon," she said. "Those were your friends."

"I had things to look over."

"You don't have to run away from me, you know," she said. A hint of the fragility he'd sometimes seen in her peeked out from beneath the fierce scowl she wore.

"I've stopped running away from things that upset me a long time ago."

"So I'm one of those things, am I?"

He grinned. "If you were a thing I could put in a box so I could stop thinking about it, all of this would be easy. But you're not, are you? You're a..."

"What?"

He shrugged.

"I think the word you're looking for is *wife*. With an independent mind and a beating heart and a..." She licked her lips and Dev felt a bolt of lust shoot through him. "I decided to let you be for a little while since you looked like you were upset."

He refused to answer.

Her lower lip trembled. "Regretting this already?"

"Not really," he said, loath to hurt her. "But you're right I'm not…in a good mood."

"Okay, that's fair enough," she said, that lost expression receding from her eyes. And Dev knew in that moment what was bothering him so much.

He didn't want to hurt her. He didn't want to be the reason the fierce light that was at the heart of Clare was diminished or even extinguished. He didn't want to be another man that made her think she was less than she was.

She wasn't that weak, he reminded himself. She'd understood what this arrangement of theirs meant. She'd accepted it.

And yet he couldn't shed this sense of responsibility he suddenly felt toward her. He turned the gold band on his finger, feeling the solid weight of the metal.

Her gaze flicked to the action and then up to his face. But her expression remained steady. And Dev knew he was just being unreasonable now.

"Do you want me to leave?" she asked.

It felt as if even the breeze and the world and time itself stood still to witness his answer. He rubbed a hand over his face. "No. I don't want you to leave, Clare."

She didn't quite smile. Her wide mouth softened.

"If I stay, I have some demands of you."

"Don't push it, sweetheart," he growled.

She laughed then. "If I stay, I'm going to want to exercise my marital rights. If you're not in the mood to accommodate me, or don't have the energy it requires, you should tell me now."

He burst out laughing, just as she'd intended. He licked his lower lip, sending a leisurely, thoroughly lascivious look up and down her body.

To his delight, pink crept up her neck and cheeks. "I'm always in the mood for you, Ms. Roberts," he said with a wicked grin.

She cocked an eyebrow. "You forget that I'm Mrs. Kohli now."

He fell back against the headboard. Warmth and something else suffused his chest. "That used to be Mama. I haven't heard that title in a long time."

Her fingers went to her chest and she bit her lip. "I'm sorry, Dev. I didn't mean to poke fun at it."

"Don't be," Dev said. This time, the mention of his mother didn't leave a painful void in its wake. Not here, with the only other woman who saw through his surface qualities. Who'd always looked at him as if he could be more. As if he was more. More than the world thought him to be. More than he thought himself to be. "I have a feeling she'd have liked you."

Clare's smile put the moonlight to shame. "You think so?"

Dev nodded, feeling a sudden stab of such overpowering grief mixed in with this new feeling of joy. "Yes. She'd have especially liked how often you keep me on my toes."

She smiled. "You miss her a lot."

He shrugged. "Yes, each year, I miss her more."

"She sounds like a wonderful woman."

"She was. She...had the knack of seeing through to a person's heart. And finding something to love in everyone."

"Will you tell me more about her?"

His chest rose and fell as Dev considered this woman...his wife. She always wanted more. More of life. More of herself. More of him. "I will. But some other time. Not tonight." He beckoned her closer. "Tonight is about you and me, Clare. Only you and me." Now that he'd made peace with that fact, the slumbering need in him had risen keenly to the surface.

Why had he even been fighting this so much?

She blushed prettily, even as she demanded he give her what she wanted. "I have a wedding present for you."

Dev felt like he had been knocked over the head. Although he didn't know why he should be so surprised. She'd already told him that she wasn't going to pretend this was a cold, dry business arrangement.

"I have nothing for you."

She clearly wasn't disappointed by that. "I didn't expect you to get me anything. I saw this when I went shopping with Angelina and it made me think of you. Don't worry, Dev. I know what I want from you."

He raised a brow, unashamedly eating her alive with his eyes. He could see the shadow of her nipples through the nightgown, the slightly rounded shape of her belly when it was plastered to her body by the friendly breeze, and a darker shadow at the apex of her thighs. "I should tell you, Clare, that I don't have either the patience or the inclination to be overly gentle tonight."

She swallowed and he saw the flutter of her pulse at her neck. "I never asked you to be gentle with me. It's your own fault if you catered to me. But then, that's what you do, don't you?"

He frowned. "I have no idea what you mean."

"That night, I didn't ask you to be gentle with me. I didn't tell you that it was my first time. It was what I needed and you simply gave it to me. That's who you are, Dev. Why fight it?"

"And here I thought you dwelled in reality, Clare."

She was hurt by that. He'd only meant to pierce the false image of him she was building in her head. Because he sure as hell couldn't be that man.

But instead of backing down, she covered the distance between them. Now she stood close enough that he could smell the lily of the valley on her. The taut buds of her nipples taunted him. "We all need a dose of cold reality most days, I agree. But as I realized recently, a little dreaming never hurt anyone. In fact, it was the thing that sustained me through so many difficult years."

When he opened his mouth, she pressed her palm to his lips. "It's okay. I don't want to argue tonight. I have other plans—devious plans," she said with a naughty grin.

Lust kicked through him. "I should very much like to be part of your plans, Clare."

In one easy movement, he picked her up and brought her onto the bed. She landed on her knees, on the duvet, his legs still buried beneath it. The scent of her skin enveloped him and he breathed it in, like a junkie.

He took the square package with the neat bow and was about to toss it aside when she grabbed it and held it up to him.

"So that's how it's going to be, huh?" he said, burying his face in her neck. The uproar that had begun in his chest hours earlier calmed at the feel of her soft curves in his hands.

"I want you, Dev. I want to spend tonight with you. More than anything in the world. But..."

He pulled back and smiled. "Okay. I guess it's true what they say about marriage, huh?"

Her eyes widened and she played along. The twitch of her mouth made his heart swell in his chest. "What do they say about marriage, Dev?"

"That the sex dries up and your wife rules you."

"Hey," she said, swatting him on the shoulder.

Dev took the wrapped package from her hands. "All right, fine. If this is what it takes..."

Her teeth digging into her lower lip, she looked at him from under her lashes.

Curiosity took over and he ripped the wrapping off.

To find a cardboard box in his hand—an audiobook of an autobiography of a black American athlete who'd found success despite numerous obstacles. Dev had been sent an autographed copy by the gentleman. It was the one book he didn't have in audio.

So of course, he hadn't read it.

Dev stared at it for what felt like interminable seconds, alarm coursing down his spine. Tension burst into life around them, replacing all the desire and humor that he'd felt so drunk on.

He looked up to find Clare watching him.

He had no idea what she saw in his face. A nervous laugh escaped her mouth. "I noticed that you don't have the audio-book for this title."

"When?" he said. Because he had to say something to cut the awkwardness. Because to say nothing at all would betray his shock.

"Oh, I told you, I loved that library of yours. It's so well categorized that it wasn't hard to see that this one was missing."

"Yeah, I meant to get it."

"Are you angry, Dev?" Her mouth was pinched, her eyes wide. "I didn't do it to pry. Like I said, that library…it was like a part of you. I thought I…"

"No, you aren't prying," he said, stunned by how perceptive she was. He rubbed a hand over his face. "And I'm not angry." But there was something in his tone that even he couldn't identify.

Was it still just shock that had him struggling to form thoughts and sentences? Only Derek knew. It had been him who'd insisted that Dev get diagnosed. That it wasn't too late. Never too late. And of course the therapist that Dev had gone to after he'd been diagnosed knew. Not even Diya had guessed or asked.

"It's not something I ever discuss," he said, his voice hoarse. "If I'd had the diagnosis of dyslexia as a child, then it might have been different."

If he thought she'd nod and agree and close the subject, he was wrong.

Clare frowned, her palms on his bare shoulders, grounding him.

"In fact, your success, your company…you're the symbol of what one can accomplish despite being wired differently."

"Before you ask, no, I'm not ashamed of being dyslexic, Clare."

He felt that maybe he should have moderated his curt tone,

but right now, the last thing he felt like doing was pacifying her or anybody else for that matter. He had always struggled alone in his life. Nothing was ever going to change that.

"I didn't think you were, Dev."

"I wasn't diagnosed until very late. Not until I was seventeen."

"But you come from such an affluent, educated family."

He laughed then, and it was the hollowest sound he'd ever heard. "You want the whole sorry story then?"

She nodded, still touching him. Still anchoring him.

"I was a very…rambunctious kid. As Deedi tells it—that's my older sister—I was slow to speak. My mother apparently schlepped me around to a lot of speech therapists. So it was decided at a very early age that of the four of us, I wasn't the brightest bulb."

"Who decided that?" Clare asked with such a fierce scowl that Dev rubbed his fingers against her brow.

"My father. But Mama wouldn't listen to him. She tried her best to help me sit down and focus. And I tried. For her, I tried so hard. But letters and words were nothing but a jumble to me. The more I tried to pin them down, the more they escaped me.

"So I started cutting classes. I started paying a friend to do my work for me. I manipulated Diya into doing my homework. I cheated as much as I could. Anything and everything to not disappoint Mama. Anything to avoid telling her the truth. Because the one thing I couldn't do was bring myself to admit that I just couldn't read. That all the books she bought me…she might as well have asked me to walk to the moon.

"After a while, all my schemes were found out. Diya got into big trouble. My friend was forever banished from seeing me. I begged Papa to not have him expelled from school. That it was all my fault. That I had manipulated them all into helping me. Mama was crushed. I've never felt as low as I did that day when she realized I'd been cheating when she'd thought I'd been getting better."

"Oh, Dev. I'm so sorry."

"I hadn't wanted to disappoint her. And I ended up crushing her. Betraying her faith in me."

"Then?"

It felt as if there were shards stuck in his throat. "She still tried. I got expelled from three different private schools for getting into trouble. She tried private tutoring and every other option out there. I'd hear them arguing at night. Hear him call me useless and stupid and her fighting with him to not call her baby boy that. Arguing that academic success wasn't everything. That she'd spend her life helping me if that's what it took. Papa was furious with me. I think more than that, it scared him. He couldn't see why one of his children wasn't like the other three. He couldn't fathom that his son was such a loser. That I resented him and argued with him and gave him attitude at every turn didn't help our relationship, either."

"But you were a kid, Dev. Just a kid. We shouldn't have to make allowances for adults and their feelings." Dev held her, hearing the pain he'd once felt echoing in her voice.

"Please tell me he didn't abuse you to your face," Clare whispered against his shoulder. "Please tell me your mother stopped him."

Dev shook his head. "He didn't call me a dumb loser, no. That was one of the names I called myself. He called me lazy, incompetent. A rogue who didn't appreciate the privileges he had. A boy who was good for nothing. Then when I was twelve, Mama died."

Clare's arms were around his neck now, her own trembling.

Dev pressed his palms to her back, glad to have her here. "The worst part is over, sweetheart."

She pulled back and glared at him. "How can you be so cavalier about this, Dev?"

"Because I can't let it be more, Clare. It's taken me years to not think of myself as a failure. Hours of therapy to realize that my brain's just wired differently. That not being able to read—

something my mother loved to do with me—didn't mean the world of books wasn't cut off for me. Whenever I thought about the past, I had to develop a degree of emotional separation from it. Or I'd have ruined my life with my own hands."

"What did your father do then? After she died."

"He packed me off to military school barely a week later. Diya told me Deedi and Bhai had a huge fight with him about it, but he wouldn't listen to anyone. His grief found an outlet in me, I think. And I was happy to leave a place that no longer held the one person who'd loved me unconditionally."

"You haven't been back there since, have you?"

Dev looked into her eyes and shook his head. "No. And the thought of going back now is painful. But for Diya... I have to."

"How was the military school?"

"In retrospect, it was the best place for me. It was rigorous and disciplined and when night came, I was simply too exhausted to think of my shortcomings. I met Derek there. And one of the coaches found something to nurture in the both of us. The rest is history."

"You're a testament to—"

Dev pressed his finger to her lips. "I don't want praise, sweetheart."

She nodded, and he smiled. "I want the wedding night that I was promised. No, that you demanded that I give you. I want you to look at me as you always do."

"You think hearing this has changed how I see you?" she asked with a frown.

"Does it?"

"Of course not, you arrogant man. It only makes me want to jump your bones even more. There, is that what you want to hear?"

"Yes," Dev said, before dipping his mouth to hers.

It shouldn't have made a difference that she knew about his childhood. About the difficulties he'd had to overcome. Some he still lived with to this day.

But as Dev swept his tongue into her welcoming mouth, as he filled his hungry hands with her curves and kissed her harder and deeper, he felt as if for the first time in his life, someone knew who he was. What he'd achieved to get here. He felt... whole. Even though he hadn't realized what he'd been missing.

Hands wrapping around her slender shoulders, he gathered her closer to him.

"Yes, please. God, yes, Dev. Now," she replied. The throaty need in her voice undid Dev just a little bit more.

The taste of her skin under his tongue felt like peace and joy and contentment like he had never known before.

She was trembling as he nipped and kissed his way from her neck to the soft, silky smooth skin of her jaw. He couldn't touch her enough. Couldn't taste her enough. He licked the delicate lobe of her ear.

She shuddered, a long moan rasping out of her throat and pressed herself against him. Her breasts crushed against his chest, her lips sought his. Dev devoured her mouth as if he was a drowning man. As if the taste of her could bring him back to shuddering life from the cold, sterile reality he'd existed in for so many years.

Suddenly his life before she'd come barging into it felt... flat, one-dimensional. A glittering mockery of the real thing.

Dev had no idea who pushed the duvet out from between them. He had no idea if he was the one who pulled up the flimsy little thing that she was wearing and threw it off. He didn't know if she demanded, or he had created a space between his thighs for her.

But as their frenzied kiss deepened, he filled his hands with the slight weight of her breasts. She straddled his hips, moving up and over him, until she was exactly where she wanted to be.

He nipped her lower lip when she rubbed herself against his hardness, and then flicked his tongue over it. Her fingers sneaked into his hair and tugged imperiously.

"Inside me, now, Dev," she whispered frantically.

He suddenly hesitated.

She moved his head so she could see into his eyes, her own feverish with desire. "You said you had no inclination to be slow or gentle tonight. I find that I'm desperate for hard and fast tonight. So how about you make good on your promise?"

Filling his hands with her slender hips, Dev lifted her up. She moaned as he lowered his thumb to her core. Slowly, he drew it down, down, down until his thumb was notched at the entrance of her sex. Her dampness drenched him. His erection lengthened further as she wound herself around him like a vine, thrusting her pelvis into his hand.

"I love how greedy you are, sweetheart," he whispered, dipping his finger in and out of her, feeling anticipation bunch his muscles rock hard.

"You make me like this. Only you," she whispered, her face buried in his shoulder.

Dev took another few seconds teasing her out, though it felt like an eternity. With his other palm, he stroked the warm, damp planes of her body. Rubbed the tight knot of her nipple between his fingers. Up on her knees, she thrust into his hand with a frantic urgency that made his throat dry.

Her eyes closed, her neck thrown back, she was lost in sensation. "Do you like this?" he growled, wanting to hear her voice.

"Faster, Dev. Damn it, give me what I want. Please."

He laughed, and she opened those blue eyes and bent to kiss him. Hard and rough, winding him up even more.

"I love it when you laugh," she said, and Dev felt like he was drenched in her shy smile.

He flicked at her sensitive bud gently and felt her responsive shudder. She moved forward and back, her breasts rubbing against his chest, pleasure painting her face a lovely pink. He tormented her for little while more, loving her moans and whispers that told him she was getting closer to ecstasy.

Just when she was hovering right on the edge of the abyss, he pulled back to quickly sheathe himself.

Lifting her with one hand on her buttock, Dev took his shaft in the other and slowly, carefully, slid himself inside her soft, wet heat.

She was incredibly snug around him, and he thought he might have died a little with sheer pleasure.

Her long, guttural moan mingled with his.

Her blue eyes deepened into a darker color, glittering with raw pleasure. She brought his palm to her left breast and sighed.

Dev kneaded her breast obediently, the tip of her nipple pressing into his palm. He didn't move his hips for long minutes. He didn't want to move, even though his body was screaming for release. He intended to savor this moment.

He kissed her brow and tasted the dampness from her skin.

Her gaze held his, shining so brightly that Dev wanted to look away.

But he forced himself to hold it. To see this woman who was a fighter just like him.

"You feel like you're inside me, all the way to here," she moaned, and then she threw her arms around his neck and held him tight.

Dev started to build their pace with slow, deep thrusts. He had a feeling he was never going to get enough of her. That one fine morning, he was going to wake up to find she'd changed him forever.

She matched his rhythm perfectly, bearing down when he thrust up, meeting him stroke for stroke. He glided his palms all over her silky back, following the curve of her hips, and chasing a drop of sweat trailing down her cleavage, before moving to take the begging tip of her dark pink nipple into his mouth. He bit back a groan as she shuddered as she approached her own peak.

And when she was close again, this time he pushed her over the edge with his fingers.

She orgasmed with a low cry, her nails clutching his shoulders, marking him. And in the hold and release of her climax, Dev chased his own.

With one swift movement, he turned her back against the sheets, and then he lost himself in the arms of his wife.

CHAPTER ELEVEN

THE KOHLIS' HOUSE in California was really a mansion. Even knowing that this trip was mostly about Dev and not her—which meant she was hoping she wouldn't be under too much scrutiny from his big family—Clare couldn't help being nervous.

Fake marriages were not easy. Especially when you were married to a gorgeous hunk with kind eyes and complex emotional depths. Especially when she and Dev made it all too real when it came to passion. Especially when during the two weeks since their wedding, she'd seen how much they had in common.

She tried to bury her anxiety by telling herself that he needed her to be confident and charming and perfect. Not because she needed to impress anyone in particular. But because that was the only way his family would believe that he'd fallen for her.

She *was* all of those things, she reminded herself. The only playacting that they needed to engage in was convincing everyone that they were hopelessly in love with each other. That was the part she was looking forward to.

She couldn't wait to see how Dev was going to pull it off.

Tall Oaks stood in solemn welcome, straddling a wide pathway with lush, green vegetation on each side for almost a few kilometers before they arrived at the residence.

By this time, Clare was used to the grandeur and affluence

that followed Dev wherever he went. But as she stepped out of the chauffeured Mercedes and stared up at marble facade of the gigantic mansion, Clare wasn't quite as composed as she'd have liked to have been.

A lump filled her throat.

She couldn't stop imagining Dev here as a little boy. Rambunctious and full of energy, yet confused by his incapability to understand the written word. Being surrounded by a genius brother and overachieving sisters, while letters and words escaped him.

And when he'd finally begun to realize that there might be a reason for that, he'd already lost his champion—his mother.

Tears filled her eyes as she recalled what he'd told her about his father's treatment of him, and Clare blinked them back. She could imagine him here, running wild, losing himself in the woods. Trying to free himself from the stifling expectations and his own shortcomings.

Feeling like he could breathe again.

She sent him a sideways glance, knowing he'd hate to be pitied. But Clare had always known herself. Had always faced her truths.

What she felt for Dev wasn't pity at all.

She reached out and took his hand in hers. He was stiff at first, his jaw tightly locked. But slowly, he tangled his long fingers with hers and his breath came out in a long, painful exhale.

He met her gaze only once. But it was enough for Clare. It was more than enough.

He knew she was here, in this moment with him. He knew he wasn't alone. And with that one glance, he acknowledged it. It told her that her presence did make a difference to him.

Clare knew he couldn't give her any more than that. Knew that he might never look any deeper at what their marriage had morphed into. Knew that she might have to wait a long time, maybe even forever, to hear what he felt for her.

But she didn't care.

She was happy to be here and share this moment with him.

She was relieved to find that her father's betrayal hadn't put her off forging new connections with people.

She was also ecstatic and a little terrified that she might be falling in love with her commitment-phobic husband whose scars ran so deep.

"So how did you and my brother meet?"

Clare looked up from the intricate swirls the henna artist was drawing on her left palm with a dexterity that left her in awe of her talent.

To find about twenty sets of eyes on her.

Her heart beat to the rhythm of the Bollywood Hip Hop fusion music that was blaring out from cleverly hidden speakers in the backyard. Despite the noise, it felt as if everyone and everything around her had fallen silent just to hear her answer.

And there was a lot going on.

Whatever she had read previously about Indian weddings, Clare had discovered that the reality gloriously outmatched the theory. It wasn't just people dressed in beautiful clothes, long-lost cousins greeting each other, kids from old family friends eyeing each other now that they were grown up, interfering aunties sizing up brides for their sons and vice versa, it was the sheer joy that pervaded the atmosphere. Diya had laughed and told Clare that by marrying Dev she'd apparently saved him from a huge peril in the form of a pushy auntie who wanted to matchmake for him.

It was also the ceremony after ceremony of teasing the bride and the groom, of dancing and food, of being a part of something that was much bigger than yourself.

Oh, Clare knew there were bound to be downsides too, but she didn't care. Not when smiling aunties and uncles she didn't know looked her up and down, kissed her cheek and demanded she—Dev's lovely new bride—take their blessings for a long, prosperous marriage.

It had taken a giggling Diya to explain that in this context, prosperity was all the children she and Dev might have in the future.

And at the thought of children—her and Dev's children—of a boy or a girl with their father's twinkling eyes, his beautiful jet-black hair, and that sheer determination to conquer life, Clare had known it was too late for her.

She badly wanted this marriage to be a real one. She wanted that future with Dev. She wanted...so much she knew she couldn't have.

Ever since they'd arrived here, he'd changed. Oh, he'd laughed and joked with people, played the doting uncle to a number of nieces and nephews, chatted with Diya for a bit, sitting in the lighted courtyard while the groom, Richard, and Clare had waited patiently.

There was a sadness in him, Clare could tell. If he had expected to feel different returning here as a successful businessman, as a world-renowned billionaire, she knew he had failed.

She saw it in his eyes.

She felt it in the silence he imposed between them at night when she crawled into bed after a long day of festivities. When he reached for her and made love to her with a dark passion, as if he needed escape.

Clare loved sleeping next to his large, warm body. Loved it when he cuddled her body against his, whispering soft endearments in her ear.

But it was clear that being back in his childhood home had cast a darkening spell on him. Clare knew that his twin looked at him with concern. But he'd shrugged her concern away in front of Clare. Had then evaded a more in-depth conversation with Clare as if he didn't trust his own words.

As if he could only communicate with his mouth and his fingers and his body.

So Clare let him. She let him take whatever he needed from her. Because she loved him with all her heart.

She finally knew it for certain when she washed off her hennaed hand and saw that the artist had inserted Dev's name so cleverly into the swirls on Clare's palm.

She rubbed at his name with her finger and took a deep, shaking breath.

Knew that he'd carved himself into her heart too.

Whatever she told herself, or however well she prepared herself for the worst didn't matter.

She'd fallen in love with Dev Kohli, and there was nothing she could do about it. Most of the time, Clare didn't want to. Because loving him meant being her best self. Seeing herself through his eyes. Seeing the very fabric and future of her life shift with him in it.

God, she wanted him in it so desperately.

"Clare?"

She looked up to see Dev's older sister—and everyone else— still waiting for an answer as to how they'd met. "Sorry, I drifted off there for a moment!" She strained her brain trying to think of the right story to tell while the artist took hold of her other hand.

She spotted the tall figure of Dev's dad hulking against the back wall, listening. to whom apparently, appearances were everything.

When Dev had first introduced her to Anand Kohli, he had greeted Clare with a warmth she hadn't expected. And when she'd trotted out her qualifications as the CEO of her own company, approval had glinted in the brown eyes that were so much like Dev's.

But the similarities had ended there. The older man didn't appear to have the warmth her husband did. Neither did he seem to possess the kindness and generosity of spirit that was so much a part of Dev's personality.

A tall, broad man like his son, he had retained his good looks and stature. Clare had tried to imagine him angry and impatient with a little boy who couldn't put his troubles into words.

As a hard man who demanded perfection instead of seeing the lonely, lost child.

Clare had never felt an anger before like she had felt it then, on behalf of that young Dev.

In a booming voice, he'd prodded Dev about not informing his family about his nuptials.

And Dev had simply shrugged. Refusing to pretend as if everything was normal between them. As if he had any obligation to his father. He's simply walked away, leaving them both staring after his retreating back.

Clare had automatically turned to apologize to the older man for Dev's behavior but managed to swallow it. This man didn't deserve an apology. Not when he was responsible for all the scars that Dev bore.

And yet...as she'd stood there facing him, she'd thought of her own father. Of how angry she'd have been if she had ever laid eyes on him again. How she'd have demanded an explanation for what he'd done.

How, if he'd offered even a tiny excuse, she'd have tried to forgive him. Would he have been genuinely sorry was a question she was never going to get answered.

But Dev's father was here. Alive. Despite everything, there was something about him that had made her feel sorry for him too.

"He likes you," Mr. Kohli had said then, a hint of shock in his voice. Whatever flash of raw ache she'd seen in his eyes gone now.

Her hackles had risen. "The last thing you should be doing now, Mr. Kohli, is criticizing your son's choice of wife."

He'd smiled then, as if he was some maharaja granting a boon to a peon. "Oh, I wasn't criticizing his choice, Clare. I was surprised, that's all."

"By what?" she'd demanded, more curious than angry now.

"I never thought he'd marry. But not only did he tie the knot, he seems to have traveled a different route to it than I or any of his siblings expected him to."

"Again, I'm not sure if you're insulting me or complimenting me."

His gaze dwelled thoughtfully on where Dev had stood not a minute ago. "After all the women that have paraded through his life, I'm glad he's chosen a wife that suits him so well. The real him. His mother would've been happy to see you with him."

Clare had been struck mute that father and son would think the same thing. "Why do you say that?" she'd asked, fishing for more.

Mr. Kohli's dark eyebrows had tied together. "It's clear that he's happy with you. Even though he thinks I don't know him."

"But you don't," Clare had whispered. She'd walked away then, without waiting for his reply.

"Clare?"

Diya's hand on her arm brought Clare back to the present once again. She forced a deep breath in and smiled. Lies were easier if they were mostly truth embroidered, weren't they? Not that she'd ever come back here and see these lovely faces again.

"Oh, I...snuck onto Dev's yacht," she said with a dramatic roll of her eyes.

A barrage of whoops and questions came back at her.

She laughed. "I had one date with him and after that he blew me off. So when I had the chance to attend a party aboard his yacht, I crept into his bedroom. And demanded that he—"

"She demanded that I either give us another chance or toss her overboard," an amused voice finished behind her.

Clare tilted her head back to find Dev looking down at her from his great height. He was wearing a half-white kurta with gold piping across the Nehru collar, and he looked gorgeous in a more subdued than usual kind of way.

Laughter and cheers surrounded them. More questions came, but Clare couldn't look away from his dark gaze. She must have moved her other hand to keep her balance because the henna artist was suddenly muttering away in Hindi.

Her heart thumped wildly as Dev fell to his knees behind her. His arm came around her waist, taking her weight and keeping her hand steady for the artist. And then he was dipping his head—uncaring of all the eyes watching—and kissing her.

More squeals abounded them, a deafening jumble of catcalls and whistles, and Clare thought she might cry at the tenderness with which he kissed her. Softly, slowly, almost reverently.

As if he were seeking a benediction. As if he were asking for something he couldn't put into words.

Clare wrapped her free hand around his neck and held on. Her heart racing so fiercely that she thought it might pound right out of her chest.

It had been like this ever since their wedding night. One kiss led to more. A hundred kisses led to everything. Everything led to her being suffused by emotions for this man.

His fingers held her jaw for his tongue's foray now. If he weren't holding her steady, Clare knew she'd have melted right onto the marble floor. She sighed when he finally let her go.

"What was that for?" she asked, rubbing her fingers tentatively over her swollen lips.

He jerked his chin back for a second. As if he found the question unexpectedly daunting. As if he couldn't think of the right words. Something shifted in his gaze and then he said, "Did I tell you how lovely you look in your lehenga?" he said, a smooth charm back in his voice.

Disappointment flooded Clare. Not that she believed his compliment to be false; the traditional outfit Diya had presented her with was gorgeous, with gold embroidery enhancing the stunning pale pink color. But because he had pushed away whatever it was that had tugged him to her in this moment. Whatever he'd been silently telling her with that kiss was now neatly forgotten again.

"Thank you," she said inanely. "How did the male bonding go last night?"

He grinned. "It was boring… Bhai doesn't drink. Richard is quiet. Then Derek showed up and it felt like a party."

"Did you and your brother get a chance to talk?" she asked, knowing that Dev had been evading his brother too.

A shutter fell over his expression. "Let it go, Clare."

Clare refused to indulge in the hurt that splintered through her. This wasn't about her. This was about him.

"I came to see if they were bothering you," he said in a loud whisper that was intended to reach his sisters.

Clare leaned back against his broad frame, feeling as if she was being torn between joy and a searing longing for more.

"Oh…pshh…your bride is safe with us," Diya answered her brother, while most of the crowd turned back to the business at hand. And then she dipped her head and planted a kiss on Clare's cheek.

Dev stared at his twin, while Clare felt as if she'd just been given a wonderful gift. She clutched Diya's hand, a prickle of tears in her throat. "What was that for?"

Diya grinned, and her eyes were glittering bright with their own wetness. "Just for coming into his life. He… I haven't seen him like this in a long time. A very long time."

Before Dev or Clare could stay her, Diya walked away, leaving a sudden silence behind.

Clare would've given anything, anything in the world, to have Dev acknowledge what his twin had just said.

She willed him with everything in her to say one word. Something. Anything.

Time ticked away, seconds to minutes, leaving her desperately aching.

She shivered, the chill coming from inside her rather than out. His body was there instantly, warm and hard. She felt his chin touch her head, his kiss at her temple. But this time, Clare wanted the words. Needed them like she needed air to breathe.

She was just beginning to think she was going to have to wait forever again. Just as she'd waited for her father…months upon months, melting away into years after years. Believing. Hoping. Sustaining herself for so long on so very little.

His hands stayed around her waist. "I have something for you."

"My wedding present?" she said, asking the same question for the hundredth time.

It had started as a joke between them. A game. But now, as his gaze met hers and held it, it became something more. Something portentous.

"No," he said, shaking his head. "Even better."

Clare pouted playfully. "Tell me."

"My security team has been in negotiations with the mobster. He's finally agreed to let me…" He trailed off then, looking slightly uneasy for a moment.

"Let you what?" she asked suspiciously.

"Let me buy you off him."

"The absolute gall of the man!" she erupted. "I'm not a camel!"

Taking her chin in his hand, Dev bent and dropped a brief kiss on her lips. "I know, sweetheart. But you're forgetting the bright spot in all this. You'll be free, Clare, very soon. You'll never have to be afraid of anyone again. Ever."

Clare threw her arms around him. He held her through the shiver that went through her at the realization she was finally free. "Thank you," she whispered.

When he let her go and stood up, she couldn't help saying, "But that pushes us one step closer, doesn't it?"

"To what?" he asked, looking confused.

"To dissolving this…arrangement. Once we've sorted out your reputation too, we can be done with each other. And as there are already lots of positive stories in the world's media about your wedding, as well as the interviews we've done with Ms. Jones and your sisters, I'd say we're nearly there already."

For once, Clare didn't wait to see what he would say. She didn't think she could bear it if he simply agreed with her. Or made a joke of it.

So she carefully held the hem of her gorgeous pink skirt with one hand and walked away, wondering why she was feeling so odd when she was on the cusp of having her freedom again.

She'd never wanted more in her life to be called back. Never wanted to hear her name on his lips so badly.

She didn't even have to give up her company. Yes, she'd pay Dev back what he'd had to pay the mobster, even if it took her years to do it, but it wasn't a deadly sword hanging over her head any longer.

Yet, instead of elation, all she felt was desolation.

As if she'd been left all alone in the world again.

CHAPTER TWELVE

"ARE YOU GOING to talk to him?"

Dev had known this was coming. He'd seen the combative look in Clare's eyes over the last three days. He knew all her looks now.

Her "I'm ready for battle" look.

Her "I want you so I'm going to have you" look.

Her "Do you really want to try me?" look.

And Dev adored them all. But this look indicating that she was going to prod and push, he disliked with a vengeance.

Her chin tilted high, her wide mouth pursed in dissatisfaction; she'd been retreating from him ever since he'd told her that she was going to be free of the crime lord. Irritation flickered through him. He hadn't expected her to fall on him in gratitude but he had expected... What?

She'd reminded them both of their agreement. That they were getting much closer to being able to end this charade. It was a reminder he'd desperately needed.

A reminder he shouldn't have needed, given how busy they'd been continuing to make his halo shine.

They hadn't been free for even one evening.

If it wasn't some wedding ceremony that Diya insisted they both join, it was attending a charity auction where Clare had trumpeted to the media about the annual charity retreat Athleta held with star athletes. Another afternoon had been spent at an inner-city youth hostel that Dev had always supported financially.

Derek and Angelina had been there at the hostel, all their issues resolved. Although he was pleased for his friend, something about how in tune they'd been had grated at Dev, amplifying the disconnect between him and Clare.

They had spent a perfect California afternoon—Derek and he playing flag football with the teens while Clare and Angelina spent more than two hours in conversation with the warden and the press that Clare had invited.

If he wasn't so wrapped up in his own thoughts, Dev would have laughed at how dictatorial his wife could get when she was on a schedule. How dedicated she was to her job of making him look good.

How easily she'd weaved herself into his life. Into his family's affections.

He'd seen his brother—who was even more allergic to having heart-to-hearts than Dev was—have a long, involved talk with her. He'd even seen his father voluntarily strike up conversations with her. Not that it was a big leap to find Clare interesting.

He'd seen Diya and his older sister with her—their heads bent together, laughing at one joke or another. And then Clare would look up—as if she had some kind of sensor for locating him—and they would stare at each other across the room, that ever-present desire shimmering like an arc between them, connecting them.

He would normally have winked and smiled at her, and she'd have blushed. Whatever the time of the day. Wherever they were.

Except she'd stopped smiling and blushing at him during the last three days. She didn't chatter away asking about this aunt who'd run away with her girlfriend twenty years ago creating a huge scandal or that uncle who'd maintained two families for years. She had retreated from him.

Each night, Dev had crawled into bed, expecting to be given the cold shoulder there too. Dreading it, in fact. Because he wasn't sure he could stand if she turned away from him there as well. Not just because he wanted to make love to her again. That desire for her was always there. He'd made peace with that.

But because those nights with her had become his escape from the grief he still felt being back here, in his family home. From the pain of feeling like a stranger among his own family.

Holding her, kissing her, making love to her had become the anchor he needed to shore up his days.

But to his shock and unending relief, her slender body had pressed up against his. Her palm on his chest, she'd burrowed into him.

She'd done it again last night too. The soft warmth of her body had instantly set him on edge.

"Clare, what's—"

She had pressed her palm over his mouth and shook her head. "I don't want to talk, Dev. Please, will you just...make love to me?"

"Yes," he had whispered, taking the easy way out.

Then she'd pulled him on top of her. The dark night had swallowed up his ragged moan as he entered her in one deep thrust. The breeze buried her gasp as he took her with a desire that didn't abate until he'd driven them both to a glorious release.

And when he'd found her cheek damp afterward, Dev had simply held her while her breathing slowly returned to normal. While she slipped into sleep. But he had stayed awake. Thinking.

He had no idea what the hell he was expecting from her or himself. They weren't, after all, truly married.

"Are you just going to pretend that I'm not standing here haranguing you?" she demanded now, interrupting his thoughts.

"You sound like a proper fishwife, sweetheart," Dev said,

determined to make her smile today. He looked up and his own smile disappeared. He felt as if he'd been kicked in the stomach. Hard.

Today, she was wearing a light blue kurta that made her beautiful eyes pop, with a wide round neck and flared pants. A tiny red bindi between her eyebrows sent shock waves through him.

Eyes wide, he stared at the delicate black bead necklace at her throat with a diamond at the center.

His fingers were shaking when he pushed his hair back. "What—" he had to clear her throat "—what are you wearing? I thought all the ceremonies were finished last night."

A wariness entered her eyes, and she touched her fingers to her throat. "They are. Diya and Richard are leaving for Malibu in two hours. This…your aunts and Deedi and Diya…they had a small ceremony for me first thing this morning."

"What?" he barked.

But she didn't back down. "Since we cheated them out of attending our wedding, they sprang a surprise celebration for me. To welcome me as the daughter-in-law of the house. Your father was there too. They all gave me presents—jewelry, clothes. And this…" she said, touching that necklace again.

"It belonged to my mother."

"I know. Diya told me. I told her I couldn't just take it like that. They didn't listen. She kept saying your mother would've wanted me to have it. That she'd have been overjoyed if she'd been here today."

Dev looked away, feeling as if his heart had crawled up into his throat. "Of course."

"You don't have to be upset about this," Clare said to his back, her voice all matter-of-fact. He wondered if she could sense the chaotic mess his heart was in. If she could see how much he wanted her to have it. How much…he was struggling with that want.

He wanted to let this thing between them grow into what it had the potential to be. He wanted to lean into it with all his being and yet…something stopped him. Something always held him back.

Being here, in his childhood home, didn't help.

"I'm not planning to steal it, Dev. I figured it was easier to go along with what they wanted and then just return it to you afterward. Unless you wanted me to tell them that I'm nothing but a fake bride."

He jerked his head back to her and saw the anger in her eyes. "Hell, Clare. I didn't think you were stealing it."

She shrugged and turned away. "It's obvious from your face that it means a great deal to you."

"What does a trinket mean when she's not here? When you can't bear to…" *To even look at me*, he meant to say. But he caught the words. "You should keep it. It's not like I'm going to run out and get another wife anytime soon. Or ever."

"I don't want it," she insisted stubbornly. "Not when it's an empty gesture. Not when it comes without…"

"Without what?"

"Without what it truly represents."

Dev's voice rose. "I can't believe we're fighting about that necklace when there's…" He raised his palms and sighed. "I'm sorry, Clare. I'm not myself. Not in this place."

"I get that, Dev, I do." Her expression softened. "I promised myself I'd be polite and calm with you today."

"As opposed to the sweet and tart woman that pushes and prods?" he said with a laugh.

She walked over to the bedroom door and closed it. "Dev, talk to your father please."

"You really want to pick a fight with me today, don't you?"

She frowned, her beautiful blue eyes not leaving his face. "Not at all. But I'm not going to back down from it, if that's what it takes."

Dev gave in. "Fine. Why would you push me to have a heart-to-heart with the man who crushed me when I was young?"

"Because I think he's finally realized he's made a mistake. Because he doesn't know how to ask you for your forgiveness."

"Why are you on his side, Clare?"

Only when he heard it did Dev realize how pathetic he sounded. How childish. How he seemed to have morphed back into a needy, temperamental pre-teen inside these walls.

Was it this that had been bothering him? That Clare got along so well with his family, with his father? That he...wanted her to be his and no one else's?

She was his. Only his. The first and only woman who'd seen more in him than he himself did.

She came and took hold of one of his hands. Lifted it and pressed her mouth to his knuckles. Cradled his palm to her face. "I'm on your side, Dev. Always."

"Then why do you ask me to do this when you know how impossible I'd find it?"

"Because I care about you." She pressed her hand to his chest, boldly. As if she was staking a claim on his heart. As if she was laying claim to the whole of him. His pulse rushed deafeningly, but the look in her eyes was calm. She was composed and elegant and the most beautiful woman he'd ever seen. "Because I think that talking to him, letting him say his bit...whether it's to ask for forgiveness or to justify his attitude back then... I think it will help you. I think it will finally burn away the resentment and anger that's been building up inside you for so long. Because I think until you face your past and gain closure, there's no possibility of a happy future for you."

"I'm here, aren't I?" he retorted.

"But are you, really? Did you let your brother get close to you? Did you let Diya see the real you? Or did you only come to show off to your father? To prove to him how rich and powerful you've become. To thumb your nose at him. I've spent some time talking to him recently, and for a sixty-five-year-old man stuck inside his own rigid set of values, I think he knows he wronged you and he's really been trying to change."

"Of course he's changed. But only because I've changed, can't you see? I'm not the lazy, useless, rogue he used to call me. I've become something more. I've amassed all this wealth and power and I finally made the family name proud. He can afford to be proud of me now. He can afford to call me his son."

"But it's not just recently, Dev. That's what Deedi was trying to tell you. He's followed your progress for years. Your entire swimming career, your first company, your first takeover, your work with Athleta. He's been proud of you for a very long time now."

The bitterness inside him was so deep and dense that nothing she was saying impacted on it. Dev wanted so badly to shift it. To cleanse himself of the poison. If not for himself, then for her. To be open to whatever it was she was trying to bring into his life. But he couldn't. "It is easy for him to say he's changed, Clare. Easy for him to give me the approval and the love he denied me once."

"But it's you who's denying all those things now, Dev. Don't you see? You're measuring yourself by his standards from back then. You're letting ugly things from the past dictate your present and your future."

A frustrated groan fell from his mouth. He grasped her shoulders. "Why are you forcing this discussion on me?"

"Because I've seen the shadows of loneliness in your eyes these past few days. I've seen how you look at your nieces and nephews, as if you're an ocean away from everyone. I've seen you say no to almost every overture and invitation that Diya and Deedi have made to you. I've seen you shut them all down repeatedly. Hold yourself apart."

"Because I'm angry and hurt and I…want so badly to belong. But I think…" Dev pressed his fingers to his temples, hating the sick churning in his stomach. "I don't know how. I've stayed away for too long. I…"

She wrapped her arms around his waist and held him, this woman who had a core of steel at her center. "Then take the first step, Dev. Talk to him. Try and sort it out. Make peace with your father. For yourself, if no one else. Despite what he did, if I had one more chance to see my dad, I'd take it."

Dev held her for a few seconds but his breath didn't settle. He felt as if he was standing on the outside again. Not knowing how to read or what to say.

"I can't," he said abruptly, letting Clare go. "I can't open myself up to all that pain again. I can't give him or anyone else the chance to…"

"Hurt you again," Clare finished sadly, stepping back from him.

Dev swallowed and shrugged.

"So what does this mean for us then?" she asked quietly.

"What do you mean?" he asked, feeling like a fool. "It doesn't change anything. This was just another part of our agreement, Clare. This was just you…giving me a hand with getting through some difficult days. Nothing has changed."

She didn't answer. And Dev felt a helplessness that he hadn't known in a long time.

He pulled her to him and she came.

"I want to kiss you," he said, plunging his fingers into her hair. "I need to taste you, sweetheart."

"Yes, please," she whispered.

He felt as if he'd conquered the world. He took her mouth, employing all the skill he possessed to push her to the same sense of desperation he felt. She was sweet and warm, like light in a cave of darkness.

And when he let her go, she looked up at him. Her long fingers cradled his cheek with a tenderness he didn't deserve. "I'm planning to leave for London tonight on the red-eye."

Dev's ferocious scowl told Clare everything she needed to know. She knew that she was pushing him when he wasn't himself. But as she'd already learned, there was no right or wrong time to do this.

To tell the man she loved that she…was an absolute fool for him.

"I'll have the jet ready in an hour or two. We can leave together."

"No." She stepped away from him, feeling as if she was cleaving herself in two. "I'd prefer to go alone. I haven't been to the office in weeks, and Amy and Bea, I know, are wondering where the hell I've got to."

"So I'll be in the way of your reunion with your friends?" he asked harshly.

"No. I just want to get my head on straight." She pressed her hand to his mouth, incapable of not touching him.

He pulled her hand away but didn't let go. "I don't understand what you're talking about, Clare."

"I've fallen in love with you, Dev." Her hand went to the black bead necklace at her throat. "I… I want this marriage to be real. I want to be Mrs. Kohli. I want this family to be mine as well as yours. More than anything, I want to share my life with you too. Are you happy to modify our arrangement to suit my needs?"

He didn't blink. He simply stood there, staring at her.

Clare laughed bitterly. "Yeah, I didn't think so. This is why I pushed you. Because I know how it feels for past scars to dictate your future. To have been so hurt badly that you close yourself off to everything. Even love. I waited for my dad to come back to me for years, Dev. Decades. You know he never did. You know what he ended up doing to me. You saw what it took for me to come back from it. You restored my faith in human nature just when it was ready to be completely shattered. But I can't wait around like that again for a man to love me. I can't… because it will break me this time. Because I love you so much and you're just not ready for it—if you ever will be. You don't want love in your life, do you? So, yes, I have to go. I have to start putting the pieces of my life back together again. I have to decide who I want to be…next."

Clare walked up to the man who'd become her entire world in such a short space of time. She kissed his bristly cheek and breathed in the delicious scent of him.

"Loving you has only made my life better, Dev. That will never change," she whispered. "But you have to choose happiness, Dev. With me. You have to decide if I'm worth trusting. If I'm worth taking a chance on. If you can finally let me into your heart."

CHAPTER THIRTEEN

DEV DIDN'T KNOW why he was still there—at his parents' house in California. In this house where he had never felt like he fit.

Derek and Angelina were long gone. Diya and Richard had left for their honeymoon a couple of hours after Clare had left him. His older brother and sister and their boisterous families had left too. His family had all bid him goodbye with a wariness that he knew he was the cause of. Both his sisters had asked why Clare had left so abruptly.

When would he bring her back for a visit?

When was he going to let them throw a party for him and Clare to celebrate their marriage? Had he convinced Clare yet to move to California with him so that they would all be closer together?

As if he were a stranger they couldn't communicate with without the bridge Clare had provided. As if she had...opened up something between him and them again.

As if she'd rekindled a spark in his cold heart.

There were a hundred things requiring his attention, tens of meetings he was missing with each day he didn't leave. And yet he had stayed, a strange lethargy weighing him down.

Instead of that agitated energy he'd felt during the first few days after his return, Dev sensed something different within the house this time. The walls looked brighter. The sight of him in the family portrait above the giant fireplace—the one he'd tried to get out of being included in—suddenly didn't feel like a joke of the worst kind.

As the hours and days passed, he felt as if the house gradually changed around him. As if for the first time in years, he could breathe here. Or was it him who had changed?

Or was it Clare who had made life so much better for him that the past no longer held such significance anymore?

As he sat down in the huge library with the vaulted ceilings and rows and rows of books that had always seemed like alien things forever out of his reach, Dev realized he didn't feel the resentment that had been his childhood companion for so long. He didn't feel caged anymore.

Because now, whichever wing he walked into, whatever nook or corner he looked into, he saw Clare.

He saw her laughing with Diya and Deedi.

He saw her turning bright pink as she tasted the spicy *pakoda* his nephew had popped into her mouth when she'd been laughing.

He saw her looking up from where she'd been sitting amid all his cousins and relatives on her knees, her lovely, warm gaze finding him wherever he was and smiling at him.

He saw her dragging him through room after room, laughing, asking questions, determined to know all the hijinks he'd gotten into as a mischievous boy. He saw her kissing him, needing him, telling him he was loved with her eyes, her kisses and her generous heart.

But her words…the very words he didn't even know he'd needed to hear so desperately, the very words that were in his own heart…when she'd finally said those words to him out loud, he hadn't been able to hear them.

He hadn't been able to see what it had cost her to say them to him. How far she'd come to be able to trust him, and want him, and…love him.

His father was still there, Dev knew. The palatial mansion meant he and the old man didn't have to cross paths even once during the day if they so pleased. While Papa had rarely approached Dev, he constantly sensed his father's presence, in the weighty silence that seemed to follow him wherever he walked.

In the pregnant hope that filled the very air.

"The house is yours," his father had declared, the one time Dev had come close enough to him for a conversation.

"I don't want it." The words had risen to Dev's mouth and yet…something had arrested them. No, not something. Someone.

Clare.

"That wife of yours," Papa had continued in his booming voice, "she will like the house, I think. She will want to raise a family here with you."

Dev had looked up, stunned. For the first time in his life, it seemed his father and he had been thinking along the same lines. The picture of her, in this house, with him, was such a clear image that Dev hadn't been capable of responding.

The two of them together in this house, building a family together…

And for the first time in years, Dev saw himself fitting into this house again. Fitting in with his family. Fitting in with who he'd wanted to be all his life—a man worthy of love.

And Clare had made it all possible by simply loving him.

By giving him what he wasn't even sure he'd earned.

"Who the hell are you?"

If Dev didn't feel as if his heart was lodged in his throat, if he hadn't felt like a total idiot, he'd have laughed at the two women who blocked his way as he walked into the offices of The London Connection.

One tall and elegant, the other a little shorter, with strawberry blond hair—they looked like sentinels guarding the gate against him. Guarding their best friend.

A part of him found relief in the fact that Clare had these women to support her. That she wasn't alone. That she…

"I'm here to see Clare," he said, trying to hide the impatience he felt.

"We heard you the first time. Our question was who are you?" asked the blonde.

Dev pushed his hand through his hair. "You damn well know who I am. I'm your best friend's husband."

Shock seemed to quiet them for once. Until he heard one muttering away and the other one squealing. Something like, "Oh, my God, he's here!"

"I don't think you should be here," the taller one said.

"Wait, Bea, we don't know that. She might want to see him. You know what shape she's been in since she returned. Also, he's our biggest client right now."

Before they drove Dev completely crazy, Clare appeared behind them. Peeking out of the back door, leading to a separate office.

"What's going on…?"

Her words fell away as she straightened. Wariness shone in her eyes as she tucked a lock of dark brown hair behind her ear. "Hey, Dev."

Dev swallowed, trying to dislodge the torrent of emotion that seemed to crawl upward from his chest into his throat. He didn't say anything in the end. Just nodded at her. Stared at her hungrily.

She looked a little gaunt but elegant in a white blouse and black skirt. She looked lovely and fierce and his breath came back in a rush, as if he'd been merely functioning until now, instead of living.

"I didn't know you were coming to London." Her tone made it clear she'd have been three continents away if she had. "Did I miss something on the calendar? I thought we'd finished all the PR for Athleta."

"No. That's all wrapped up," he finally said. "I'm sure you've seen the articles. I'm now being praised as a twenty-first-century model CEO."

"With most of his female fans crying over the fact that he secretly married his English wife," added the one called Bea.

Clare flushed. Her arms wound around herself in a gesture of defensiveness that tugged at Dev's heart. "It's okay, Bea. He'll be back on the market soon enough." Her blue gaze pinned him. "In fact, now that you're here, maybe we can finalize—"

"No, I won't," Dev said loudly. Enough was enough!

"You won't what, Mr. Kohli?" asked the blonde who must be Amy.

"I'm not going back on the market," he snapped. "For anything." And before she could shoot him down with another question, he caught up to her. "I want to talk to you in private."

Her breath quickened as he neared her. "I don't see what we have to say to each other. I'm not interested in playing Mr. Kohli's adoring wife anymore."

"No? I thought you were pretty damn good at it," he said, grinning. Gaining a little of his confidence back. He'd have to beg, yes, but she'd forgive him. She loved him. And the one thing he knew about Clare was that she didn't give her heart away easily.

And once she did, she was never going to take it back again. God, he'd been so foolish.

The woman he'd married was not the flaky type. She wasn't going to kick him out of her life just because he'd been slow to see what was right in front of his eyes.

"Did you get the profile of that last magazine interview I sent you?"

Her blue eyes grew huge in her face. "I opened it just now... I...it's a brave, big move publicizing your dyslexia like that."

Dev smiled. "I didn't do it to be brave or big. I did it because I realized you were right. I was still measuring myself by someone else's standards. And failing. In truth, telling the world I'm dyslexic is a selfish act, Clare. Really, I'm doing it to prove to myself and to you that... I choose happiness. That I choose love. That I choose...you. I love you, sweetheart. I want a future with you, if you'll still have me. I'll even give up the monstrous, gigantic, oversized yacht if it means my tomorrows are filled with you..."

Tears filled her eyes and fell across her cheeks. She looked so stricken that Dev felt a flicker of fear.

"Do you still not trust me?" he muttered hoarsely.

She shook her head, and then she was throwing herself into his arms. "I trusted you from that first night. You gave me my heart back, Dev." A world of joy filled her eyes. "You were just so determined to stay a bachelor."

"But that was before you stormed into my life, Clare." He kissed her temple and held her as she trembled in his arms.

Dev heard a couple of masculine voices behind him but ignored them. The only one who mattered to him, the only person he ever wanted to see was here in front of him.

"I love you. I think I fell in love with you when I found you sleeping in my closet. You're so brave and sweet and I can't imagine what my life would be like if you hadn't come storming into it, Clare. Forgive me for being a foolish man. For not seeing what you were giving me, sweetheart." He opened the top couple of buttons on his shirt and there lay the necklace she'd left behind on his nightstand.

"I want you to be my wife, Clare. Forever and ever. My father has been trying to give me the family home, but if you don't like the idea, I want you to help me pick a house for us wherever you want to live. I want you to have a big family with me. Because I know that's what you've always wanted. I want you to teach our children how to be strong and brave like you. I want you to give me a chance to love you like you've always deserved to be loved, darling. And I promise I'll never again keep you waiting. Not another minute, not another second."

And then she was burying her face in his neck and murmuring through her tears.

"I do love you, Dev. With all my heart. I…"

Dev kissed her quiet. "Shh…sweetheart, no more tears. I'm here. I'll always be here for you."

EPILOGUE

"Do we have to change the name of our company now that we have offices on two continents?"

Clare looked up to find her friend Bea considering the question thoughtfully, the way she did everything else. Her husband Ares was sitting by her, his arm around her on the couch. Amy and Luca, on the other hand, sat squashed up on the opposite recliner together, still arguing over where they were going to spend Christmas.

She smiled as strong arms came around her waist and she was pulled against a hard body. Warmth exploded in her blood as the familiar scent of her husband enveloped her.

"Are you going to answer Bea's question or are you just going to grin like a fool?" Amy demanded, laughing at what Clare was sure was a blissful look on her face.

"Luca, please advise your wife not to call mine a fool."

Luca grinned while Amy continued. "Well, your wife is the CEO of our company and since she's made the executive decision of ditching us and moving to California to open the US branch of our business, Bea and I have been wondering."

Clare straightened, hearing the hint of uncertainty in Amy's voice. When she looked at Bea, she found the same.

Her friends weren't worried about the business or their share of it. But The London Connection had brought them together when they had nothing else in the world. Nothing but each other.

"Of course, we're not going to change the name," Clare said, clearing her throat. "I'm just one flight away from you. And remember, ladies, we're all about the modern woman."

"What Clare means, Amy," Bea chipped in, while smiling at Ares, "is that Ares and Luca and Dev know better than to expect that we'll put them before the business."

Amy laughed and Clare joined in. She couldn't believe all three of them had met and fallen in love with such wonderful men.

With Dev by her side and her friends near enough to see regularly, she finally had everything she had ever wanted—love and a big family and a place to belong.

* * * * *

Keep reading for an excerpt of
The Greek's Secret Heir
by Rebecca Winters.
Find it in the
Mediterranean Men Blockbuster 2024 anthology,
out now!

PROLOGUE

"MONIKA? I'M SO HOT I'm going for a quick swim before I'm burned to a crisp."

Her sandy-haired friend didn't open her eyes. "I'll join you in a few minutes."

Alexa Remis, almost eighteen, got up from one of the rental loungers set out along the semicrowded Perea Beach outside Salonica, otherwise called Thessaloniki, Greece. The August temperature had climbed to the high eighties, perfect for her three-week vacation before school started again on Cyprus, nearly a thousand miles away. This was only her second day of freedom from books and tests, but it would go too fast and she wanted to make the most of it.

After wading into a surreal world of turquoise water, she kept going until she could immerse herself in the deepening cobalt blue beyond. Talk about paradise! On impulse she did a series of somersaults and ended up colliding with a hard, male body who gripped her arms to steady her.

"I'm sorry!" she cried after lifting her head. Once he let go, Alexa had to tread water to stay afloat.

"It was my fault, *despinis*." The sincere apology, spoken in Greek, came from the gorgeous guy staring straight into her eyes. In the afternoon sun she couldn't tell if his eyes were black or brown between those black lashes. "I'm Nico Angelis."

"I'm… Mara Titos." She'd almost made her first mistake by telling him her real name. Her grandfather was the Greek ambassador in Nicosia in Cyprus. For security reasons he and her grandmother had made her promise never to reveal who she really was to anyone while on vacation. With so much political unrest there, they didn't want Alexa to be a target for enemies.

Meeting this Adonis out swimming had thrown her off-balance. "Where did you come from, Nico?"

He pointed to a sleek white cruiser in the distance, revealing his well-defined chest. "My friends and I have been racing each other."

"And I ruined it for you by being in your way."

His gaze wandered over her, making her feel a voluptuous warmth that was completely different from the effect of the sun. "I didn't watch where I was going, but believe me, I'm not complaining about running into a beautiful mermaid. I didn't know they came with long chestnut hair and sea-green eyes." She smiled as he asked, "Do you live here?"

"No." *Remember what you're supposed to tell people, Alexa.* "I live in France with my mom, but am on vacation until school starts."

"You're a long way from home. I've just turned nineteen and must join the Greek navy in three weeks to do my military service."

They swam around each other. "Are you looking forward to it?"

"Not particularly. I'd much rather stay right here."

The comment sounded so personal her heart picked up speed. "How long will you have to be gone?"

"Two years." He studied her features, lingering on her lips. "At the moment a year sounds like a lifetime."

"One more year in a strict French schoolroom before college sounds like a lifetime to me too." After he chuckled, she heard voices in the distance coming from the cruiser. "I think your friends are calling to you." But Alexa didn't want their conversation to end.

"That's okay. They can wait. I have more pressing matters here." His compelling mouth broke out into a smile, turning her body to liquid. "What about you?"

Remember for security reasons that Monika has a different name too. "My cousin Leia is sunbathing. I'm staying with her and the Vasilakis family during my vacation."

"How long are you here for?"

"Three weeks."

"That's perfect. It gives us time to make some plans."

He had a masterful way about him that made her breathless. There was no guy in Europe or anywhere else who acted or looked like Nico. The dark hair plastered to his head reminded her of a copy of a statue of a young Emperor Augustus in the Archaeological Museum of Salonica she'd seen yesterday.

Monika's parents, the Gatakis, who'd only recently begun working at the embassy with Alexa's grandfather, kept a house here. They'd insisted the girls have one day of intellectual pursuits before hitting the beach for the rest of their holiday.

As far as Alexa was concerned, Nico, with his chiseled features and firm jaw, could have been a model and was so handsome, she couldn't take her eyes off him.

"What did you have in mind?" She knew she was being picked up. Other guys had tried. Before now she'd never been tempted to break her grandparents' rules, but this guy was different. She decided to go with it and see what happened.

"Tell your cousin you're swimming to the cruiser with me. I know a place along the coast where we can buy food and eat on deck while we get to know each other better. I'll bring you back before it gets too late. Wherever I'm stationed in the military, I'd like a happy memory to take with me."

That worked both ways. "What about your friends?"

"I'll drop them at the pier."

So it was Nico's boat. Alexa made a snap decision. "I'll swim to shore and let her know."

His smile faded. "If you don't come back, I'll know this meeting wasn't meant to be after all and you really are a mermaid who'll disappear on me."

Alexa took off for the beach, haunted by what he'd just said. She reached the lounger dripping wet and told Monika what had happened. "He's going to take me for a boat ride."

Her friend jumped to her feet. "Are you crazy? Don't you know who that is?" She sounded almost angry.

"Should I?"

"Nico Angelis is the only son of the billionaire Estefen Angelis, the famous Angelis Shipping Lines owner in Salonica. I've told you about him before."

Alexa didn't remember.

"Over the last year he's been in the news—he gets around." At least Monika knew of him. Alexa's grandparents couldn't object to that. "There've been times when he's played volleyball here on the beach with some of his highbrow friends, picking up girls. He's the last guy on earth you should ever get mixed up with."

Whoa. How could Alexa have known something like that while she'd been living in Cyprus for so many years with her grandparents? "He's still out there waiting for me."

Monika laughed. "You really think so with a line like the one he just fed you? A mermaid? How naive can you get."

Alexa felt foolish. "Maybe I am. But all the same, I'm swimming back out." She hurried into the water once more, wondering, fearing that he'd disappeared. Somehow the idea of never seeing him again disturbed her.

"Mara?"

He was still there. Alexa had almost forgotten that was the

name she'd given him. She had her answer and knew she was going to spend the next few hours with him no matter what Monika said.

"Nico!"

NEW RELEASE

BESTSELLING AUTHOR

DELORES FOSSEN

Even a real-life hero needs a little healing sometimes…

After being injured during a routine test, Air Force pilot Blue Donnelly must come to terms with what his future holds if he can no longer fly, and whether that future includes a beautiful horse whisperer who turns his life upside down.

In stores and online June 2024.

MILLS & BOON

Subscribe and fall in love with a Mills & Boon series today!

You'll be among the first to read stories delivered to your door monthly and enjoy great savings.

WE SIMPLY LOVE ROMANCE